SUMMER SKIN

kirsty eagar

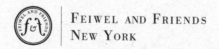

FEIWEL AND FRIENDS
NEW YORK

A Feiwel and Friends Book

An imprint of Macmillan Publishing Group, LLC

175 Fifth Avenue, New York, NY 10010

Our books may be purchased in bulk for promotional, educational,
or business use. Please contact your local bookseller or the Macmillan
Corporate and Premium Sales Department at (800) 221-7945 ext. 5442
or by e-mail at MacmillanSpecialMarkets@macmillan.com.

Library of Congress Cataloging-in-Publication information is available.

ISBN 978-1-250-14600-7 (paperback) / ISBN 978-1-250-14599-4 (ebook)

Book design by Danielle Mazzella di Bosco

Feiwel and Friends logo designed by Filomena Tuosto

First edition, 2018

10 9 8 7 6 5 4 3 2 1

fiercereads.com

For Jeanette

1.
I Go Over

Jess Gordon reached the third story of Gallagher Wing and paused for a breath on the landing, taking the opportunity to tie the laces on her high-tops and pull up her tube socks. She only knew it was Gallagher Wing because a smug gold plaque near the bottom of the stairwell had told her so. It was typical of Knights' pretensions. At Unity, Jess's residential college, they didn't have wings; they had blocks. Knights had been built using bricks and sandstone and something indefinable that suggested learning and Latin mottoes, while Unity was constructed from concrete and steel, with the unfortunate appearance of a jail. Unity was coed; Knights was all male. Just act like you're meant to be there, Jess had been told—advice that completely ignored the fact that it was technically impossible without a penis.

Jess wondered if Leanne, giver of said sage advice, was having better luck. Then she forgot about it, hit by an upwelling of nausea that made her clamp a hand over her mouth. There, a wooden door with a glass insert—that had to be it. She pushed inside, hoping for a bathroom. She was in luck. The place appeared to be empty, thank God, providing sweet relief from Brisbane's swampy heat, although it smelled faintly of ammonia and urinal cakes.

Jess made it to the nearest stall, slamming the door shut before a series of convulsions squeezed out the contents of her stomach in layers: a gush of water, more water, frothy spit, and, finally, teeth-stripping, neon-yellow bile.

"Okay," she breathed to no one in particular, wiping her mouth on her T-shirt. Feeling weak and spent, she leaned back against the stall door, vowing to never drink again—and she meant it this time—absentmindedly patting down the front pockets of her denim cutoffs. But she'd forgotten her Zippo lighter. Damn. Her palm itched for it.

Then someone shuffled their way inside, and Jess froze. She turned her head, listening to the footsteps pass the toilet area. Much closer there was a sudden blare of synthesized music that made her jump. Ella Thompson's voice wailed through the space, echoing off the tiles, and Jess ripped her phone from her back pocket.

It was Brendan. She hit Ignore, cutting off the ringtone abruptly.

For a moment there was only silence, as though the other person had stopped to listen, then the footsteps resumed. A door swung shut and Jess exhaled, switching her phone to vibrate before the message notification came through. Because she knew Brendan would leave one. She wished she'd stayed calm and let his call ring out instead of cutting it off—Brendan would read all sorts of shit into that. But then she remembered that Brendan and his paranoia were not her problem anymore, and she experienced a brief, floaty feeling of euphoria strong enough to propel her from the stall as soon as she heard the splash of a shower starting.

Emboldened, Jess visited the sinks before she left, washing her hands and rinsing her mouth out, forcing herself to drink a few mouthfuls of water. So thirsty—she hadn't been able to hold anything down all morning. This time she'd try the little-and-often approach. She patted some water on her face and rubbed viciously at the mascara smears beneath her eyes. Normally, she was okay with how she looked. Her face was a little too long and thin perhaps, but a few freckles and her slightly crooked, once-broken nose gave her something like character, while her shiny hazel eyes and smile made people notice her. But right then Jess couldn't find anything redeeming about her appearance. Her eyes were bloodshot; her smile was MIA; she officially looked like shit. On top of that, she smelled like a nightclub: beer, cheap wine, and tequila, so help her God, steaming through her pores; her hair a stale, smoky curtain. The only upside was she looked the part for the walk of shame, a plausible enough excuse for being at Knights—if you could call that an upside.

Jess left the bathroom and started down a long, gloomily lit hallway. Each time she came to a door, she tried the handle. Locked, all of them locked, which probably meant the rooms were vacant. The returning student body wouldn't arrive until later that afternoon. Right then, the residential college's only inhabitants were its freshman intake and its student council. Jess was hunting for a room belonging to a member of the council. There were fifteen of them, and something like two hundred and eighty rooms in the college, so the odds weren't great. The good news, though, was that for the next hour or so she could safely assume council members were not in residence, preoccupied with hosting a ceremonial lunch.

"Leaving Home" was blasting out of an open door at the far end of the hallway. God, what was it with that song? Did they put explicit instructions in the orientation week handbook? *Thou must playest Jebediah at all times.* It had been the same at the beginning of last year, when Jess's peers at Unity had pumped it out of their rooms day and night; never mind that most of them had been in diapers when the song was first released; never mind that playing it when they had literally just left home was possibly, just maybe, being too literal.

Jess paused long enough to tap out a text to Leanne—**U found one??? So over this!!!**—then continued on, trying doors without success. By the time she'd reached the "Leaving Home" room, she'd decided on a more direct strategy.

"Hi. I was wondering if you could . . ." Jess's voice trailed off as she took in the state of the room, noticing the lump under the sheets on the bed—probably human. The stale smell of morning after enveloped her: a fog of booze, cigarette smoke, body odor, stinky beer farts, and musty mouth. Whoever he was, this guy was in a worse way than her. The thought gave Jess an odd sense of comradeship. Clothes littered the floor, and there was a collection of empty beer bottles on the desk, along with an open pizza box displaying a pile of crusts. "Leaving Home" finished, only to start up again. It was on repeat. The place was hell.

Jess spotted an MP3 player docked on the shelf above the desk, and she killed the song. Then she opened the window in another act of mercy. To do it, she had to step around a couple of traffic cones and a road sign that had become a self-fulfilling prophecy—HAZARD AHEAD—and she wondered why Brisbane City Council never seemed to figure out that roadwork equipment shouldn't be left unattended in the suburbs of St. Lucia, Toowong, and Indooroopilly. Running shoes and turf boots were clumped in the corner of the room, leaking dirt. Knights College was big on the perfect male specimen; there was a definite preference for athletic types, especially ones proficient in the rah-rah sports: rugby and rowing.

Jess noticed the lump's schedule pinned to the corkboard over the desk and peered at it closely. He was doing some kind of engineering, and all the subject numbers started with one, so he was a freshman. He wouldn't have what she needed—at least, not yet.

Her phone started to vibrate. She checked the screen, hoping for a text from Leanne saying she'd scored and they could go home. Instead, it was another call from Brendan. Jess felt her empty stomach hollow further. She let it ring out this time, putting the buzzing phone down on the desk. The phone finally stopped, only to start up again, and, just for something different, it was Brendan. Jess gave the screen the double bird and a silent scream of agony: *Fuck off!*

At that point, a groan startled her. Pocketing her phone, Jess turned to see the lump move. She'd forgotten about him. The sheet was thrown back to reveal red hair and a flushed face, eyes screwed up against the light.

"Zat you, Griggsy?" he croaked in a hoarse voice. The guy needed water. A lot of it.

"Yep," said Jess.

"What time is it?"

"Nighttime. Go back to sleep."

The guy snuggled into his pillow, making loud smacking noises with his mouth, and a moment later he started to snore.

"Wait a minute," Jess said. The snoring caught and then stopped, so presumably she had his attention. "Do any of the student council guys live on this floor?"

"Mmm . . . tat dowine."

"Tatooine? It's not *Star Wars*. Hey, I asked you a question."

With effort, the redhead dragged himself out of sleep, squinting at her. "Who are you?"

"Not Griggsy. Look, I'm trying to find the student council guy. You know, the one in this block."

"Wing."

"What?"

"Do you mean Jarrod Keith? Because he's . . . he's not, um . . ." The redhead's voice trailed away, and his eyelids flickered closed.

"Wake up," Jess hissed, poking him in the shoulder. "Where's Jarrod Keith's room?"

The redhead groaned. "First floor."

"What room number? Come on, help me out here."

"Dunno," the guy mumbled. He added something unintelligible and toppled back into sleep.

Jess left, closing the door behind her. On the landing, she stopped dead, assaulted by the sudden glare and cicadas that sounded like summer chainsaws. Her phone started vibrating as if in response. As Jess squinted at the screen, she felt the beginnings of a headache, and she wondered which part of her not answering Brendan had trouble processing. She turned the thing off. First floor, Jarrod Keith. If that yielded nothing, she was done, she decided, starting down the stairs.

As she was passing the second floor, Jess became aware of voices below her. She rounded the landing and slowed. Five Knights boys were coming up the steps in a clump, as though relying on one another for body warmth.

"Did you see Henryk—"

"Freshman Gobbler."

A high-pitched giggle. "That's right. Freshman Gobbler."

"Puked all over Tolu's shirt."

"But what about that milkshake thing? That was disgusting, brah."

Freshmen. They sported camouflage paint and towel headbands, and each and every one of them was wearing their special O-week shirt, which that year featured a pumped-up-looking knight brandishing a big barbed spear, his knees bent with its weight, his pelvis thrust forward. Above it, a screaming red font proclaimed: LIVE BY THE LANCE!

Knights and its subtle euphemisms.

The boys spotted Jess and their talk and laughter stopped

abruptly. Acting as one, they put their heads down, huddling closer so that they could pass her two abreast. *Relax*, she wanted to tell them. *Haven't you ever seen a female before?*

But what she said was, "Hope they're taking it easy on you guys," lowering her voice, because she'd read somewhere that the lower the voice, the greater the authority. One of the leaders mustered up enough courage to look at her. "Where's Jarrod Keith this year?" she asked him.

The question caused them to stop and go into groupthink mode.

"Do you mean the—"

"He's president of the—"

"I think he's at that lunch thing."

"No, I mean, where's his room?" Jess asked. "Isn't he on the first floor here?"

"Not here."

"He's over at—"

"Turnock Wing. First floor there."

"Right," Jess said. "Thanks."

They started up the steps again.

"Who was that?" one of them whispered, but none of them dared look back at her. Jess watched them go. They seemed so harmless; you'd never guess what assholes they were going to become. The backs of their shirts read ALL KNIGHT LONG. Probably the amount of time spent playing with their lances.

She sighed, about to give up. She had no idea where Turnock Wing might be, and it was too late to ask the freshman group if anyone else from the student council lived in that block . . . wing . . . whatever. She heard a door swing open on the landing below, and she glanced over the railing, catching a glimpse of a tanned forearm and a net bag full of clothes slung over a shoulder.

The laundry room. So simple. Why hadn't she thought of that before?

Jess took the rest of the stairs two at a time. She peeked around the bottom doorway and then followed the guy down a path that stretched along the back of the next building, heading toward the river. He had an easy, relaxed gait, and she admired his wide shoulders, the muscular triangle of his back. His nice ass. It was a shame more Unity guys didn't place the same emphasis on being perfect male specimens. A lot of them had video gamers' shoulders and were pale, unfit, and grungy. This guy's blond hair was neatly cropped, the sort of cut a Unity guy wouldn't have been seen dead with, and, even viewed from behind, he had an aura of confidence.

At that point Jess's perving was abruptly interrupted, because the guy turned around and started walking toward her.

Shit, she thought. And then: *Just act like you're meant to be here. Smile, say hello.*

He was wearing the O-week shirt, too, so he was probably a freshman, but he didn't seem anything like the guys on the steps, his angry blue eyes flickering over Jess in a way that eventually forced her to look away. She felt busted, even though she hadn't done anything wrong—yet. They passed each other in a prickling silence.

Why had he turned around? Had he known she was following him? Jess risked a glance over her shoulder to see him disappear through the doorway they'd just left. Maybe he'd forgotten something. She started to run, which did nothing for her headache, and was relieved when she spotted clotheslines ahead. When she peeked inside the laundry room, she was even more relieved to find the place empty. It was similar to Unity's: a cavernous room smelling of laundry detergent and hot air, with a bank of commercial washing machines along one wall and three large dryers at the far end. One of the dryers was on, the clothes inside flopping from the top to the bottom in a steady rhythm.

Jess started with the piles of dirty clothes on the table in the middle of the room, picking through them. Underwear and socks, shirts and shorts . . . but no cigar. Okay, the dryer then. The machine stopped as Jess opened the door and checked its contents—jeans and a couple of T-shirts—and in the sudden quiet she realized she could hear faint music. It was coming from an old clock radio on a side bench, its neon display reporting it was after one. The student council lunch would be finishing up soon, but her more immediate worry was Blondie's return. The dryer started ticking as it cooled, the sound heightening her sense of urgency.

Jess could feel the back of her throat growing slippery. Oh, not now! She swallowed furiously, walking the length of the washing machines, most of which seemed to be churning water. Except one: It was spinning. The lid made a hollow clanging noise as Jess slammed it open, and she watched the chamber grind to a halt, feeling dizzy. She leaned in and tugged at the circle of clothes, trying to loosen them, her skin breaking out in a clammy sweat.

As Jess pulled a shirt free, she noticed the name tag on the collar: MITCHELL CRAWFORD. *Mummy still tagging your clothes, Mitch? Probably a leftover habit from when she sent you away to that rich boarding school. Lord knows why she didn't just get everything monogrammed.* Then she peeled back a pair of jeans—also Mitchell Crawford's—and hit the jackpot. Attached to thick cotton was the Knights' coat of arms and the words *Virile Agitur*, which could probably be translated as *We're better than you*. Despite the fact that she was suffering from a rush of blood to the head and was about to vomit, Jess gave a delighted laugh.

The jersey was at the very bottom. She leaned farther into the machine, her fingers scrabbling to get hold of the thick cotton, trying to pull it free.

And that was when she heard someone clear his throat.

2.
Alpha

Jess froze. There was a guy. Watching her. Well, technically, he was watching her ass—of all the times to be wearing cutoffs. Worse, the guy in question was probably *that* guy. She didn't know what to do, so she did nothing, just stayed in position, her heart racing madly. Absurdly, she identified LOLO BX playing on the radio and was glad they were getting airplay.

But then he said, "Can I help you there?"

Jess turned to look at the speaker, feeling woozy as the blood drained from her head. It was Blondie, all right, his bag of clothes and a box of laundry detergent on the table in front of him. So that's what he'd forgotten: laundry detergent. His face was expressionless, but Jess had the feeling he'd been standing there for a while. She tugged at the frayed hems of her cutoffs, giving him a nervous smile.

"You really scared me!" she gushed. Then she turned around and started pulling clothes out of the washing machine, piling them onto the lid of the machine beside her. Because what else could she do? She had to ride this one out, act like she was meant to be there. In an all-male college. Going through a stranger's laundry.

"I said, can I help you there?" The words were friendly, but his tone was not.

As Jess straightened again she finally lost it, starting to heave and retch, puking onto the concrete floor. Each contraction wracked her insides so thoroughly that on the final violent heave she thought her actual stomach might make an appearance, but no, that seemed to be it. All that came up were the little-and-often handfuls of water she'd drunk in the bathroom.

"Sorry." Jess wiped her mouth, feeling dazed. "What were you saying?"

Most guys would have at least come closer and hovered help-fully, but Blondie hadn't moved a muscle. He'd just watched the free show. Unimpressed.

"Someone's going to have to clean that up now," he said with distaste.

"Oh. Right. Sorry." Jess patted her front pockets, finding a wadded tissue that she used to smear the tiny puddle. Then she suddenly wondered what the hell she was doing: squatted down, cleaning up a smidge of *water*, in a *laundry room*, while he stood over her, inspecting the job. She straightened abruptly, taking aim, and tossed the tissue at the trash can.

It missed.

Jess glanced at Blondie, expecting at least a smirk, but he was expressionless. He should have been cute, with that blond hair, that snub nose, that body. But there was a hardness to his face and a tension in the way he held himself that meant he wasn't cute at all. Or stupid, as Jess would have liked to have assumed; if a guy was rich, good-looking, and athletic, she usually drew the circle wide enough to include arrogant and stupid as well.

His blue eyes were cold, the pupils down to pinpricks. "You should pick that up," he told her.

Jess stared at him. Blinked once. Slowly. "Sure," she said with a sudden smile and picked up the tissue, dropping it in the trash can with a flourish. She showed him her hand, fingers splayed, displaying her post-drinking tremors. "I had a big night, that's all. And it's so hot today." She made a fist, rubbing it on her thigh, working sweet and ditzy. "I'm used to heat, not used to drinking."

"What are you doing here?"

"My boyfriend's at that lunch. The intercollegiate thing?" That's it, just keep talking, Jess told herself, stepping back to the open washing machine. Spray him with stupid. "And he asked me to put his laundry in the dryer. But maybe I should have tried a Hydralyte or something first." She giggled—a high, clear, bubbling sound. Seriously, she was like an Aero bar: full of nothing. If he hadn't been making her nervous, she would have been impressed by her own performance.

"You're a freshman?" he asked.

"Hmm." Jess was expecting him to ask her which college she lived in—she'd go with one of the all-female ones, the preferred hunting grounds for knights—but instead he seemed to dismiss her altogether, picking up his things and pushing past her. She flattened against the washing machine, aware of his body, sure it would brush hers. It didn't. He stopped in front of an empty machine and tipped in the contents of his laundry bag.

Jess watched him warily for a couple of seconds, then turned back to Mitchell Crawford's clothes, hastily scooping them into her arms, careful to keep the jersey on top. She hurried to the dryer, walking the long way around, so she didn't have to pass Blondie.

"I know you're lying."

Jess whirled around. "Excuse me?"

Blondie wasn't looking at her; he was measuring out laundry

detergent. "The song," he said calmly. "They're the words, aren't they?"

Jess realized he was referring to the song now playing on the radio. "Yeah, I guess," she said. He'd been repeating Meghan Trainor's lyrics, but was there a subtext?

"You should know. It's one of yours."

"What do you mean?"

He sprinkled detergent over his clothes, his tone dismissive. "It's a chick song."

There was a subtext: He was a dick. "I didn't realize music had a gender," Jess said.

"You want me to open that for you?"

"What?"

Blondie slammed the machine's lid closed, and the noise made her jump. "The door. Of the dryer. Would you like me to open it for you?"

"Oh no. I'm okay, thanks." Jess dumped her pile of laundry on the table and opened the dryer. For a freshman, he was pretty sure of himself. Come to think of it, he looked kind of old to be a freshman, but perhaps that was the stubble shadowing his jaw. Maybe he'd taken a gap year or something.

She was hoping he would leave, but he didn't. Instead, he sat on one of the plastic chairs at the end of the table, riffling through a stack of magazines before selecting a well-thumbed-through copy of *Maxim*. Jess started shoveling clothes into the dryer, and, even though he didn't look at her once, she felt watched. Her nerves were shot. Soon only the jersey was left. *Distract him*, Jess thought.

"How's your O-week been?" she asked.

"Predictable."

"They haven't been too rough on you?"

"Not as rough as they've been on you, by the look of it."

Jess slammed the dryer door closed with more force than was

necessary. The machine hummed to life, and she immediately felt bolder, shielded by sound.

"You forgot the jersey," Blondie commented, turning a page. He looked up, meeting Jess's gaze, his eyes weirdly bright. She noticed him swallow, and she wondered for a fleeting second if she reminded him of somebody else, if that was his problem. But then the moment passed. He raised his eyebrows, an arrogance to the gesture suggesting he expected explanation.

"He doesn't want it going in the dryer. My boyfriend. He's worried it'll shrink."

"Well, aren't you a good little girlfriend? Running around, doing his laundry for him."

Jess gave him a good-little-girlfriend smile and said in a good-little-girlfriend voice, "I try to be!" Then she grabbed the jersey and headed to the door.

"Who's your boyfriend? You didn't tell me his name."

Jess stopped, conscious that she still had to pass him. "Oh, didn't I? Mitchell Crawford. Do you know him?"

"Not well, obviously," he said, dismissive once more. Did that mean he was a freshman? Jess wondered. "I'm curious, though."

"Hmm? About him?"

"No, about you. How did you meet?" Blondie put his magazine down, giving her his full attention. "I mean, you're"—he tilted his head to the side, eyeing her with an expression that suggested whatever she was, it was lacking—"a freshman. And he's not. So . . ."

"Actually, I met him over the holidays. We're from the same town."

"Yeah? Where's that?"

"Rockhampton. We got together one night when we were out. At the Heritage. That's a pub there. I mean, a club. Well, a pub-club.

In Rockhampton." Jess gave a little cough, covering her mouth. "Where are you from?"

He leaned back in his chair, his hands linked behind his head, letting his gaze come to rest somewhere below her eyes. "Not Rockhampton."

"Well, that's lucky. For you, I mean," Jess said, ignoring the urge to cross her arms. "You know what? I'd better go. I think I'm going to be sick again." She said the words mechanically, pointedly, not bothering with the charade at all now. She expected him to stop her, or at the very least tell her to leave the jersey, and she didn't even care. Let him try.

But to Jess's surprise, Blondie did nothing, just turned his attention back to his magazine. Maybe he had bought her act after all and he was only giving her a hard time because she was a woman, and that was the Knights way. Only, when she reached the doorway, she couldn't stop herself from turning back one last time. Because she'd won. And boys like Blondie always turned Jess into a bad sport.

"Well, I guess I'll see you around then," she told him, singsonging the words, a smug little smile of triumph pulling at the corner of her mouth.

Blondie looked around in a way that suggested he'd forgotten she existed. His face changed as he processed what she'd said, and he let his gaze tally up each and every facet of her bedraggled appearance, his expression somewhere between amusement and . . . yes, it was pity.

When he answered, he showed his teeth, like he'd enjoyed a joke. "I doubt it."

3.
Pictures

Back at Unity, the first thing Jess did was take a shower. When she returned to her room, she left the door open, sliding one of the slatted closet doors across to screen the doorway instead, hoping to generate cross flow—the closet doors were on tracks for that very purpose. When none appeared, she scraped a coin from the pile of loose change on the desk and stood on the bed, setting to work on the screw that held the window's tracking. Windows at Unity were immense, stretching the width of each room and over half the height. It was probably for safety reasons that they were restricted to opening only by a foot—unless of course you busted the tracking, in which case they'd swivel to horizontal and beyond. Everybody did it.

Jess secured the window in its new position, using the belt of her robe as a temporary tie, flooding the room with sky. As she did so, the sprinkler system on the lawn below flared into life. Her room looked toward the river. An afternoon breeze pushed through the room, bringing with it the scent of water and a hot smell Jess associated with restlessness. Summer. It made the schedule she'd pinned to her corkboard dance.

She ate some chips from the open packet on the shelf above her desk—salt and vinegar, good hangover food now that her nausea seemed to have finally abated—and looked at the bags clumped on the floor. She should finish unpacking. Outside, she could hear the voices of her floormates in the process of doing just that, doors open so they could shout to one another from their rooms—ten of the twelve of them had been on T-floor the previous year, so it was a reunion of sorts. But what Jess did instead was blow-dry her hair properly, using a large rounded brush, stopping from time to time when her arms ached. When she was finally done, her long toffee-brown hair was at its full-bodied best, her fringe feathered. Then she tweezed her eyebrows, her robe gaping as she leaned toward the mirror above her dresser. She stopped suddenly, studying her reflection. Made a face.

I doubt it. Her tone was sour.

Dropping her gown to the floor, Jess rummaged through one of the bags and pulled on undies and a tank top. Then she slumped in her chair, legs up on the desk, examining the stolen jersey while she finished the last of the chips. It was still damp. The funny thing was, according to the tag, it wasn't Mitchell Crawford's but, rather, Julian Lloyd's—whoever the hell he was. The person Jess's thoughts kept returning to, however, was Blondie. *I doubt it.* Using nail clippers, she carefully unpicked the label and then pitter-pattered her hand across the desk like a spider, finding her Zippo. She opened it with a flick of her wrist, spinning it around her middle finger before hitting the flint-wheel with her thumb. *Flick-spin-scritch!* Jess did this so quickly it wasn't a party trick anymore but a twitch, a nervous condition.

She smiled at the flame, feeling an answering glow somewhere deep inside her. Then she burned Julian Lloyd's tag to a blackened, charred crisp, holding it with her tweezers.

She'd just dropped it in the empty chip packet when a military *rat-a-tat-tat* shook the frame of her closet door. Jess hastily scrunched up the jersey and shoved it in the pigeonhole above her desk.

"Still burning shit?" Leanne asked, shoving the door aside with such vigor that it rattled along its track and smashed into the wall. "You should get that looked at."

"Do you have to do that?" Jess asked with a pained look at the door. She exhaled. "I thought you were Farren. Are you just now getting back?"

Leanne nodded, pushing inside the room with some difficulty, a large canvas bag slung over one shoulder. She pulled off the cap she was wearing, ditto the sunglasses, then slung the bag onto Jess's bed and unzipped it.

"Check this out," she said, sounding pleased. "It's one of those cool retro ones." She held up an aqua-colored toaster, showing it to Jess. "What? I needed a new one."

"You're getting crumbs all over the floor. Did you even look for a jersey?"

Leanne glanced at her, her face untroubled. "Yeah." Her voice suggested it was obvious. Over the holidays she'd had her dark hair dyed Rihanna-red and undercut. It made her startling green eyes even more startling. "Didn't find one, though. Look! Got this for Allie." She held up a sandwich press, and Jess groaned. "Relax. No one saw me."

"There are cameras."

"I was incognito. Anyway, I went out by the river." Leanne stepped backward so she could peer at Allie's room, directly across the hall. The strumming guitars of Wish emanated from her open doorway. "Damn. Where is she?"

Allie always turned her music up as she was leaving her room—like she could take the music with her, or she didn't want her plants to feel lonely while she was gone. Jess wasn't even sure it was a conscious decision. Leanne would know: She and Allie were both from Mackay and had gone to the same high school, back when Allie was Allison.

"No idea," Jess said.

"Check Instagram."

Jess laughed. "Funny one."

"Yeah, because it's true." Leanne snatched Jess's phone off the desk. "Why's it off? Who turns their phone off?" She pushed the side button, and Jess's Nokia returned to life with a series of little chimes. Leanne studied the screen and laughed. "Okay, that makes sense." And Jess knew she'd seen the missed calls.

"Use your own phone," she said sulkily.

"The screen's wrecked. I need a new one. Hey, on that—I think we should sell the Telstra shares."

"You don't sell shares in Telstra just so you can buy a phone. That's a terrible trade. This way you're making money off all the suckers who do own phones."

"My share is only a couple hundred bucks. Not like it matters. I'm broke."

"It will matter, though. Trust me," Jess said patiently. "They've just announced they're doing dividend reinvestment. Do you know how big that is?"

"I don't even know what that means," Leanne said, her eyes still on the screen. "But, okay, Buffet, I'll take charity then." She tapped away for a very long time before Jess processed what she was doing.

"What are you up to?" Jess tried to snatch the phone from her, but Leanne moved away. She showed Jess the screen, and Jess peered at it, starting to laugh at the comment Leanne had left on

Allie's latest upload: *Show us yer personality!* Then realization hit her. Jess's eyes widened, and it was Leanne's turn to laugh. "She'll think I said that!" Jess protested.

"How'd you do, anyway? Score?" Leanne asked.

Jess felt a surge of pleasure that blew away the vestiges of brooding. She pulled the jersey out of the pigeonhole and unfurled it like a flag, trying to play it cool. Usually Leanne did all the daring shit.

Leanne gave an admiring whistle. "Way to go, Flash."

"Just got lucky," Jess said modestly, feeling stupidly pleased.

"Here, put it on." Leanne held up the phone. "Let's take a snap."

"What if Farren sees it?"

"She's not even on Instagram."

A slow smile spread across Jess's face. "Okay. But make sure it's not obviously a Knights' jersey." She frowned. "And I want to look good. *Allie* good."

She pulled the jersey on and posed as Allie would have done: looking seductively over one shoulder, her long hair teased and arranged around her face, pouting even—and Jess never pouted.

"Filter?" Leanne asked when she'd taken the shot, like she might say, "Sauce?"

"*All* the filters," Jess said. "I told you, I've got to look good. And caption it. Say, 'Doubt this, asshole.'"

"That's a bit strong for you, Smiley," Leanne mused, tapping the screen.

"Private joke."

"Done and done," Leanne said, finally handing over the phone.

Then both girls froze, because from out in the hallway, a booming voice said, "Where's Jess? Is she in there?" Another voice answered in the affirmative.

"Farren. *Fuck*." Jess ripped the jersey off, shoving it back in the pigeonhole. "Quick, hide that bag! It's got the Knights' crest on it."

But what Leanne did was throw the bag down on the floor with the others, kicking it over so the crest couldn't be seen. Just in time, because Farren Ghosh came through the doorway like the human tornado she was—a tornado wearing purple Docs, a galaxy-print miniskirt, and a Unity jersey from two years ago—entering the conversation as she always did: as if they were midway through a different conversation.

"Now, look, don't make it difficult for me. We've got half an hour to have that barbecue set up. I want the freshmen to meet their mentors before the headmaster starts making speeches."

"Use your minions. What's the point of being president if you don't?" Leanne said, sidestepping her with a smoothness Jess admired.

"I *am* using them. But we need more hands," Farren said, swiveling around as she spoke because Leanne was already at the doorway. "Allie's helping,"

That made Leanne pause. Jess, too, was surprised. "She is not," Leanne said.

"She is. Come on, don't make me beg."

"Okay, I won't then," Leanne said, and left.

Farren made a huffing noise and turned her attention back to Jess. Frowned. "Don't you want to get dressed first?"

4.
Known Better

"**O**kay! There are several ways to tie a toga, but I'm only going to show you one. If you don't listen, you'll have to work it out yourself, because I am not your mother and I don't repeat myself," Farren bellowed.

Jess, standing beside her, snickered. "Rehearse that much?"

"Start by making a loop," Farren said loudly, giving Jess a look. She clicked her fingers impatiently, and Jess handed over her sheet.

As Farren started winding the tall of the sheet, Jess looked around, pressing her beer to her cheeks and neck. The first few days of the term had been oppressively hot, the air syrupy thick, but for the first time that week there were clouds in the sky, and, now that the sun was setting, the stillness seemed charged, expectant: a thrumming beneath the murmur of music and voices. Ahead of that night's intercollegiate toga party, Farren—president of Unity's student council–had decided to split the college for the pregame.

The girls had gathered on Unity's flat concrete roof; the boys were down in the bunker.

Most of the freshmen were paying rapt attention, sitting directly in front of Farren and Jess, sheets bundled in their laps, all of them in bikinis or one-pieces—a sea of summer skin. The older girls had already wrapped their togas and were farther back, only pretending to listen. The T-floor girls, Farren and Jess's floormates, weren't even pretending. They had their backs to the presentation and were absorbed in pouring their drinks over the railing—presumably they hit their target, too, because there came a distant shout.

Farren turned to Jess. "Arms up, sunshine." She was British Indian and still had traces of her English accent despite having lived in Australia for eleven years. Jess, accordingly, held her arms out wide as Farren started wrapping the sheet around her trunk. Tightly.

"Jesus, Farren, it's not a corset," Jess said. A mistake, because if anything Farren pulled it tighter. Farren was yet to tie her own toga, or maybe she didn't intend to. It was draped around her shoulders like a cloak, paired with a black crocheted bikini top, red velvet shorts, fishnet stockings, and her purple Docs, her long dark hair in two braids. Jess wished she could work a look like that. She felt conservative by comparison in her cutoffs and Black Milk Pixie Dust zippered one-piece (limited edition, thank you very much).

"When you've wrapped it, loop the roped tail around your neck and tie it off with the other tail." Farren stood back to admire her handiwork. "If you want more shape, tie some cord around your waist, or under your boobs."

The freshmen broke into a polite round of applause.

"You're kidding," Jess said.

"They're terrified of me," Farren murmured, looking pleased.

Jess glanced past her at the T-floor girls. Leanne finally seemed to have remembered she had a part to play and had stopped dicking around. Giving Jess a theatrical thumbs-up, she shouted, "Hey, Farren!"

Farren turned, and Leanne held up her phone. Jess's phone, actually—Leanne had demanded a working prop. "Mikey called. He needs you down in the bunker."

"Why didn't he call me?"

"That's what I asked him. Do I look like your secretary?" Leanne said, appealing first to Farren and then to Vanessa Ng, who actually was Farren's secretary. Vanessa shook her head.

Farren left, muttering dark things about the usefulness of her vice president. Jess knew they didn't have to worry much about their cover story, because when Farren reached Mikey she probably would discover he needed her help with something. As soon as Farren was gone, Allie, standing near the sound system, dropped the volume on Meg Mac.

"Okay!" Jess shouted, trying to get the girls' attention. "We're going to have to make this quick, so listen up. Guys? Hey!"

"Shut the fuck up, bitches!" screamed Leanne, joining her in front of the group, and there was a sudden silence.

Jess coughed, nodding her thanks, feeling nervous with all attention now focused on her. It was different standing up there beside Farren; Farren just sort of filled a space. "So, last year, at the toga party, the guys from Knights ran the inaugural Dragon Slayer Sweep." With those words, the quiet seemed to take on a different quality. The girls had not only stopped talking, they'd stopped moving.

"Yeah. Most of you know what I'm going to say. But for those of you freshmen who don't—it was a cash prize that went to the first knight who slept with a Unity girl. Given that we don't actually have a herald, take the dragon label as a further insult."

"The guy who won it slept with Farren. She went back to his

room. Obviously, she knew nothing about the sweep—none of us did." Jess's voice grew raspy, her face starting to burn. She cleared her throat. "And she also didn't know that the asshole was going to stream everything to two other guys—the judges—in another room. Thanks for that, Skype. So, you can imagine how she felt when—" Jess broke off, unable to finish the sentence, shaking her head. Even now, it made her so angry she wanted to kill somebody. Because she'd been there when Farren returned to Unity, been witness to her distress.

One of the freshmen put up her hand, which reminded Jess of high school, and in that moment she was aware of the vast distance between who she'd been back then and who she was now.

"Speak," Leanne scolded. "Don't put up your hand, just speak."

"Did Farren take action?" the freshman asked, and it wasn't really a question so much as a prompt, an expectation.

Jess opened her mouth, then closed it again, glancing at Leanne, who made a don't-look-at-me face. "Um, no, she didn't," Jess said eventually. "It was kind of complicated. She didn't want— Like, she felt that if she did, she'd be admitting there was something to be ashamed of, and . . ."

A different freshman started to raise her hand, realized what she was doing, and lowered it again. "Are they still living at the college?"

"The guys who did it?" Jess shrugged. "We don't know. She never told us who they were. And no one from Knights would say anything—they protect their own like that. The whole thing kind of got hushed up. So . . ." Her voice had grown raspy again, and she coughed. "The thing is, tonight brings it up again. We want to make tonight about something else—"

"Cutting it short, we're holding our own competition," Leanne said, putting Jess out of her misery. "The inaugural Knight Rider challenge. I came up with that, by the way, so feel free to clap." That broke the tension. A wave of laughter passed through the girls, followed by applause, hoots, and cheers. "But don't be misled by the name," Leanne continued. "To participate, you do not ride a knight. In fact, under absolutely no circumstances are you to—"

"Sit on their lance," Jess finished for her.

Leanne barked an appreciative laugh. "Exactly. No sitting on their lances, no letting them *Virile Agitur.* Do not sleep with a boy from Knights—"

"Ever," Jess added, extra vehemence in her voice because she'd had a sudden memory of Blondie standing over her while she swabbed a concrete floor. "Because if you do, you're like a traitor to Farren and every other girl in this place. And—and—well, just every girl. Full stop."

"That was so beautiful," Leanne said, patting her on the arm. "So we've all got the point? If you make jiggy-jiggy with a knight, Jess will ask you to leave the college. Obviously, tonight you won't get them back here on the promise of a coffee alone, though, so you are going to have to pretend you're up for it. Then, when you've got a live one, the first thing you'll need to do is restrain him. If you pick a freshman, chances are he'll pass out anyway, but we've also got a whole bunch of these."

Leanne nodded at Allie, always her willing assistant, who stepped forward, holding a plastic bag. Her sheet wasn't fashioned in a toga. Instead, she'd wrapped it around her like a towel, securing it with a badge of the Aboriginal flag, displaying her ample cleavage. She probably had a strapless bra or bikini top on beneath it, but you couldn't be sure—nothing like suspense as an attention getter. Jess glanced around the faces in front of her, saw all those eyes focused on Allie, and she knew the thoughts going through their minds as they toted her up: Wearing her sheet that way might have showed off her rack, but it didn't do anything for her chunky shoulders. With her golden-brown skin and blond hair worn loose and tousled, she had the beach-girl look down pat, though. Her makeup was minimal, smoky eyeliner and glossy lips. And her legs were good, but were they good enough for the slits she'd cut up the sides of her costume, nearly to her waist? Wasn't she a little too girl-next-door to be acting like she was a goddess?

And driving all these questions was their real question: What did she have that they didn't?

The answer was the kind of self-fulfilling prophecy that messed with girls' heads. Allie had the numbers: a mind-blowing following on Instagram.

Leanne reached into the bag and held up a plastic cable tie; such a small object to be greeted with such a loud round of applause and cheers. And Jess realized, with some surprise, that the girls were onside—always a fifty-fifty proposition with a Unity crowd.

Leanne smiled, pleased with the reaction, and said conversationally, "If you need to use them, I find they work a lot better if you secure the person's arm to an object, like the leg of a desk or the arm of a chair, instead of just binding their wrists together." Jess and Allie side-eyed each other. "If you're worried about going one-on-one, go two-on-one. Tell the knight that you and your friend are going to make all his schoolboy fantasies come true. But the main idea here, in case you haven't already worked it out, is to give him a makeover."

Jess listed some of the many ways they could get creative, drawing hoots and cheers with each point—it was heady, really; she was starting to understand why Farren liked giving speeches so much. "Oh, and don't forget to record your efforts. Allie will be your judge this evening—" Allie bowed to the gathering, one arm clasped to her cleavage, scoring whistles and whoops. "—and she's going to need photographic evidence. In fact, we all want to enjoy it, so load it to Instagram or Facebook."

Leanne took over: "Goes without saying, the person who does

the most impressive job will become an instant legend, but they'll also be awarded tonight's prize, kindly borrowed last Sunday by Flash here—"

"Ah-aahh!" the second and third years chorused on cue, echoing the song by Queen, and Jess grinned. She'd always secretly loved her college nickname.

Allie held up the Knights jersey with a flourish, showing its front and then the back to the crowd. UNITY KNIGHT RIDER was now screenprinted on both sides.

When they saw it, the gathering erupted. Allie turned the music back up. Everybody was definitely pissed, but it was hard not to get caught up in the energy of the occasion. Jess and Leanne glanced at each other, laughed, and then looked away.

"You and your stirring emotions," Leanne said, nudging her with a shoulder.

"Oh, fuck off," Jess said placidly. "Farren's my best friend." They watched Allie, handing out cable ties. "Hey, what's *Virile Agitur* mean, anyway?"

Leanne made a snorting noise. " 'Do the manly thing.' "

"Oh God. That is so funny."

"It gets better," Leanne assured. "Do you know what our motto means?"

"Didn't know we had one," Jess said, surprised.

"Read your handbook. It's *Nemo me impune lacessit*." Leanne paused for effect. " 'No one wounds me with impunity.' "

5.
Boys Like You

By ten o'clock, the downstairs part of Building 33 was jammed with sweaty, frenetic, sheet-clad bodies, many of them drunk, which was to be expected when the ticket price to an event included all the alcohol you could drink. Somehow, the DJ pulled off a segue from Arctic Monkeys to 360 and Gossling, and a fresh wave of people pushed onto the dance floor—Jess, Farren, and the Z-floor boys among them. The Z-floor boys hadn't bothered with togas but had cut holes in their sheets, wearing them poncho style. They seemed to be hearing their own music, floating around in a knock-kneed kind of way, probably on something—Jess could never tell with that lot—but Callum left his bubble long enough to pat her on the back and ask, "You all right, little fella?"

He was a cherubic-looking engineering student, with an odd blend of shyness and high excitability. He was also, apparently, suffering some sort of short-term memory loss, because he'd asked Jess that same question five times in as many minutes.

"Why wouldn't I be?" she asked, shouting to be heard over the music. Then she frowned, distracted. "What's going on with your glasses?"

He obediently bent toward her. The lenses were smeared with what looked like Vaseline, although Jess was pretty sure it was actually lubricant. She cleaned them using his sheet, and he put them back on, blinking at the world around him with an air of revelation.

"Thanks, Jess! The guys must have done it. I was really scared. Thought something was wrong with my eyes."

"Right," Jess said. Some nights you just weren't drunk enough to deal with drugged people. Then she noticed Brendan, and she stopped moving. Callum's size-eleven boot stomped on her sandal, causing her to double over in pain.

"No, I'm okay," she muttered, hobbling. Callum hadn't even noticed.

Brendan's presence explained why Callum had kept checking on her. He must have known Brendan was there—they used to be floormates, after all—and assumed Jess did, too. But it hadn't even occurred to her that Brendan would go. He'd left Unity.

She tried to dance again, feeling like a puppet pulling its own strings. Brendan's arms were slung around a pair of Unity girls, and he lurched them from side to side like he was having the best time in the world, his pretty eyes hidden by his long fringe. His sheet was wrapped around his waist, probably to show off the tattoos on his neck and chest. He was lean, without an ounce of body fat, and Jess knew it was the hungry, restless energy burning in him that had whittled him down to muscle, sinew, and bone. She'd been attracted to that energy. And she'd escaped from it, too.

She watched him, he ignored her, and after a moment she realized that most of the surrounding Unity crowd was sneaking glances at the two of them. So nothing had changed; they were still providing the entertainment.

Jess glanced at Farren, who was dancing with Davey Walters, Z-floor boy and her boyfriend. Farren frowned, as if to say, *What the hell are you still doing here?* It was all Jess needed. She turned away, pushing through the crush of bodies to reach the outside area, where there were fewer bodies and more air. Brendan hadn't followed her—if he had, his hands would have been on her already. Parting the skirt of her toga, she dug her Zippo out of the pocket of her cutoffs and flicked it on. She watched the flame, desperate for some kind of relief. *He's left Unity, you're out of the relationship, so breathe*, she told herself.

When she was calmer, Jess headed back inside, but through a different doorway, one farther down.

"Flash."

Jess turned to see Allie, leaning against the doorway, clutching an empty plastic cup, and a naughty little voice in her head captioned the moment: *Just hanging at the toga party, looking miserable.*

"Hey, what are you doing here by yourself?" Jess asked.

But Allie only gave her a funny smile, as if she didn't trust herself to speak. She reached out, touching Jess's cheek, and Jess caught her hand, squeezing it.

"You okay, Allie?" she asked, concerned now. Allie didn't seem like herself at all. Definitely not the girl who racked up hundreds of comments every time she posted something online.

Allie shook her head. "I'm okay, I'm just . . . You know."

"Did somebody say something to you? Who?" Jess asked, her voice sharp now. It happened from time to time—guys who recognized Allie and seemed to think that because she was accessible online, she was just as accessible in the real world. Jess put an arm around Allie's shoulders. "I guess, if you put yourself out there, you're going to cop the wrong sort of attention sometimes, too."

It wasn't the right thing to say because she felt Allie tense.

Dropping her arm, she tried to smooth things over. "Well, just so you know, I'm in hiding, too. I just saw Brendan."

Allie finally looked at her, giving her a pinched smile of sympathy. "Bet that went well. What'd he say?"

"Nothing. He didn't get a chance. I ran off—very mature of me. But we've talked about it, and talked about it, and I can't keep explaining myself. It's over. Does he really think that if he keeps pushing I'll change my mind?"

Allie didn't seem to be listening, her attention fixed on someone in the crowd of people outside.

"Um, so, anyway," Jess finished lamely. She sighed, leaning back against the wall beside Allie. Then she straightened, spotting Brendan through a gap in the crowd. He was looking around, as though searching for someone. "Shit. There he is. Come upstairs with me?"

ON THE TOP level things were less feral, but the line for the bar was five deep. Jess joined the back of the line and felt exposed and vulnerable until a pair of boys took up position behind her. She didn't know what was more shocking: seeing Brendan for the first time since their breakup during summer break four weeks ago or her reaction to seeing him again—a hot panic that made it hard to think. The problem with Brendan was when he'd been drinking he liked to escalate things, typically in ways that were humiliating for her.

Then someone grabbed Jess's toga, jerking her backward and temporarily choking her.

"We've got drinks," Leanne said, dragging her through the crowd and out onto the deck, where a couple of Unity girls were sitting on one of the heavy outdoor tables, bracketing a large collection of white plastic cups filled with black liquid. They were playing admiring audience to four knights holding lightsabers, who staged a mock battle in front of them.

Jess glanced around the deck, realizing that a large proportion of the people there were either Unity girls or knights—easily identifiable as such because they'd painted their faces with blue zinc cream. "I forgot about that."

"We invented it!" Leanne sounded offended.

"I know, but . . . I want out. Any chance you'll walk me back to the college?"

"Not unless I'm riding a knight," Leanne said. "Why?"

"Brendan's here."

"He probably just wants you to get better," Leanne said, a smirk pulling at the corner of her mouth. Leanne, like Brendan, was doing psychology. With the fullness of time, Jess had come to wonder at how that course was full of truly fucked-up people. "Come on, drink it out, bitch." Leanne handed her two of the cups, then took two for herself. They clinked and downed each drink, one after the other, and Jess made a face. Bourbon.

"Here, this will cheer you up. Meet this guy." Leanne grabbed one of the dueling knights as he passed them. "Jess, this is Richie. Richie, Jess."

"Richard," the guy corrected good-naturedly. He was tousle-haired, rosy-cheeked, and wet-lipped—a freshman, for sure.

"Now, now, better Richie than Dick," Leanne admonished him. "Richie is studying economics, Jess. Just like you. Maybe you should take him home tonight and find out whether he's micro or macro."

Jess watched Richie/Richard flick rapidly and vigorously at his eyelid with his fingernails. "Maybe you should," she told Leanne.

He gave them an overexcited laugh. "Maybe you both should!" Then he did the thing to his eyelid again. The skin above it was purple, Jess noticed. Birthmark?

"Richie has eczema," Leanne explained.

"Yeah, something's set it off. This place is really dusty."

"Richie, do you mind?" Jess asked. "I want to talk to my friend."

"Sure," he said and skipped back to the duel.

"I feel sorry for him," Jess hissed at Leanne.

"I don't," Leanne said. She tapped her ear spike. "In fact, I'm going to use this to pierce his—"

"Uh, uh, uh!" Jess warned, shaking a finger. "Nothing they can sue over. We talked about that, remember? Listen, what's up with Allie?"

"Don't tell me there's no Wi-Fi."

"I know you know. You're the only person she trusts, the only one she talks to." *And that's the paradox of people,* Jess thought. Because before her eyes, Leanne seemed to soften, basking in the words like a cat in sunshine.

"Don't. Say. Anything," she warned, handing Jess another two drinks and taking two for herself. She led Jess across to the spot where the deck's siding met the wall. From there, they had a clear view of the grassy area downstairs, and Leanne pointed at one of the outdoor tables. Michael Azzopardi, Knights' student council vice president, was there, alongside his best bud, Duane, the two of them talking animatedly, entertaining a group of girls from one of the other colleges.

"Who am I looking for?" Jess asked.

"You're looking at him. Mikey."

"Okay, what about him?" Jess asked. Mikey may well have had liquid brown eyes and been tall, olive-skinned, and athletic—the sort who wouldn't be out of place at Knights—but he'd never done anything for Jess. Well, he might have once: in the moment during O-week last year when she'd first spotted him, right before he'd opened his mouth. She frowned, trying to decode the situation. Mikey's attention seemed focused on one girl specifically. Was she a clue? Was she connected to Allie somehow? Jess had seen her around but didn't know her. She was laughing at something Mikey had said, flicking her glossy black hair over her shoulder, gripping his arm.

"Work it out," Leanne growled.

Jess blinked. "Mikey?" Her voice rose. *"Mikey?"*

Leanne shushed her. "They got together on Sunday night."

Jess giggled. "But it's . . . Mikey."

"Oh yeah. This from the woman who ended up with Brendan." Inexplicably, that made Jess giggle more. "Thing is, Allie really likes him. And Mikey . . ."

"Is Mikey." Jess tried to get it together. "Oh man. So that's why she was helping set up for the barbecue."

"She's liked him for ages."

"Really? I never knew."

"How would you? Allie just howls inside."

"You think?" Jess had never really seen Allie as being that way. Allie never complained, never explained. A lot of people took her as being aloof, but Jess, never able to stop herself from letting it all hang out, admired Allie's restraint.

"Shit, yeah. If her Instagram account isn't the most passive-aggressive demand for attention ever, then what is it? Social media was made for introverts."

Both girls froze. Down below, the girl who'd been flirting with Mikey had turned to one of her friends, their hands sliding over each other's shoulders. With Mikey and Duane watching on admiringly—the whole thing was for their benefit, after all—the two girls shared a slow, lingering kiss.

"Oh yuck," Jess said crossly.

"Evolve, bitches," said Leanne.

Without pause or hesitation, each threw a drink. And in one of those precise, perfectly orchestrated moments of fate, the plastic cups traced twin arcs through the air before smashing into the head of the girl who'd been the object of Mikey's attention.

"Yeeeewww!" With that, Leanne disappeared into the crowd.

"Oh shit," Jess breathed, ducking down behind the siding.

"Good shot."

Jess turned to see the guy from the Knights laundry room standing against the wall a short distance from her. She should have been shocked to see him, but she was actually more shocked by what she'd just done. He also seemed interested, craning his neck to see what was happening below.

"Are they looking up here?" she asked, watching his face for clues.

"Why? Are you having regrets?"

"Not really," Jess admitted.

"Well, you're in the clear. Because despite all laws of trajectory, they seem to think it came from somewhere downstairs. She's not happy, though. You've messed up her hair."

"Good."

Blondie gave her a questioning look. "Don't tell me you like Michael Azzopardi?"

"Not me."

"Are you going to stay down there all night?"

"I don't know. What's happening now?"

"She's leaving. Mikey's not very happy about it."

Jess snorted. "Mikey. That's what we call him, too. Hey, how do you know him, anyway?"

"Come over here and I'll tell you all about it."

Jess did no such thing. Instead, she sat on the siding, turned sideways to see him, her back against the wall. For a moment, they just stared at each other. Unlike last time, Blondie was clean-shaven, but his toga was awry, his hair stuck up in tufts, and his blue eyes glittered. He seemed a little loose. Jess wasn't displeased to see him. In fact, she'd been hoping for it. If this was round two, bring it on.

She frowned, noticing the way his fingertips were digging into the brick. "What's wrong? Are you afraid of heights or something?"

"Yeah, so come over here. I can't talk to you while you're sitting there."

"It's not even high," Jess said, leaning over to check.

"It's more of a structural thing," he said quickly. "Like, the railing might— Do you have to do that? Just come here."

"Your voice is different," Jess said, without moving.

"Yeah? How?"

"Sort of chummy. You didn't strike me as chummy last time we met." Jess tilted her head to the side. "Old chap."

"When you were showing me your ass?" he asked. Jess took a sip of her remaining drink, aware her face was betraying her, flushing. "Not that I minded," he added. "You've got a great ass."

"You're not really a freshman, are you?" she asked, deciding to change the subject.

"I never said I was. You did, though. And you failed to mention you were from Unity."

Jess was glad he'd figured it out. It made the stolen jersey sweeter. "You failed to ask."

"What'd you do with it, by the way?" he asked, as if reading her mind.

"Wouldn't you like to know."

"What I'd like is for you to get off that ledge. Please."

"No, thank you. Why were you back at Knights early then? If you're not a freshman, are you on the student council?"

"No. I just needed to be reindoctrinated. You're looking more glamorous this time around."

"I pulled myself together in the hopes of seeing you again."

"I would have preferred your hair down."

"I'll make a note. Got any cigarettes?"

He shook his head. "Filthy habit. I'm sure your boyfriend says the same thing."

"Mitch? Mitch loves me smoking."

"That's right. Good old Mitch. What do you think of him?"

"That's a very personal question."

"Only for Mitch. I bet he's a fucking asshole. Actually, I know he's an asshole. It's a fact. Coroner certified."

"Coroner certified?"

"It means it's official. He's not the guy for you."

Jess narrowed her eyes at him. "Are you only pretending to be drunk?"

"Haven't had a drink all night. What are you pretending to be this time?"

Jess thought about it, then smiled. "Interested."

Blondie tipped his head back and laughed into the night. "And she's funny."

Jess took note of his muscular neck, the width of his shoulders, and the V of his chest, and she felt something flutter in her stomach. She'd never been with a body like that. It was what girls were supposed to want, but she'd always been attracted to the personality, not the package. And maybe it was also because when a guy looked like that she automatically counted herself out.

Blondie hadn't moved, taking a deep breath and exhaling slowly, staring at the stars like if he joined the dots he'd find an answer. And the moment pierced Jess, because it told her something about him she hadn't expected. But then City Calm Down came on, and his head snapped back.

"Great song," they said at the same time.

"Wow, one thing in common," Jess said.

"Let's go back to your room and find the second."

This time it was Jess who laughed. "And he's quick. But we haven't introduced ourselves."

He shook his finger at her. "No names."

"Okay, Blondie." Jess considered him, tightening her ponytail. "I take it you're after the jersey. Or are they holding another sweep?"

"What sweep?"

His face was blank, but she wasn't buying. For all she knew, he could have been one of the three. "The one where the first knight to sleep with a Unity girl wins."

"That's a bit presumptuous, Jersey: thinking I want to sleep with you."

"Not at all. It's true to your type."

"My type?"

"A fully paid-up member of the boys' club. You'd be doing it to teach me a lesson."

"You'd secretly want it, Jersey. Your type loves my type."

"Really?" Jess asked, one eyebrow raised. "And what's my type?"

"Competitive."

Jess opened her mouth and then closed it again, conceding ground with a smile.

Blondie laughed, but in a nice way, like he appreciated her honesty. "And the smile! It's all right, Jersey. I guarantee you'll finish the night disappointed. I'm a reformed man. You won't be getting any."

Jess made a coughing noise, searching for a putdown, but was distracted by Leanne and a couple of the other Unity girls taking Richie-the-knight's arms and pulling him inside. As they did, she spotted Brendan standing in the doorway.

"Oh shit." She dashed across to the wall beside Blondie, flattening against the bricks.

"You keep saying that. What's wrong now?" he asked, turning

toward her, which was good because it meant she was blocked from view.

"Nothing, I just— Nothing."

"Something's wrong. You've gone white," he said. Jess snuck another a glance at Brendan. "Are we hiding from someone?" Blondie asked, looking over his shoulder.

"Don't," Jess said in a terse voice. "Please."

"Indie squid in the doorway?" Blondie asked, his voice sharp. "You should have told me you were with someone else." He went to move away, and Jess, terrified that he'd leave her exposed, grabbed his arm.

"I'm not with him. We broke up a while ago, but he's not taking it very well, so please just . . ." She stared at him in a mute appeal, her eyes wide, and eventually he settled back against the wall.

And while they waited for Brendan to go, or to find them, Blondie watched Jess the whole time. But she didn't care. Because how many times had Brendan accused her of looking at other guys when they'd been together? How many drunken arguments had they had? Him needling her for hours and hours and hours, until she'd wanted to lie and say, yes, he was right, just to get some peace, just to get some sleep. And all those times there'd been nothing, only drama he'd invented. So what would happen if he saw her talking to this guy? Because this time, despite her better instincts, despite even the fact of him being a *knight*, there was more than a flicker of attraction, and Brendan would know it. No matter that they were no longer together, he was still capable of making a scene.

"He's gone," Blondie said, and Jess realized he'd swiveled to take another look.

"Are you sure?"

He nodded slowly, eyes narrowed like he was trying to work her out. "That was quite a reaction, Jersey. I've got to say I'm surprised." He paused while Jess finished most of her drink in one go, the cup rattling against her teeth. "I didn't think you'd take shit from anybody."

Jess met his eyes, her expression raw. "You've only seen me at my best."

Something changed then. The tension that was in him released, his face no longer seeming guarded. He studied her with curiosity in his eyes, as if she'd somehow changed shape. And Jess, in turn, remembered how he'd stared up at the night sky, that drawn-out release of breath. She realized he'd told her the truth when he said he hadn't been drinking, and he hadn't painted his face blue like the other knights. She wondered if these things meant anything, and the swirl of the world around her quieted.

I doubt it.

He glanced down at his arm, and she saw she was still holding him, but she didn't let go. He was keeping her grounded. Then he moved, leaning forward until his head was near hers, and she could smell the hot, woody tang of his aftershave. They looked down into the space bracketed by their bodies; they watched him take her drink.

"Do you mind?" he asked. But he didn't drink from it, just dropped it so he could pull her closer, and there was the warm shock of his skin. He pressed his mouth to her ear and murmured, "You want me to walk you home?"

"Be my knight in shining armor?"

"Why not? You need one."

It was all to script, but still Jess hesitated. Then she sighed, heavily, because there was no way to forget about sweeps and challenges and examples that needed to be made. At least it was easier like that: not looking at him.

"Okay," she said.

6.

Games

Blondie's arm tightened around Jess's shoulders as they left the balcony until her cheek was pressed to his chest, and she realized he thought Brendan might be on the other side of the doorway. She kept her eyes down, pretending to be more out of it than she was, and then they were through and in the clear and Brendan was nowhere to be seen.

The DJ was playing Alison Wonderland, and the room's atmosphere echoed the energy of the music. Guys were sliding, running across the wet tiled floor, and smashing into groups of people, knocking them over for the hell of it. Somebody must have recently collided with the group that included Leanne and Richie, because they were on the floor, trying to disentangle themselves.

Farren was standing at the back of the line for the bar, surveying the room like a general watching a campaign unfold. She did not look impressed. The guy talking to her was a knight but, in Jess's view, an unlikely one: pale-skinned and soft-looking, with thick brown hair and a matching hipster beard, freckles—visible despite the blue smeared over his face—his glasses giving him an earnest look. Farren was nodding, as if she agreed with whatever he was saying. Why was she even talking to him? But then her eyes flashed as she spotted Jess. She didn't pay Blondie much attention, and Jess took it as evidence that he couldn't have been one of the three guys involved in the sweep, but the look on Farren's face suggested she might suspect Jess of having something to do with the sudden attraction Unity girls felt toward knights in general. Unnoticed by her companion, Farren shook her head at Jess, her expression tight. Jess quickly looked away, getting a twinge of something.

At that moment, a stocky guy with curly hair and a blue face blocked Blondie's path, addressing him as "Killer" and telling him it was the Paddington Tavern for the after-party, acting like he couldn't see Jess tucked under Blondie's arm. He probably thought he was being subtle. And Blondie played right along: widening his stance as if experiencing a sudden and significant surge in ball size, speaking in the drawl used by guys who are fluent in Brah.

"Yeah, right, the Paddo. Not gonna make it."

At that, the other knight finally focused on Jess, and she decided she didn't like his eyes. "Roger that." He smirked. "Killer."

Jess rolled her eyes. Her moment of doubt on the deck seemed like a long time ago. Actually, if this guy was indicative of Blondie's friends, it had been more like a temporary spell of insanity. Did she really want to go through with this? Letting this pig assume for one second that she'd been successfully groomed seemed like far too high a price to pay. She started to pull away and then stopped. Not because Blondie's arm had tightened, but because right at that moment her eyes locked with Brendan's on the other side of the room. When his flared, she decided to let the roger-that guy gloat, meekly allowing Blondie to shepherd her past him and toward the spiraling staircase that led to the roof and what was actually ground level—the building having been built to make the most of a sloping site. Escaping cleanly, Jess felt, with no small measure of relief, was worth that price. She'd let Blondie walk her home and decide what to do about the challenge when she got there.

Their exit coincided with the entrance of a large group of people, forcing Jess and Blondie into single file. He took her hand, leading her, the two of them hugging the curved wall. At the tail end of the arrivals was a smaller subgroup of girls. The first two passed Blondie without seeming to notice him, but the third crossed to block him, veering so abruptly that the two girls following nearly knocked her down the stairs. They stopped also, and Jess, not realizing what was going on, drew level with Blondie, so that the three of them formed an unwilling audience to what was obviously going to be a confrontation.

"Killer. How nice to see you. What's it been? A year?" The girl's voice was high and clear, but the glitter in her green eyes suggested adrenalin was coursing through her system.

Blondie looked shocked. No, he looked hunted. He glanced past her, as if calculating the possibility of escape, his hand tightening on Jess's to the point where it hurt. He'd forgotten she was there, she was certain of it.

"I actually didn't think you'd be back. But here you are," the girl mused.

"Here I am." Blondie's voice was even, but his grip hadn't eased.

"You know, I'm not surprised to see you again. But I am surprised you didn't get in touch. Not once." The girl said this so carefully that Jess had the impression it had been rehearsed.

"You're surprised?" Blondie's tone was flat. "Really?"

For a moment, the two of them just stared at each other, something close to hatred on the girl's face. Then she blinked, back in control, and turned her attention to Jess, who immediately wished she'd stayed behind Blondie, in the shadows. This girl was like a diamond; she drew the light. And she had a way of reflecting it that made you feel exposed. Her pale blond hair tumbled over her shoulders in loosely styled curls. Her makeup was immaculate, lashes so thick and luxurious they had to be false. But they weren't tacky, they just made her more exquisite. For the first time Jess understood how looking like that was a kind of armor. Nobody would ever say *I doubt it* to her.

"And who's this?" she asked, her voice sweet.

"Nobody," Blondie answered, blocking her.

The girl gave Jess a small smile of sympathy. "I'm sure he doesn't mean that." She seemed to reconsider. "Well." And Jess felt humiliated, even though the insult was largely intended for Blondie. "Isn't it amazing?" the girl asked, her attention back on him. "Everything that's happened, and you haven't changed at all. I almost admire it."

"When you're done."

"When are you going to be done, Killer? That's what I want to know."

Blondie shook his head, angry now. "I don't need this." He pushed between her and her companions, dragging Jess along behind him.

Jess heard Diamond Girl laugh, and then she and Blondie passed through the doorway and out onto the roof, where the vibration of the music could be felt underfoot and cigarettes looked like fireflies in the dark.

Where it was quiet enough for Jess to hear his uneven breathing.

BY THE TIME they reached the tunnel that cut beneath the physiology building, Jess couldn't stand it anymore. Not one word had passed between them since they'd left the toga party, Blondie's pace quickening to the point where he was breaking records.

Ducking out from under his arm, she placed both hands on his chest. "Stop. Just stop. I want to get off."

His jaw was clenched, and it took him a moment to return from wherever he'd been. Even in dim light, Jess could tell that it hadn't been a good trip. She had the sneaking suspicion he'd forgotten she was there. "What's wrong?" he asked, irritated.

"I can walk myself home from here. You're too angry."

"I'm not angry," he said, sounding angry.

Jess touched his fisted hand, and he batted her fingers away. For some reason that stung. Badly. Maybe because she was drunk. Maybe because the exchange with Diamond Girl had clearly affected him and, with his defenses down, Jess had expected soft-ness. But he was a knight, she reminded herself. Her expectations should begin and end there.

"Okay, you're not angry, and I'm just fine, so thanks for the lift. Next time I want someone to put me in a headlock and march me home, I'll be in touch." With that, Jess walked off.

She thought that was it, that he'd just let her go, but after a moment she heard, "Hey!" And then: *"Hey!"*

She spun around. "I'm sorry, are you talking to me? Or is there an invisible dog in the vicinity?" It would have been perfect, except she was walking backward and nearly tripped on her toga, which had started to unravel. Blondie laughed, pissing her off, and she took it out on the sheet, tugging at it violently until she had the whole thing off, bundling it up and throwing it on the ground.

"Nice exit!" he called.

"Interesting mental problem!" she shouted back.

This time Jess counted her strides, deciding that two hundred of them would put an acceptable distance between her and him. But she'd only reached five when she heard the soft pad of his sneakers behind her.

"What the fuck's wrong with you?" he asked.

"Nothing, now that I'm leaving."

"You can't leave yet—"

"Watch me."

"—you haven't got what you wanted."

"And what would that be?"

"Your good-night kiss. The part where I try to take things further, and you act like you don't want it."

"Jesus, both hands on your lance," Jess muttered. More loudly: "You can kiss my ass. How about that?"

"Wouldn't mind. Is this because I said you were nobody?"

"Hardly."

"You sure? Because you've got an ego, Jersey. Even I can see that."

Astonished, Jess whirled to face him. "You say that like it's a bad thing! Oh, I get it." She jabbed his chest with a finger. "In your world that is a bad thing. God forbid a woman actually has an ego. Well, listen up, my friend, because you may find this next part a bit controversial." She leaned closer, her voice low and breathy: "My ego is enormous. I have a *big* . . . *thick* . . . *ego* . . . and I love it. It's the reason I'm able to tear myself away from you. I'm just dying to get home so I can play with it." She winked. "Roger that, Killer?"

But he grabbed her hand as she turned to go, pulling her around to face him, catching her other wrist as he did it. "Don't go, Jersey," he said, sounding much too in control for her liking. "Is that what you want me to say?"

Jess didn't bother trying to pull free. Instead, she lashed out in a different way. "No, let's talk about your ex-girlfriend. That's going well."

His grip tightened, and she knew she'd scored a direct hit. "It's nothing like that, so don't project your shit on me."

"Oh, I'm sorry." Jess watched the muscles working in his jaw, feeling a nasty sense of triumph. "She's current?"

"I don't do girlfriends."

"Your own or other people's?"

"Why don't you shut your mouth?" The aggression in his voice was like a slap.

Shocked, Jess stared at him. "Well, congratulations."

"On what?"

"On being the guy I thought you were."

"You don't know me."

Jess gave a hollow laugh. "I do now." As soon as the words left her mouth, she tensed, wondering if she was about to be hit by a guy for the first time in her life.

Instead of exploding, Blondie seemed to crumple, his face stricken, dropping her wrists and slumping back against the wall of the tunnel. For a moment he stared straight ahead, his eyes glassy, then he turned his head away, and she could see the rapidly beating pulse in his neck. His breathing was ragged, hitching in his throat like he was having some kind of anxiety attack.

Jess, on the other hand, had stopped breathing altogether. Realizing this, she sucked back air that sat high in a tight chest. "Are you okay?"

Blondie wiped a palm across his forehead and then frowned down at his own sweat. "Too hard," he said, talking to himself, not her, his voice scratchy. He swallowed, eyelids flickering. "Can't do this. It's too . . ." He focused on Jess, looking at her without really seeing her, using her as some kind of distraction, something to hold on to.

"Well, I'd offer to walk you home, but . . ." Jess shrugged, making a face.

Blondie seemed to return to the here and now, his blue eyes sharpening. "Look at me. I'm a fucking joke," he said, his voice harsh.

"Really, it's okay. I'm not judging. I think people should be—"

She broke off with a gurgle of alarm as he pulled her abruptly into a hug, burying his face in her neck.

At first, she held her arms out to the sides, her body rigid and tense. But he held her for such a long time, long enough for the shock of being held by him to give way to an awareness of him: the warmth of his skin, the hint of sandalwood in his aftershave, and, beneath it, the spice of his sweat, the feel of his cropped hair brushing her cheek—so militaristic, so different from the carefully mussed locks sported by Unity boys. Long enough for her hands to come to rest on his hips. Long enough for a silence to become expectant.

When his face finally moved toward hers, Jess closed her eyes.

But just before their mouths touched, Blondie whispered, "Question for you, Jersey. If I'm the guy you think I am, then what are you still doing here?"

Jess froze, feeling the world tilt and spin away from her. As her eyes opened, he ran his lips along her jawline, murmuring, "Seems to me you want it."

Jess pushed roughly at his chest, stepping backward, away from him, more humiliated than she'd ever been in her life. She'd only been going to kiss him because he'd been vulnerable, she told herself—and he *had* been vulnerable; he'd completely lost it. Was that it? He was punishing her because she'd seen him like that?

Blondie smirked, holding his palms out as though offering her a deal. "It's either that or I'm not the guy you think I am."

Jess said nothing, her heart thudding, her hands sliding into her pockets of their own accord, seeking out her Zippo. And her fingertips brushed the cable ties she'd stuffed in there at the beginning of the night, what seemed like a hundred years ago.

Eventually, Blondie dropped his swagger. He shifted, clearing his throat, glancing back the way he came, as though wondering if he should make his exit.

And Jess finally spoke. "Do you want to come back to my room?"

7.
Hands

People had already started trickling back from the toga party. Alpine blared from a C-floor window, and somebody's bedroom had been transported to the courtyard outside the dining room, reassembled there perfectly.

"Wow. Different college, same shit," Blondie murmured, sliding an arm around Jess's waist and feigning innocence when she looked at him. "What? I might get lost." Jess gave him a demure smile. "Not buying it for a second, Jersey. You're pissed."

"And yet you're here."

"Wouldn't miss it for the world."

"*Killer!*"

Jess glanced back to see a pair of M-floor girls and Leanne supporting Richie-the-knight. Leanne gave Jess an evil grin, and Jess got another twinge of the kind she hadn't wanted to examine the first time she'd felt it: when she'd spotted Farren near the bar.

"Hey, Killer!" Richie shouted again when Blondie didn't respond. "*Killer!*" He sounded like a bawling calf.

Jess dropped her pace, only to be forcibly dragged along. "Slow down, there's a legend behind you. He's got three girls, and he needs your approval."

"I don't want to talk to the freshman dickhead."

"But you're his hero," Jess pouted. "Killer."

Blondie shot her a look.

The other four peeled off, heading toward the M-floor steps, while Jess led Blondie through the reading room. She stopped at the vending machine outside the office.

"I'm going to need a drink for this," she said by way of explanation. "I've got rum in my room."

He let go of her reluctantly. "I'll get it."

"I didn't say you had to buy it for me. I just said I'd need one."

"And I said, I'll get it."

Jess patted her heart. "Oh my, a gentleman. Coke, please."

Blondie tried without success to find a way into his toga and then just ripped the sheet off and threw it on the ground, revealing a pair of black Canterbury rugby shorts and a chest so well-defined it made him seem more tightly skinned than ordinary people. Jess bet he shaved it. He bought two cans of Coke.

"Thank you," Jess said, and, despite everything, she meant it. Brendan had insisted on splitting every single transaction—unless, of course, Jess had wanted to pay.

Blondie seemed bemused. "And thank you. Most girls just seem to expect it."

"I'm not most girls," she told him flatly, walking off. When she realized he wasn't following, she turned around. He hadn't moved.

"If that's the case, you want to tell me why we're here?"

Jess stared at him for a moment, savoring a strong dislike. She covered the distance between them in four quick strides, stopping only when she was right up in his personal space. Close enough for his expression to change. Close enough to feel the heat trapped in his skin.

"You're here because you want something," she said, taking one icy can and pressing it to his left nipple. Blondie flinched but otherwise didn't move, his eyes locked on hers. "And I'm here to give it to you," she continued, taking the other can and pressing it to his right nipple. She held the cans there, enjoying his discomfort.

When she'd removed them, he asked, "Are you talking about the jersey or something else?"

"Whatever gets you up in my room."

"Up? How high is it?" Jess just smiled. Blondie's gaze traveled upward as he made the calculations. "Of all the rooms in this place, you have to have one on the top floor?"

"I know. It's like we were never meant to be."

Seven flights of stairs later, they reached a deserted T-floor, and Blondie stopped for a moment to press a palm to the wall, perhaps reassuring himself that the place was structurally sound. Jess didn't wait for him, but when she opened the door to her room, juggling the cans of Coke, he was right behind her, his hands closing on her hips in a way that made her skin fizz with risk. They were alone.

Inside, she checked her phone. Six texts from Brendan that she didn't bother to read. Blondie was closing and locking her door, each sound seeming to have a grim finality. She touched her pocket, considering what she was about to attempt. She could feel the rushing of her own blood.

Blondie turned to look at her and then baulked. "The window."

"Oh. Right. That."

Jess untied the cord that held her window at a perfect horizontal and let it swivel to a more moderate gap. It was possibly for the best: There was sheet lightning in the east, and in its flashes she saw heavy-bellied clouds gathering to mount one of Brisbane's summer storms. There was no wind yet, though, no thunder, only suspense; the air was still and swollen.

Blondie stood, looking around him. Jess's room, now unpacked and tidy, was a blend of the sporty, the feminine, and the bookish. There was a basketball clumped in the corner alongside her high-tops and two pairs of running shoes. Scented candles and silver-framed photos lined the shelf above the desk, in keeping with the white linen quilt and lace cushions on the bed, and instead of prints or posters on the walls, covers of her favorite books were strung from a wire that stretched the width of the room, displayed there like scalps.

"Where's the rum?" he asked.

Jess hesitated, wanting him sitting down, not roaming around, but her hands were full with tying the window into its new position. "In the fridge. Which is in the closet." Blondie pushed open the sliding door on the left, revealing the dresser. "Other end," she told him, but he acted like he hadn't heard, opening the top drawer, exposing her underwear. "Hey! Do you mind?"

"No." Blondie shut that drawer and opened the next, working his way down.

"You won't find what you're looking for."

He slammed the bottom drawer shut and started flicking through the clothes on hangers, pausing when he saw her college jersey. She thought he might take it in retaliation, but he kept going, stopping again when he reached a black hospitality apron.

"What's Q-P-A-C stand for?" he asked.

"A little inconvenience called work. You may not be familiar with it."

"I've worked."

"That's past tense. And a week of high school work experience doesn't count."

"Full-time. All last year."

"You weren't here?" It tallied with what Diamond Girl had said, Jess realized. *What's it been? A year?* And it was firm confirmation that he'd had nothing to do with the sweep. She sat on her bed, waiting for him to say more. He didn't, flicking through the rest of the hangers. "Where'd you work?" she asked.

"Sugar mill."

"Why?"

Blondie ignored her, peering into the closet at the floor space beside her dresser, the part where she kept her shoes. Then he pushed the slatted doors across to reveal her fridge. It opened with a smacking sound, the glasses inside clinking together.

He glanced at her, eyebrows raised. "You keep T-shirts in your fridge?"

"Only when it's hot." There were bras in there, too, and Jess was mildly disappointed that he didn't comment on it. "You said you weren't a freshman. Does that mean you took a year off?"

Blondie poured a hefty slug of rum into one of the cold glasses. "Ice?"

"Yes, please. Wait. Aren't you having one?"

He screwed the lid closed and returned the bottle to the fridge. "I haven't had a drink in over a year, and even if I was drinking, I wouldn't drink rum. Can't stand the smell of it."

"Sugar mill, hates the smell of rum . . . You're not from Bundaberg, by any chance?"

Blondie dropped a handful of ice into the glass, then looked at Jess. "On second thought, let's not get to know each other. How about that?"

He was so cold. Jess felt off-balance, intimidated. It occurred to her that he'd probably just leave when he couldn't find the jersey, and she also realized it might be a good thing. She was starting to doubt herself.

"Fine," she said, turning away so he couldn't see the look on her face, pressing keys on her laptop. Jackie Onassis started faintly, then the brass kicked in and Jess jumped, hastily turning it down.

"Tell me you don't really like that shit," Blondie said, slamming the fridge closed.

"I'm playing it, aren't I?"

He moved to the desk, topping off the glass with Coke. "Yeah, but you like City Calm Down."

"That doesn't mean I can't like Aussie hip-hop. I might have democratic tastes."

"Yeah, and you might also have a pair of cowboy boots, hardly worn, a pair of Doc Martens, hardly worn, and a pair of high heels, hardly worn. Adidas high-tops and Asics running shoes. In other words, you don't know who the fuck you are or what the fuck you like. My guess is you play that in an attempt at irony. That's part of the whole Unity deal, isn't it? And being different . . . along with all the other people being different." He handed Jess her drink, looking down on her.

Jess blinked, stung by the attack. "Yeah, that's the Unity thing," she told him, placing the glass on the floor. "You're probably also threatened by the fact that the guys here can cope with women in contexts other than porn. Not like a bunch of little lords who hate women because they secretly prefer getting hot and sweaty with one another under the guise of chasing a leather ball around a field." Jess tightened her ponytail. "Killer."

"Pitch."

Jess, mishearing him, fired up. "*Excuse* me?"

"It's called a pitch."

"Go fuck yourself."

"Oh, that's ladylike."

The sneer in his voice. As though she wasn't worth even a

pretense at courtesy. It hurt. Jess dropped her gaze, reaching for her drink, the fizzing Coke burning her nose and making her eyes water.

"You forgot to say that a lot of your friends are guys," he said after a moment, still standing over her.

"A lot of my friends *are* guys," Jess said, sliding out from under him. She stood at the desk, emptying her pockets—not just the loose change and her Zippo, but also the cable ties. She wasn't up to this. Her eyes were still watering.

"They're not your friends. They're just guys who wouldn't mind doing you, and they've worked out that familiarity gives them an advantage."

Jess flicked her Zippo on and stared at the flame. "You're telling me this because a lot of your friends are girls?"

"None of my friends are girls."

She snapped the Zippo shut. "And that's a good thing, is it?"

"At least I'm honest."

As Jess turned to face him, he made a motion with his hand, obviously expecting her to resume hostilities. But there was a flicker of confusion on his face when he noticed her eyes.

"Well, what do you want me to say?" she said in a dangerously quiet voice, her cheeks burning. "You don't even know me, but you hate me anyway. Because I'm a girl. And I can think that you probably hate a lot of things, but that doesn't make me feel better. You have humiliated me by laughing at me when I thought you were going to kiss me, you have insulted my taste in music and, somehow, my taste in shoes. I'm not only unladylike, I don't know who I am, and you've also gone to the trouble of assuring me that none of my male friends respect me, either. Basically, you have made me feel the opposite of special in every possible way. But guess what? You're too late. Because somebody's already done that."

There didn't seem to be any oxygen in the room. All Jess could see were unblinking blue eyes. When she couldn't bear it any-more, she groaned, covering her face with her hands. "We're done. Just go."

"Jersey." His voice was completely different.

"Please," Jess said into her hands.

"Look, I'm sorry, all right?"

"Whatever. And don't worry, I'm not weepy. It's just been a pretty full-on night, what with Brendan, and you, and all the drink-ing, and all the other nights."

His hands closed on her wrists as if he was about to uncover her face, and Jess knocked them aside before he could do it, squinting at a spot just to the right of him.

"Hey. Jersey." He leaned forward, trying to get her to look at him. "Sorry." The word sounded just as rusty the second time around.

"It doesn't matter." Jess blinked several times and then focused on him as the thought occurred to her. "But I genuinely do like Aussie hip-hop, so you can go suck it on that one."

He nearly smiled but squashed it.

"Go," she told him, pointing at the door.

"I would . . ." Blondie sat down in the study chair, his long legs trapping her between him and the desk. "But now I don't want to."

"Well, you should, because there's nothing for you here. You won't find the jersey, and you won't win the sweep. I might have been going to kiss you, but I would *never* sleep with you. Not in a million years."

"That's all right. I wouldn't sleep with you, either." It should have been an insult, but something about the way he said it meant it wasn't. He leaned back in his chair, placing his hands behind his head, exposing tufts of fine, golden hair, still holding her hostage.

"Honestly, I'm too tired for this shit." As Jess said it, she felt it. *"Exhausted.* Do you know I've been out every night for the last six nights?"

"You're a legend."

"That's what I was aiming for. Legend status."

He smiled, squeezing her with his thighs. "Sit down."

"No." Jess paused, overcome by a yawn. "And you should go."

"Can't."

"Why not?"

"Because you're not what I expected, Jersey."

"What'd you expect?"

"You know. Just a chick." Jess's eyes narrowed ever so slightly. "Oh, come on. It's a compliment."

"Right," Jess said. They stayed like that, her trapped between his legs, and if Jess's face was thoughtful while she studied him, Blondie seemed perfectly comfortable with the scrutiny. "Okay," she said eventually, and he eased the squeeze just enough for her to perch on one of his thighs. "Now what?" she asked, looking sideways at him.

"Now . . ." He repositioned her so that she faced forward, one arm hooked across her waist like a seatbelt. "I make it up to you. Give you a massage."

Jess giggled, in spite of herself. "Oh, wow, you've got all the moves."

His free hand closed on her shoulder, starting to knead the muscles there with a quiet assurance, and she grew still, wary. He paused long enough to push her ponytail out of the way and resumed using both hands, and Jess realized, surprised, that he genuinely intended to give her a massage. When that sank in, she leaned forward, resting her forehead on her folded arms on the desk, surrendering until further notice; yielding. She wasn't stupid. She knew it was probably the next stage in a strategy: flirt, flay, soothe, and lay. But it felt so good, she'd take it anyway.

Besides, it would have been hard to knock back something so unprecedented. She'd never been touched like that before. Her high school hookups had been furtive territory wars, with the exception of a sweetly sincere boyfriend at the start of senior year who'd done nothing but kiss her for months—eventually scoring the jackpot one day, just because she was so bored. And with Brendan, touching had been passed over entirely in favor of elaborate, competitive sex, the two of them moving through a series of strangely sterile positions, more posed than felt. If high school was all about whether or not you'd give it up, college seemed to be about nothing but giving it up. Suddenly, inexplicably, the rules changed, and—*bam*—you were Adult-with-a-capital-*A*. There was no means to the end, there was just the end, just sex, and you pretended to keep up. Sometimes Jess had felt it, the flaring of her own appetite, but she'd rarely let herself go. Too busy performing.

She remembered something: Brendan slapping her ass, right in the middle of things. Her mouth filled with spit. Out of all they'd done, that (relatively minor) act needled her still. Because he hadn't asked. Because she'd been reduced to a prop, while he pretended to be something he'd seen. She should have slapped him back. No. She should have laughed her head off.

"It's just a massage," Blondie said, and Jess realized her fists were clenched.

She exhaled, trying to leave her head and return to her body. Slowly, under the firm, continual pressure of Blondie's hands, she did it. Anger, resentment, a biting sense of the ridiculous—it all faded. A lot of things faded. Even the awareness that she was being massaged.

Until her head was finally, blessedly, empty.

8.
You Can Be the Boss

Eventually, though, something pulled Jess out of her pleasure coma. It wasn't that her playlist had finished. Or that the storm had arrived and was close to breaking, thunder reverberating through the air. No, what made Jess resurface was a change in pressure of a different kind: Blondie's hands were softer, slower, more thoughtful, somehow. Then he wasn't massaging her at all, but rather stroking her flesh with his fingertips. Her one-piece was low-backed, and he drew patterns all over her skin, sometimes dipping below the gaping waistband of her denim cutoffs in a way that was delicious, but also only just bearable. Soon he was stroking the skin under her arms, the sides of her breasts, circling her armpits . . . areas so sensitive that Jess couldn't help it: She squirmed.

And he stopped.

Jess waited, breath held, hoping he'd keep going. But he didn't, resting his palms on her shoulders where they'd begun. She shifted, turning her head to the side as though listening, and her gaze came to rest on a small group of objects she'd laid out in preparation for the night. Hair dye. A razor. Shaving cream. More cable ties. They looked like pieces in a game of chess.

The words were so low she hardly heard them, scraped from the back of his throat: "Can I touch you?"

Hot white light flashed in the room, and the thunder accompanying it was so loud and so close that Jess jumped, wondering if the sky had cracked apart. Next came the first few drops of rain, the gin smell of it wafting through the window.

"Sorry," she said. "I got scared."

"That's okay." His voice, like hers, jarred.

"My heart's beating so fast."

His hand snaked around her body and pressed against her chest. "I can feel it."

Jess cringed. But then the rain came down hard, drowning out their sudden awkwardness. Blondie slid an arm beneath her legs as though he was about to carry her off and turned her sideways across his lap so that her knees were hooked over the armrest. Jess pressed her flushed face to his neck. She'd known it would go this way—was counting on it, in fact—but things seemed confusingly real. The beat of his pulse against her lips: a rapid, hot rush. He felt it, too.

Blondie tugged on her ponytail, pulling her out of hiding. She thought he was about to kiss her, but he said, "You didn't answer my question."

"I'm not going to sleep with you."

"That's not what I asked. I just want to touch you."

After a moment, Jess nodded. She was turned on. It was that simple and that complicated. Blondie reached for the zip on her one-piece, and she watched the shiny purple fabric split apart to reveal vulnerable white skin. Her nipples were hard, visible through the material. His hand slid inside, and as he cupped and squeezed her he started to breathe through his mouth. Then he was tugging at the straps, pulling them over her arms so that she was bare-chested, sitting on his knee like a lap dancer. For a moment, he held her away from him, staring at her body. He said, "Oh, that's beautiful," as though he was talking to someone else.

Then he leaned over, grabbing the unopened can of Coke from the desk.

Jess grabbed at his wrist. "No!" Half laughing.

"You taught me." Blondie held the can there, just out from her breast, until she looked at him. And when she did, his eyes were so intense that she released his wrist. She gasped when he pressed the can to her nipples, first one and then the other, but then he replaced it with his mouth, sucking each nipple in turn, his hands supporting her, and Jess closed her eyes, her breath catching. She arched her back.

"You like that?" he asked, but it wasn't a question, because he knew. He started to suck again, his mouth more insistent now, his stubble scratching her skin, and she wrapped her arms around his head, her fingers grasping his hair. As his mouth drew her in, she felt it all the way down below: a tugging sensation.

Then Blondie stopped abruptly, repositioning her again so she was facing forward and leaning back against his chest, and she could feel his erection pressing against her as he unbuttoned her cutoffs.

Jess's hands clamped down on his.

"It's all right," he told her. "Nothing's going to happen."

"Liar." Jess shifted against him. "You're hard."

In answer, he pushed a hand down the front of her underwear and gripped her crotch. "And you're wet."

It was sudden and shocking and Jess gasped, knocking his hand away. "God, you're such an asshole."

"It's true, though, isn't it?" he asked in a mocking voice. "Admit it. You're wet."

Jess hurriedly pulled the straps of her one-piece back on, zipping it up. "Would you stop saying that? Anyway, so what? It doesn't mean anything." Jess went to stand, but Blondie grabbed her hips, holding her there.

"Well neither does the fact I'm hard. You're not irresistible. I told you before, it's not even on the table. We're just messing around." He wrapped his arms around her, and Jess could feel his breath on her cheek. "But that's all right, isn't it? You don't want anything more than that anyway, do you?"

Jess shook her head, her face flaming. Her gaze fixed again on the little zoo of objects on her desk. Blondie was too busy enjoying himself to notice. His mistake.

As suddenly as it had started, the rain stopped. But what followed wasn't stillness. There were voices, a slamming noise, shouting, some giggling right outside the door, and then Lana del Rey—old stuff from before she got famous—played loud.

"The others are back," Jess said, feeling the need to explain the obvious.

"We'll be quiet," Blondie said, as though she'd asked a question. "Come over on the bed. I swear, no sex." He went to stand, one arm around her waist, but Jess gripped the edge of the desk.

"Not yet. I'm embarrassed, okay? I can't even look at you."

Blondie stopped moving, saying nothing, but Jess knew he'd like her feeling like that. He'd try to exploit it somehow. She was counting on it.

A slow minute passed. When he spoke again, his voice was completely different. Harder. "Take these off then." He tugged at her cutoffs.

"On one condition."

"What's that?"

"You can't touch me unless I say so," Jess said, placing his hands on the arm rests.

"You'd better get off me then."

Jess climbed off his lap and turned to face him, leaning against the desk. She let her cutoffs fall to the floor.

"Take your hair down, too." A command, not a request.

"What's the magic word?"

"*Fuck*," he said, drawing the word out. "But we're not doing that."

Jess said nothing, just pulled the hairband from her ponytail and shook her hair loose.

"Turn around."

"No touching?"

He gripped the armrests. "No touching." So Jess turned around for him. "Bend over." Jess did, resting her elbows on the desk, hearing him suck air through his teeth. "For the record?" he said, his voice rough. "If I was going to do you, it'd be like that. Over the desk."

There were a number of things Jess would have liked to have said to that. Instead, she swapped her hairband for two of the cable ties, tucking them into the front of her one-piece.

This time, she gave the instruction. "Now you take your shorts off."

"And why would I do that?" he asked.

"Because you want to see me on my knees."

There was a coughing noise. "I didn't think you were that kind of girl, Jersey."

"What kind of girl is that?"

"The sort who will do things."

Jess said nothing. After a moment, she heard him shift in the chair, the snap of elastic, the rustle of fabric. Quick, eager movements.

"Underpants, too," she said.

"Way ahead of you," he told her, and Jess rolled her eyes. Then she turned around to face him, her skin prickling with adrenaline.

Blondie was slouched in the chair, fully naked, his elbows resting on the armrests, his legs planted apart, his whole positioning seemingly about displaying his cock, because that was all Jess saw, jutting up from the soft purse of his scrotum and a neatly trimmed patch of golden pubes. As she stared down at it, he tensed so that it pulsed, and she glanced at him in surprise. He smiled at her, but there was a cold burn in his eyes, and she wondered if he was angry or turned on, or whether, for him, they were exactly the same thing.

Holding his thighs, Jess got down on her knees, suddenly unable to look at him, her nerve failing. When she didn't do anything more, Blondie took hold of his penis and reached out with his other hand.

"No touching!" Jess jerked back, glaring at him. "I don't want you holding my head, driving things. That would make me feel—"

"Choked," he said apologetically.

"—used."

He blinked. "Okay," he said, clamping his hands to the armrests. "No touching."

He wanted it bad, that much was obvious. For some reason it helped Jess feel more in control of the situation. She cleared her throat, picking up his shorts. "I'm going to tie you there," she told him, her voice brisk, businesslike. "I don't trust you otherwise."

Blondie exhaled, shaking his head. "Fine. Whatever it takes." He watched as she used his shorts and underpants to tie his wrists to the armrests, obviously not threatened at all. It wouldn't stop him if he wanted to break free.

"Why so impatient?" Jess asked.

Blondie looked at the ceiling. "It's been a long time, all right?"

Then his head snapped back as Jess took hold of his penis, feeling it thick in her palm, pulsing in response to her touch. His hands tightened on the armrests, and he narrowed his eyes in concentration, looking like he was in a rocket, preparing for blastoff. Jess slowly licked her lips, watching his eyes glaze, then lowered her head, her mouth opening, showing the tip of her tongue . . .

And she stopped, letting his penis snap back against his stomach. "I don't want you watching me, either."

"You're killing me."

"I'm embarrassed. I mean, I hardly know you."

"All right," he said through gritted teeth, closing his eyes.

"Not enough," she told him, grabbing her cutoffs and sliding them over his head. Blondie started to protest, but shut up as she cupped his balls in her hand. So soft. So vulnerable. She stroked them gently, taking out the cable ties. Then she leaned over, letting her hair brush his penis and balls, his inner thighs. He groaned. She did it again, and as she was doing it, she threaded the cable ties loosely around his wrists. Then she straightened, gripping his knees. "Ready?"

"Take a wild guess."

Jess pulled on the cable ties as hard as she could, snapping them tight.

"Hey, what are you doing?" Blondie asked sharply, not *really* worried yet. That came a moment later when Jess pulled the cutoffs from his head and he had visual. "What the fuck?" He turned his head, straining to see her, then shuffled the chair around in a way that might have been comical if the stakes weren't so high. "What is this?" he demanded. "You take them off right now! Right. Fucking. *Now!*" He screamed the last word out, flexing against the ties, his face reddening with the effort, the cords in his neck strained, his teeth bared. And Jess's heart stopped, because she really thought he'd snap them, and when he did . . .

There was a frenzied knocking on the door. Blondie and Jess froze, staring at each other like coconspirators.

"Hey, Jess! Is everything all right?" The voice was as familiar as family, but, for a moment, Jess couldn't place it. Blondie looked to be having the same struggle with returning to reality. Then she realized it was Allie.

"I think so!" Jess shouted. "Just hold on a sec." She lowered her voice, asking Blondie, "Am I okay? Or do I need help?"

"You can do anything you want. *Anything*," Blondie hissed, violently shaking his head, "but don't let them in. Do not let them in!"

There were muffled giggles and whispers outside the door. Due to interest in the Knight Rider challenge, the whole of T-floor might have been collected there, if not most of the girls in the college, Jess thought. Blondie seemed to have reached the same conclusion.

"You can't struggle," Jess warned. "You just have to take it." He nodded in frantic agreement. "No, I'm good!" she shouted. "He's going quietly."

Blondie exhaled, looking down at his dying erection, and Jess suddenly lost it, wracked by silent giggles. It was the only way to release the adrenaline still zinging around her system.

"Yell if you need us, okay, girl?" Allie shouted. "We've got your back."

The giggles and whispers outside the door faded. Then Blondie and Jess were alone again. Their eyes met, and Jess winced. He looked murderous.

"*Nemo me impune lacessit*," she told him.

"Latin?" he said in a sour voice.

"No one wounds me with impunity."

"S'pose the blow job's off the menu then."

"Afraid so."

"Not that kind of girl?"

"Not for you, anyway."

"Are you sure about that, Jersey? Because I felt how wet you were, remember? I think you're pissed because I said I wouldn't fuck you. You wanted it."

Jess coughed a laugh. Then she smiled, shaking her head. Because for the first time that night she held the balance of power, and it wasn't because he was tied to a chair.

It was because he was wrong.

"I doubt it," she said.

She walked around behind him, sliding her hands over his shoulders and down his chest, murmuring the words in his ear, her voice low and throaty: "Let me tell you something. I *was* wet. I got turned on. I liked you touching me. For a moment there, I even liked you telling me what to do. But that doesn't automatically mean I wanted to have sex with you." She stroked his nipples, feeling them tighten, watching his erection return. "You're not irresistible. All it means is that I've got a body, just like you. And in that body, there's a heart and a brain. I'm *human*. And if you think about it, that's the complete opposite of what you seem to have mistaken me for."

"A slut?"

She flicked the head of his penis, and he swore with pain, deflating rapidly.

"A blow-up doll."

9.
Teeth

Jess slumped lethargically over the desk, her head resting on her outstretched arm, and used her room key to scratch *STU* into one of the desktops in Unity's library. It was a gloomy space punctuated by shafts of sunlight from tall, narrow windows: a graveyard of old desks and bean bags, ancient textbooks and dust-covered ferns. Jess had dragged herself down here thinking she'd start the year off well by getting ahead on her assigned readings. Well, that, and she was avoiding Farren; this place was one of the only locations in Unity where you could truly be alone. The problem with that, though, was she only had a hangover and gloomy thoughts for company, and her laptop remained closed. Maybe she should have gone for a run instead.

Someone knocked on the door, making the glass pane rattle, and Jess started.

"It's only me." Leaving the door open behind her, Allie drifted across to sit on the edge of Jess's desk, propping her feet on the back of a chair. She was definitely more girl-next-door than goddess today: her hair lank and in need of a wash, the eyeliner she'd worn to the toga party still smeared around her bloodshot eyes. She was in a pair of leggings and an old stretched T-shirt that she kept pulling over her knees as if trying to make a tent to hide in. All signs that Allie had entered the down phase of the Allie Mood Cycle.

"So this is the library. How exciting!" she crooned with a small smile, raising her shoulders. But her heart wasn't in it. "Been missing this?" She handed Jess her phone.

"I've been looking for that everywhere! Where'd you find it?"

"Leanne was using it."

"God, she's a ratbag."

"She wants Farren and me to convince you to sell the Telstra shares."

Jess, about to flick her phone case open, placed it on the desk instead, giving Allie a worried look. "Do you want to sell?"

Allie shrugged. "Don't care." As if aware that she'd slipped and sounded as flat as she felt, she laughed. "It's your show, girlfriend."

"Okay, I'm gonna hold on a bit longer then," Jess said, running a hand through her hair. It was a relief to focus on something other than the dramas of college. To focus, instead, on something related to her future, which, to Jess, was like a bright, shiny city, one where she had it all going on. "Everybody thinks the board is going to have to make an announcement soon because the—" She broke off, noticing Allie was holding up a hand, making a face.

"Don't care. *Won't* care," she said with gentle emphasis.

"Okay, okay." Jess had convinced the other three to go in with her on the trade, not because she needed them, but because she'd been so certain about it at the time that she hadn't wanted them to miss out, and by lumping their money together they only paid one lot of brokerage. But now she was worried in case it didn't come off. Allie, like her, worked part-time, and Jess knew that was where her dollars had come from. Thanks to her parents, Farren was always solvent. But Leanne—God knew where she'd got the dough; it was best not to ask. *Didn't mean she didn't need it, though*, Jess thought, and she grimaced. "Do you think I should sell some off for Leanne?"

"Little Miss Now? The only reason she's pushing for it is because you're not giving her what she wants. Make her wait. It'll be good for her. And don't put too much pressure on yourself. If it doesn't work out, it's not the end of the world."

"Oh, thanks, Al," Jess said, giving her a grateful smile. Her voice changed, becoming more cautious. "How're you doing today?"

"Fine, honey. Why wouldn't I be?" Allie's voice was bright, but her smile faded.

"Okay." Jess nodded. "That's good."

"Anyway, I should scoot." Allie stood up, pasting the smile back on. She twinkled her fingers at Jess. "Laters, lovely."

But just before she reached the door, she turned around. "Hey, Jess? As someone said to me recently, if you put yourself out there, sometimes you cop it, but you don't let the haters get you down, okay? You just block 'em and move on. Post something with a big smile, show your teeth. Because . . ." She shrugged, her eyes a little too bright. "Well, good or bad, the fact they're there is a kind of power. Look at me—nobody used to know I existed. Girls like you and Farren, you're loud and quick and funny, and you've got opinions. But for people like me, that's hard. Then one day, I just thought, *Fuck it. I'm going to* pretend *to be confident*. Tits, tongue, and teeth. That's how easy it is, really. Just don't ever let them see they've gotten to you. Act confident." With that, she left.

"Oh-kaaay," Jess said, blinking at the empty doorway. It didn't occur to her that Allie's shake-it-off speech was for her benefit; she thought it was solely a reaction to the comment she'd made the night before. Bad timing, because she already felt fragile, but maybe it was good that Allie was opening up. Jess turned her attention back to the heavily abused desktop, scratching out a *D*, then *STUT*. Someone had written, *I'm from F-floor*, which was kind of funny. Unity's floors were named alphabetically, but with quite a few gaps. So while there was an E-floor and a G-floor, F didn't make an appearance. It was a phantom floor.

She was working on a new line, *S* followed by *L*, when a call came through on her phone, and she let it ring out, knowing without checking that it was work. The ringtone was Lady Gaga and chosen specifically. She scratched out *U* and *T*, and then listened to the message. After eight months of working for her boss, Vivian, Jess knew you never tackled her head-on. You listened to what she wanted and gave yourself a chance to formulate your excuses *before* you spoke to her. But it wasn't a big deal. Vivian only wanted her to start half an hour earlier than scheduled.

She tapped Home. Four missed calls from Brendan, three texts from Brendan, one text from Farren and—*holy shit!*—196 notifications on the Instagram app. She'd never reached triple digits before! It was probably due to the photo of Blondie she'd loaded in the wee small hours of that morning. Jess tapped the screen, feeling her spirits lift, sure she was about to read a wave of praise and appreciation from the Unity crew.

The first comment was from a username Jess didn't recognize: dudisbigyo. *You fucking disrespectful slut. He should have done you up the . . .* And it was all downhill from there.

"Oh my God." A creeping cold came over her skin. The other comments were just as bad, if not quite as graphic. Sprinkled among them were positive comments from Unity people, but Jess didn't even take those in. They were drowned out by what seemed like a flood of bile evenly split between the photo of Blondie and the photo Leanne had taken of her in the Knights jersey: *Look at her posing. Thinks she's hot. HA HA HA HA! Dirty thief.*

Jess clamped a hand over her mouth. That pose, that stupid, stupid pose. *Pouting*, for fuck's sake.

How could so many of them have known who she was already? The answer was obvious, but Jess checked Allie's account to be sure. Allie had re-grammed all the Knight Rider challenge photos, giving full credit to those responsible. Why? Because she'd been asked to—Jess and Leanne had wanted maximum coverage of the knights' humiliation.

At that moment, the glass pane in the door started to rattle. A rhythmic thudding from outside in the hallway grew closer and louder, and Jess froze. Then Farren strode into the library, bouncing a basketball, little clouds of dust rising from the carpet with each thud.

"There you are!" she demanded. *Thud*. "Didn't we agree this was practice time?" *Thud*. "I want to suck less this year." *Thud*.

"Sorry, I forgot," Jess said, trying not to sound guilty. She wished she could see Farren's eyes. She was wearing her aviator sunglasses, along with an old O-week shirt and a pair of board shorts Jess was sure belonged to Davey Walters. "You are the only person I know who wears pom-pom socks."

"And not even ironically. What's this?" Farren peered at Jess's handiwork.

STUD

STUT

SLUT

"Stud to slut in two moves," Jess told her.

"I can do it in one."

"Change the attitude?"

"Remove the penis." *Thud . . . thud*. "What are you doing down here, anyway?"

"Oh, nothing. Reading and . . . freaking . . ." Jess held up her phone, then realized it was nothing she could share with Farren and snapped the case shut. "My boss called. She's kind of—I don't know, scary."

Thud. "She's good at her job, though, right?" *Thud.* "I mean, would you rather your boss was a warm, mothering idiot or a woman who is actually on top of what's going on and doesn't appreciate having her time wasted?"

Jess licked her lips. "Are we talking about Vivian or you?" *Thud.* "Can you please stop doing that? My head's killing me." Farren caught the ball, lowered her sunglasses, and fixed Jess with a death stare. "Okay, I'm sorry I didn't tell you about the Knight Rider challenge," Jess blurted. "But I knew if I did, you wouldn't let us do it."

"Damn straight I wouldn't have let you do it. Do you know what that was like for me last night? Standing there, listening to Jarrod Keith—"

"The beard?"

"Yes, the beard." Farren's tone was curt, her dark eyes flashing angrily. "The beard who is president of the Knights student council. The person who went out of his way to find me so he could tell me that things were going to be different at Knights under his watch. To tell me that the three guys involved in the sweep didn't get their applications for residency approved this year. He also said that he'd discussed things with the master, and, while they couldn't do anything official without my taking things further, the master will certainly be honest if he happens to get a call from a potential employer asking for a character reference—which happens more than you'd think, old boy network and all that."

"Well, that's good, isn't it?" Jess asked in a small voice.

Farren made a noise at the back of her throat and pegged the ball at her head. Jess, luckily, ducked, and the ball bounced off the wall. "No! No, it wasn't good. Because while Jarrod was telling me these things, I was forced to stand there and watch you and all the other idiots taking matters into your own hands and royally fucking them up!"

"But we did it for you!"

Farren stabbed the air with her finger. *"Don't!* You did it for yourself. Because what happened to me made you feel angry and helpless, so you did something to make yourself feel better."

"That's bullshit."

"Is it?" Farren asked, widening her stance. "I know everyone here thought I should have taken it further. Taken a stand—put myself *on* the stand, more like it. And that's my problem with the whole thing. People save their strong opinions for women. Why don't they look at men? If I have to read another book or see another movie about a woman being courageous, I'll throw up. Where are the books and movies about the men who do this stuff? But no, it's always about the women. They not only have to get through it, they're supposed to stand up, become a symbol, allow their whole lives to become derailed and defined by it. What if you don't want to? What if you just think, *Okay, so two guys watched me having sex without my consent.* It wasn't pleasant, but so what? Big. Fucking. Deal. I refuse to sacrifice myself to that."

"Okay," said Jess.

"Oh, I'm not finished." Farren planted a hand on the desktop. "Because here's the thing. As far as I'm concerned, I'm already a hero. You know why? Because I did the one thing nobody thought I would do after that. I ran for president. And you know why that makes me a hero? Not because I was making some big, brave statement, but because it's what I'd always intended to do. I did not allow my life to change. Not even to make other people feel better. People bang on about women having the right to make choices—well, they need to realize women have the right to choose in these matters, too." Farren glared at Jess a moment. "You got that?"

Jess nodded rapidly.

"Good," Farren said with a satisfied sniff. She pushed off the desk, flashing Jess a smile that was disconcertingly normal and suggested she hadn't been quite as angry as she'd seemed. "Let's go shoot some hoops."

10.
Fever for
the Flava

Jess didn't bring up Instagram until they were en route to the basketball courts.

"Okay, the trick to dealing with backlash is to get off the Internet," Farren told her, puffing slightly because Jess had insisted they jog there as a warm-up. "Look around. It's not here, is it? Not in the real world. It's an electronic mirage."

Jess smiled wanly, dribbling the basketball as she ran. "But it feels real. I don't think I'll ever go online again."

"And there's your silver lining," Farren said with a case-closed air. "There is simply no excuse for being on social media. Not even if it's just to check out what the stupids are doing." Jess bounce-passed to her, realizing for the first time when Farren's aversion to social media had started. "I mean, look at what it's done to you." Farren's voice changed subtly. "Turned you into a pouter."

Jess groaned, but not loudly enough to drown out Farren's laughter. "Don't! I'm already embarrassed enough about that stupid photo. I posted it after I stole the jersey. I'm going to delete it. Actually, I'm going to delete my whole account."

Farren's laughter ceased, and she passed the ball back to Jess harder than was necessary. "You are not deleting anything. There are freshmen who did things to three other knights because you told them to. They're copping this shit, too. You owe it to them to ride it out. Leanne's cool with that—"

"Yeah, and she's also a maniac," Jess muttered.

"She's been leaving comments on their accounts. Supportive comments. And I want you to do the same. Right now, they don't care about the backlash, because you two are right there in the trenches with them. They think they're legends. Don't you dare ruin it."

"You're right. You're absolutely right." Jess exhaled, dribbling the ball a couple of times. "When we see them we should give them high fives and stuff."

Farren snorted. "Where do you get this shit?"

"You. You do that all the time, and people love it. I think that's why the council would lie down and die for you. You're always good-jobbing and high-fiving. People love to feel appreciated."

For once, Farren was silenced. It didn't happen often, but it did happen. "Oh," she said eventually. And then, because Farren never stayed silenced: "You have to apologize, by the way. Leanne's already rung the freshman dude and offered something that was about as close to an apology as she gets—only because I was standing on her ass, mind you, but still."

"Well, she won the Knight Rider challenge. I bet she wanted to tell him that as well." Jess winced. "Is he okay?"

"Not really. Pretty shaken up, I think. And humiliated—it's not like the knights would be forgiving."

Jess sighed, feeling bad for Richie. He *had* seemed like a nice kid. Fuck. She wished she could rewind time and take him out of it. "I'll call him later, too."

"I meant you should call your guy."

"Can't." Jess's voice hardened. "And won't. I have no idea who he is, but even if I did, he's a misogynistic pig who fully deserved it. The only thing I'm sorry about is Richie, but I'm not sorry for anything else. I reserve my right to choices, too, and I choose to behave badly. So there."

"Ooh," said Farren. "So you're *feisty*." And Jess stifled a giggle, knowing all was well between them again and feeling lighter for it.

Their footsteps crunched on the dirt path that linked Unity to the rest of campus. Any signs of the previous night's storm were long gone, the girls' sneakers already covered in dust. Every time Jess noticed they were out of step, she slowed down. Farren was short, and, beside her, Jess, at five-foot-seven, felt like a lanky giant. In every other aspect of life besides running, Farren moved like a bullet, fast and straight and true, whereas Jess liked to wander. Farren was a third-year arts and law student who got involved, changing the world from the inside out. Jess was a second-year economics slacker, allergic to committees of any kind. Farren analyzed things rationally, looking at them from all angles. Jess operated on gut instinct. Farren was an only child, the offspring of two lawyers, now divorced. Jess was one of three siblings whose parents hadn't made it past high school. Both had lived on T-floor the year before, and the birth of their friendship had been fast, furious, and forever. Obviously.

A once-vacant lot near Research Road had been transformed over the summer break. Now it was a construction site. It was disconcerting. Jess hadn't even realized it was a vacant lot until she saw it cordoned off by a chain-link fence. Surely they couldn't fit a building in there? But apparently they were going to—its footprint marked out on the cleared ground by wooden framing and steel mesh. Four builders were pouring cement for the foundations.

Another group was sitting in the small sliver of shade thrown by the site office, having their lunch.

"Okay, I need candy," Farren said, slowing to a walk.

"We only just started! That's what we do after."

"For my eyes."

"Oh," Jess said, nodding understandingly. The two girls stopped, hooking their fingers through the chain-link fence. Wet cement gushed out of a hose that looked like an elephant's trunk, and the throb of the mixer seemed to beat in Jess's bloodstream. It was like she was overly sensitized, sliding through the heat in a state of aroused shock.

Can I touch you? She could *hear* his voice. And every time she thought about it a thrill passed through her body, like electricity through wires, lighting up the hot zones. But then her mind slid into what came after, and she felt confused and upset. And angry.

"Why is this an open fence? Shouldn't it be boarded up or something?" Farren asked, peering over her aviators. "I didn't think you were supposed to be able to see into construction sites. Although I never understood why. Maybe it's to stop busybodies from reporting health and safety breaches."

"Maybe it's to stop girls from leering at the builders."

Farren laughed. "Or vice versa." She nodded at the clump of guys on their lunch break who'd been surreptitiously perving but immediately pretended otherwise. "They're checking out your legs in those running shorts."

"I think they're looking at your socks." The two girls stared the builders into submission, emboldened by the privacy afforded by their sunglasses. An orange extension cord ran from the site office to a portable stereo, and snatches of ads reached them in between gusts of wind. "I bet you a million dollars that's tuned to Triple M," Jess said, pushing her Ray-Bans up to hold her hair back from her face. "Triple M *rocks* your work site."

"Are you being a snob?"

"Can't be. My dad used to work on building sites."

"You should ask him about fencing regulations."

"I'll do that, Farren. I'm sure he's right up on it."

"If they had boarding, this could be like a peep show. Hey, just quietly, I think something's gone down between Allie and Mikey."

"Get out of here."

Farren wrinkled her nose. "So you knew already."

"Well," Jess said modestly. Then she added: "Not sure it's good, though."

"No, probably not. Mikey has trouble coming."

"What? *What!* Oh, I didn't need to know that. When?"

"Before your time. Our first year. Why? Judging me?"

"No, I'm just reeling, that's all," Jess said. Part of Unity's culture was a curiously discreet approach to sexual intrigue. Who people were doing, and who they'd done, was never really discussed, and it made Jess, who'd only had one sexual partner the entire time she'd been there, feel like there was a whole world of covert stuff going on that she knew nothing about.

As if to illustrate this, Farren said, "After him was Widget. That's how I got to know Davey. I'm sure Davey's been with Katie Millhouse, but he won't admit it. And do you know why Davey was crying at last year's Unity Ball? Because I kissed Ben Kerevi. And at Paulie's twenty-first—you know how Callum kept trying to mediate between us?"

"I never knew what that fight was about."

"It was about Davey sleeping with Gemma Wickham."

"What?" Jess coughed.

"It upset me, but what I really hated was that he wasn't honest about it. I wanted to get him back—Callum didn't just mediate. Although I had to initiate it, of course. You know what Callum's like."

"Are you joking?"

"Five times. That night. I was *very* angry," Farren said. Jess didn't doubt the sexual marathon. She'd long associated Farren's room with a kind of musty tang she suspected came from the sheets. "Retaliatory sex is the worst. You're using them and using yourself. I'm not proud of it. But mistake made, lesson learned, I'm trying. I think that's what this part of life is about—making mistakes. Because no one I know is getting married."

"I don't know about getting married, but you and Davey *are* meant to be together. I can tell you that right now."

"Why do you say that?" Farren asked, and there was the most delicate note of hope in her voice. It made Jess want to hug her.

"There was this moment at the end of last year—I can't remember where we were, but everybody was really drunk. You said something funny, blurted it out, and I saw the look on Davey's face. He was just, I don't know, *delighted*. Taken by surprise. Then he gave you this big hug."

"Oh, thank you, Jess," Farren said, with an embarrassed smile. "That's lovely."

"When I saw that, I knew what to aim for. And I knew I didn't have it with Brendan."

"Byron," Farren corrected: her nickname for Brendan. As in, Lord Byron. As in mad, bad, and dangerous to know. "He asked me to give you a letter. I told him I didn't want to get involved."

"You should have gotten involved right from the start. Asked me what I was thinking," Jess said gloomily.

" 'Cause he's soooo sensitive, you know?" Farren said, on her own riff and not listening at all. "Authentically low-fi. He uses paper. Pens. So cool."

Jess snickered. "Crafty-cool?"

"No, no—cooler. Thoreau-cool. Like he went into the woods, and he made the paper, and then he made the pen, and he used his own blood for ink, squeezed from the heart you broke, to write you a letter."

"He was my Edward." Jess grinned, tickled by the thought. "Why didn't you ever say anything? About him?"

"I'm your friend, not your manager. Anyway, he was probably necessary for your evolution. The mistake you had to make. We couldn't work out why you stayed with him for so long." Farren frowned, obviously still wanting the answer.

"God, even I know that. I stayed with him"—Jess made an elaborate flourish in the air with her hand—"because he kept telling me I wouldn't."

Farren snorted in appreciation. "You're probably right." She turned her attention back to the builders. "Why *do* they like milky drinks so much?"

The lunching builders had grown bolder. They now seemed to be openly discussing Jess and Farren. Jess wondered how much they could hear—the wind was blowing that way. Then a young guy with dreadlocks and his hard hat worn at a rakish angle spun the stereo around so that it faced the girls directly, turning the volume right up on Hot Action Cop. Presumably so they, like his cheering workmates, could appreciate his lip-synching and crotch-grabbing skills.

"You owe me a million dollars," said Jess.

"Walk, don't run," said Farren.

As they turned to go, a lone wolf whistle split the air, and they stopped dead, turning back abruptly. The builders suddenly appeared to be very occupied.

"Oh, you're so brave. You're so brave now!" Farren shouted.

Their second retreat was met with a cacophony of wolf whistles. The girls squealed and then started to run, laughing so hard they couldn't breathe.

"You know what's really bad?" Jess asked, when they'd slowed back to a jog.

"We were being objectified? I kind of liked it. I never get objectified."

"He took my schedule—the guy from Knights. Said nothing, just ripped it off the corkboard. You know when someone's so angry they are just *ice*? Didn't slam the door, closed it very carefully. Maybe he's going to get me back."

"Maybe he likes you."

"He called me a slut."

"Generation Porn, Jess. Consider it a term of endearment."

11.
I Don't Wanna Hear It

Saturday night, Jess jaywalked toward the arched windows and elaborate fretwork of the Royal Exchange Hotel like she was pleased to be introduced—although they'd met before, of course, and the place was the RE to its friends. Once inside, she headed for the public bar, deciding she'd get served a lot quicker in there. The place was busy, J. Roddy Walston and the Business blasting out. To Jess, wanting to cut loose and catch up with the night, the music was stirring, anthemic.

She got in line at the bar, digging around in her messenger bag for her wallet. While she waited, she sought out her reflection in the blur of faces in the mirror behind the service area. Georgie, one of her coworkers, had made her over while they'd been on break, which was the sort of dumb thing you agreed to when you had time to kill. Her long hair was piled on top of her head with a few wispy bits pulled loose. And her makeup? Theatrical. Jess had since rubbed some of it off.

Then Jess caught a flash of pink. Even before she saw his

reflection, she knew it was Blondie, just by the way other people were turning to stare. When his face appeared in the mirror behind hers, her heartbeat stuttered. He was standing so close she could smell his aftershave.

At that point, the bar guy stopped in front of her, ignoring a couple of others to serve her early—she was still in her work clothes, and black-and-whites looked out for one another. "What can I get you?"

"A rum and coke, please." She nodded at Blondie. "And whatever he wants."

Blondie looked at her, his eyes heavy-lidded. "I want my Wednesday night back."

"Okay, apart from that. Come on, let me buy you a drink. We should celebrate."

"Celebrate what?"

"Your new look," Jess said, trying not to giggle and failing. Nervous.

"Decided?" asked the bar guy, placing the rum on the bar.

"A Coke, thanks," Blondie answered.

Jess paid for their drinks and then carried them across to Blondie, who'd moved to a spot against the far wall. "Cheers," she told him, handing him his Coke. When he didn't respond, she clinked his glass. "Oh, come on, where's your sense of humor?"

"Haven't seen it since Wednesday. How long does this shit last, anyway?" He made a gun using his thumb and forefinger and attempted to blow his head off.

Jess stared at his hair—formerly blond, now pink. "It's semi-permanent. But the good news is that it's also very conditioning. I mean, spare a thought for me. I'm the one who had to buy a new toothbrush." Blondie remained impassive. Jess winced. "At least your eyebrows are starting to grow back."

Apart from those minor details, he looked good, in jeans and a Western shirt, the sleeves rolled up and showing his forearms. Jess had recently realized she had a thing for forearms. Golden-haired, muscular forearms. She looked away, taking a sip of her drink.

"Happy with yourself?" Blondie asked in a sour voice.

"Come on, it could have been a lot worse."

"Oh yeah, that freshman dickhead."

The thing is, one of the M-floor girls had later told Jess, with the blank-faced look associated with shock, *if we hadn't stopped Leanne, she would have kept going. She was having the time of her life. Sometimes I think there's something wrong with that girl.*

If you lived on T-floor you'd know there was, Jess had responded.

"They didn't just shave his eyebrows," Jess said, nodding.

"Yeah, I saw. They did his head."

"And his arms, and his chest, and his legs. But they didn't need to shave his"—Jess whistled, pointing downward—"because apparently the kid's an optimist."

"If some guys had done that to a girl, there'd be hell to pay," Blondie muttered.

"Oh, I don't know," Jess snarled, hit by a rush of blood to the head. "Nobody seems to mind when *some guys* watch things without permission. I guess the assumption is that girls who have sex deserve everything they get."

"What?"

"The sweep. Last year."

"I don't know what you're talking about. I wasn't here last year."

They were interrupted as a guy wearing a sunset-hued Hawaiian shirt passed them saying, "Killer" in a low, guttural voice, his gaze flickering over Jess.

"I thought they'd have to be around somewhere," Jess said when he'd gone. "You guys hunt in packs, don't you? And it's probably crucial for morale that you teach me a lesson."

"Don't flatter yourself. He's not from Knights. He went to high school with me. St. Luke's. He wouldn't have a clue who you are. You have that much in common."

"Actually I object to that," Jess said, with more passion than necessary because the memory of him dismissing her on the basis of her footwear had annoyed her for days. "You're wrong. The fact that I can get away with lots of different identities means I have a really strong sense of identity. Who I am is not determined by what I look like. And it means I've got a sense of humor."

"Yeah, you're not rabid at all." Blondie calmly moved the bag she'd dumped at her feet so he could see her shoes—black Docs— then let his gaze travel higher: black stockings; black knee-length skirt; a white blouse, which, thanks to Georgie, had an extra two buttons undone; her made-up face; the cigarette tucked behind her ear. "Oh, we're a working girl. That's an interesting identity."

The second connotation was intended. Jess gave him an unimpressed look.

"So how was work?" he asked. "At the Queensland Performing Arts Center." Jess was thrown for a second, then remembered he'd seen her apron. "Remind me to catch a show sometime," he added. "You can serve me."

"Wow, you're like a double-entendre machine. Listen, I've got a problem. I don't know what to call you anymore. It can't be Blondie, not now you're so pink. And Killer's stupid. I'm thinking of Mitchell Crawford. How do you like that for a name? Because I'm pretty sure it is your name, unless of course it's Julian Lloyd. Hard to know really."

Blondie's face changed—a kind of closing off. "Easier than you'd think."

"I'd say Mitch. You don't look like a Julian. And most of those clothes were tagged as Mitchell's. It was only the jersey that said Julian. Do you want to know how I figured it out? You were doing your whites when I saw you in the laundry room. And one thing I've noticed at Unity is that people usually do their colors first, so it was probably your second trip. When I remembered that particular detail, it all made sense."

A muscle twitched beneath his eye. "You're quite the detective."

"I was impressed. It's not often you meet a man who separates."

Blondie shook his head. "You and your mouth."

"What's the problem? Don't like lippy women?"

"Only if they're sucking my cock."

It was such an ugly thing to say. Which, of course, was why he'd said it.

"You know what? You're boring." Jess grabbed her bag, about to walk off, but Blondie gripped her arm.

"What'd you do with it? The jersey."

Jess was startled by his intensity. "It was the prize for . . ." She waved a hand at his hair. "And I didn't win. The girl who made over the freshman dude did. What's the big deal? It's just a jersey. Is this Julian guy giving you grief over it or something?"

Blondie opened his mouth, then just shook his head. They had reached an impasse.

It was broken by a third party. The guy, in his midtwenties and probably the only person in the RE wearing a suit, was tall and thin, with a thick mop of dark brown hair. If he felt hot, it didn't show, his skin pale and freckled. His sudden appearance was startling, like receiving a surprise visit from an undertaker.

"I'm going," he said, his gaze on Blondie, the statement delivered as a demand.

"And?" Blondie asked, aggression to spare.

"And do you need a ride?"

"Nah."

The newcomer waited—perhaps for Blondie to grow up. Evidently, he realized it might be a while, because he looked pointedly at the glass in Blondie's hand and then at Jess, radiating disapproval, and said, "So straight back on the horse, are we? Good to see you haven't learned a fucking thing." With that, he left, shaking his head.

Blondie stared after him, glassy-eyed, anger leaching the color from his face. "It's a Coke!" he shouted in a strangled voice.

"And I am not a horse!" Jess shouted, just as angrily. To Blondie: "I'm going."

"What do you want? A round of applause?" His gaze raked over her. "You'll find the ferals out the back."

12.
Shut Up and Let Me Go

Jess charged into the beer garden feeling like she wanted to start a war. Most of the Unity crowd—her people, the bunch of state-schooled, regionally grown, subversive, disorderly individuals who she called friends and Blondie called ferals—were clustered around two tables near the bar. She spotted Brendan among a satellite clump of skinny-jeaned, flannel-clad Knights old boys just a short distance away, and a second later, as though he'd somehow sensed her presence, he saw her and *glowered*. It made Jess feel slightly sick, but not enough to leave. If he wanted to make a scene, well, good. She was in the right mood for it. Still, she gave him a wide berth as she pushed through the crowd. Then someone kicked her in the back of the knee, making her leg buckle and pulling her up short.

"Hola!" Leanne held up a beer jug in salute.

"Just once, can you greet me with something other than violence?"

"It's how I show I like you. You want cerveza, little girl?" Jess glanced at her rum, realizing she'd finished it. Leanne was already tipping the jug over her glass, crowing, "Look at the head on that!" She was obviously in one of her maniac moods. Her red hair was slicked back, and her T-shirt read: NEVER TRUST A GINGER. Jess didn't know if she was relieved or disappointed—there was every chance Leanne could have chosen to wear the Knights jersey. With Blondie in the vicinity, it might have proved interesting.

Jess sliced the froth off her beer with a finger. "Where's Allie?"

"Where do you think?" Leanne said.

"Really? Azzopardi?"

"Yeah, he's gonna have a party. In Allie's pants."

Jess glanced around, spotting Allie at the end of the neighboring table, playing on her phone. Mikey had his arm around her shoulders and was busy conducting a conversation with another guy over Allie's head. "I thought they were done. She seemed pretty down the day after the toga party."

"That's 'cause she found a used condom in his trash can. She went over to his room the morning after. Knew he was in class."

"Whoa. That's pretty . . ."

"Grade-A disturbing," Leanne finished for her.

"Yeah, and not fair," Jess said. "I mean, Mikey can't read situations at the best of times, let alone minds. He's not a bad person, he's just . . . Mikey."

"Now, now. Much easier to have sex with someone than to tell them you like them," Leanne pointed out. "That's why she put up that selfie. Told ya—rages inside."

Jess knew the one Leanne meant: *No tan lines!* Allie had posted it late in the afternoon of the same day. It was her sunbathing on the roof, her hair framing her face in a freshly washed golden cloud, her lipstick red and matted, her white teeth gleaming. You couldn't see her eyes, though—she'd been wearing sunglasses. Jess had noticed the shot when she'd gone back on Instagram to block users from her account.

"Not that I judge," Leanne added with a smirk.

The smirk annoyed Jess. "Remind me, what's Allie studying?"

"Multimedia design."

"And what does she want to do afterward? Job-wise."

"She wants to get into the educational market. Design learning games and stuff for kids. Likes them for some reason."

"Well, see, I didn't know that."

"So?"

"So why don't you stop acting?"

"Oh." Leanne's eyes widened in amusement. "Smiley's getting disillusioned."

"I know you care," Jess told her. But if Leanne did, she'd never admit it. It wasn't the Unity way, a code that seemed to fit Leanne to a T: care, but not too much; observe, but don't get involved; irony over earnestness, at all times.

Don't judge, but don't give a shit, either—say it in Latin, and you had a motto.

Jess sighed. "You're annoying, and I've got to sit down. I've been standing up all day."

She found a seat beside Callum, who interrupted the conversation he was having to nudge her with his shoulder. "How are you doing, little fella?"

"Yeah, okay, considering Brendan's here. Notice how he's specially cut out the neck of his T-shirt? Yes, okay, we get it— you've got tattoos!" Jess grimaced. "Sorry. There goes my dignified silence."

Callum shrugged, not particularly bothered. "It's a messy situation. But you know I'm here if you ever need to talk about it. I told him the same thing. He's just hurtin', that's all. He was so far gone on you that it'll take him a while to come back."

Jess smiled. Callum always made her feel better. It might have been the slow, lilting way he talked, or because he was gentle, an irony-free zone—she thought he was, anyway; she was never quite sure what irony actually was. She gave him a wink. "Are you offering your counseling services?"

"What?" Callum said, puzzled. Then his eyes widened behind his glasses and he said, "Hoh!" He gave an embarrassed laugh, and his baby face flushed. "Did Farren tell you? Don't ever bring it up in front of Davey Walters, hey. Things between him and me got pretty rocky there for a while."

Jess frowned. "She only did it because he'd slept with someone else."

"Yeah, but still . . ." Callum shook his head. "How would you feel if one of your best friends did that to you?" He was visibly upset, and it pulled Jess up short. That's what Unity did to you, she realized. Made you treat everything as a joke. And in his own quiet way, Callum was pointing out that this joke wasn't funny. "Pretty big, huh? Forgiving your friend for that. I've got to wear that, too."

"Sorry, Callum," Jess said, flushed, distressed.

Callum ruffled her hair, relaxed once more. "Don't worry about it, Jess. I know you. We're friends. You didn't mean anything by it."

Jess frowned. "We are real friends, aren't we? You're not just doing it because you think familiarity will give you an advantage?"

Callum looked confused. "Have I done something?"

Jess laughed, squeezing his shoulders. "No. I was just settling an argument."

He looked past her, the expression on his face changing to one she didn't understand until she realized Brendan had joined them. It was a wonder she hadn't felt the vibrations, all those wires pulled tight. Callum slipped away, joining the other Z-floor guys. Leanne and Farren were there, too, and Leanne glanced back at Jess, her face amused. Observing but not getting involved.

"Hey, Brendan," Jess said in a subdued voice.

She wanted him to look at her, but he kept his head bowed, his face hidden by his long fringe. The same old pattern. Withholding. Making her draw him out. He'd removed his ear gauge, and the sight of his flaccid, holey lobe made her feel sick. She reminded herself that she didn't have to play—she could even leave if she wanted. But there was a difference between knowing it and owning it, and that difference was habit.

"How do you think that made me feel, Jess?" Brendan asked suddenly, his voice low, compressed with feeling. "Seeing you leave with another guy."

"It wasn't what you think! It was for—"

"Why won't you answer my calls? My texts, e-mails?"

Jess didn't answer, crushed by a familiar sense of claustrophobia. *Because if I keep responding you'll never, ever let go*, she thought. And she couldn't understand how someone would rather you pretend to care than be truthful.

Brendan pulled a wad of paper out of his pocket. "I wrote this for you."

But when he tried to hand it to her, Jess leaned back, refusing to take it. He was still for a moment, then he drew his fringe back in that careful way of his, and there was the shock of his pretty green eyes. He was crying. Jess felt worse than she had when she'd broken it off with him in the first place. When he'd gone, she realized she was holding her breath.

AFTER THAT, JESS made a solid attempt at getting drunk, joining in with the T-floor jug rounds. It didn't work, only left her feeling numb, no longer a participant in the night but outside it somehow, sitting on the table, playing with her Zippo. Farren arrived and told her to buck up, plucking the cigarette from behind Jess's ear and breaking it into small pieces. But she rubbed Jess's arm while she listened to a blow-by-blow of the exchange with Brendan. Then she left to go clubbing with Davey and the Z-floor guys, after trying to convince Jess to join them. Shortly afterward, Jess noticed Allie and Michael Azzopardi kissing—messily—while behind them a couple of guys started to push one another around, and the whole night took on a slow inevitability that made her hope the other T-floor girls would get bored soon so she could go home. But when Michael approached the table, everything about him suggesting a strong headwind—his braced shoulders and lifted chest, the way he bounced on the balls of his feet rather than rolling from the heel—she straightened, suddenly alert.

"Mikey!" Jess grabbed his shirtsleeve as he passed. "Where did Allie go?"

"Bathroom," he told her, startled. Then he recovered. "*Michael*. You know I hate you guys calling me that."

"Just come here." She pulled him down until they were face level. "What's the score with you guys?" she hissed urgently. "Have you talked about what's happening?"

"Aw, come on, Flash. No need for that." Michael gave her an embarrassed grin, pushing at his glasses, which were fashionable and suited him. "We're good."

Jess dragged him closer. "You need to listen to me," she told him, speaking slowly and enunciating her words as if he was hearing impaired, not just drunk. "Just because someone acts like it's casual, doesn't always mean that to them it is just casual. Do you understand what I'm telling you?"

Michael's eyes went up, Michael's eyes went down, Michael's eyes went side to side. He finally focused on her, frowning. "I think so."

"Good." Jess released him abruptly. "Now get away from me. She can't see us talking." Ignoring the wounded look he gave her, she lay back on the table, hands behind her head, the movement causing a slight dizziness that made the stars above her spin. It occurred to her that she might be drunk after all, but when people started jumping to The Ting Tings, she didn't feel drunk enough.

It was then Jess noticed the people on the balcony, primarily because most of them were wearing Hawaiian shirts. Blondie was the odd man out. Not only had he failed the dress code, he was standing apart from his friends—back from the railing. He was staring down at her, his expression the one people have when they're looking at you but thinking about something else. Jess met his gaze, showing no surprise, no reaction at all. And for one curious moment the world was still.

"Bit awkward for you. Him being here."

Jess tilted her head back to see Michael's upside-down face. He was standing on the other side of the table, behind her, and must have witnessed the exchange.

He glanced back up at Blondie. "If he gives you any trouble, let me know. Can't stand the arrogant prick."

"You know him?"

"Yeah, from rugby—the intercollege comp. I actually didn't think he'd come back, you know."

"Come back from what? His year off?"

Michael frowned down at her. "You don't know? I thought somebody would've told you."

Jess sat up, twisting around to see him properly. "What are you talking about?"

But Michael was staring at a point somewhere beyond her right shoulder, deep in thought. "I'd love to know if he's playing again this year. Did he say anything to you?"

"We didn't talk about rugby, Michael. We didn't even get around to names. Is he Mitchell Crawford or Julian Lloyd?"

Michael's eyes snapped back to Jess. "Well, he can't be Julian Lloyd."

"Why not?"

"Because Julian Lloyd is dead. That's Mitch Crawford. They're both from Bundaberg. Went to school together, used to play rugby together. Best friends. Julian died in a car crash while they were home for the Christmas holidays. Mitch took last year off because of it."

Jess gripped the table, feeling like she was in free fall. Finally, she understood why Blondie—why Mitch—had kept asking her about the jersey. She looked up at the balcony, meeting his gaze. When he saw her face, he obviously realized what Michael had told her, because he turned away and started pushing his way through the crowd.

Jess stood, grabbing her bag. "Oh God. This is so bad."

"Hey, don't worry about it. If he didn't tell you, how were you supposed to know?"

Jess took off without saying anything. Michael didn't know whose jersey she'd stolen. No one did. Because she'd taken the tag off. By the time she reached him, Mitch was nearly at the door.

"Mitch!" The impropriety of using his name, like she was trespassing.

He turned back automatically, frowning when he saw her, one hand held up to ward her off. And then someone grabbed Jess's arm, spinning her around.

"So you *are* doing him now." Brendan. In a frenzy, drunk and ridiculous, spraying her face with spittle. "Don't forget to make sure his laptop's closed. What I want to know is, who'd you fuck back in Rockhampton, Jess? Who broke us up?"

Jess gaped, feeling the attention they'd gathered press down on her. All those eyes. She glanced at the doorway, hoping Mitch had gone, but he'd stopped to watch, too, his face completely devoid of anything approaching empathy. "No one," she finally managed. "You're being—" She reeled backward as he flicked her in the face with the letter he'd written. "Brendan!"

"Who?"

Jess stared at him, beyond humiliation now, her cheeks and neck burning. "Everybody," she hissed. "The whole damn town. All eighty thousand of them. Now leave me alone, you fucking psychopath."

Her words vibrated through the air, drawing coughed laughter from the assembled peanut gallery. Brendan's eyes grew slitted, mean. He turned from her, heading for Mitch, swaying slightly, and for one wild moment Jess thought he was about to throw a punch. Mitch looked to have reached the same conclusion, his arms held slightly away from the sides of his body. He was much bigger than Brendan.

But true to form, Brendan proved to be a dirty fighter. What he did was hand Mitch the letter, saying, "Here's the menu."

13.
Get Free

There was nobody waiting at the bus stop, and that was a good thing, because Jess did not want to be near another soul at that moment. Normally, she would have been nervous about waiting somewhere alone at night, but there was a lot of traffic on the double-lane road, and the bus shelter was directly beneath a streetlight. She took a seat, watched with interest by a carload of boys pulled up at the lights, Major Lazer blasting from their stereo.

Her mind worked its way through a rosary of fucks. What the fuck was in that letter? Fuck, Brendan. She should have taken the fucking thing from him in the first place. Fuck, she needed a cigarette. How the fuck was she supposed to have known Julian Lloyd was dead? Fuck, fuck, fuck.

The lights changed, the car moved on, and the music faded. Too agitated to sit, Jess got up, checking the bus schedule. Sixteen minutes to go. She left the footpath, collecting twigs, dead leaves, and dried grass from beneath the gum trees a little farther down the hill, then returned to the bus stop, sitting cross-legged on the concrete at the end of the shelter, carefully arranging the stuff in front of her—dried grass and leaves on the bottom, some of the smaller sticks teepeed over the top. When she was satisfied, she pulled out her Zippo. The grass flared first, then the leaves caught with resinous zing, the thinner twigs caught next, burning through quickly and leaving a neon-orange line, something skeletal, before disappearing altogether.

And up until then, Jess had been shaky, but with the fire came something like calm. She slowly fed it the remaining twigs. A car beeped as it passed, but Jess hardly noticed. It was only a small fire, burning on concrete, no wind around. Nothing for anybody to get excited about.

She heard the slightest noise, a scrape, and she shuddered, knowing instinctively that she was being watched.

Mitch. She wondered how long he'd been there.

"I didn't . . ." Jess's voice faltered. She didn't know what to say to him, and he didn't look like he wanted to hear it anyway. He handed her Brendan's letter, neatly folded, then strode off down the hill. Jess watched him go, too shocked to do anything for a moment. Then she got to her feet, stamped out the remainder of her little fire, and ran after him, her messenger bag clonking against her hip.

When she reached him, he didn't slow his pace at all, so she had to dance along sideways because she needed to see his face. "Hey, I'm sorry," she said, already breathless—from nerves rather than any great exertion to catch up with him. "I'm so sorry, okay? I had no idea. And if I had known, I would never have taken that jersey."

"Don't worry about it." In the gloomy light, the look on Mitch's face was intimidating.

"Can you just stop for a second? Please."

"You've said what you wanted to say, I heard you, so we're done, aren't we?"

"But I don't want to be done," Jess told him, and he made a noise that was part laugh, part bark. "I feel so bad. I'd get the jersey back for you, if I could. Actually, I probably could get it back, for a significant sum of money—"

"You want me to pay you to return the jersey that *you* stole from *me*?"

"No! I meant I'd pay the money. To the girl who won it. She's kind of a mercenary—heartless, really—and that's the only way she'd give it back. It doesn't even matter, though, because the thing is, it's been defaced. So I'm not sure if you'd want it now anyway. And you've got to know that nobody from Unity knew it was his. I took the tag off. And I'd offer to at least return that to you, but I don't have it anymore, either."

"Where'd it go?" he asked. "Did you sell it to somebody?"

"I burned it."

"What are you? A pyro or something?"

"*Ish*. Pyro-ish. I am responsible."

"Well, he was cremated. Does that get you going?"

Jess stopped walking abruptly, her hand over her mouth. Mitch turned back. They were near a streetlight, and his face was in shadow while hers was in the light. He would have seen how shocked she was.

"Okay, I'll leave you alone now," she told him in a small voice, dropping her hand. "I know that's what you want."

Mitch didn't move. She wished she could see his face. She waited, seconds sliding by. It was only as she was turning to go that he finally spoke.

"Why'd you burn the tag?"

"Because you annoyed me so much. That day in the laundry room."

"Yeah? How so?"

"By thinking that . . . you're better. Than me." Jess's halting answer was not so much about attacking him as admitting something about herself.

She heard Mitch draw a heavy breath. When he spoke, his voice was rough but warmer. "Seriously, Jersey, there's no danger of that."

There was a run of traffic then, a relief for both of them. Jess watched the bus for the university roll pass, undulating in the way that accordion buses did. She caught a blur of faces, people locked safely away inside their bubble of light. When the road had drained, she was surprised to find Mitch still standing there.

"Was that your bus?" he asked, and things felt different.

"Doesn't matter. I'll wait for the next one. Unless you wanted to walk back together? I won't talk, I promise."

"I'm not going back to campus."

"Oh. Sure. Okay," Jess said, nodding. "Where are you going?"

"Well, I *was* going to Depper Street. This chick I used to fuck lives there now."

Jess blinked at him. Then she swatted him with the letter. "Why do you do that? You always slap me in the face with the sex stuff, just when I start to think you're all right." Then she went *"Aarrgh!"* and started walking back up the hill.

But he was right beside her, his hand closing around the back of her neck, so tightly it made her wince. "But *now* I feel like a swim," he said, guiding her through a semicircle so that she was once again heading downhill. "With you." Jess glanced sideways at him, her shoulders hunched. "Don't flatter yourself, Jersey. If I wanted that, I'd go to Depper Street. Are you coming or not?"

"Seems like it," Jess said on a sigh. They were passing beneath the streetlight again, and she did a double take. His eyes were more electric than ever, maybe because of his missing eyebrows or the pink hair. "You look really beautiful, by the way," she told him, not making anything of it, just giving him the truth.

Mitch dropped his hand like she'd burned him. "How about I stop slapping you in the face with the sex stuff and you stop calling me beautiful?"

Jess laughed. "Deal." They were starting to stride out, and she did a little skip so that her strides matched his—left, right, left. He gave her a sidelong glance. "Just a habit," she told him.

"How many compulsions do you have, exactly?"

"Enough to keep me busy."

"I'm Mitch, by the way. Mitch Crawford."

She smiled, acknowledging what he was doing. "Jess. Jess Gordon."

"As in Jessica?"

"As in Jess. Just Jess."

"Do people ever call you Flash? You know, because your surname is Gordon."

"No, no one in the whole world has ever made that connection. You're the very first."

"Sarcasm," he scolded. "And what are you studying, Just Jess?"

"You already know that, Just Mitchell. You took my schedule."

"Not tonight, I didn't. This is a time-out. From that and everything else." He looked sideways at her, his eyes more intense than his tone. "All right with you?"

Jess nodded, thinking it over. "I mean, we're probably never going to speak to each other again, right? So we could just be free."

"If that does it for you."

"It does." Jess gave him a wan smile. "Because, as you've probably noticed, things are going so well for me at the moment. Where are we headed?"

"That apartment complex before Ryan's Road."

A little way on, they came across an abandoned shopping cart.

"Seems a shame to waste it," Mitch said. "You want a ride?" And Jess smiled and nodded, because now the night felt soft, like things could be fun. He held the cart still while she clambered into it, her Docs making the metal ring. She faced backward so she could look at him. They set off again, Mitch pushing the cart, or, rather, stopping it from running away down the hill.

"Lucky we're in a time-out or I'd be nervous," Jess told him.

"Don't be."

"So what are you studying?" Jess asked, the rattle of the cart vibrating her voice. It was good it was so noisy; it relaxed things between them.

"Commerce and law."

"Huh. Because you wanted to? Or because you didn't want to waste a high entrance score?"

His manner changed, becoming stiff. "Ah . . . because I didn't get into medicine." Jess laughed. "What?" he asked.

"Just the way you can take something as impressive as getting into commerce and law, and turn it into a failure."

Mitch blinked. "Never thought of it like that before. Why are you studying economics?"

"Economics takes you where the money is."

"That's a pretty right-wing answer for a girl from Unity."

"I wouldn't admit it to anyone there, but you'll understand. You're from a rich family."

"How do you know? We might just be comfortable."

"You live at Knights, you went to St. Luke's, and when you were getting those Cokes the other night, you dropped some change. It was nothing, maybe fifteen cents in total, but you fished it out from under the machine. If you were middle-class, you would have just left it. So you respect money. Your parents probably drummed it into you."

"I feel like I'm being dissected."

"But I'm right, aren't I? I think about this stuff a lot."

He nodded. "What about you then? What is your family like?"

"My family are the type of people who take their pillows with them when they travel."

Mitch sucked a breath. "Man, you are brutal."

"No, I'm just giving you the quickest snapshot possible. We don't actually travel, but if we did, we'd hit Surfers Paradise. Your people, I imagine, prefer Noosa." Mitch's eyes widened, and he gave her a nod. "Dad distrusts 'The Southeast Corner'—which makes him sound dumb, but he's not. He didn't go to university, went to a trade school instead, and he gets moody about it, sort of sabotages himself, I think. But he's smart by any other definition, reads a lot, asks people questions. Mum works at Kmart. And, for the record, they'd laugh their heads off if they heard what I just said about the pillows. We dissect ourselves all the time. It's family policy. Dissect yourself, dissect everybody else, don't let people push you around, and always bear in mind that hotel pillows, even the expensive ones, are full of dust mites and other people's grease. My family is probably your family's worst nightmare. Other people worry about climate change; we worry that Ford will stop making V8s. I'll know I've arrived when I buy a Jet Ski."

"And you're the eldest." Mitch looked like he might be starting to enjoy himself.

"Dissecting *me* now? Twin brothers. Twelve-year-olds. How'd you know?"

"I can't puncture it by explaining my method."

"In other words, you guessed."

He ignored that. "Always been treated like you were something special?"

"*Very* good. The downside is I'm expected to live up to it."

"That's not so bad if you're the great shining hope. I'm worried I'll let the side down."

"Poor baby. So how many brothers do you have?"

"Just one. But let's stay with you." Mitch studied her. "I wouldn't have picked that as being your background."

"Really?" Jess said, and the word had the faintest tint to it. Hopefulness, or pleasure, or something else that made her flush.

"Morphing?"

"I don't know. I guess I take notice of things. I read a lot, and I'm intelligent—"

"Of course."

"Not boasting," Jess said. "It's a fact. I'm aiming for a place on the honor roll."

Mitch grinned and then said, "There's another reason."

Jess brightened, finding her own dissection weirdly enjoyable. "What's that?"

"I've been in your room, remember? Docs, two pairs of Ray-Bans, one hell of an Adidas addiction—"

"It's the only true brand. Iconic."

"Yeah, but that stuff's not cheap."

Jess frowned. "I never said we were poor. Hello! Heard of the mining boom? I believe it visited Bundaberg. Dad's been working fly-in, fly-out for the last eight years. But perhaps you're insinuating that I have *taste*, and, in that case, I've got a fairy godmother. Dad's the black sheep of a family that probably isn't too different from yours. We don't talk to his parents, but Aunt Heather's always kept in touch. Did town planning, married an architect, nice big Queenslander home. Wears linen shirts because she's got a cleaning lady who irons them for her. She's a Brisbane sophisticate, gets obsessed with things like salmon confit. They don't have kids, so I'm her project. She wanted to help with my living costs, but Dad wouldn't let her, so every year she gives me three grand for textbooks behind his back." Jess smiled. "Between that and work, I'm kind of rolling in it. *Nouveau riche.*"

"I spend less than five hundred on textbooks, and I'm doing a double degree," Mitch said, sounding disapproving.

"Don't be literal."

"So what? You just spend it on stuff?" Mitch sounded even more disapproving.

"No, I put most of it into bank shares. And I bought a little Telstra."

"Smart. Good dividends."

"You know about dividends?" Jess shook her head. "I told you. Rich."

Mitch's gaze slid to the side, his mouth open, as though he'd never realized that this was unusual. "But you know about dividends."

"That's because I *intend* to be rich. Slightly different thing."

"It must be. Because the money I've got invested is money I earned."

"Oh yes," Jess said, mock seriously. "At the sugar mill." Then she giggled.

"What's so funny about that?"

"I keep seeing you hot and sweaty in overalls and a hard hat. Calendar stuff."

"I was in the office."

"*Nooo,*" Jess wailed. "Disappointed."

"Not so sexy now," he told her.

They were on Sir Fred Schonell Drive by this stage, which wasn't as well lit, and Jess was glad—she'd had a sudden recollection of him sucking her nipples.

"So you study economics, and you go where the money is, and then what?" Mitch asked. "Who will you be?"

"Just someone," Jess said vaguely. She sniffed, giving him a decisive nod. "All I know is I want to travel a lot."

"And you'll take your pillow."

"Proudly," said Jess, and they grinned at each other. "You know what?" she mused. "You're fun." Mitch snorted, dismissively. "Oh yes. I think this is who you really are. Not the other guy."

"What other guy?"

"The one from the laundry room. But don't worry, I won't blow your alpha cover. So, who's the dude in the suit?"

"You're so smart, you tell me."

Jess considered it, wrinkling her nose. "I'm thinking secret service. Or your mother."

"Close."

"*That's* your brother? He's nothing like you at all. He's so . . ."

"Uptight?"

"Hot," Jess said, and Mitch rewarded her with a laugh. He sounded puffed, and she realized it was because they were going up a steep hill. "Hey, do you want me to get out?"

"Nah, you're all right. Just keep talking. About anything you want."

Jess smiled, because the way he said it made her feel good. Then her smile faded. "I've run out."

"Didn't think that could happen. Can I ask you something then? How in the world of fuck did you end up with the head case?"

"Careful."

"Your words, don't let anybody push you around."

"No, my dad said that," Jess corrected. "And if he's in one of his moods, we all get out of his way."

"Waiting."

Jess sighed, loudly and with a distinct lack of grace. "His name is Brendan, and he wasn't always like that. Well, maybe he was, but in the beginning I thought all the drama was passion or something." She frowned, hit by a sudden realization. "I was going to say it was because I cared about him—only because, for you, it might be a revolutionary idea. But the truth is, it's because he wanted me so bad. There is something totally addictive about being the focus of another person's attention. My downfall was sleeping with him. Sex tricks you into caring about the other person, even if they are a possessive head case."

"Depends on the sex."

Something in Mitch's tone jagged Jess's attention. "Oh my God, you read the letter, didn't you?" Even his smile looked guilty. "Bastard!"

"Don't worry, it's covered by the time-out. It doesn't go any further than me. And I did respect your privacy to a degree. I skipped the sappy stuff, and the parts where he seemed to be pressing charges. I only read the dirty bits."

"Why? So you could call me a slut again?" Jess asked, her voice heated.

"Oh, come on, you didn't take that seriously, did you?" Mitch stopped the cart.

Jess wouldn't look at him, staring at the houses on the other side of the road. "Of course I did. Given you don't actually know my sexual history—forgetting for a second that it's irrelevant—I can only assume you said it because for a minute there I enjoyed myself. I hate that way of thinking."

"I said it because I was tied to a chair with my pants down and a dick so hard it hurt. I was pissed off."

"See, I won't accept that. You could have said anything, *anything* else. But not that. It was below the belt. And no snide remarks, thanks. I realize it's a poor choice of phrase."

"Jess, when it comes to me, there is no belt," Mitch said, and something in his voice stilled her. Resignation? Defeat? "I am the other guy. Worse than that even. What do you want me to say? I take it back?"

It wasn't exactly an apology, but for some reason it was enough. "No," Jess said with a sniff. "I want you to revise your attitude. Women, amazingly enough, are allowed to like it. If that's news to you, then you're not doing it right."

"*I've* never had any complaints." Jess said it at exactly the same time as Mitch, and then lost it, giving in to a laugh that vibrated her whole body and sounded vaguely like the *wukka-wukka-wukka* of chopper blades. Shaking his head, Mitch started to push the cart again.

"It's not my fault you're predictable," she told him, wiping a fingertip under each eye. They were over the crest of the hill now, heading down the other side, speeding up. She dug around in her bag, finding her Zippo, and unfolded Brendan's letter. *Flick-spin-scritch!*

"You're not even going to read it?" Mitch asked, and something in his tone made Jess wonder just what, exactly, Brendan had revisited. Thank God she'd never let him film anything.

"How bad is it?" Jess asked with a grimace.

He smiled. "Why do you think I'm here?" Jess groaned. "Oh, relax. I'm just messing with you." He was silent for a couple of strides then added, "Bit porny."

"You can talk!" Jess exclaimed with scorn. She deepened her voice: "That's it, baby, bend over. Yeah, that's how I'd do you. Like a boss."

Mitch coughed. "At no stage did I use the terms 'baby' or 'boss.'" He sounded embarrassed, though, which pleased Jess. "Anyway, you liked some of it. You admitted that much."

Jess snapped her Zippo shut. "Don't say 'admitted' like you scored a point. I told you that quite willingly—"

"Just before you killed my dick."

They were hit by a weird silence, unable to meet each other's eyes. Things felt loaded, what they'd done pressing down on them. When Mitch cleared his throat, Jess tensed.

"Listen, is he harmless, or . . . I'll have a word with him, if you want."

"What? Oh. No, I don't need saving, but thank you and everything. Really, this is the worst he can do." Jess held up the letter. Then she blinked. "Wow. A guy trying to shame a woman sexually, motivated by a sense of entitlement. Who would have thought that could happen?"

"Yeah, all right, all right," Mitch said. As Jess flicked her Zippo on again, he added: "Why don't you subvert the patriarchy by doing a reading?"

Jess giggled. "Too risky. What if you got all hot and bothered and left me rolling down the hill while you went to visit your girl on Depper Street?" She held her Zippo up so that light from the flame illuminated his face. "Tell me about her."

"Nothing to tell."

"Is she the girl from the toga party?" Jess asked, keeping her voice light but suddenly desperate to know.

Mitch stared at her a moment, his blue eyes unreadable. "No."

One word, but unmistakably a roadblock. Jess ignored it. "So who—"

"I told you, Depper Street is just a girl I used to fuck," he said firmly, offering a detour. "I haven't seen her in more than a year."

"Huh," Jess said, allowing herself to be diverted. "So you'd just— What? Turn up when you were horny?" Mitch nodded. "Now, see, a girl could never have an arrangement like that. It's not fair."

"What are you talking about? She had an arrangement like that."

"Did she ever visit you?"

"No."

"I rest my case."

Mitch leaned forward, pulling the cart closer to him, and she caught a whiff of his aftershave. "Why? Would you want an arrangement like that?"

Jess swallowed, pretty sure he was asking a theoretical question, but not 100 percent. "Maybe. But I don't see how it would work. At least not for me."

"Pretty straightforward, if you ask me."

"No, you think I'm something I'm not, because of the other night, and because of this." Jess held up the letter, then set fire to it. "But I'm actually a control freak. I've only slept with two guys: Brendan and my high school boyfriend senior year." She glanced at Mitch, expecting him to say something snide, hoping he wouldn't.

"Okay," he said, carefully.

"I mean, I've hooked up with people, sure." It occurred to Jess that technically he was one of them, and she flushed, shaking the sheath of paper gently to give the flames more air. "But I can't have sex without trust. Actually, it's worse than that. I have to be sure they care about me. Too bad if I could do better, just so long as they're safe."

She turned the wad of paper over to slow the burn, holding it by a corner. "It's frustrating, really. Sometimes I'm gagging for it. You know when you've been studying for too long?" Mitch laughed, acknowledging what came of those circumstances. "But if it came to the crunch, I wouldn't be able to do it anyway. It's hard being me." Jess tossed the burning stub toward the road, where it landed in the gutter. "I wish I was more like you."

The stub would have gone out unassisted, but Mitch let go of the cart to stomp on it. It took Jess a moment to comprehend what that meant, and by the time she did, she was rolling away from him, traveling backward down the hill, getting faster and faster, feeling the rattle of the cart in her teeth.

Mitch looked up abruptly, realizing what he'd done, and sprinted after her. "What the fuck, Jess?" He jerked the cart to a stop, glaring at her, his shoulders rising and lowering as he took audible breaths. "Why didn't you yell out or something?"

"I don't know," Jess told him, as shocked as he was. "I just knew you'd get me."

He shook his head. "Are you fucking insane?"

Jess laughed, looking up at him, hit by that mix of lightness and warmth otherwise known as relief. "Maybe," she breathed, unpeeling her hands from the sides of the cart. "But you did."

She saw how his face changed. Charmed, even though he didn't want to be.

14.
Warm Water

To reach the apartment complex's swimming pool, they had to scramble over a brick wall fronting the road. It wasn't as difficult as it might have been due to the fact that you could climb up a small embankment and haul yourself over from there. Jess had already ripped her tights getting in and out of the shopping cart; going over the wall added to the damage.

"Don't look up my skirt," she grunted at Mitch, throwing a leg over the wall.

"Hard not to," he said dryly.

For some reason that sent Jess into hysterics, and she could only lie there on top of the wall giggling helplessly until it passed.

"Hurry up!" Mitch hissed, smacking her on the butt. "There are cars coming." Jess swung her legs to the front and jumped down onto the lawn on the other side. Seconds later, Mitch landed beside her. He started to say something, but Jess gripped his sleeve, cutting him off with an urgent "Shush!"

"What's wrong?" he hissed, frozen beside her.

"I love this song! Banks. Listen. You can just hear it."

Mitch muttered something, pulling away, but Jess was mesmerized. The music, faint and haunting, wafted down to her from somewhere up high in the two apartment blocks. It made the moment seem magic, unreal, the pool glowing blue in the night, throwing light patterns onto the wall of the amenities building that fronted it. How strange that she was there with him, about to go swimming.

She checked her phone. There was a text from a number she didn't recognize, which puzzled her until she realized it was Leanne using someone else's phone: **Where u at dickhead!!!!! L.** The concern was in the five exclamation marks. Jess replied with: **Got a cab to my aunt's J xo.** Technically, not a lie, because she hadn't said *when* she'd done this. There was a missed call from Farren, which must have come through when she was at the RE— impossible to hear anything in there. She'd left a voicemail, also nearly impossible to hear because she seemed to be shouting the words over the background of a live band:

"Okay, I'm just saying this while I'm pissed, and tomorrow I'll pretend it never happened, so don't bother bringing it up, but . . . Sometimes it makes me so angry, Jess. You're a good friend. The toga party reminded me I'm not alone. That I've got friends. Loyal friends. So, thanks. Yeah."

Jess slipped her phone into her bag. She looked across at Mitch's muscular back, watching him pull his jeans down to reveal black boxers, her mouth dry. *It's a time-out*, she reminded herself. *Tomorrow, you'll be loyal again.*

Mitch dived in, splitting the water's skin cleanly. Jess untied the laces on her Docs, kicked them off, and started to unbutton her blouse. Was he watching? She couldn't bring herself to check, suddenly terribly self-conscious. She should have been wearing big occasion stuff, but no, she had to be in cotton hipsters and a sports bra. *Cut to the tights,* she thought desperately, *and sell these babies like Wall Street.* They were stay-ups, and therefore sexy. She stepped out of her skirt, placed her foot up on a lounge chair, and rolled down one sheer black leg and then the other—delicately, as though they weren't already ripped to bits.

Then and only then did she look at the water.

Mitch was floating on his back, arms outstretched, not watching her at all. Feeling sheepish, Jess thanked God that only she knew how ridiculous she'd just been. Then she grinned, running silently to the side of the pool. She leaped high, bringing one leg up to her chest, and bombed him in the water. When she surfaced, laughing, residual drops from the splash she'd caused still rained down on her head.

Mitch shook his head, his mouth open. "You wait."

She shrieked, going under and pushing off the side to get away from him. But he got her when she surfaced, clamping both hands on her shoulders and forcing her under again. She came up coughing because she was still laughing. When it had subsided, they regarded each other warily, treading water.

"Graceful entrance," he said.

"Snobby dive," she said.

Jess freestyled to the other end, tumble-turned, and then completed the next lap underwater, surfacing with a gasp. Floating on her back, she looked up at the apartment building, wondering if they'd get busted. But there was nobody glaring down at them. Most of the units were in darkness. She flipped over and stood up, waist-deep in the water, eyeing Mitch. "Hey, want to play Sharks and Minnows?"

"How *old* are you?"

"What about Marco Polo then? *Please.*"

But Mitch just ignored her, pulling himself out of the pool. She turned away, giving up on him, but a second later he whistled, holding up a tennis ball. He jumped back in the pool and then threw it to her, treading water, his throw soft, measured, and careful.

Jess caught the ball one-handed. "Oh my God, how embarrassing."

"What?"

"You can't throw for shit," she said, pegging the ball at him as fast and hard as she could, using the sideways action her dad had taught her, just like the cricket players they'd watched on TV. Mitch caught it, which was lucky, because otherwise it would have smacked him in the face, and he shook his head at her, sucking air through his teeth, pretending to be pissed off. It gave her a secret thrill.

But then she forgot about all that, slapping the water excitedly. "I know, I know! Let's play Classic Catches!"

"Yeah, all right," Mitch said.

———

LATER, AS THE water calmed after a series of spectacular catches from each of them, Jess watched Mitch glide toward her underwater, as sure as a shark. She shivered as he surfaced, flattening her back against the pool wall. He wiped his face, blinking the water from his eyes, then placed one arm on either side of her, their bodies close but not quite touching. After that he didn't seem to blink at all.

"Jess."

"Hmm?"

"Just saying it."

"It's cold now, isn't it?" Jess said with a shiver, hugging herself.

Mitch rubbed her leg with his knee. "How'd you get those hamstrings? You're ripped."

"Running. Intervals, mainly."

"Times or distances?"

"Both. Like, I might do four-hundred-meter intervals, but the fast lap has to be under a certain time, and the recovery lap has to be within a certain time, too."

He raised his nonexistent eyebrows. "Hard-core."

"I've done a lot of reading on it—how to improve your VO_2 max—the lactic acid thing. I guess you'd know all about it because of rugby."

"So, is this a serious thing, the running?"

"No. I mean, it was, till I got down here. Then I wasn't winning anymore. There are girls I can't beat, you know? They've been doing little league since they were three or something. Or maybe they're just better, I don't know. Like, I am competitive, but only when I've got a chance of winning. So now I just compete against me. Sorry, talking too much. Nervous."

"Why are you nervous?"

"You know why."

"Tell me."

"Because you're . . ." *Too close.* "Examining me. Tell me about the rugby thing."

"Not much to tell. I'll play for Knights. And I'll try to make the university team. But because I had the year off I'll have to work hard and prove myself all over again." He started to stroke the skin under her eye with a thumb. "What's with all the makeup?" he asked, and Jess realized that courtesy of Georgie's efforts she probably looked like a raccoon. "I didn't think you were the type to wear a lot of makeup."

"I don't normally," Jess said. But she was thinking about Diamond Girl from the toga party. She'd been wearing a lot of makeup. Therefore, what Mitch was really saying was Jess wasn't his type. *I doubt it.*

He smoothed away her frown, running his thumbs over her eyebrows. "What's that about?" he asked.

"I'm confused myself." Jess drew a sharp breath, trying to relax. He drew a line around her ear and tweaked her lobe. "Don't," she said, clapping her hands over her ears and giving a nervous laugh. "I know they stick out a bit. It's embarrassing."

"No, it's cute."

"Cute is for baby ducks."

"Okay, it's sexy. You've got very sexy, only-slightly-sticking-out ears."

"Stop it!" Jess wailed.

"Well, what are you worried about your ears for? You're hot. I'm the one without any eyebrows." Mitch leaned closer, close enough to make Jess stop breathing, his fingertips brushing her cheek, his eyes narrowed.

"Had a cigarette when I finished work. Sorry," she blurted, worried about how she'd taste.

Mitch shrugged, completely unconcerned. "I can't smell it."

He hadn't been going to kiss her, Jess realized. Probably hadn't even thought of it at all, until she'd made it obvious.

"What happened to your nose?" he asked.

"I broke it," Jess said in a flat voice and turned her head.

"What's over there?"

"Nothing. I'm trying not to breathe on you. That's the only reason why I said that about smoking, by the way. I'm cold. I'm getting out." She tried to push him out of the way, but he didn't budge.

"I just don't do kissing, Jess." He gave her an odd smile—wry, sympathetic even. There was no smirk in it. "It's not you. I've never been into it."

Jess was still. She could have kept up the pretense, but it would have been difficult in the face of that steady, blue-eyed gaze. "I wasn't wanting it, honestly. But when it looked like that's what you were going to do, I thought, Oh well, it's a time-out. It might be nice." She sighed. The night had been popped like a bubble, all the magic gone. "I feel so dumb."

"It's not dumb." Mitch hooked his hands under her thighs, lifting her effortlessly in the water and pulling her to him, and Jess wrapped her arms tightly around his neck, her legs around his waist, more comfortable pressed against him than having him look at her. "Anyway, other things might be nice," he murmured and then kissed her cheek.

"I thought you didn't kiss," Jess said, with another shiver.

"I do, just not like that. But I'll kiss you here . . ." He kissed her jaw. "Here . . ." He kissed her neck, making her squirm because she was suddenly ticklish. "And on your sexy, sexy ears."

Jess giggled, hunching her shoulders as he went to do it. "Would you shut up about my ears?" She pulled back to look at him and was still, overwhelmed by a feeling of being caught somehow. She touched his hair gingerly, then traced one of the pale-pink rivulets running down his neck, the only sounds their breathing and water lapping at the sides of the pool. She gently rubbed her knuckles along his jawline, feeling the rasp of his stubble.

"Should I have shaved?" he asked.

"No, I like it." Jess ran a hand over his chest, feeling regrowth. "You shaved this for the toga party?" He nodded. "And you trim downstairs, too."

"I might have let myself go. You should probably check."

Her laugh was high and breathless. "No, I'm okay. I was just curious."

"Jess?" Mitch said, and Jess sucked in air that was too thin, like she was getting it through a straw, before finally, reluctantly, meeting his eyes. "Can I touch you?"

"I'm sorry. I'm really sorry. But I can't," she said in a rush. "I'm trying so hard to relax, honestly, but it's just not working. I think kissing was probably it for me."

There was a beat while Mitch adjusted to the gap between what he'd thought was going to happen and reality. "That's okay." He nodded for a bit. "That's all right." An awkward moment followed, the two of them looking at each other as if to say, *Now what?* "You still cold?" he asked.

"Little bit," Jess said, relief in her voice. "But listen, I—"

"Want to go?"

It was unbelievable, really, how quickly he could become that other person.

———

THIS TIME AS Jess scaled the wall there were no jokes about Mitch looking up her skirt. He went first and waited for her on the other side, staring blankly in the direction of campus. The shopping cart looked lonely on the other side of the road, abandoned for a second time. As they headed off, Jess skipped to get into step and regretted it immediately. They stayed that way, though, striding out efficiently like some four-legged piece of machinery, harvesting the night. And the silence between them didn't just feel uncomfortable, it felt uncrossable.

Things changed when they turned into Carmody Road. Mitch started to pull ahead, walking faster and faster, as though he had some urgent appointment to get to at one o'clock in the morning. By the time they neared the roundabout, the distance between them was big enough to be symbolic. If it wasn't for the fact that they'd never talk to each other again, Jess might have just let him go. As it was, she wanted the last word.

"Hey!" she shouted. Mitch didn't show any signs of having heard her. "Oh, come on, who else would I be talking to?" He slowed reluctantly, stopping under a streetlight without turning around.

"I love how the time-out ended as soon as I said I wouldn't do stuff with you," Jess said when she reached him. She stared at his profile. "Really, you should have thanked me. I bet I'm the first girl you've ever just talked to."

"No, that's not right," Mitch said, his voice carefully neutral in a way that was meant to block her. "I used to talk to this other girl sometimes."

"Well, I hope you treated her better than this," Jess said. "Me? I wish that you'd never let me take that jersey."

He lifted his chin at her. "We finished?"

"Oh, we're finished," she told him. Mitch started walking. "Actually, no, we're not." He stopped again. "Why *did* you let me take that jersey? Just tell me that."

Jess thought he wasn't going to answer, but eventually he turned around, facing her for the first time. "You want to know why? Because Julian's dead, and I'm alive, and I hate myself for that every fucking day. His parents gave me that jersey when they found out I was coming back. They thought I should have it, because I was his best friend. His mum hadn't even washed it, because it used to smell like him—" Mitch broke off, swallowed. "That's why I washed it. In case it still did."

"Mitch, stop," Jess said, her hands pressed hard against her chest. "I'm sorry."

"And then you show up," Mitch said, his eyes wide and haunted. "You're going to steal it—this jersey that means so much to everybody. And just for that moment I wanted you to. I thought, Good. Take the fucking thing. You carry some of it." He rubbed his eyes, and Jess thought he was crying, but when he pulled his hands away, she saw he wasn't.

Then he started to walk again. Jess trailed behind him the rest of the way. Even though he wasn't walking fast anymore.

15.
Cherokee

Jess woke late the next morning, and while she'd never liked Sundays—too saggy, too melancholy—this one stretched before her like an interminable wasteland. Everybody had disappeared, T-floor echoingly empty, a wind tunnel. She streamed Triple J, just to hear some noise, but Cat Power was playing, which only heightened the ache. And when she showered, she noticed that her fingertips, pruned when she'd gone to bed, were smooth again, the smell of chlorine faded from her skin.

Perhaps that was why she ended up stalking Mitch online. She wanted proof of him. Or more of him. But he didn't seem to have a social media presence, or to be anywhere else for that matter: St. Luke's hadn't been online for long enough to include his time there, and the Knights newsletters were protected. There were a couple of fleeting mentions of him in articles about the university rugby team, but the fact he'd made an impressive debut didn't really do it for Jess. There was a funny taste in her mouth when she searched for Julian Lloyd instead, along with "car crash" and "Bundaberg."

She found three articles. The first was a perfunctory news piece: A man had been killed at around 1:30 a.m. following a New Year's Eve party, when the car he was driving left the road and crashed into a tree. He was the sole occupant of the vehicle.

The second article confirmed the man as being Julian Lloyd, aged twenty, and the use of the word "man" seemed incongruous in relation to his age. He was a boy, like Jess was still a girl. The article included a photograph of an emergency service worker near what was supposed to have been a Holden truck, but it was unrecognizable as any sort of vehicle—the driver's seat had been eaten by a mash of metal; the front wheel was kinked toward the body of the car at a right angle. There was a second circular shape beneath the driver's seat, resting on the road, and Jess eventually realized it was the car's steering wheel. The article quoted a police spokesman who said that the crash was under investigation, and it was believed speeding and alcohol had been contributing factors. The police were to prepare a report for the coroner.

Jess remembered Mitch talking about himself in the third person on the night of the toga party. *I bet he's a fucking asshole. Actually, I know he's an asshole. It's a fact. Coroner certified.* He'd been at the party, she was sure of it, and he felt he should have stopped his friend from driving. It was the sort of thing from road safety campaigns—*Real friends don't let friends drive drunk.* But, to Jess, one small detail made the horror involved in Julian's death very real: the misplaced steering wheel. Julian's hands had been holding it. If it had ended up down there, what had happened to his hands?

The third article was more of a tribute piece: PROMISING FUTURE CUT SHORT BY TRAGIC CRASH. And even before Jess read the headline, her breath caught, because she'd seen the photograph: Mitch standing with another guy who could only be Julian, both of them wearing their school blazers. It had clearly been taken a few years earlier, but Mitch was still so recognizable, so immediately Mitch, it made Jess want to understand the things that made him who he was. Oddly enough, with Julian there, it became possible.

Julian. While Mitch was tanned, Julian was so pale that it made his tousled hair seem impossibly black by comparison, inky. It might have just been the photograph, but his eyes weren't brown as you would have expected, but a deep, dark blue. He was thin-lipped, his mouth open, showing white teeth and the tip of his tongue, and that, combined with the upward tilt of his chin, made his expression challenging, almost sexual. No. To Jess, it was sexual. She felt the punch of his presence. He was the type of guy that she would have crushed on but never approached. If he wasn't interested, he would have been cruel, and if you'd had to approach him, he definitely wasn't interested. If he approached you, the flirting would have been flinty, the opening negotiations to something even more dispassionate.

His arm was slung around Mitch's shoulders, his forefinger and thumb cocked like a gun.

Beside him, Mitch seemed more reserved, facing the camera squarely, his arms held loosely in front of his body, maintaining the *T* of his frame, even as Julian leaned on him. Resisting? Maybe. As always, his blue eyes pierced her, and he looked older than Julian, mature for their age, his chin shadowed by stubble. But there was something about his brow, a hint of tension, the slightest pull between his eyebrows, that marked him as less sure than his friend. It was an odd thing to notice, another small detail, but to Jess it was crucial. Of the two boys in that photograph, Mitch was the one she didn't know.

16.
Team

Jess wound her way through the tables at La Dolce Vita, red-faced and sweaty and slightly underdressed in running shorts and a T-shirt featuring a Rolling Stones–style tongue framed by forked fingers, her hair in two loose braids. She wasn't a huge fan of the place. For a start, she found it geographically confusing, what with a replica Eiffel Tower mounted directly over an Italian restaurant. The tower itself was meant to signpost the entire complex of shops and eateries, which was named *Savoir Faire*, but no one ever called it that. People referred to it as Park Road, Milton, and they adopted a superior air, running the three words together: *Park-Road-Milton*, like Paris-France, or, in this case, Paris-Italy. The people who had most cause to refer to it were keen on alfresco dining and drinking coffee in the same indefinable way that they were keen on Tuscany: as an attitude, a state of mind.

Heather frequented Park-Road-Milton a lot. That was one of the things Jess actually liked about the place: its association with her aunt. She stood as Jess approached, smoothing her skirt over her ample hips and taking a certain pleasure in it, giving Jess's T-shirt a discreet nod of approval. And maybe it was the Pavarotti piping through the sound system that made Jess's heart feel too full, or perhaps it was something quieter to do with family and safe havens.

"Hello, darling," Heather breathed, ignoring Jess's protests that she was too sweaty and engulfing her in a hug.

Jess ostentatiously kissed Heather on one cheek and then the other. "Sweetie."

"Little shit," Heather scolded, and then made an *Aaack!* noise as Jess licked her nose. She sat down, her expensively streaked, ash-blond bob ruffled and looking better for it, smiling as she dabbed at her nose with her napkin. She was wearing a muslin scarf loosely knotted at the neck of her linen shirt, which must have been the new thing among patrons, because at Jess's work quite a few patrons of the arts had been wearing their scarves that way, too. Jess felt comforted just being near her aunt. Someone who knew her and where she was from.

She went to dump her backpack on the ground, knocking her knuckles against the table edge. "Ow! Fuck!" she cried, making people at the nearby tables turn around.

Heather, unperturbed, glanced down at her runners. "Did you jog here?"

"Yeah. I'm going to keep going after, too. Run to work," Jess said, flicking her hand. "I've got my shoes and clothes in the bag. I can shower there." She thumped into her seat. "But if Vivian finds out, I'm toast."

"If you need money for buses, darling, just let me know."

Jess smiled. "Thanks, but I think you've done enough. I'm doing it because I like it. It stops my thinking. Well, I do think, but only about my breathing."

They ordered drinks, then Heather leaned in to tug one of Jess's braids. "Been doing a lot of running lately, Jessie?"

"I don't know, maybe. Why?"

"You look thinner. Dark moons around your eyes. Are you getting enough sleep?"

"Yeah," Jess said, her voice suddenly croaky. "No."

Heather waited.

Jess sighed. "I met the wrong guy."

"Oh, sweetheart, I knew something was up." Heather paused, appearing to pick her words carefully. "Wrong like Brendan? Or a different wrong?"

"Different. Completely different. He was muscly, and he was smart, and he was rich, and hot—so hot. And we could talk. He kept up with me. Do you know how rare that is?"

"Do you mean to say this boy is dead?" Heather sounded shocked.

"No, it's not him who's dead," Jess said with a frown. "Oh, I get it. Past tense. Yeah, funny how I did that. He's not dead, but he might as well be, because I haven't seen him for weeks. Even if I did, he probably wouldn't talk to me, and I definitely shouldn't talk to him. Uh-uh." She paused and then added in a doleful voice, "We played Classic Catches."

"Classic Catches?"

"You know, when one of you throws the ball, and the other one has to dive into the pool and catch it before it hits the water. Like cricket."

"Darling, I'm familiar with Classic Catches. It's the context that threw me."

Jess charged on, hardly hearing. "And now he's in my *head*, all the time. I think I'm going crazy. Nineteen years old and I've got an imaginary friend. Seriously, he was with me when I walked in here, making comments about my ass and saying, 'So this is the famous Heather.'"

"Well, he sounds wonderful," Heather said, rolling with all this in her usual effortless way. "Bring him over for dinner. Tell him you need a date and use it as an excuse for getting in touch. I'll make salmon confit."

Jess laughed, and then sighed, and then laughed again. "That will never happen." She pressed her fingertips to her temples, staring at her aunt. "I'm so stupid. He wanted me to do stuff with him, and I wouldn't. And now, all the time, I keep wishing I did." Heather raised her eyebrows. "Don't look at me like that," Jess huffed. "I've got a libido."

"You get that from our side, sweetheart," Heather said, patting her hand. "And that's not why I'm looking at you. I've been wanting to talk to you about this business, but I haven't known how to broach it. I don't want to overstep the line. I'm not your mother, after all."

"That's all right. I like having a team behind me. What business?"

"This pornography business."

Jess started to laugh. "Have you been watching porn?"

"From what I can gather, everybody's watching it," Heather said, and then thanked the waiter as he placed a cappuccino on the table. "I have something for you," she told Jess, opening her purse and placing a fifty-dollar note on the table.

"I said I don't need bus money."

"It's not for that. It's for a website."

"What sort of website?" Jess asked suspiciously.

"Make Love Not Porn. I watched the founder's TED talk. She says that people need to see real-world sex rather than porn sex all the time. She worries that young women, like you, darling, will agree to things that you don't want to do because porn has left you thinking that it's normal. The only thing is, you have to pay to view. There's this lovely—"

"Oh God, Heather, that's disgusting! It's all real people having sex, and some of them are old and really hairy—" Jess shut up abruptly when she noticed that all the same people had turned around again.

"Why *are* girls today so frightened of hair?" Heather asked calmly, spooning froth from her cappuccino.

"Actually, it's not just girls. That guy I'm telling you about? He shaves his chest. And trims the garden, if you know what I mean."

"Well, hip, hip, hooray. Finally I can sleep knowing that we've achieved equality."

Jess laughed in surprise. "Snarky!"

Heather's face was serious. "What did this boy want to do with you, Jessie?"

Jess looked away, her voice low and ashamed. "He said it would just be a couple of his friends. And a donkey." Heather flicked froth at her, and she grinned, dropping the act. "I don't know. He said he wanted to touch me."

There was a short, charged pause.

"Oh," Heather said.

"*I know.*" Jess leaned forward, feeling alive, lit up. "And I think he might be good at it, too. Touching, I mean."

"Well, thanks be," Heather said with some passion. "Because with all those camera angles, there is *no* touching in those movies. That's what's been lost. Women aren't participants, they're receptacles."

"Um, thank you," Jess said to the waiter as he placed an iced chocolate on the table. And then, to her aunt: "Okay, can you stop talking about porn? Because it's fucking weird."

Heather ignored her. "How on earth are you going to run after drinking that?"

"Slowly."

"So why did you say no to him?" Heather asked, back to the subject at hand.

"I can't do the one-night-stand thing." Jess attacked her iced chocolate, shoveling cream into her mouth. "I think there's something wrong with me."

"But what if he genuinely only wanted to touch you?" Heather asked.

Jess thought about it. "Even if he had meant it—and that is an enormous, unicorn-size 'if'—he's from Knights and I'm from Unity. So it can't happen. Ever."

"Two households, both alike in dignity?"

"Yeah. Except not so alike. What's the definition of a bitch? A girl who won't sleep with you. What's the definition of a slut? A girl who has. That's what they're like. Complete misogynists. And Romeo's no exception. Doesn't like women." Jess slurped at her drink, ignoring the straw.

"Then he doesn't like himself." Heather rubbed a fingertip over her top lip, and Jess, prompted, did the same. "Oh dear."

"I know. So as far as I'm concerned, we can never be. Because look!" Jess used her spoon to draw a circle in the air around her aunt's face. "Some of the best people I know are women."

"Special girl," Heather said, with a look of such love that Jess shifted in her seat. "Why don't you help him then? Let him get to know a woman. Be friends."

"I don't think he wants friends. I don't think he wants anyone at all." Jess stabbed at the island of ice cream in her iced chocolate. "He's fucked up. His best friend died in a car accident last year."

"Oh, the poor boy. You can't hold that against him, Jessie."

"I'm not. It kills me that he's so alone. Do you know I've never seen him text anyone? Not once."

They stared at each other for a second.

Jess dropped her eyes. "But even if he didn't want to be alone, he wouldn't want me."

"What are you talking about?" Heather scolded. "You're beautiful and smart and funny—"

"Good to know. Wait, aren't you my aunt?"

"—and very independent," Heather finished, ignoring her.

"Three thousand bucks says I'm not."

"You know what I mean."

Jess shook her head. "It's okay, I don't need boosting. What I mean is, there's someone else. I don't know what went on between them, but it's obvious he's still really hung up on her. And compared to her, I'm . . . I don't know what I am, but I'm not a diamond girl."

Heather straightened, pulling at the hem of her linen blouse, her tone brisk: "What you aren't is a second-place girl."

"Oh, thanks, Heather," Jess said, touched. "That's lovely."

"You're a competitive little shit."

At that, Jess laughed. Which helped.

———

WHEN THE BUS stopped near the Regatta Hotel on Coronation Drive and a large, rowdy group boarded, Jess took little notice. She was staring out at the Brisbane River, her forehead resting against the cool glass of the window, thinking she'd run past that spot that very same day on her way to meet Heather, but it seemed like a million years ago. She was listening to Lorde, and she was aware of the new passengers in the same way that she was aware of the music or the lights reflected on the water: They were just background to her mood. She was tired from work, and the better for it. Calm. Well spent. Plus she'd pulled the tongue T-shirt on over the top of her work blouse for the trip home, guaranteeing she wouldn't have to share her seat.

One of the new arrivals took the seat in front of Jess, though, and turned sideways to look at her. He mouthed something, seeming vaguely familiar.

Jess removed an ear bud. "Sorry?"

Curly brown hair, solid build—he might have been cute in an amiable boy-next-door kind of way, if not for his eyes, which were cold, reptilian. The eyes helped Jess place him, and when she did, her heart came loose in her chest. He was the one who'd stopped Mitch and her as they'd been leaving the toga party. She glanced up at the tail end of the group, the two guys shuffling past her, both of them wearing Knights jerseys, and she got a sick, falling-away feeling. Lagging behind them, as though leaving room for an entrance, was Diamond Girl. She had two other girls in tow—literally, a chain linked by hands gripping shoulders—the three of them moving in a slow-motion way that suggested they'd been hitting it hard, mountaineers trudging their way through a blizzard. They lurched to one side as the bus pulled out, tottering on high heels.

"Mr. Bus Driver, if you could drive a little more chaotically, please?" Diamond Girl called over her shoulder in a clear, ringing voice. "Hit the brakes or something? That would be super."

Her friends disintegrated into giggles. It was then she spotted Jess and gave her an exaggerated wink, before continuing to lead her friends to safety, staring shortsightedly at the aisle stretching ahead of her, and Jess wasn't sure if it was a case of not being recognized or not being worthy of a reaction. She was acutely aware that her T-shirt smelled faintly of sweat, paranoid that the knight in front of her could smell it, too.

He'd been temporarily distracted by Diamond Girl—probably everybody had, the girl had that quality. But now his attention was back to Jess. "Hey, Mitch! I told you it was her," he shouted, directing his words toward the back of the bus.

"Is this really necessary?" Jess asked, trying to sound bored and instead sounding every bit as anxious as she felt.

His gaze flicked to her without interest, as though further input from her was irrelevant, then he straightened in his seat, focusing on someone behind her, a sudden wariness in his demeanor. Jess glanced around, expecting to see Mitch. But the guy leaning across her seat was stocky and dark-skinned, a sleeve of Polynesian tattoos covering his left arm.

He gave Jess a polite nod, then turned his attention to the knight in front of her. "Give it a rest, okay, Dud?" he asked, his voice deep and relaxed. "No need for this."

"Aw, come on, Tipene," the other knight protested. "You know what she—" he broke off as Tipene cuffed him across the head, hard enough to knock the smart-ass look off his face. Violently enough to make Jess jump.

"Sorry about that," Tipene apologized to her. To the guy he'd called Dud: "You've got ten seconds to pick another seat." With that, he was gone.

Dud sat there looking sulky for maybe half of his allotted time—trying to save face, Jess thought—then joined his comrades down the back. Jess exhaled, replacing her ear bud, and leaned against the window again. But now she was only pretending to listen to the music. Their voices were loud and they carried.

"What the fuck, Tipene?" Dud's voice, whiny and querulous.

"It's not right, man," Tipene answered him.

"Is that the one from the toga party?" someone else wanted to know. "The one who—"

"You didn't say she was hot, Mitch."

"Should've got her to shave your pubes, too."

Mitch's voice, slow and insolent: "Why do you think I'm sitting funny?"

There was a round of loud laughter.

Jess's jaw was clamped so tightly, it hurt her teeth. What an asshole. He hadn't done anything to call his dog off, and now he was acting like she didn't matter at all. She'd mythologized him in the four weeks since she'd seen him last, forgotten who he really was: one of the boys, a knight. She was such a fool—the way she'd gushed to Heather! She'd been yearning for someone who didn't exist.

Diamond Girl's bell-like voice cut through the laughter: "You're so honorable, Tipene!"

"Aw, nah, Sylvie," Tipene replied, sounding embarrassed. "Just, you know, not right to treat a girl like that."

Sylvie. So that was Diamond Girl's name. Unexpectedly soft and old-fashioned, but silky, too. A name for something precious.

"I think it's honorable," Sylvie told him. "You rugby boys are like that, aren't you, Tipene? You do the right thing. It's like a code, isn't it? Hang on," she added, as though something had just occurred to her. "Why didn't you defend her then, Killer? You're a rugby boy."

"Why don't you fuck off, Sylvie?"

"Oh, look at Tipene," Sylvie exclaimed. "He's just dying to tell you not to talk to me like that. But he can't, can he, Killer? Because you're not just rugby boys, you're knights. It's all right, Tipene. I'm not scared of the big bad Killer."

"Sylvie, hon," another girl's voice said uncertainly. "Maybe you—"

"Maybe you shouldn't drink." Mitch's voice could have cut flesh from bone. "Your impulses are no good when you're drunk, Sylvie. You get shrill. Lose your class."

There was a dry coughing sound. "Class? *You* want to lecture *me* about class? Oh, this should be good. Let's talk about class, Killer. And while we're going, why don't you tell these guys about loyalty—"

"Shut up."

"—and respect for your friends. Why don't we talk about—"

"Guys!" The voice was Tipene's, and it cut through the argument like a hand clap. "You gotta stop this, all right?" he begged, his voice impassioned. "What would Julian think if he could hear you two going on like this? It would kill him." There was a pause. "Shit, I didn't mean to say that. I'm—"

"It's okay, Tipene," Sylvie said, her voice subdued.

There was silence from the back until the bus stopped to let some passengers off, then a couple of the knights started a discussion about whether Betfair or Sportsbet paid the best odds, but they were using the hushed, careful voices kids use when Mum and Dad have been fighting. When the bus finally reached the university and turned onto Chancellor's Place, the tension broke and the knights started filing down the aisle, their conversation loud and raucous again, obviously happy to be making an escape. Jess kept her head down, wrapping her ear buds around her phone and tucking it into her bag, but when she heard the click of heels stop beside her seat, she glanced up, curious.

"*You!*" Sylvie exclaimed, pointing at Jess. "My hero." She held up her hand for a high five, looking unsteady on her feet as the bus jerked to a stop. After a moment's hesitation, Jess clapped palms with her. She watched Sylvie totter off, trailed by her attendants, until she was blocked from view by the knights who followed. She thought Mitch was the last of them, and, when Jess saw his retreating back, she was hit by a confusing mix of hurt and relief. His hair was back to blond again. She caught the faintest whiff of a warm, spicy smell: his aftershave. And she realized that none of the knights had seemed to know anything about their time-out. But maybe he just hadn't told them because to him it wasn't significant. He hadn't scored.

Then she gasped and yelled "Ow!" clamping a hand to her head. Mitch turned around.

"You going to invite me back sometime, too?" Dud asked, his

jovial voice a complete mismatch for the vicious way he'd pulled her plait. "I've never been to Unity."

"Oh sure," Jess said, rubbing her head. She looked up at him, pushing her backpack into the aisle with a foot as she did so. "Come and visit. I'm on F-floor."

"F-floor, huh?" Dud said, and she knew everything she needed to know from the look on his face right then. Girls didn't usually play along with him, and he had no idea what to do when they did. "*F* for fuck?"

"*F* for fun," Jess cooed, giving him a sweet smile.

Confused, he looked away, blindly starting to walk off. And as he did so, he tripped over her bag, falling with a loud smack.

"*Nemo me impune lacessit,*" Jess told him.

It went unheard because the driver bellowed at them to get off his bus, and Dud pulled himself to his feet, scrambling past Mitch, red-faced and eager to escape. Jess picked up her backpack and started down the aisle, stopping when she reached Mitch, who hadn't moved.

"Let me guess," he said, taking in the details of her T-shirt. "There is no F-floor."

"That's what I like about you," Jess told him with a tight smile. "You keep up."

"Hey, listen, I'm sorry I didn't—"

"It's the only thing I like about you," Jess said. "Can you move, please?"

138

17.
Hey, Ladies

Econometrics was a hard thing to face first thing on a Friday. It was the second-to-last Friday of the term, and Jess was struggling to find the motivation or the momentum. When Farren arrived, Jess had showered, dried her hair, and pulled on a skirt, but that was the extent of her preparations.

"Yo, 'tis I," Farren announced, leaving the door open and doing the Running Man in the middle of the floor. Jess was playing hip-hop, but you couldn't assume the two things were related; Farren's version of the Running Man always seemed to be to music only she could hear. She was wearing a men's white business shirt, paisley tie, red velvet shorts, fishnet leggings, and Converse sneakers. Jess admired Farren's outfit, then ignored her, selecting a polka-dotted bra and a tight white T-shirt from her fridge. Morning sun flooded her room, and it was already a hot one. "Ready to go?" Farren asked. "Leanne's waiting."

"Sure." Jess slammed the fridge shut and walked out the door bare-chested. Luckily, there wasn't anybody around at that moment.

Farren's laugh rolled out into the hallway after her. Jess returned to the room, giving her a huffy look. "Well, obviously, I'm not ready to go. You're early, and my boobs are out. Why even ask? You know it annoys me, but you do it every time."

"Because you react every time," Farren told her with a big cheesy grin. "Nice tits, by the way."

"They're small—"

"Why can't small be nice?"

"If it wasn't for the pill, I wouldn't have anything at all, thanks to running. I'm still on it, even though I'm not getting any. It plumps them up."

"Vanity," Farren scolded. "You should totally get off it. I have. There's nothing sexier than how your body feels when you're cycling naturally. I love it."

Jess glanced at her. "What about Davey?"

"Condoms. I prefer them. Less mess."

"Huh." Jess pulled on the bra and T-shirt, sucking air through her teeth, because before the cold was good it was painful. "God, I hate mornings. That's why I like sleeping through them. I don't like being this cranky."

"It's not just mornings," Farren observed helpfully. "You've been cranky for days. Weeks!"

Jess squeezed paste onto her toothbrush and started brushing more vigorously than necessary, suddenly paranoid Farren might do the sums and solve for causation. She'd been briefed on what had happened with Mitch at the RE, but Jess had ended the report with Mitch handing her the letter and walking off. Farren knew nothing of cart rides and night swims and the strange and wild aching that haunted her still—even, maddeningly, despite that bus trip. Between those lapses of judgment and the messy aftermath of Brendan, it had been a grim term. Jess was just focused on making it to the Easter break, so she could wipe the slate clean and start again.

"Well, while we're not on the subject," Farren said, and dropped a significant pause. Jess stopped brushing, mouth full of foam, heart full of guilt, not sure how Farren knew everything, just sure she did. "Byron called me last night."

"Oh for God's sake. I thought he'd given up," Jess said, the words gargled. "Anyway, what happened to not getting involved?"

"Trust me, you're going to want to hear what he had to say."

Jess spat her mouthful of toothpaste out the window.

"Or maybe not," Farren said. There was a dim shout, presumably from someone walking along the concrete path three stories below.

"Sorry!" Jess shouted out the window, keeping out of sight. To Farren: "Okay, what?"

"Our Brendan has met someone else," Farren said grandly, her eyes shining. "I regret to inform you the ship has sailed! He wanted you to hear it from him first, and he knows you ignore his messages, so . . . I think it was one last flare of ego. I told him you'd only be happy for him."

Jess whooped, sending flecks of foam flying. Suddenly, inexplicably, she was sure things were about to turn around, and she realized how desperately she'd been waiting for it. "Back in the game, baby!" she shouted, bouncing on the bed. "I've always wanted to say that."

Farren was doing the Running Man again, joining in with the Beastie Boys. "Hey! Hey! Hey . . ."

"HEY, LADIES!" LEANNE shouted as they neared the building site. Over the last few weeks their exchanges with the builders had become a regular thing, secretly relished. That day, aside from the usual nine guys, there was also a clean-shaven man in a short-sleeved business shirt and chinos, straddling a briefcase and consulting what looked like architectural drawings, his hard hat pushed back on his head. The site foreman, a barrel-chested guy with a beard who reminded Jess of a leering pirate, looked strangely subdued, engaged in an earnest discussion with the visitor. The stranger's presence might have also explained why the radio was off and the other guys were hard at work on the framing.

"I think we've just been burned," Jess said.

"You're right," Farren said, her tone incredulous. "They're completely ignoring us."

The guy with dreadlocks, crouched down using a circular saw, gave them a little wave, and a couple of the other builders glanced across, but that was it. They were the very picture of a team who could do it on time and on budget, with no place for distractions.

"It's like we meant nothing to them," Jess said, hooking her fingers through the wire mesh of the fence and sagging despondently. "Who's going to ogle us now?"

"I feel used," Farren agreed. "Cast aside for some honcho from head office. And now I'm not being objectified, my sense of self is suffering. I'll have to get back on Facebook."

"God, you two go on with some shit," Leanne said. She brought her forefinger and thumb to her mouth and whistled.

Dreadlocks responded like a meerkat, standing up with a start, his head swiveling their way, and then to his coworkers, as though begging permission to react. The other builders grinned but steadfastly refused to look at the girls. The foreman, though, moved like he'd received a rocket up the ass, clapping a hand on his visitor's back and shepherding him briskly out of the site gate, heading toward the parking lot. He glanced back over his shoulder at the girls with wide eyes that were begging for a head start.

The two sides regarded each other silently—that moment of tense contemplation you see in all good Westerns just before the shooting starts. Then the foreman and visitor disappeared from view, and the builders downed tools, letting loose with a volley of wolf whistles.

Dreadlocks planted his legs apart in a stripper's pose and gave them a series of pelvic thrusts. His workmates started cheering.

Leanne bawled, "Wait! Is that a peanut or a penis?"

Dreadlocks yelled, "It's a jackhammer, baby!" And the builders roared their approval.

"Yeah? 'Cause all I see is a tool!" Jess shouted, earning a high five from Farren.

"Show us yer tits!" This from one of the other guys.

"Show us yer bolt!" This from Farren.

"Yeah, sure! If you'll just hold these two nuts for me!"

"Why? I'll bet you don't even know how to screw!" Farren responded.

"I've got a big hard thing!" yelled a guy who'd been marking out a sizeable plank of wood.

"See, from here," Jess shouted, "it just looks like you're holding a stubby little pencil!"

"He's a carpenter! He'll teach you how to hammer!"

"But hammering's no fun when the nail's too small!" Leanne boomed jovially.

"I could drill you instead!" offered another guy helpfully.

Farren, starting to lose it, gasped out: "Yeah, they say that's a two-second job!"

At that, Jess howled, doubling over. When she straightened, still completely at the mercy of her special helicopter laugh, she caught sight of someone walking past. Someone with cropped blond hair and electric-blue eyes, a pen tucked behind his ear in the way that she might sport a cigarette. Someone who wore his navy polo shirt well, stretched across the type of chest a girl could curl up on. Someone Farren and Leanne didn't notice at all, because they were busy with the builders.

The moment was so close to perfect. By chance, Jess had put a rinse through her hair the night before, so it looked glossy and rich, and as she'd spotted Mitch, she'd been drawing it back from her face like she was in a shampoo ad, but completely unselfconsciously—the only way to pull off that maneuver. And while he'd caught her unawares, there couldn't have been a better time for him to do it, flanked by two friends, trading innuendos with a site full of builders, laughing her head off, seemingly unaffected by her four encounters with him. Things couldn't have played out better . . . except for one small detail.

When Jess noticed Mitch, she did a double take.

It was only after he'd gone that she realized he'd slipped up, too. When she'd seen him, his face had been impassive, his eyes as unreadable as reflective sunglasses—quite a feat, given he would have heard the whole of their exchange with the builders. But at the last moment, when his gaze had slid past her and was once again focused straight ahead, his mouth twitched.

And he smiled.

18.
Catch Me

Wednesday night, Jess climbed the lecture theater stairs to take her usual seat. Political economy and comparative systems—could life get any better? She had her ear buds in, listening to The Jezabels, and she needed the music, feeling tired and down and kicked around. Too many nights spent in a fever, sweating into her sheets, her eyes wide but unseeing, suffering a heat of her own making. Too many days spent waiting.

She just had to hold out for term break. Then she'd be at her aunt's, away from school and the constant, exhausting possibility of seeing Mitch again. Five days had passed since the morning at the building site, and she could wonder why he'd even been there in the first place—how could it have been coincidence when knights never went that way and he knew her schedule?—but all it was doing was making her sick. No. She made herself sick.

Jess sighed, pulling out her notepad and stowing her phone. Then she propped her chin on her hand, watching Professor Meakin get set up at the front of the room.

"Earth to Jess." A hand waved in front of Jess's face.

She blinked, focusing on Roger. "Oh, hi. How are you?"

"Not bad," he said, filling the seat beside her, and Jess grabbed her notepad so he didn't knock it to the floor. Roger wasn't fat, but he liked to make himself at home, one of those people who automatically claimed a shared armrest. His tie was loosened and skewed to the side, and he had a receding hairline at twenty-five. He was also the only person Jess had ever met who treated a lecture as a networking opportunity, changing seats every week. Because it was a night lecture, most of the attendees were mature-aged students who worked full-time like he did. The fact he hadn't excluded Jess was oddly flattering and meant she was more tolerant than she might otherwise have been. Roger had a few quirks.

"Big weekend?" he asked, opening his laptop, then answered his own question before Jess could: "We ended up at Friday's. It was pretty messy. Cam got escorted outside by the bouncers . . ."

Jess had no idea who Cam was, but Roger always talked as though she was intimately acquainted with his friends and world. And his weekends were always messy. She thought he was having some kind of reaction to having gone straight to work after high school. She tuned him out, watching her fellow attendees fill up the front half of the theater. She was probably the youngest person in the room. Then she straightened in her seat.

Mitch was standing in the entrance.

He looked around the theater, finally catching sight of her, and Jess almost laughed when he shook his head, because even though she couldn't see his expression from that distance, she could read his mind: Of all the seats, in all the rows, in all the lecture theaters in that town, she had to choose one of the highest. She held her breath, wondering if he'd leave, faced with that. But he crossed the floor, his gait unsteady. From that, and the way

Professor Meakin glanced sharply at him as he passed, she realized he'd been drinking.

Oh boy.

He started up the stairs strongly enough, but by the time he'd reached the midway point, he'd slowed and was grasping the back of each seat as he passed, as though needing to haul himself up, stopping every now and then to warily glance back over his shoulder. He was in jeans and, in a nice touch, an old Just Do It T-shirt.

"What's this joker want?" Roger asked, breaking his monologue.

"I was wondering the same thing," Jess replied, sounding distracted.

"You know him?"

"Kind of. Actually, Roger, you might want to move."

But Professor Meakin had pulled up the first of his PowerPoint slides, and Roger tapped Jess's notepad with his finger. She started jotting down notes and Roger copied them, his fingers rattling the keys of his laptop. When Mitch finally drew level with them, he shot Jess a look that made her feel like she'd been hit by blue lightning.

Rather than attempt to push past Roger, he edged along the empty row behind them, his breathing labored. Jess could smell the alcohol on his breath. Then, moving like he was in slow motion, he slid belly-down along the seat tops on the other side of her and tumbled into their row. Professor Meakin's voice trailed off as he stared up at them, which made everybody else turn around, too—a sea of annoyed mature-aged faces all glaring at Jess, as though the interruption was her fault. Roger hissed "What is he doing?" and Jess didn't know whether she wanted to laugh or cry, one hand clamped over her mouth, her face burning.

Mitch, oblivious to all this, maneuvered himself into a sitting position, one white-knuckled hand locked onto the back of the seat in front of him, his face pale and clammy.

"As I was saying," Professor Meakin said, looking up at the projector screen for a prompt, clearing his throat. "Ah yes, Milton Friedman. One of the most notable proponents of monetarism . . ."

Jess met Mitch's glassy eyes and whispered, "Great entrance."

That's when she really knew he was drunk, because he had no comeback, just looked sheepish, nudging her clumsily in a way that made her smile. He was moving like an astronaut, either afraid he was about to be sucked into space or having some kind of weird reaction to being under the influence. Then the *tap-tap-tap* of Roger's finger got Jess's attention, and she returned to her note-taking, Roger studiously copying her.

Mitch leaned closer, and Jess tried to ignore the thrill that passed along the length of her body. "I need paper and a pen," he murmured, and while his words weren't slurred they were definitely smudged. "Please."

As Jess handed him these things, Roger tapped her folder again, and she thought about jabbing him in the eye with her pen but resisted. Instead, she frantically scribbled down the rest of the slide before Professor Meakin changed to the next one, aware that Mitch was observing all this.

The lecture could have been in Latin for all Jess knew. She was writing on autopilot, unable to think past the fact that Mitch was beside her, his shoulder pressed hard against hers. Beneath the booze, she could smell his aftershave, and every cell in her body was lit up and pulsing like the lights of Las Vegas.

Mitch wrote something, then pointedly tapped his pen to get Jess's attention, mimicking Roger. Her smile faded as she read his words. She returned to her note-taking with a vengeance. Mitch tapped his pen again. When she didn't respond, he did it more insistently: *TAP-TAP-TAP!* And he drew a circle around what he'd written: *Have you been thinking about me?*

Jess shifted uneasily in her seat. She did not want to lie, and maybe that was because the term had been a sleepless hell, but there was so much risk.

So she wrote: *Why?*

And by the way Mitch's face changed, Jess knew there was risk for him, too. She returned her attention to the front of the room, feeling lightheaded. Nothing passed between them for the next forty minutes, until Professor Meakin announced that they'd take their usual ten-minute break. At that, Roger groaned, snapping his laptop shut and making a big show of stretching. He glanced from Jess to Mitch questioningly, as though waiting to be introduced. But Jess didn't respond, her rapidly beating heart sounding out: *Please go, please go, please go.*

Roger said, "Might head out for a coffee. Coming, Jess?"

"She doesn't want one," Mitch answered.

Roger bristled but had nowhere to run with it, because Jess gave him a quick smile and said, "I'm okay, thanks."

When he'd gone, Mitch asked, "Who's the"—*tap, tap, tap*—"dude?"

And Jess spurted some of the nervous laughter that had been collecting ever since his arrival. "His name's Roger. He's short-sighted; can't read the screen from up here. So he copies my notes instead."

"Why doesn't he get glasses?"

"I don't know. I don't really know him. He doesn't normally sit with me."

"Yeah? He really is blind then."

There was a funny beat between them. Mitch pulled his drink-sticky gaze away from her face, facing the front.

"When I saw you on Friday . . . What were you doing there?" Jess asked.

"Checking out the builders," Mitch said. Jess made an exasperated noise, and he gave her a sidelong look. "Obviously, I was trying to run into you."

"Why?"

When Mitch finally spoke, he sounded belligerent. "Because I can't stop thinking about you, all right? You are in my head, all the fucking time. Everywhere I go, it's like you're there with me, making your little smart-ass remarks—and don't say anything because I know it sounds crazy."

"It is a little weird," Jess said with a funny look on her face.

"Yeah, well, I've tried to stay away, believe me. But here I am, telling you all this shit, so . . ." Mitch exhaled, long and slow. "So now I just want to know. Have you been thinking about me, too?"

"I've heard about you," Jess sidestepped. "Do you know I've actually had girls from other colleges coming up to congratulate me on your makeover? Seems you're well-known. An absolute slut, apparently."

"I thought we didn't use that word."

"We do when it's nonstereotypical. But you're also very cold. That adjective came up a lot. Not big on cuddling afterward, or even acknowledging the girl's existence. Is that why you're not online? Worried they'll try to contact you? Friend you?"

"I went offline because if I read one more inane message about Julian on my timeline I was going to punch somebody. Otherwise, for a guy like me, social media is a catalog."

Jess looked away, feeling winded. "Wow. You're a whole other level."

"You think it's just me? Everyone at Knights wants to bag that Ellie chick—"

"Her name is Allie."

"But she's playing the game, too. That's why she's got all those photos up. It's advertising—"

"Too passive. She calls it power."

"—but you're not like that." Jess blinked at him. "Yeah, I've looked," he told her. "I saw the roasting the boys gave you after the toga party, by the way. You'll be glad to know that Jarrod Keith's tried to call them off, asked them to be bigger than the situation. I'm sorry you had to wear that. Some of it went too far."

"Really? You don't seem to mind when it happens in person."

Mitch rubbed his face. Then he focused on her, suddenly looking tired. "Okay, Jess, I'm sorry. I should have said something that night on the bus. But if I had it would have made it obvious that there's a bit more to us than people think, and—I don't even want to go there, all right? It's complicated and it's ugly, and it's nothing I'm proud of, okay?"

Not ugly at all, and not that complicated, Jess thought. Only two words: Sylvie Wawn. She now knew Sylvie's surname because she'd found her Facebook profile. Actually, first she'd found Tipene Taiapa's profile, via Jarrod Keith's profile, then searched through Tipene's 1,012 friends until she'd found Sylvie—not obsessed at all. But apart from a stunning profile pic and a header showing Sylvie and some girlfriends dressed as if for a ball, Jess learned nothing more. Sylvie kept her information locked down.

She'd also found Dud. His real name was Owen McCaffrey.

"Why do they call him Dud?" she asked abruptly.

Mitch blinked, thrown for a second. "Because he's a dud."

"Why do they call you Killer?"

A shadow passed over his face. "It started with rugby. Sometimes it means lady-killer."

"God, that's so lame."

Mitch leaned forward. "Jess, everything you've heard—it's all true, okay? I'm not pretending otherwise."

"Have you ever done something somebody didn't want?"

He frowned. "I'm not a rapist."

"Are you sure? I mean, you're from Knights, you may not have known the difference." Mitch met Jess's gaze steadily, looking angry now. "Sorry," she said eventually. She swallowed, her voice dropping: "Who's Sylvie? To you, I mean."

"No one," he said. Without hesitation. Stony-faced.

Liar, Jess thought. "I thought you didn't drink."

He leaned back in his seat, suddenly lifeless. "Special occasion."

"You had to be drunk to see me?"

"Birthday."

"Happy birthday."

Mitch shook his head. "Not mine."

Jess stared at him. "It's *his* birthday?"

Mitch's eyes met hers, his face leached of color, his expression so bleak that she had to look away, but as she did she reached across and squeezed his hand. And he clamped his other hand down on hers, gripping it like a drowning man who'd been thrown a rope.

Jess heard Mitch swallow, heard him take a jagged breath. With impeccable timing, Roger decided to return, looking comically wary as he approached, and Jess knew from the way he stared blatantly at Mitch that Mitch had turned his face away. Roger's gaze flicked to their entwined fingers as he told Jess he'd give them some privacy, rapidly grabbing his things. She didn't even care.

When he'd gone, Mitch said, "Jess," his voice low and scratchy. She looked at him, careful to show no reaction to his bloodshot eyes, his haggard face. "Aren't you surprised that I'm here? Now. Like this. Falling to fucking bits."

She shook her head.

"I am."

She gave him a funny smile and squeezed his hand again. "I know."

Then Professor Meakin started the second half of the lecture, and Jess copied down the slides as diligently as ever, forced to turn pages one-handed, because Mitch showed no signs of wanting to let go, sniffing quietly in his seat. And somehow she knew, beyond any doubt, that while Mitch Crawford had slept with a lot of girls, and Mitch Crawford had probably done a lot of dirty things, Mitch Crawford had never held hands with anyone before—not until that night.

19.
Left Hand Free

By the time Professor Meakin ended the lecture, forty-five minutes later, Mitch had sobered up some, seemed more comfortable with heights, and was in a considerably different mood. He was using a fingertip to draw slow, suggestive circles on Jess's palm, ignoring her when she tried to pull free of him, a smile tugging at the corner of his mouth. Everybody else was gathering their things, rushing out the door. Professor Meakin was talking to the small group of students who stayed behind to pick his brains every Wednesday night. The group left together, not seeming to notice that Jess and Mitch remained in the theater.

And then they were alone. The realization prickled through Jess's body.

"Can I have my hand back now?" she asked.

"I don't know. What are you going to give me for it?" After a moment's undignified struggle, Jess managed to wrestle it free, mainly because Mitch let her. While she packed up her things, Mitch used the paper she'd given him to make a plane. "You know what?

You didn't answer my question," he said, throwing it. The plane swooped through the air in a graceful arc before crashing into the second row. "Have you been thinking about me?"

"We'd better get you down these stairs."

"Why won't you just admit it?"

Jess licked her lips, which were incredibly dry for some reason. "Because it's a dead-end street."

"Well, then, it can't hurt, can it?"

"All right, yes. I've been thinking about you."

"A lot?"

"All day, all night."

"Good stuff?"

"Filthy."

"Fantasies?"

"Only the one."

"Tell me," he said, lifting his chin, and he was a long way from broken now.

Jess looked away, wishing he'd stayed open a little longer. "It's the shipwreck fantasy. You and I are shipwrecked on an island together, and I can do everything and anything I want with you, because nobody will ever know."

"Nobody has to know."

Jess made a noise like a laugh. "Oh, that is a fantasy. In real life, people always find out, even if I could trust you to keep quiet."

"Have I said one word about the night we went swimming?" Mitch sounded offended. "No, I have not."

"Look, it's more than that. I stood up in front of every girl in my college and told them that they could never get with a knight after what happened to my best friend."

"Are you talking about the sweep?"

Jess looked at him. "I thought you didn't know anything about it."

"I didn't. I asked around because you kept bringing it up."

"Well, you can see why loyalty might be an issue for me." Jess hesitated, trying to hold back, but then the words gushed out: "And it's not just that you're a knight, it's that sometimes you act like it, too. And I don't like you when you're like that. Brendan was a mistake, but if I follow him up by getting involved with you, I'm worried the problem might be systemic. Something wrong with me. No offence."

"Getting involved?" Mitch laughed. "Geez, Jess, I'm not talking about anything serious. Even I know I'd be a bad deal."

Jess frowned at him, confused, and more than a little embarrassed. Her heart was racing, pushing blood through her body too fast, and she felt flushed, agitated. "So . . . What? An arrangement? Like your Depper Street girl?"

Mitch held up his hands. "No, you've got it wrong. I don't want to sleep with you. And you've just outlined all the reasons why you shouldn't sleep with me. That's what makes this perfect. Besides, if we don't have sex, what have I got over you, anyway? This way works for both of us. No sex. No relationship. We get each other out of our systems and move on." Mitch ended his spiel confidently and then stared at Jess with an expectant face, as though waiting for her to sign on the dotted line.

She blinked. Several times. "Sorry, I don't get it. What exactly do you want?"

For the first time Mitch seemed nervous. He coughed, bowing his head. When he looked at her again, his blue eyes snapped with electricity. "I want to touch you. That night—the toga party—I really got off on it. And I keep thinking about it, all the time. I just want to . . . do things to you."

Jess, suddenly weak, leaned back in her chair, drawing a hot breath.

"I'm talking about a couple of time-outs, that's all. On the quiet. What do you think?" Mitch waited for her to answer, muscles working in his jaw. "Come on, Jess," he urged. "What do I have to say?"

Then everything went black. They were in sudden darkness, the only illumination the rectangle of light coming through the doorway to the lecture theater, a long way down and the green exit sign above it. Jess was frozen, swamped by her worst fears—this was all an elaborate ruse Mitch had planned with his Knights friends to get her back. She was about to be humiliated in the worst possible way.

But then Mitch swore and said, "The lights must be on a timer."

And Jess listened, but she couldn't hear anything except the sound of their breathing. As far as she could tell, they were still alone. But in the dark, something changed.

Mitch shifted, turning toward her, his voice bolder: "Can I touch you?"

Jess's voice sounded like she was in pain. "Can I *trust* you—to keep it quiet?"

"Yes. *Yes.* But I don't know how to make you believe it."

"Well, you're going to have to somehow, Mitch, because the thought of guys like that Dud person finding out and turning it into something else makes me sick."

It seemed they'd reached an irresolvable stalemate.

But then Mitch exhaled. "I know how." And there was something horribly bitter about his voice as he said, "I swear to you on Julian's ashes that nobody is going to know about this from me. And I won't try to sleep with you, either."

Jess's hands went to her head. "Oh God, I didn't ask you to—"

"I know you didn't," Mitch snapped. "But I want to hold myself to that. No sex. So what do you think?"

Again, he waited; again, she didn't speak.

"Look, I'm not going to beg. If it's a no, just turn the lights on when you leave, and—"

Mitch didn't get any further with his instructions, because Jess gripped his forearm, his lovely, golden-haired, muscular forearm, and said, "I've got one condition."

"Anything," Mitch said, his voice strangely hoarse.

"No matter what we do, no matter what happens, please don't ever slap me on the ass. I hate that."

There was a surprised pause. And then, "You got it."

SOMETIME LATER, MITCH followed Jess down the stairs of the lecture theater, his hands on her shoulders. Getting him down was easier than it should have been. Maybe because it was dark. Or maybe because, like her, he was feeling too dazed to worry about falling. By unspoken consent, they staggered to the bathrooms, and Jess stared at herself in the mirror while she patted water on her flushed face. Her eyes were too bright and too big. Her denim skirt had twisted around to the side and she straightened it, but she left her hair the way it was—pulled loose from its ponytail.

They shared an awkward hug, then Mitch followed her back to Unity to make sure she got there okay, staying well behind in case anybody saw them. And Jess was glad, because it meant they didn't have to talk. She wouldn't have known what to say. But when she stopped at Unity's gate, she hesitated. There was nobody around, so it was probably okay to at least look back at him. Was that the etiquette in this situation? Or was she supposed to pretend that nothing had happened? As his footsteps approached, she was in an agony of indecision. What to do?

In the end, Mitch solved the problem for her. As he passed, she heard his low whistle.

After that, Jess left earth and flew, *flew*, back to her room, bolting up the seven flights of stairs to T-floor, her legs a blur. She passed a group of freshman boys, and something about the way she was traveling made them stop in their tracks, yelling, "Flash! Ah-aaah!", and they clutched their hearts, pretending to fall at her feet as she passed, and she laughed but didn't stop, because she could hear music blasting out from T-floor—"This Head I Hold" by Electric Guest—and by the time she was running down the hall-way, the sidelights blurred lines in her peripheral vision, she'd real-ized it was coming from her room, and when she ripped the door open at exactly the moment when the song progressed from piano to full band, Leanne and Allie cheered and hooted like maniacs, and Jess had no fucking idea why they were in her room, but that sort of shit never bothered her. They were lying sideways across her bed, their legs up on the windowsill.

"Who happened to you?" Leanne demanded, sitting up and looking Jess over.

"Nobody. Just in a good mood."

"Uh-uh. Jessie's got a *luuuurver*," Allie purred, viewing her upside down. "Look at you. You're glowing, girl."

"I wish," Jess protested, but she couldn't stop smiling. She jumped on the bed and started bouncing up and down between them, and after a moment they joined her, and none of them fell out of the window, so it was a golden moment, the three of them shouting out the chorus of the song. But then Leanne leaned across to sniff at Jess, who pushed her away, suddenly paranoid she'd smell what she'd been up to.

"Fahrenheit, right?" Leanne said with a shit-eating grin.

"What?"

"Your aftershave."

***

ONE O'CLOCK IN the morning and Jess was smoking out of her win-dow, not even attempting to sleep. T-floor was quiet, her neigh-bors' windows in darkness, but somebody on the floor below was playing alt-J softly, the music climbing to her on a ladder of still air.

She sucked on her cigarette, hearing the paper crinkle, watch-ing the tip flare, but it was nothing compared to the way her heart was blazing in her chest. Everything with Mitch had been worth it for that bonfire, flames that made her hungry for things she couldn't define. And she realized that feeling was the thing, the reaching not the getting, but thoughts were slippery, and all Jess really wanted to do was burn. Burn for the light it made, burn for the ache it gave, burn so she could breathe the smoke and feel alive.

She watched the night prowl past like a giant dark beast, and she wished she could slip out of her window and ride its back. To where? To him?

No. She just wanted to ride.

Was he awake now, thinking about her? He better be. She ran her fingertips over her thigh. *Can I touch you?* The thought made Jess smile. She ground out her cigarette and lay back on her bed, staring up at the ceiling. She'd overheard a discussion between the Z-floor boys once, about how they sometimes jacked off with their less adept hand so they could pretend it was someone else. That's what Jess did then, remembering what had happened in the lecture theater.

She used her left hand and pretended it was Mitch.

———

HIS HAND STROKING her inner thigh, fingertips circling their way up sensitive skin, reaching the V of her legs only to retreat again so that she grew impatient, and when he finally pulled up her skirt, she helped him do it. His hand nudging her legs apart. His hand brushing ever so lightly across her mound and then returning to her thighs, as though she'd only imagined it, teasing, because by then it was all she could think about, her whole body thrumming for him to touch her there. She slid lower in her seat. And, finally, his palm cupping her, feeling her push into him. His hand, sliding into her underpants, a finger slipping inside her. His sharply inhaled breath. "God, you're so wet."

"Don't start that again," she said, embarrassed. "I can't help it."

Mitch's voice was rough: "No, it's great."

He found her clitoris and rubbed it gently with a fingertip, making the tiniest circles, keeping up a light, steady pressure without trying to make her come, like they had all the time in the world. It took away the need to perform. Jess stopped feeling self-conscious, stopped thinking, and instead just concentrated on the sensation, the whole of her body responding to that tiny spot. Eventually her breathing caught and her legs shifted restlessly, and she tilted her head back, pressing on his hand, wanting him to rub her harder, faster, directing him; and she'd never been like that before, at least not while she was sober. She came abruptly and violently. And that was different, too, because normally it was something she had to work for, a peak that had to be climbed.

In the aftermath, Jess turned toward Mitch, breathing hard, wanting to tell him that she'd never come with anyone but herself before. But of course she couldn't say that. Instead she gripped his wrist, and said, "More."

"More?" he asked, surprised.

Jess might have got embarrassed then, but there wasn't time, because he'd leaned across and was using both hands, hampered by her underpants, which somehow made it better, his fingers on her and in her, bringing her to another orgasm, eagerly and quickly, as though he was curious to see if it could be done.

It could.

"That's fucking great," he whispered.

"It's no big deal. Most girls can." Jess sighed the words, slumped in her seat, not quite returned to him yet. "It's not just me."

"Yeah?"

"I mean, through touching they can," Jess corrected herself. "I've talked about it with my friends. Some girls can make themselves come just by crossing their legs in lectures. Again and again. It's just a thing." She yawned sharply, a reaction to holding her breath. "Called the clitoris."

"That's good to know." Mitch reached down once more.

She pulled weakly at his arm. "It wasn't a challenge."

"Let me," he said. So she gave in, her head falling back. This time, he took things slower, teasing her, holding off every time he felt her stiffen, and laughed when she slapped his wrist. "Wait." He shifted, unbuttoning his jeans. Jess heard the rasp of denim on skin, the snap of elastic. He reached for her hand and she tensed. "Is that okay?" he asked.

"Yes. But can you show me . . ." Jess's voice failed her and she swallowed. "I've never done that before."

"A hand job?" he asked, sounding amused. "Seriously?"

"Don't laugh at me," she wailed. "I'm just being honest."

"Shh. It's okay." His hand slipped back into her underpants, his fingertip resuming its slow circling, but Jess couldn't relax, feeling miserable now. He whispered, "Lick your palm."

So Jess did as he said, understanding why he'd told her to do it, feeling stupid for not knowing in the first place, and then reached down to touch him. His hand closed over hers, and he rolled her palm over the head of his penis, and then guided it down the length of him and back up again. As she got the rhythm of it, he let go, leaning back in his chair. He was still touching her, but Jess hardly noticed, stopping to lick her palm again, loving the feeling of him responding to her, wanting to make him helpless to it. When Mitch climaxed, he groaned, and his hand closed over hers, making her grip the head of his penis, and she felt it swell as he came.

Then they were still. Jess drew her hand back, wiping at it. And as their breathing returned to normal and the silence between them stretched out, she began to feel worried.

But then Mitch said, "I knew I should have studied economics." And she laughed, suddenly lighter.

20.
So What?

The next morning, Jess woke feeling irritated and anxious. She sat on the edge of her bed, flicking her Zippo on and then snapping it shut, over and over. That's how the big kids play, she told herself, getting the weird flare of pride that sometimes accompanies spent innocence. It faded quickly, though, and when it did, the gnawing feeling in her stomach returned. Sick of being alone with it, she trudged down the other end of the hallway, passing one of her floormates, who raised her eyebrows at what Jess was wearing: the shirt from the previous night's lecture and a pair of panties.

Half a minute passed between Jess's knock and Farren unlocking and opening her door. Farren was wearing her Valley markets find-of-the-century, a genuine Pucci dress—which didn't make sense to Jess until she spotted Davey Walters in Farren's bed, bare-chested and obviously naked under the sheet that was pulled up to his waist, and she realized the dress was probably the first article of clothing Farren had pulled out of the open suitcase on the desk.

"Have I interrupted something?" Jess asked, sounding sulky.

"Sleep," Farren said, equally sulky. "What are you doing up?"

"I don't know."

"It's six thirty."

"Is it? Sorry, I'll go."

"Don't be stupid." Farren returned to the bed, pulling the pillow out from under Davey, his head hitting the mattress abruptly. She doubled it beneath her neck so she could see Jess, who'd curled up like a cat on other end of the bed, resting her head on Davey's bony knees. Farren's room had a definite aesthetic: scarves and pot plants hung from the window; gig posters for My Morning Jacket, Sonic Youth, and Pretty Girls Make Graves lined the walls—not because she'd been to the gigs, but because she was a fan of Travis Bone, the artist; and orange-spined Penguin classics were trapped between the textbooks on the shelf above the desk, alongside wine bottles topped with the wax of dozens of candles.

The window was open, but the room had the smell of sleepy bodies and a hint of what they had been doing before they went to sleep.

"This place is a sex nest," Jess said. As an afterthought, she added, "Hello, Davey."

"Flash." Davey craned his neck to see her, his bleary eyes having trouble focusing. He was so tall his feet reached the edge of the bed, and he had a head full of dirty-blond corkscrewed curls. When he danced, he looked like a crazed scarecrow. He was also, singlehandedly, bringing back the goatee. Like Callum, he was an engineering student.

Farren nudged him. "You can tell the guys you woke up with me and Jess."

Davey gave a sheepish grin, eyes closing again. "Already thought of that."

"Just don't tell them you tooted your morning horn," Jess told him, and she and Farren laughed as his hand clamped down on his nether regions.

Then Jess groaned. Loudly.

"That's it?" Farren asked. "You woke me up for that? I'm catching a plane home in four hours, so speak now or forever hold your peace."

"I went for a drive last night," Jess said, shooting her a significant look.

Farren looked blank. Then she made an *Oh!* face and held up her hand.

Jess shook her head. "Not a high-five situation."

Farren frowned. "Did you use an airbag?"

Jess rolled her eyes. "Always so subtle, Farren. And no—we didn't go that far. You know I don't do one-night . . . crashes."

Davey, suddenly wide awake, pulled the pillow out from under Farren's head and doubled it up under his own neck. "Tell Uncle Davey all about it—*vroom vroom*. Manual or auto?"

Jess had to laugh at his enthusiasm. "Manual. Definitely manual."

"Handled well?"

"Very responsively."

"Many previous owners?"

"Dunno, but the vehicle in question has given a lot of rides. A *lot* of rides."

"But who was it?" Farren asked, her tone puzzled.

Jess looked away.

"That wasn't very good," Davey scolded. "You should have asked something like, Big gearshift? Or, Do you think you'll try the backseat next time?"

Farren ignored him. When Jess finally met her eyes, she asked, "Do I know him?"

Jess shook her head, feeling incredibly uncomfortable and incredibly disloyal. Maybe she should have stayed quiet rather than lie, but she'd felt so bleak, and Farren always made her feel better.

Besides, Farren would hear Leanne's and Allie's aftershave theories at some stage, so it was better to volunteer the information and control it. And behind the obvious reasons for not being honest—how hurtful it would be to Farren and how humiliating to admit she'd broken her own very publicly announced code—there was another reason, wrapped around something more vulnerable. If she thought about it too much, Mitch telling her that he was happy to fool around but had zero interest in getting involved didn't feel very good. Even if she didn't want to get involved, either, his certainty on the subject had been a kind of dismissal.

"It was a guy in my class," she said eventually. "We left last."

"Knew I should have studied economics," said Davey.

Farren slapped his arm, giving Jess a penetrating look. "That's unusual for you." When Jess said nothing, she asked, "Well? Was it good?" And Jess nodded, looking miserable. Farren frowned. "What's the problem then?"

"Why, just because there was something physical, do I want more? We had a moment—so what? Why can't I just enjoy it for what it was?"

"It's not your fault," Farren assured her. "You're going up against years of conditioning—this idea that for every woman there's a singular male who will haunt her, fascinate her, for the rest of her life. Look, from the moment they start reading fairy tales to us, we're encouraged to isolate ourselves, put ourselves in a tower or in a deep sleep, hang out in our room at college, and *wait* for this mythical being to turn up."

"Right," Jess said slowly, narrowing her eyes. She shook her head and focused on Davey. "Tell me what guys do in this situation. I want to be like that. You wouldn't mope. You wouldn't give a crap. You'd probably just slap yourself on the back, readjust your tackle, and say, *Well, played, brah*, and . . . And what? What would you do?"

Davey, in a voice that was deeper than normal, said, "I'd take my mind off it. Go play touch football with the guys or something."

Farren snorted. "Okay, he's full of shit, and you're sexist. The person you should be asking that question of is *me*. Because, after we got together for the first time, Davey followed me around with his tongue out, making whining noises and looking pathetic. He even sent me a text asking if we could do it again with—get this—multiple-choice answers."

For the second time that morning, Davey looked sheepish. His shoulder twitched. "You didn't have to say the bit about it being multiple choice."

Jess squashed a smile. "Okay, tough guy," she said to Farren. "What'd you do then?"

Farren stretched luxuriously, giving Jess a high-wattage grin. "I played a lot of P!nk. And I felt fucking good."

Jess gasped, one hand pressed to her chest. "You like P!nk?"

"Girl, I'm from Cairns. Of course I like P!nk."

Jess shifted position so she was kneeling, reaching out to grasp Farren's hand. "I never knew. I mean, you're so cool and—"

"Seriously, I'm a fish on a bicycle," grumbled Davey.

"Shush," both girls told him sharply.

"*I* like P!nk," Jess told Farren, her voice full of feeling. "I'm from Rockhampton."

They stared at each other, simultaneous smiles blooming on their faces.

"Oh my God," Davey squealed, waving his hands. "It's like you're meant to be."

WHICH WAS HOW Jess came to be pounding her way around Sir William MacGregor Drive at eight thirty in the morning with an iPod borrowed from Farren. She only planned on doing four kilometers, but she was struggling by the halfway point, her breathing labored, unable to find the groove she normally slid into after the first five minutes. It was far too early for a start, and to top it off, the day was hot and humid.

But no matter how bad Jess felt during a run, at some point she always committed to trying to beat her best time, and that morning was no exception. In fact, it became a point of pride. She went all out, using her usual mind games to do it: For some unspecified reason she actually *was* Flash Gordon, savior of the universe—the female version—and, for some other unspecified reason, she had to complete the third kilometer in four minutes or everything was doomed. And then she was down to the last kilometer, heavy-legged, exhausted, but the music helped her lift. For a fleeting moment, she glimpsed Mitch in among the cheering crowds at the finish line, hoping she would save them all . . . but then she changed her mind, wiping him out of the scene altogether, deciding he could watch her on the news instead.

Consequently, on a stinking-hot day, in the *morning* no less, as scratchy-eyed and tired as she was, Jess Gordon broke her own four-kilometer record. And maybe it was the endorphins, or it might have been the P!nk, but when she pulled up, dripping with sweat, spaghetti-legged, hands on her head to let more air into her burning lungs, she felt fucking good.

She felt like she'd just saved herself.

21.
Closer

"Honestly, these freshmen," Farren complained when she finally returned to Jess, Allie, and Leanne on the RE's balcony, bearing a fresh jug of beer. She plucked the cigarette out from behind Jess's ear and threw it over the railing, ignoring her protests. "Just had a little chat with a girl who's been here for exactly one semester and informs me she'll be running for council next year." She refilled the girls' glasses and then her own. "Is there anything more ridiculous than a political animal?"

"Is that a rhetorical question?" Jess asked, eyebrows raised. "Madam President."

"Excuse me, I'm there in service, not for status. I don't object to people wanting responsibility, but I do object to them wanting power." Farren placed the jug at her feet. "When I asked her why, she said, and I quote, 'I just think it'd be cool.' Honestly. Makes me want to stick around."

Jess glanced at Leanne and Allie, but they weren't paying attention. Leanne was doing a sly pour over the balcony rail, Allie watching on, giggling. "What did you just say?" Jess asked Farren sharply. "The last bit."

"That'll make it grow!" Allie called to someone below. She and Leanne turned their attention back to Farren and Jess. "Bald," Allie explained, tapping her head.

Farren sipped her beer, then wiped foam off her top lip. "What?" she asked Jess defensively. "Don't you ever fantasize about moving out?"

"You mean, like, doing your own shopping and cooking and cleaning and paying electricity bills and stuff?" Leanne asked. "Growing up?"

"Yeah."

"Nah," Leanne said, shaking her head.

"Don't look at me like that," Farren said to Jess.

"I'm not looking at you like anything. You must be feeling guilty."

"I've got to get my GPA up if I want to get into the honors course, and I'm not like you, Jess. You can work and go out and day trade and just cram for exams, and you still pull As and Bs. I've got to study consistently. But being president is taking a lot of time, and I've already decided I'm not doing it next year. It's on my résumé now. But if I stay at Unity and my replacement does a shitty job . . ."

"So much for loyalty."

"Excuse me, but I haven't decided yet, and if I do decide to go, who's the first person I'd ask to go with me?"

Jess stared at Farren, feeling even more uneasy, like everything in her world had just shifted three degrees off center.

"Enjoy the suburbs," Leanne told her with a grin.

"Don't fight, darlings," Allie scolded. "Here, let's drink to me, instead." The four of them held up their glasses and clinked. "To me," Allie said, so brightly Jess nearly made it to a smile, because when Allie was on form she couldn't be bettered, and for some reason she was really on form that night. Allie held up her phone to document the occasion, and Jess, knowing it'd be on Instagram later, asked not to be tagged, not wanting to elicit more comments from the knights.

Before Allie could load it, Leanne pinched her arm. "Ouch!"

"Well, tell them."

"I got an internship," Allie said, rubbing her arm, reticent and proud at the same time. "Two weeks during the midyear break. It's this company that is developing a software package to teach kids languages. There are heaps of educational benefits to learning a language, and they're bundling it with voice recognition. . . . Anyway, the market will be huge if they can get it right. I mean, it's not off the ground yet. But they just got some venture capital funding and they've done other stuff, so . . ." She smiled, hunching her shoulders. "Yeah."

"That's great!" Farren said, giving her a high five.

"You're going to be in a start-up," Jess breathed. "You'll probably end up working for them and getting shares in the company, and then you'll make a killing when they go public. You'll keep me in the loop, right?" Allie laughed and agreed, and Leanne beamed like a proud parent until she noticed Jess watching her, at which point she slouched and looked nonchalant.

"Thanks for the support, lovelies." Allie downed the rest of her drink. "Don't wait up, okay?" She kissed Leanne on the forehead, and then she left.

Farren licked her thumb and rubbed the lipstick off Leanne's forehead. Leanne, surprisingly, submitted.

———

AFTER THAT, JESS ignored Farren. And Farren didn't call Jess on it like she normally would have. So Leanne got to play piggy in the middle, the three of them staring out at the crowd, their elbows resting on the railing. Jess was very careful not to look at Mitch—she'd spotted him not long after they'd first taken up position on the balcony. Instead, like Farren and Leanne, she watched Allie making a beeline toward Michael Azzopardi, who was standing with a couple of Unity third years near the DJ's table, his arm slung around his best friend Duane's shoulders. The group of guys seemed to be recounting something, all of them shouting to be heard, their eyes glazed, their grins slobbery, the beer jugs they clutched in their free hands angled in a way that meant they were nearly, but not quite, about to spill. First Sunday night back from midterm break and even the air was amber-hued.

"What's Mikey like in council?" Leanne asked.

Farren gave a sudden laugh. "I thought you were going to ask what he's like in bed. He's actually really good. Takes it seriously. Gets things done without me having to ask—not like some of the other tourists."

"What's Mikey like in bed?" Leanne asked.

Farren snorted. "Not as good as he is in council." She topped up their glasses. "Do you know he told me once that I was too sure of myself? This came with care, right? He was looking out for me. He said that if I wanted to be more attractive to the dudes, I should stop acting like I was all that. And I said, 'That's funny, because the dudes have been lining up to take your place.'" Jess burst into laughter, then remembered she was ignoring Farren.

"That guy," Leanne said fondly. "You're an only child."

Now, Michael and Duane sandwiched Allie, looking down at her in a way that was warm, covetous even, but that made it clear she wasn't one of them. Unwittingly, Jess remembered the photograph of Julian and Mitch that she'd saved to her hard drive. Had they talked about the girls they'd been with? Shared conquests? Of course they would have.

Why was that thought so acidic? Girls talked, too. All the time.

And yet . . . Whatever the difference was, it was the reason she'd always been so careful. But nobody else seemed to care. It made Jess feel lonely, like she was a freak, crippled by the pointless urge to knock up against someone and feel something real. And what confused her still, was that for a second there, she could have sworn she'd seen the same thing in Mitch. Only then did Jess realize it might have been something different entirely: the antidote.

Wanting the answer, she allowed herself another look at him. Mitch saw it, his eyes locking with hers for far too long, inducing a heady rush and the growing certainty that a second time-out was very much on the table, if she wanted it. Farren and Leanne didn't notice. Mitch was standing with a group of guys on the parking-lot side of the beer garden, and none of them noticed, either, not even when he put his arms out—telling her, Jess presumed, that he'd catch her if the railing gave way. Dud was with him, and a couple of others who'd been on the bus that night, but not Tipene.

"Do you judge a guy by his friends?" she asked abruptly, interrupting Farren and Leanne's conversation.

"Only if they make him feel like he has to choose," Farren said. She must have assumed they were still on Mikey, because she added, "Duane's as dumb as rope, but he's okay. He's not like that."

Jess flicked her Zippo on and stared at the flame. The DJ was playing Tegan and Sara, who sang that it wasn't just physical. Jess, on the other hand, hoped desperately that it was.

Leanne nudged her, holding up her empty glass. "Next round's yours, Smiley."

"Yeah, that's what I thought." Jess snapped her Zippo shut. "Wish me luck."

———

DOWNSTAIRS, JESS HOVERED in front of the cigarette vending machine, not far from the spot where she and Mitch had talked once before—surely the logical place for a rendezvous? Maybe he hadn't noticed that she'd left the balcony yet. When she passed the point where you'd normally stop dithering and make a purchase, she paid a visit to the ladies' room instead, joining the line. Oddly, for such a busy night, the bathroom was empty when she emerged from her stall, and she was grateful for the moment of peace.

Her reflection stared back at her with a face full of doubt. "What?" Jess demanded. But still she didn't move. What was she waiting for? A sign?

The door swung open, making her jump, and she did a double take. Sylvie, on the other hand, seemed expectant, which suggested it wasn't a chance encounter.

"Hey," Sylvie said, her voice aspartame-sweet.

"*H-eyy.*" Jess strangled the word so badly she coughed and tried again. "Hey."

Sylvie clip-clopped to the wash basins and blinked at herself in the mirror, mouth slightly open, showing the tip of her tongue and sharp little teeth. She took a tube of lip gloss out of her fringed shoulder bag and popped the lid, offering it to Jess.

"Oh no, I'm cool, thanks. It's Jess, by the way."

"I know." Sylvie widened her eyes, dabbing on gloss. "My hero."

Flustered, Jess washed her hands, glancing in the mirror again as she turned off the tap. Sylvie had thin lips, she noticed—not in a bitchy way, more looking for clues. What made you want to watch this girl? Her halter-neck dress exposed the swell of her breasts, but she pulled it off without looking desperate because she was so delicate; it wasn't a dress so much as wrapping paper.

"Your eyes are warmer," Sylvie said. "Good hair, too."

"Sorry?" Jess asked, startled.

Sylvie looked Jess over: cowboy boots, jeans, black raglan tee, shiny big-buckled belt. "And you've got style, grunge cowgirl."

"Not really," Jess assured her. "I'm just easily bored."

"If I wore those boots I'd look like a munchkin. I want your legs."

"I wasn't comparing!" Jess said, with an abashed smile. "Just staring. You're stunning."

"And there's the big money," Sylvie said, thoughtfully. "The smile."

Jess laughed, embarrassed, looking from Sylvie's reflection to her own, and just for a second she saw what Sylvie meant. Somehow, the humor and light in her hazel eyes, the kindness in her face, her *vibrancy*, rendered Sylvie's perfect symmetry irrelevant.

Then she grew still. Were Sylvie's eyes watering? As though wanting to hide, Sylvie leaned forward until her nose nearly touched the mirror, and she huffed on the glass to fog it up.

"Anyway," Jess said, feeling like she was intruding, "I'd better, um . . ."

"Can I touch you?" Sylvie asked. She looked sideways at Jess, smiled at her shock. "Did he say that to you? On the night of the toga party?"

Jess licked her lips nervously. "How did you know?" she asked, and she might have sounded normal but her mind was a traffic jam.

Sylvie's laugh was high and resonant, a knife tinging crystal. "He says it to everybody." She wiped the mirror clean with her hand. "Julian used it, too."

"Nothing happened." Jess licked her lips again. "It was just a college thing."

"You were taking him down." Sylvie said, nodding. The warmth on her face faded and she seemed to turn inward, staring at Jess without really seeing her. She looked waxy, like a doll, not a person. Her eyes were a clear, pale green. "If he's not careful, I'll do it myself one of these days."

"What do you mean?" Jess asked, and Sylvie blinked.

"Don't worry about it." The look Sylvie gave Jess wasn't unkind, but it did suggest she was clueless.

"Did you find out about Depper Street?" Jess asked. "Is that what happened?"

Sylvie frowned. "Depper Street? What happened on Depper Street?"

Jess backed off, realizing she'd blundered. "Nobody—I mean, nothing. I was confusing you with someone else."

"Ooh, intrigue." Sylvie said playfully. "Want to know a secret? I am someone else. Nobody knows the real me."

Jess opened the door, sick of being toyed with, wanting to get away. Her voice was flat. "You're a girl. It's the same for all of us."

MITCH WAS OUTSIDE, waiting in the same spot where they'd talked to each other back when he'd had pink hair. When he saw Jess, his eyes sparked and he stepped forward, about to say something. "I can't talk to you," she said, cutting him off. "I just saw Sylvie in the bathroom, and she'll be out in a minute. I don't want her to see us together."

"Sylvie?" Mitch's face was blank. The shock he felt was in his voice. "What'd she say?" When Jess tried to push past him, he gripped her arm—too hard.

"Ow. Don't!" Jess shook him off. "I've got to go."

"Well, meet me in the parking lot then. I've got my brother's car. You can't leave things like that. Just talk to me. Please," he begged.

Jess met his eyes, and when she did she couldn't look away. She'd never seen Mitch like that before. Worried. No, stressed.

"Okay?" he asked.

"Okay," she said.

22.
Lovers in the Parking Lot

Mitch inserted the key into the ignition of his brother's silver Mazda 6 so he could roll down the windows. Solange honeyed out from the stereo, momentarily overriding the rumble coming from the RE. Then they were back to stewing in silence.

"Have you told them about us?" Jess burst out.

"No. *No.* You know what I swore on. Why?" When she didn't answer, Mitch said, "I'm not going to wait it out, Jess. Just tell me what's going on." He sounded nervy, on edge, not at all like himself. As if aware of it, he spoke more slowly. "Can you put me out of my misery?"

So Jess told him what had happened in the bathroom with Sylvie, staring through the windscreen, her voice clipped. "And the thing is, I felt so guilty. Like, any second she was going to work out what was going on. Between you and me, I mean." She glanced at him. "She already hates your guts, but I didn't want her to hate me."

"Hang on. You think I was involved with her?" Mitch gave a disbelieving laugh.

"That's why you were happy to keep this quiet, isn't it?"

"*Fuuuuuuuck.*" Mitch tipped his seat back until it was nearly flat, staring up at the car's roof. When he finally spoke, his tone was completely different. Calm. Patient, even. "Jess, do you even know who Sylvie is?"

"You said she was no one, but she seems to have a bit more presence than that."

"She's Julian's girlfriend. *Was* Julian's girlfriend."

Jess blinked. "Oh," she said.

"Yeah. Oh." Mitch pulled his seat upright again. "So you're absolutely right. She does hate my guts. I think it's probably safe to say that she would like to see me dead. But it's probably good she doesn't know about us." Mitch frowned, seeming to have trouble finding the words. "Because if she knew that I was getting on with things, after . . . like, when Julian can't . . ." Jess heard him swallow and touched his leg.

"It might be hard for her to take," she finished for him. He nodded. She exhaled, slowly. "I don't know what to say."

"Say we're all right. 'Cause you are the reason I came tonight. I'm not lying about that."

Jess hesitated, thrown by his choice of words. "Just tell me there's nobody else. At the moment, anyway—while I'm around. I'm not making a claim, I just can't do that. Because even if they don't find out, it's still not right."

Mitch looked at her, seeming angry, or hurt. But Jess held her ground. It was a reasonable question.

"There's nobody else," he said finally.

"Promise?" she asked.

"Promise," he said.

She frowned.

"What now?" Mitch asked, sounding resigned.

"How come Sylvie knows that you say that?"

A car engine started nearby. Mitch's blue eyes were luminescent in the shaft of light thrown by its headlights as it turned out. He stared at Jess, blank-faced, then shrugged. "Julian probably told her. Maybe I did. We all used to hang out together."

"I thought you didn't have girls as friends."

"She wasn't my friend. She was my friend's girlfriend. There is a difference."

Jess thought of Davey and Callum and Farren. "Not always, Mitch." She stared at him, feeling a dissatisfaction she couldn't pin down. How could things between him and Sylvie have got to this? They'd both lost the same person, and, in those circumstances, didn't they need each other? Sylvie could blame him, but what was the point? It was obvious Mitch blamed himself. And even then, perhaps Mitch should have stopped Julian from driving, but she was pretty sure he hadn't made Julian drive, either.

Mitch held up his hands. "No more, Jess. I can't go back there, all right? It doesn't do me any good."

"Sorry," Jess said. A good half a minute passed. "But you know what? I *hate* knowing you've said that to other people, too."

Mitch grimaced, rubbing his jaw. "Okay, so maybe I recycled, but I couldn't risk untested material with you. It had to work."

"You're a douche."

"You already knew that."

"And a slut."

"You knew that, too. You've always known exactly what I am, Jess. You're smart. But here's something. Every other time I've said it, it's just been a gateway to sex. With you, I actually, genuinely, wanted to touch you."

Jess gave him a look. Suddenly, surprisingly, they both laughed. She hit his arm. "You don't need to reassure me."

"It's the truth." Jess made a scoffing noise, but fell silent as he reached across to pull at her seatbelt, his body pressed to hers.

"Let's go for a drive," he said, buckling her in. "You can tell me what we got up to on the island over the break."

"Didn't even think about you," she said, her voice too high.

"That's funny." Mitch started the car. "Because I went blind thinking about you."

———————

AS THEY TURNED onto Coronation Drive, Jess checked her phone. It had to be done. "What do I tell my friends? I was supposed to get the next round. They've probably died of thirst."

"Say you've left and you'll see them tomorrow."

Jess glanced across at Mitch, surprised. "I thought we were just going for a drive."

"Adrian's away for work. He has his own apartment. I have keys. We could drive there."

"Who's Adrian?"

"My brother. What do you say?"

Jess rolled her window down. The wind pushing against her face made her feel breathless, but also free. She looked at Mitch. "I'm not going to sleep with you," she told him earnestly.

Mitch took her hand, his voice also earnest: "Okay, I trust you."

"Smart-ass. And I want you to drive me home tonight. You know, after."

"Done." He squeezed her hand and then let go.

Jess tapped out a text to Farren—pretty much what Mitch had suggested. A response arrived pronto: a lewd-looking devil emoji and **Fahrenheit???** Jess hurriedly switched off her phone. She leaned out the window, letting the wind whip and snarl her hair. As the buildings of the city approached, she retreated inside again to ask, "Where's your brother live?"

"Far, far away. It's a long drive. You might want to tilt your seat back. Get some rest."

Jess frowned. "How far?"

Mitch put a hand on her thigh, his voice completely different. "Tilt your seat back." After a moment, Jess did it, her breathing suddenly shallow and rapid. "Pull your jeans down," he instructed, keeping his eyes on the road. Jess did that also and then lay back again, her head turned sideways to look at him, one hand pressed to her cheek. She could hear her own pulse. Mitch glanced across at her, his face hard with want. "Say it. You know I can't now."

"Can you touch me?"

This time, she bit her own fingers.

———

WHEN THEY ARRIVED, twenty minutes later, Jess was in a daze, her eyes closed. The car stopped and she heard the engine die. Then Mitch took the hand she was still holding to her face and kissed her fingers. "We're here," he whispered into her palm.

Jess opened her eyes, looked at him, sat up slowly. "Where's here?"

"Hamilton."

Old-money world. Jess fixed her clothes and got out of the car, looking up at a three-story art deco building that seemed at odds with the federation-style houses surrounding it. She heard the car's central locking, and then Mitch's arm slid around her shoulders. As they walked, her boots rang out on the concrete, and she skipped to get in step with the softer rhythm of his Timberlands. Then she had to skip again—he didn't exactly amble along—and again a short while later, before she saw his face and realized that he was lengthening and shortening his strides deliberately.

"Very funny. Hey, how come you don't have a car?"

"I did have a car. Before. But I got rid of it. Mainly to shut my parents up. They were worried. Anyway, you don't really need on when you live on campus."

They reached the entrance, and he held the stained-glass door open for her.

"Those manners," she said on a sigh.

"Doing it for you?"

"That's what's so disappointing," she admitted, and he grinned.

The apartment was on the top floor. Number nine.

"How old is Adrian? A hundred?" Jess asked. It wasn't the bachelor pad she'd been expecting. If anything, it looked like the place had been prepared for sale, with no signs of the personality of the person who lived there. Antiques, Persian rugs on a polished wood floor, plush furniture, gilt-framed oil paintings hanging from the original picture rails.

"Twenty-six."

"And he owns a place in Hamilton already?"

"It's our parents'. They have investment properties."

"Why don't you live here, too, then?"

"Dad went to Knights. Adrian went there. We all do our time."

"So what does Adrian do?"

"He's a lawyer," Mitch said. "Works for Kerrigan Todd."

"Never heard of them." Jess slid past an ornate side table. What was it with rich people and lamps? As she moved, Mitch followed. She felt like she was being stalked. No. She *was* being stalked. The evidence was there in her racing heart, the naked hunger on his face. They were officially alone. Open season.

"Where does all this come from, anyway? The money," she asked, banging her hip on the corner of the heavy Jarrah dining table in her rush to put it between them.

Mitch trailed her on its other side. "Mum's what you'd call a canny investor. Dad's a urologist, so she's got money to invest."

"Oh. Hence you thinking about doing medicine."

"Hence."

"It's probably for the best. You would have made a terrible doctor," Jess gabbled. "Imagine your bedside manner."

"You won't have to imagine much longer."

Jess flushed, looking through the window at the Brisbane River. "What's your mum think about Telstra? I mean, as a short-term punt."

"Couldn't say."

"Tell me about your dad then. What's he like?"

"So many questions."

"I talk when I'm nervous. You know that." Jess stopped short in a corner of the lounge room. There was a turntable there and, beside it, four milk crates full of vinyl. "Oh, how embarrassing. Your brother's a hipster." She started flicking through the LPs, and Mitch leaned against the wall, watching her. Ryan Adams, The Afghan Whigs, Arctic Monkeys, Bon Iver, Kate Bush, Johnny Cash . . . "I can't wait till I can afford to buy music on vinyl, instead of just getting it for free. Your brother's got serious taste."

"No Aussie hip-hop, though."

"He'll get there one day."

"Put something on."

Jess chose Sky Ferreira. When she straightened, Mitch was right behind her. She was caught. He wrapped an arm around her waist and pulled her hair to one side, starting to kiss the back of her neck. She closed her eyes, her knees suddenly weak.

"Let's go into my room," he murmured.

"And do what?"

He turned her around, pushing her along in front of him, his hands on her hips. "Cuddle. What did you think?"

23.
Everything Is Embarrassing

"This is your room?" Jess asked doubtfully, looking around. The room had a double bed, an oil painting of the sea, two bedside tables with yet more lamps, a luxurious rug, and a built-in closet with mirrored doors.

Mitch switched on one of the lamps and turned off the overhead light. "It's the room I use when I'm here." He pulled back the quilt, then started to undress, looking at her. "What's wrong? You don't want to cuddle?"

"I want to. I just can't imagine you doing it." Jess sat on the edge of the bed. "Guess I'd better take my boots off, at least."

"Actually, I was hoping you'd take everything else off and leave them on."

Jess laughed. Mitch, down to a pair of gray trunks, opened the window, and a warm breeze blew out filmy white curtains. Then he lay back on the bed, watching her get undressed, one arm under his head. She stopped at her bra and underpants and then dived into bed with him, burying her face in his chest.

"Stop looking at me. I'm embarrassed."

"You shouldn't be." But he took pity on her and dimmed the light.

And then, they cuddled.

After some time, Jess shifted, taking her bra off, before pressing against him again. Mitch made a noise at the back of his throat. She felt the same way, wriggling with pleasure.

"God, you feel good like this," he breathed, running his hands over her back in the way he'd been doing for what felt like days, weeks, months, but still not enough. "Skin on skin."

"You've got summer skin," Jess told him. "So warm."

He buried his face in her hair. "You smell good, too." And Jess was glad that she'd made the executive decision not to smoke that night.

She licked his neck, wanting to know what his skin tasted like. She kissed his shoulders. She kissed his chin. She hesitated.

"Mitch? Can I kiss you?"

"You already are."

"No, I mean like that." Jess felt him take a breath. "Actually don't worry," she said quickly. "It's all good."

"Sorry, Jess." As if to make up for it, Mitch started to stroke her again. His hand slid over her breast, and she was still. Then he dipped his head, his mouth closing firmly on her nipple, and she gave a soft exclamation, feeling the world turn over.

But too soon he stopped. "We're supposed to be cuddling."

"Shame."

"That's right. You like that, don't you?"

Jess flushed, remembering the last time he'd done it to her. "No, I *love* that."

"Good to know," Mitch murmured. Jess hoped he'd run with it, but no. "Jess?"

"Hmm?"

"The boys have asked me to be captain."

"Of what?"

Mitch stiffened. "The croquet team. What do you think?"

Jess's words were muffled because her face was buried in his chest. "Oh right. Sorry. The rugby league thing."

He pulled back to look at her. "Union. Rugby union."

"Oh, you knew what I meant," she told him, burrowing back into his chest. "That's pretty big, isn't it? Captain of the university team."

"It's not for the university team," Mitch said, sounding slightly bemused now. "The season started in May. This is for the Knights team. The college comp."

"Oh. Well, that makes so much difference. Can you just get to the point?"

Mitch laughed. He started to stroke her hair. "There's a guy called Tipene—"

This time, Jess pulled back to look at him. "I know who Tipene is," she reminded him wryly.

"Oh yeah. The bus. The guy who did what I was supposed to do." Mitch exhaled. "Well, now it's reversed. Because he's meant to be captain, but he wants me to do it."

"Who's the better player?"

"Him. He made Reserves this year."

"So why's he want you to be captain?"

Mitch hesitated, then said, "I think . . . because of Julian. Like, I represent him, or something. I mean, if it was just on merit, I'd be honored, you know? 'Cause rugby is a big thing at Knights. They're not the same level as the university team, but there's a history there. That's why it's so good, being part of it. My freshman year was fucking great because of it. But . . . yeah." Jess felt Mitch breathe in, breathe out. "I'm not captain material, Jess."

"Tipene obviously thinks you are."

Mitch was quiet for a while, then he asked, "What do you think?"

Jess was surprised her opinion even mattered. "I think actions speak louder than words. If you want to be captain material, start acting like captain material." Another thought occurred to her. "What would Julian say? I mean, if he was around. You used to play together, right?"

Mitch gave a flat laugh. "He'd just be really pissed off because he'd be sure he should be captain."

"Well, it's the guy who's not sure he's up to it who's probably the right pick. My friend always says this thing—be wary of people who are certain they should be in charge."

"Smart." Mitch kissed her on the head. "Who's your friend?"

"Unity's president." They both laughed, then Jess groaned. "God, Mitch, if Farren knew I was here with you . . ."

"This is the chick with the nose ring, right?"

"Knights usually use a different identifier."

"I'm back to being a knight? Aren't we on the island?"

"I didn't mean it that way. I just feel guilty, that's all." And in that moment, Jess did feel guilty. But it was hard to feel guilty enough to want to change anything, because he felt so good—like lying on sand in the sun kind of good. What sort of idiot left the island early?

"Do you want me to take you home?" he asked, his voice low.

"Why? Do you want me to go?"

His arms tightened around her. "No. I want to stay like this all night."

"Yeah, me too." Jess thought about that and then sighed. "Another reason why you should probably take me home."

BEFORE THEY LEFT, Jess used the bathroom. That was when she heard voices: Mitch talking to someone else. She froze, staring at herself in the mirror, straining to hear. *Oh, please don't be his brother, please don't be his brother, please don't be his brother,* she prayed, drying her hands.

The uncertain smile on her face faded as she reached the lounge room.

It was his brother.

"Jess, is it?" he asked, stepping around his bag to touch his palm to hers for a second, his skin as chalky dry as his manner. "Adrian."

Jess quelled a sudden urge to explain that they hadn't been doing anything, not really, and instead told him, "Jess Gordon." Because that was how she'd been brought up. Adrian nodded, a flicker of a frown suggesting the extra detail was superfluous, and rubbed his hands together in a nervy sort of way that made Jess wonder if her hands had been damp, or he was simply trying to rub her germs off.

"Did you have a nice trip?" she asked, in a voice that was oddly—no, stupidly—bright.

"Well, it was work," Adrian said, with another flickering frown to suggest the presence of a glaring oxymoron. "And it was Melbourne."

"I've never been to Melbourne. Is it nice?" Jess asked and then assumed a frozen expression while a voice in her head screamed, *Shut up! Please, just shut the fuck up!*

"I wouldn't know. I've only been there for work," Adrian said, flashing her a bloodless smile. He was so thin, with dark circles around his brown eyes, and had none of Mitch's pack-leader self-assuredness. You'd never have guessed they were brothers. When it became apparent Jess had no further stupid questions, he turned his attention back to Mitch with obvious relief. "Our dinner didn't run as long as expected and we managed to get the last flight back. If I'd known you were thinking of coming over, I would have—"

"Meetings go well?" Mitch asked, his face unreadable. If they seemed oddly formal with each other, Jess had the feeling it was situational, rather than the norm.

"Not bad. Had a few wins." Adrian pulled on the suit jacket he'd slung over the back of the lounge. "But listen, I've got a taxi waiting outside. I was just dropping my bag off."

"You're going into work now?" Mitch asked.

"Well, yes. It's only ten thirty, and it'll give me a head start on the week. There's a shitload of follow-up to do."

And that's the type of person he is, Jess thought. *A clock head. Knows exactly what time it is without checking.* He reminded her of the mature-aged students she'd met: work-worn and irritated, martyrs hurling down pronouncements from the cross: *You don't know how good you university students have it. Wait till you hit the real world.* Which always made Jess want to respond with a flippant *Fuck that!*

Adrian grabbed his briefcase. "Nice to meet you, Tess."

24.
My Number

Jess clapped her hands to her face and looked at her econometrics tutor, Erin Shaw, pulling her cheeks downward in her best impression of Edvard Munch's painting *The Scream*. "Do you ever suspect that a whole bunch of economists got together and said, *Hey, if we just make up some really big words, we can pretend it's a science? Heteroscedasticity—what's that, like, six syllables?*"

Erin smiled—big of her, given that there was a long line of stressed students needing time and attention outside the door, and her scheduled two-hour consultation time would probably run way over. "Eight."

Jess counted it out on her fingers. "Jesus, I can't even get that right."

"You know what you need to do?" Erin said decisively. "You need to forget about the number of syllables and concentrate on the intention. A linear regression is an attempt to model a suspected relationship. But can we trust the predictions? Statistically speaking, it might look like a relationship, smell like a relationship, but unless it passes the tests for Goodness of Fit, it's not significant."

"Right," Jess said, sounding dubious. "So then you use the different tests to see if there's anything wrong with your data, like if the coefficients are related or something, and once you know, you can fix it."

"Except it's not the coefficients," Erin said. "It's the—"

"The variables! That's what I meant. The explanatory variables." Jess groaned, laying her head down on the desk.

"Hate to interrupt your sleep, but . . ."

Jess straightened. "Yes, I know you're busy. But when I'm with you I feel safer. Like I won't fall on my ass in the midterm. And we've bonded, haven't we?"

"I've seen you twice."

"At your *consultation*, but do I ever miss a session? I know I'm your favorite."

Erin's mouth twitched. She was doing a research master's on the economics of clam farming, so Jess was probably the best thing to happen to her all day. "Out," she said.

Or not.

———

AS JESS MADE her way downstairs, she was hit once again by the same greasy, overwhelmed feeling she'd experienced *before* visiting Erin. It hardly seemed fair. Wasn't that what tutors were paid to do? Make things better? That was the problem with university: It was so easy to drift along, going out, working to earn a bit of coin, festering over your readings, typing up your lecture notes rather than actually trying to understand them, kidding yourself that turning up was enough—only to get smashed by big lumps of pressure around exams, or when assignments were due, and pay the real price for being there all in one hit.

She reached the Level Two entrance and paused just inside the doors to put her ear buds in, wanting some respite from the panic in her head. She glanced up to see Mitch coming through the doorway. From the way his face came alive, Jess knew he hadn't expected to see her—although it had only been a matter of time; economics, commerce, and law shared the same stomping grounds, after all. Without discussing it, they moved to a dead-end corridor where they were less likely to be seen.

Mitch faced her, leaning against the wall. "What are you doing here?"

"Had to see my econometrics tutor," Jess said curtly, taking out her ear buds.

"Midterm?"

"Saturday."

"Stressed?"

"Suicidal. What are you doing here?"

"Tutoring." Mitch waited for Jess to meet his eyes. "Oh, come on, you're not still holding on to that, are you?" he asked, a smile pulling at his mouth. *"Tess."*

"Of course I am! Talk about humiliating. All those questions and I don't even care about Melbourne. It was *awful*." Mitch laughed—through his nose, no less. "It's not funny!" Jess protested. "I'm actually really sensitive." And yet she couldn't help but smile, which was annoying.

"There it is. There's the smile," Mitch said. "What'd you think of him, anyway? Adrian."

"I thought he was very nice. For an alien."

"Well, he measures his time in six-minute increments these days—it's all got to be billed to somebody. He was probably just annoyed that the six minutes he gave us can't be accounted for. And he wouldn't have been expecting to walk in on that."

"Don't make it sound like we were having an orgy. We weren't doing anything."

"That's worse. He probably suspects we were reenacting *The Secret History* before he got there."

"I didn't know you could read!" Jess cried. "I *love* that book."

"Learned in my year off," Mitch said modestly. "Had nothing better to do."

Jess laughed, delighted, and in one cinnamon-sugar moment Sunday's humiliation was forgotten, simply because talking to Mitch was just more fun than talking to anybody else. It was the same for him—she could see it in his eyes, his grin.

"I'm glad I ran into you," he told her. "Thought I'd have to do the Wednesday night lecture again. All those stairs. All that tapping."

Jess held up her phone. "We could just swap numbers, you know." There was a beat during which Mitch's eyes slid away from hers. "*Jesus.* I'm not declaring eternal love for you. I just meant making contact would be less complicated."

"Yeah . . . it would . . ." Mitch scratched his stubble. "But I don't check my phone much."

"No stress. It's all good," Jess said in a bright voice. She checked the time. On her phone. "Hey, you're going to be late. And I'd better go."

Mitch didn't move, still seeming slightly evasive when he asked, "Jess? You want to line something up now?"

"Um . . . this week's kind of busy," she said with a grimace. "I mean, my midterm's coming up, and I've got a lot of cramming to do."

"How about after your exam? I've got a game that afternoon, but I could get Adrian's car and see you after that."

Jess wrinkled her nose. "I've got to work."

"I could give you a ride home."

Jess made an aw-shucks face. "We could go dancing after."

Mitch was still for a moment. He was many things but not stupid. "Sunday?"

"Sorry." Jess gave him a million-dollar grin. "I'm going to that festival."

Mitch nodded slowly. "Some of the guys got tickets for that. I was thinking about it. Maybe I'll see you there then."

"Maybe," Jess said breezily, popping her ear buds back in.

"What are you listening to?"

The correct answer was Tegan and Sara. "P!nk," Jess said.

"Really? I would have put money on you saying some sort of Aussie hip-hop. Even if it wasn't. *Especially* if it wasn't," Mitch said dryly.

Jess just stared at him. "I should go," she said.

25.
Holidays

Frozen cocktails in hand, Jess and Farren huddled around Leanne, who was holding the program. Allie, meanwhile, was busy documenting the moment, pursing her lips over her cocktail at her phone, using the others as a backdrop.

"If it's not on Instagram, did it ever really happen?" Farren asked Jess and Leanne in an undertone. Then, more loudly to Leanne: "Highlighters? You've been a busy girl."

"Green's a must-see," Leanne told her. "Acts marked in yellow are the ones to run to after a green has finished, and orange means worth checking out."

Jess took the drink Allie handed her, saying, "Don't tag me, okay?"

Allie looked at her for a second, then nodded, attention back on her screen, typing rapidly with both thumbs.

"Caption?" Jess asked.

Allie read aloud: "Surprised at how much I'm enjoying today. Hashtag—Beachland Festival. Hashtag—girls' day out."

"Can you be any more tentative?" Leanne complained. "Own what you really think. Say, *Beachland is fucking great. Hashtag—I'm here and you're a loser.*"

Allie giggled, taking her drink back from Jess and sipping it. "Mmm, that's good. What is it?" she asked Farren, who'd bought the round.

"Sugar," Farren replied. "Which is why we're all bouncing off the walls."

It wasn't just sugar, though, that had them all vibrating with the same barely suppressed energy, smiling like idiots. Maybe it was the festival lineup—dance and electronica, instead of just the usual indie staples, a mix that somehow made you feel a little more glamorous than usual. Or perhaps it was the setting: South Bank's Cultural Forecourt, a grassed area that was backdropped by the edifice of the Performing Arts Center and looked across the Brisbane River at the buildings of the central business district. Or it might have been something as simple as girls liking occasions where they could wear a mix of animal prints, denim, lace, and feathers, and feel totally confident that they were pulling it off. They were on holiday, even if just for a day.

"Expensive sugar," Leanne grumbled. "Next round, beer. I'm broke. Broke and isolated, thanks to Buffet, here."

"Actually, on that . . ." Jess cleared her throat. "I missed it at the time because I was studying for my midterm, but Telstra made an announcement during the week. Not only are they now doing dividend reinvestment—"

"That's so fascinating," Farren said. "You should blog."

"—but they just announced their new CEO," Jess continued, giving her a sidelong glance.

Farren clapped a hand to her face. "Who?"

"It's the guy everybody thought it would be."

Leanne looked up from the program. "What's that mean?"

"The guy who was second in charge. All the analysts were predicting it, and nobody wanted him, so everybody sold—which was when I bought. But then, when the announcement came out as expected, nothing happened—it couldn't, they'd already sold. So then they had to close out their positions."

"English," Leanne growled.

"The share price has gone up by about eighty cents since we bought. So that's like eighteen percent—thirty-six percent on an annual basis. And that's not including dividends. Isn't that great?"

The three girls blinked at her.

"Anyway, I'm going to sell. You'll have your money next week."

To Jess's surprise, Leanne shook her head. "No, keep mine. Do something with it. I'm kind of liking the challenge of living off-grid anyway."

"Really?" Jess said, excited. "Wow. That makes me feel like a real investor."

"Girl, you're a gambler," Leanne said, and Allie and Farren laughed. "But I think you might be good at it."

Jess beamed at that. She looked from Leanne, to Allie, and then Farren, her beautiful friends, and the moment put an ache in her chest. "Hey, let's take a photo. Of us. Now. Like this." Allie started to raise her arm. "Not a selfie," Jess said. "A photo. You know, something we can look back on when we're old. Here—I'll ask this girl to take it."

The girl said yes. And afterward they crowded around the screen, shielding it from the sun with their hands. It was a beautiful shot, very natural: just the four them, in front of the city, their arms around one another, standing tall and smiling brightly at their future selves.

"OH, I NEEDED this!" Jess exclaimed, looking up at the giant wheel as she and Allie passed beneath it, stark against an infinitely blue sky. The day was perfect: bathed in sunshine, hot but not swampy, friendly little breezes puffing through like puppy breath. The crowd was smiley. Jess linked arms with Allie, skipping to get in step. They were heading for the Rainforest Stage after splitting with Farren and Leanne, who'd decided on the Main Stage. "Miami Horror— *yeeew*! 'Cause I came to dance. Hey, I want that on a T-shirt. No! I want that on my tombstone. *I came to dance*." Jess jabbered away like this for a little longer before realizing that Allie wasn't responding. "What's up?"

"Nothing," Allie said, sweet-voiced. Her posture, though, was stiff.

Jess stopped. "Allie, don't eat it. Just this once. If I've done something, tell me. We're friends. You can say it."

Allie looked away, then back at her. "Okay. It's that thing you said about wanting a photo, not a selfie. And the fact you don't want me to tag you anymore, like I'm so embarrassing. I know you think it's hilarious that I take Instagram seriously—what was the comment? 'Show us your personality.' But what if that *is* the way I show my personality? It didn't make me feel very good. You're supposed to be my friend."

"Hey, that was Leanne, not me," Jess soothed. And she thought it was solved. Leanne was rude to everyone; Allie knew that better than most.

But Allie didn't look any happier. "You can look me in the eye and tell me you've never judged me?" She shook her head. "You know what? It doesn't matter. Let's go."

"It does matter," Jess said, clasping Allie's shoulders with both hands. "Look, the tagging thing is because I'm worried you'll get a bunch of horrible comments on your account. But . . . yeah, okay, there may have been times when I might have judged. It doesn't mean I haven't felt admiration, too, though. To be honest, Al, sometimes I envy you, sometimes I wish I had your swagger, and sometimes I cringe. But, mainly, I just like knowing you in world." Jess dropped her hands with a shrug. "Anyway, w know? If you knew half of the stuff I've been up to lately . . . All I really think is that girls are allowed to collect life experiences, too, without it meaning that they're ruined. Not that I'm saying what you're doing is a mistake," she added quickly.

"You know what it is?" Allie said thoughtfully, and just like that the tension between them seemed to have passed. "Sometimes I get so down. Depressed. And then I take a photo of what I want my life to be like. Of what *I* want to be like. And when people like it, it's confirmation—yeah, you're good, your life's good, nothing's that bad." She cleared her throat delicately, with a little smile. "And then, when things are good, I feel the need to record that, too. Just to rub it in."

Jess laughed. They linked arms again, starting to walk, and she skipped to get in step. "See? Talking helps. I talk all the time."

Allie squeezed her arm. "Really? I never noticed."

A large group of guys had stopped to consult a program in the middle of the walkway ahead, disrupting the flow of the crowd like rocks in a river. Jess recognized Tipene first and then saw Dud among them also, giving a loud, phlegmy laugh at something one of the others had said, pulling at the waistband of his jeans, looking drunk and disheveled.

She ducked her head, feeling sick but also excited, getting the electric tingle she now recognized as the precursor to seeing Mitch. She couldn't help stealing a quick glance at the group as they passed. When they were farther along and partially hidden by the crowd, she looked back once more, frowning now, because he'd known she was coming. . . .

"Listen. The set's starting," Allie said, and she grabbed Jess's arm, pulling her into a run.

A WALL OF backs confronted them as they neared the Rainforest Stage.

"This is no good!" Allie wailed, up on her tiptoes, trying to see. "Come on, let's pretend we know someone in the front." Pulling Jess along by the hand, she started to weave her way through the watching bodies, collecting an occasional not-so-accidental shove on the way—punishment for pushing in. Halfway down, the girls realized they did in fact know someone, spotting Callum in the crowd. When they reached him, they slammed into him, nearly knocking him over, and he took it with his usual affable good humor, enveloping them both in a hug.

"What are you doing here?" Allie asked, shouting to be heard over the music.

Callum reached for the stage with both hands. "Miami Horror! I love them!"

"Me, too!" Jess yelled, pulling on his sleeve excitedly. "I love that you love them!"

"I love everybody!" Callum cried, and Jess noticed his eyes were Manga-size, but maybe that was his glasses.

"Aren't you hot?" Allie asked.

Callum looked down at his jeans and black hoodie as though wondering who'd dressed him. "I *am* hot," he said, sounding surprised. "I think I'll go for a swim in the river."

Jess shook her head. "I don't think that's a good idea, Mr. Buckley."

"Okay, I won't then," Callum said, not only feeling the love but also exceptionally agreeable. He and Allie focused on the stage, raising their arms, but Jess was distracted, glancing at the crowd around her. Now would be a perfect time for Mitch to tap her on the shoulder. . . .

Jess gave an alarmed shriek as Callum's head slid between her legs and he raised her up on his shoulders. She clutched at his hair, beating her heels against his chest, certain he was going to drop her, feeling terribly self-conscious. But she didn't fall off, even with Callum constantly bouncing to the beat, and no one was paying her any attention—she was hardly the first chick to ever sit on someone's shoulders at a festival. Slowly, her spine straightened, and she let go of Callum's hair, starting to enjoy her new perspective: a sea of waving arms and raised phones.

If Mitch was in the crowd, then there'd be no way he could avoid seeing her, Jess realized. Up on another guy's shoulders, having a good time. With that, the decision not to shrink became something more flamboyant. She raised her arms, swishing her hair from side to side, really getting into it. And as she was doing this, she happened to catch sight of the object about to hit her in the head. It was a can of beer—Heineken, actually—and it turned out to be close to full when Jess felt the clunk of it, heard the sound echo around her brain.

Then the world turned to static and flickered out.

26.
'Cause I'm a Man

Three hours later, Jess tried the door to her room and found it locked. She pressed her ear to the wood and then attributed the impulse to having a swollen brain. She wouldn't be able to hear anything over the Tame Impala blasting out of Allie's room—she'd left her door wide open as usual.

She knocked, saying loudly, "It's me. Jess. Open up." At first nothing happened, and Jess wondered if she'd just imagined her call to Mitch. Well, her call to the Knights office, where a polite boy had put her through to the phone in Mitch's room without asking for her name, and the phone had rung out, going to message, and she'd hesitated for too long before she'd actually left one.

But then the door swung open to reveal Mitch, wearing shorts, a T-shirt, turf boots, and football socks, looking a little flushed in the cheeks, and Jess wondered if it was from exertions on a field somewhere, or from rushing over to see if she was okay. She chose the former. Because he also looked like she felt: fed up. Jess slid past him without saying anything, hearing him close and lock the door behind her. Dropping her bag on the dresser, she palmed her Zippo and took two painkillers with a sip of water. Mitch had retied her window, reducing the gap, and she had to bend to see outside. It was nearly dark, the dying golden light turning the trees along the river a vivid green. Then she sat on the bed. Flicked her Zippo on, snapped it shut.

And through all that, Mitch stared at her expectantly, his arms hanging by his sides.

So Jess said, "I thought your game was yesterday."

"We were just having a kick. You're lucky I even checked my messages. Normally, I'd head straight to the shower." He sounded like he wished he had.

"Okay, I'm sorry I called," Jess said. Mitch didn't seem satisfied, though, so she added, "I'm annoyed, too. I'm going to miss all the best acts."

"Are you all right?" he asked, his voice brusque.

"I got knocked out."

"You said that. Did anyone take a look at you?"

Jess nodded. "My friends took me to the medical tent."

"Why'd they let you come back by yourself?" Mitch sounded disapproving, but Jess had the feeling it was because he'd been inconvenienced. Or because she'd committed the unpardonable sin of calling him.

"Allie was going to come with me. But I told her I'd go to my aunt's place—which is what I really wanted, by the way, not this. But when I got there nobody was home, and I waited for ages before I remembered they're in Adelaide for the weekend, so then I got another cab here, and that's when I called you, because my head's still hurting and the lady in the medical tent said I wasn't supposed to be . . ." Jess broke off to take a breath, rubbing her eyes, suddenly tired and teary.

"Alone," Mitch finished for her.

Flick-spin-scritch! "And I wouldn't have called, except everybody I know is at the festival—"

"It's all right."

"—and it's so stupid that you can live at a college with three hundred other people and still have to rely on the one person who doesn't want to be relied on."

"I'm here, aren't I?"

Snap! "Yes, but you don't want to be." Jess finally looked at him. "So I'd rather be alone, thanks. Sorry for wasting your time."

Mitch exhaled, taking the Zippo out of her hand and placing it on the desk. He knelt in front of her, his hands on her bare thighs, the tension gone from his face, replaced by something much nicer. "Are you all right?" he asked again—this time the right way.

"Have you been listening at all?"

Mitch smiled. He examined the side of her skull, rubbing her hair gently with his fingertips, and Jess swallowed, feeling funny. He frowned when he found the big lump above her left ear. "Did they ice it?"

Jess nodded. "They gave me a pack at the medical tent."

But he was already opening her fridge, taking out one of the T-shirts, and throwing some ice cubes into it. "Wouldn't hurt to do it a bit more. Have you vomited at all?"

"No. I felt like it in the cab here, though."

He sat at the head of her bed, putting a cushion on his lap. "Lie down." So she did, and he held the T-shirt ice pack gently to her head. And of course she could have held it herself, but it was nice that she didn't have to.

"It was kind of funny, really," she told him. "One of my all-time great exits."

"Do you feel tired? You're not supposed to sleep after getting a concussion."

Jess wrinkled her nose at him. "How come you're the concussion expert?"

"Rugby." Mitch ran a finger over her nose. "Are you ever going to tell me how you broke that?"

Jess yawned. "Nope."

"Maybe I should stay with you," Mitch said, as if he was thinking aloud. "Make sure you don't sleep."

The fact that he was still weighing up how long he had to be there was too much for Jess. "Oh, forget it." She sat up, knocking the ice pack out of the way. "Go. *Go!* There's the door. My friends keep texting to check on me, so if I tell them I'm back here by myself, one of them will come."

"Settle down. I was only thinking about what happens when everyone gets home and I'm—" Mitch broke off as Jess covered her mouth with her hand. Then he was off the bed, handing her the bin. Jess bent over it, waiting, but the nausea gradually subsided.

"You know what? I'm going to take a shower." She breathed in through her mouth slowly, a hand pressed to her throat. "That might make me feel better." Mitch sprang to attention, grabbing her towel. "I'll be fine," Jess told him, her voice croaky, no fire left now. "See ya."

"I'm not going," he told her firmly. "You could pass out and hit your head again. People die from secondary concussions."

"Whatever," Jess said, collecting her robe and toiletry bag, moving like an old woman. Mitch took these things from her, and she let him. She let him walk her to the bathroom. But when he went to follow her inside, she blocked him, saying bluntly, "Not feeling it."

"I'm not interested in that. You can't go by yourself, that's all," he told her. When she didn't move, Mitch frowned. "Jess, it's me."

Jess looked at him for a moment, tasting the trust implied by that, then she let him in. Mitch followed her into one of the shower stalls, which were actually quite roomy, the shower at one end, a small dressing area with a bench at the other, and took a seat, suddenly becoming the poster boy for correctness, staring steadfastly at the opposite wall.

And even though she was mad at him, Jess had to smile. She pulled off her T-shirt, throwing it over his head. "At ease, soldier. We're probably well beyond false modesty anyway," she said philosophically, gingerly pulling her hair into a loose bun.

"Just trying to do the right thing," he said, his voice muffled.

Contrary to her words, though, Jess was relieved that Mitch left the shirt where it was while she stepped out of the rest of her clothes—stripping off in broad daylight required a confidence level she wasn't hitting right then. It was only as she was soaping herself that the shirt slid to the tiles.

"Look at that. It fell off," Mitch said. And not even a head injury could stop Jess from feeling embarrassed by the frank and admiring assessment he gave her. She buried her face in the flow of water, feeling her skin tighten into goose bumps, her nipples harden.

"Thought we were beyond false modesty," he commented.

"It's not false!" Jess protested. She dug around in her toiletry bag, finding her toothbrush. Aware of Mitch's scrutiny, she held it up to show him. "Just for the record? I wouldn't normally brush my teeth in the shower."

He narrowed his eyes at her. "I bet you do it all the time."

"I do. Completely gross, I know," she admitted, garbling the words through a mouthful of foam. "Sometimes I even brush them in my room and spit out the window."

"Ever hit anybody?" he asked, sounding interested.

"Walk by sometime and find out," she told him, and he laughed, and Jess loved the way he looked right then. So relaxed. Like he was enjoying himself. But all too soon Mitch's face hardened, and he watched her with a hunger she'd seen before.

Except this time it hurt. He was more than happy to hang around now.

You bought in, Jess reminded herself. She spat, rinsed her mouth.

"What's wrong?"

"Nothing," Jess said, letting water stream over her face. "It's all good."

She turned off the taps abruptly, holding out her hand for the towel. Mitch didn't give it to her, making her meet his eyes. He didn't need lines anymore. He could ask the question without any words at all.

"Not here," she told him, pulling the towel from his hands.

———

BACK IN HER room, things happened fast, like they were taking part in a coordinated military operation. Mitch closed and locked the door; Jess shelved her toiletry bag and hung her towel over the window ledge. As she lit candles, he killed the light. She heard the thud of his turf boots hitting the floor, the flick of elastic as he pulled down his socks, the soft rasp of his shirt coming off, and she wondered how far they were going to go. Then he was behind her, turning her around, stripped down to his shorts, and Jess pressed herself against him, wanting the warmth of his skin, but he pushed her back, focused on untying her bathrobe, his movements rough and urgent, not looking at her face once.

And all of it was wordless. And all of it was awful.

"Stop it!" Jess cried, not able to bear another second. "We're not making a fucking porno." Mitch froze, looking completely taken aback. "Can't you at least be gentle? Because my head really hurts, and you're supposed to—"

Care. Jess covered her face with her hands. At no point had they ever discussed care being part of their arrangement.

After some time, Mitch slid his arms around her. "Is that better?" he asked, holding her cautiously.

"No. Now I feel stupid," Jess said, burying her face against his chest.

"You're not stupid. I should have taken things slower."

"This isn't because you were rushing," Jess said with some heat. "I happen to like that, sometimes. I'm angry because I wasn't even a part of that, and I don't know who the hell you turned into."

Mitch exhaled and then said, in a tolerant voice, like he was educating her, "Look, Jess, sometimes I just want to get off. That's all. I *am* a guy."

"You think that's just you?" Jess head-butted his chest. "Because you're a *guy*?" She head-butted him again. A dull ache started inside her skull, and she pulled back to look at him. "Let me pop that bubble for you. Sometimes I want to get off so badly that I'd give anything for somebody to walk through that door and just do me. Over the desk, on the floor, standing up, sitting down, me on top, upside-fucking-down. I want to be fucked fast, fucked slow, but most of all fucked senseless, and preferably more than once. If it's the middle of my cycle, I can feel myself *throbbing* for it down below. If that makes you a guy, Mitch, what does that make me? No, don't bother answering, because I already know the way you think and it's why we'll never have sex. The *difference* between you and me is that I know my fantasy fuck buddy doesn't exist. If someone did walk through that door, they'd be an actual person, and I would freak the fuck out."

Mitch appeared even more stunned by this secondary explosion. "Okay," he said eventually.

She glared at him. "Being human isn't two separate experiences.

Get that into your thick head." Then she buried her face against his chest again.

Mitch exhaled slowly, and Jess felt him relax. That annoyed her. She breathed in his bare skin, and that annoyed her, too, because he smelled good—like salt and sunshine, in fact. He started stroking her hair. That annoyed her also, for a while, and then it didn't. And at some point she realized she wasn't tense anymore. She just felt drained, and her head hurt.

"You okay, now?" he asked.

"No."

"You gonna look at me?"

"No."

"I'd like to see you."

Jess sighed, lifting her face to his. Their eyes met, and there was an odd moment. Then Mitch kissed her nose.

"You know, I haven't smoked at all today. I have had a few drinks, but I did just brush my teeth, so I'm pretty sure I'm not that disgusting."

"*Jess, please.* Just respect the fact that I don't do that, all right?" Mitch sounded perilously close to begging. "And there is nothing about you that I find disgusting, believe me. Not even the fact that you brush your teeth and spit it on people out your window."

That knocked a smile out of Jess, but it was only a small one. "It's all right, you can go," she told him in a quiet voice. "I know I've wrecked everything."

"I don't want to go. Anyway, I'm on sleep watch." He rubbed his hands up and down her arms. "But can we lie down for a while—I mean, rest?"

So Jess threw the cushions off her bed, pulled the quilt back, and lay down. She kept her bathrobe on, but didn't bother retying it. Mitch crossed to her dresser and returned with two painkillers and a bottle of water.

"Thanks," she told him gruffly after she'd taken them. He slid in beside her, holding out his arm so she could rest her head on his shoulder, and then hugged her to his chest.

"God," he said, sounding exhausted, and Jess figured they'd reached the point where a voiceover would normally intone: *And he was never seen again.* The black humor in that bit her without warning, and she smothered a laugh.

"What?" he asked.

"Sorry, it's just . . . What a mess."

Mitch was silent for a bit, then he said, "Can you say that thing again? The fuck speech."

"Oh, shut up."

"It turned me on."

"Liar. You were terrified."

"I was." Mitch turned on his side to face her, and they smiled at each other. He touched her cheek, and Jess thought he might be about to relent and kiss her, but apparently all he wanted to do was gaze. So when he ran his thumb over her lips, she nipped him.

"Ow." He gave her a look. She gave him one back. He pushed his thumb into her mouth. She sucked it obediently. His breathing changed, his eyes glazed. She reached down and rubbed the front of his shorts. He pushed her hand away.

"Let me," she told him.

"Not yet." Mitch rolled on top of her, pinning her arms, and went to work on her breasts, scratching her skin with his stubble as he turned his head from one to the other. He kissed her nipples, bit them gently, and then sucked them swollen, and Jess moaned, feeling it again, that tugging sensation down below, as if there were strings being pulled by his mouth, and she didn't care what she sounded like, she just wanted him to keep going.

But Mitch moved on, moved lower, suddenly off the bed completely, kneeling on the floor, pulling her hips toward him.

He'd kissed his way up her thighs and had very nearly reached his destination when Jess grabbed his hair, trying to pull him up. "No, no, don't worry about that. Just do the boob thing."

Mitch stopped, frowning up at her from beneath his brow. "You don't want me to? Or you haven't had it before?"

"I have, but . . ." Only with Brendan. Only once. And he'd sucked her clitoris too hard, too vigorously, without any build up at all, and it just *hurt*, and not in a good way, either, and then he'd done this weird tapping thing with two fingers that made her want to punch him in the head, but he'd acted like she was supposed to go crazy, so she'd acted like she had, as though she'd die if she didn't have him right then, and when Farren said things like, *Davey loves it; he'll do it for ages*, she'd always thought it was an exaggeration, wondering why on earth you'd spend any more time putting up with that than you had to.

Mitch considered her, his eyes amused, as though he could hear this stream of consciousness.

"It's not funny!"

"It's not supposed to be hell, either," he told her with a frown. "So just *relax*."

"But I'm not used to relaxing! I haven't done much relaxing. I've only done sex. Sex and kissing. I haven't been with people like you, who are into touching, who are into"—Jess's face flushed, her voice dropping three octaves—"going down."

"I'm into touching *you*. I want to go down on *you*," Mitch corrected. "Normally, I wouldn't bother."

"Oh," Jess said. Then doubt arrived. "Is that a line?"

"Yeah, Jess. I'm feeding you lines so that *I* can go down on *you*. There's a situation your mother warned you about."

"But it's like you always have to teach me stuff. I'm nineteen, for God's sake. It's embarrassing."

"*Hey. Ego.* Whatever this thing is between us? It is not a competition. That is not what this is, all right?"

"Do you even know what you're doing? You've just admitted you don't practice regularly."

"I'm pretty confident," Mitch said, looking pretty confident. He grinned, waiting for her answer.

Jess made a noise. "All right, then. I mean, if I haven't ruined the moment." Mitch gave her a funny look, his mouth twisted sideways, and then he just lost it. And once he started laughing, he couldn't stop, his face screwed up, his shoulders shaking, the whole bed vibrating from it. "Mitch!" Jess cried, squeezing his shoulders with her legs.

"Sorry," he wheezed. "It's just—" He exhaled sharply, trying to get control of himself. "You look like you're going to the dentist." That set him off again. And, despite everything, Jess got pulled in, too, because it's hard to resist laughter like that.

Finally, Mitch got it together, rubbing his eyes with the heel of his hand. "God, it's good to laugh. I haven't laughed like that for ages."

"You're an idiot," Jess said with some affection.

"I'm a guy," Mitch said with some affection right back.

Then he gave her an open, easy smile, one she'd never seen before. As though, despite the fact that she was naked and he was lying between her legs, and she was from Unity and he was from Knights, and she was a modern-day riot grrrl, and he was a modern-day sexist pig, they were friends. Then his smile faded, his blue eyes narrowed, and Jess's breath caught in her throat. It was quite a thing to be looked at like that.

27.
How to Fly

Afterward, they faced each other on the bed, head to toe, Mitch at the base, propped up by cushions, hugging Jess's feet to his chest. It was dark outside, the light from the candles making it feel like they were in their own little world. Mitch raised his eyebrows questioningly. Jess made a so-so face. He dropped his eyebrows into a frown. She swooned. He nodded, eyes knowing, and he winked at her. He had a very sexy wink.

"The suck," Jess told him with an air of revelation. "The suck is the best bit. I never knew that. It can't be too hard, though, you know? *You* were gentle." Jess took a big breath, released it. "Thank you. So much."

"And thank you. How's the headache?"

"It's okay. I'll take more painkillers in a while." Jess blinked. "Oh, did you want to go?"

"No. I told you, I'm on sleep duty."

"Say if you do. The others will be back soon anyway."

He squeezed her feet. "Stop trying to kick me out. Just set your alarm for three in the morning, and I'll sneak out then. They think you're at your aunt's. The door's locked."

Jess turned away to set the alarm on her phone, allowing herself a quick, secret smile. She settled back against her pillows. They studied each other.

"You're a long way away," Mitch said.

"So are you."

He lifted his chin at her. "Come here."

She made a scoffing noise. "You come here."

"Someone has to give in."

"It won't be me," Jess assured him.

But wait . . . Mitch was *shifting*. He dived between her and the wall.

"Oh my God! Did that just happen?" Jess laughed, turning over to see him, wincing because she'd rolled onto the injured side of her head. She just caught sight of his red face before he turned her back the other way so he could spoon her. "And you're embarrassed, too! I didn't think that could happen."

"Don't make a big deal out of it," he growled, squeezing her tightly.

"Are you kidding? It's like the total breakdown of civilization. Next you'll be asking for my number." When Jess felt Mitch breathe in, she pinched his arm. "I'm joking!"

He kissed her shoulder. "I know."

Then again, she sort of hadn't been, but she let it slide. He started to push against her in a slow, lazy way that wasn't sexual so much as sensual, rubbing because it felt good, and Jess felt his growing erection through his shorts.

"Mitch?" she said softly. "Can I do anything for you?"

"I believe you already have."

"In a different way this time. Like what you did for me."

Mitch stopped moving. "No, it's okay," he said, after a moment. "You're supposed to take it easy."

"But I want to," Jess said, and she meant it. Right then she trusted him completely; she couldn't have offered otherwise. Society viewed sex as the big deal, but as far as she was concerned, girls giving oral was where attitudes got really tricky.

"Yeah?" he asked, sounding hopeful.

Jess's mind went further, and as soon as she thought it, she knew it. "Actually, I want to have sex with you."

"I thought you said you'd never sleep with me."

"I've changed my mind."

She heard him swallow. *Nervous*, she thought, smiling. Then a banging noise made them both jump. It was followed by loud, discordant voices. Allie's music was cut off abruptly, replaced by Sticky Fingers, played at volume next door, which meant two things: Leanne was in residence, and she was ready to entertain. On cue, what seemed like a herd of animals arrived.

"I'm scared," Mitch whispered, making Jess giggle.

They listened to the snippets of conversation that reached them over the music. It was fair to say the mood had been broken.

"I didn't know girls used the C-word so freely," Mitch remarked.

"Leanne does. She thinks we should reclaim it; possession being nine-tenths of the law." Jess rolled over to face him, propped on her elbow. "She's the one who's got Julian's jersey. The redhead who did that freshman over. That's her room."

"She lives next door? Jesus. Isn't she some sort of sociopath?"

"Hey, *I* can say it," Jess warned.

One of the girls in Leanne's room cried, "The Sneetches! Let's do the Sneetches!"

"Dr. Seuss. Tongue twisters," Jess explained. "Giggle games."

"Like drinking games?" Mitch asked.

"Sort of," Jess said.

"Mine needs a new hose," someone commented next door.

"They've got money in Unity's budget for new garden hoses every year. Because by the time everybody takes a couple of cuts, that's, like, sixty meters gone," Jess told Mitch.

"Use mine," a girl said insistently. "Glass is less toxic."

The window next door closed abruptly, muting the noise.

"Do you do much of that?" Mitch asked.

Jess shook her head. "Hardly ever. Too much of a control freak."

"I just get paranoid or sick. Rather be drunk." Mitch gave her a look. "But better that than smoking cigarettes."

"Don't nag. You sound like Farren."

"Who? Oh, the sweep."

Jess's face clouded. "I thought she was the chick with the nose ring."

"You know what I meant."

Jess prodded him in the chest with a finger. "Well, what I mean is, she's my best friend, she's Unity's president, she's doing arts and law, she's a latecomer to basketball—where her effort definitely outstrips her ability, and I love that about her—and nothing else is relevant."

Mitch just nodded, not reacting but also not responding.

Jess stared at him reproachfully. "Would you have done something like that? *Have* you?"

"No."

"That Dud guy would." Jess stewed some more. "Would Julian have?" She knew by Mitch's face that she'd finally gotten to him, and she couldn't understand why she'd needed to push on that. To punish him?

"Possibly." He rolled onto his back, no part of his body

touching hers now, his hands resting on his chest. "But I'm not claiming to be better than them. That's what you're really asking, isn't it?"

"I don't know," Jess said in a small voice. But she was lying, backing off in the hope that he wouldn't block her completely. Because she wanted to know everything about him, pull him apart with questions. And she realized in that moment that if anything, absurdly, she felt jealous of Julian. Sylvie, too. Because they'd known Mitch better than it seemed she was ever going to be allowed to. And Mitch had let them down. He must have. Why else would Sylvie hate him so much? If Jess knew how, maybe she could protect herself. Not care so much.

"I think I just want to know what Julian was like, that's all," she said carefully, trying to find a way in.

"All right, let's talk about Julian." Mitch's voice was grim. "You would have hated *his* attitude toward women. He had Sylvie, but he still did whatever he wanted. I never had a girlfriend, so I used to think I was more honest. But who knows? You might have preferred him. He would have kissed you for a start, but only if he thought he'd get a fuck out of it." The way Mitch said it was so ugly. Jess flinched, feeling like she'd just been offered to his dead friend. There was a sudden round of crazed laughter next door.

"He was a funny cunt, but he only liked cutting people down. And competitive—*always* with the alpha shit, had to be pressing your buttons. Now he's not around, I sometimes wonder if I even liked him. We were just used to being around each other. Primary school, high school, same college, playing together." Mitch rubbed at his forehead and then stared at his palm. "Maybe we were each other." He fell quiet, and Jess waited, tense and not sure why. When he spoke again, his voice was hoarse. "But if someone ever gave me a hard time during a game, or in a club or something, Julian would be like a sheep dog coming over the top of everybody else to back me up. And when we played together, he gave it every-thing, every time." Mitch's voice cracked on his next words: "I didn't like him, but I did love him. I just didn't know it then." He cleared his throat. "Hey, look at me. I'm alive."

Jess threw herself on top of him, hugging him as tightly as she could. "I'm sorry, I'm sorry, I'm sorry." A mantra, vibrating from the back of her throat. And at first Mitch resisted, but then he hugged her.

"It's all right." His hold eased, and he sounded like he'd given up on something when he said, "You know the worst thing, Jess? Sometimes I think all I miss is how I felt back then. Before all the cracks." Jess raised herself so she could see his face, and when his eyes met hers, he frowned. "That's how you got in, by the way. Through the cracks."

"So I'm vermin?" Jess forced herself to smile, but it physically hurt.

Mitch's face softened. "*No!* God, no." He touched her cheek. "You're great, Jess. More than great. The best fun I've ever had with a chick. I'm just saying I might not always be cracked, that's all. And you're pretty special, so I don't want . . ."

When Jess nodded again, Mitch looked relieved. She remem-bered then that he liked being honest.

They were silent for a while, then she said, "Hey, if you wanted to sneak out now, you probably could, you know. They're out of their heads, and nobody uses the back stairs much, the ones near the back parking lot. Now's the time."

A different sort of relief. "You sure?"

Exactly the same smile. "I'm fine."

"What about your head?"

"It'll survive."

He kissed her on the forehead when he left. Like an uncle. As far as exits went, it sucked.

28.
Burning

When Mitch had gone, Jess retied her window so it was horizontal, and a witchy little wind blew into the room, making
the candles above the desk flicker. The breeze had crossed the
river and brought with it a shivery premonition of change. As far as
Jess was concerned, Queensland only had two seasons. That wind
signaled the end of summer.

The music next door had switched to The War on Drugs, and
she wondered if that was irony. But then it shut off, and she heard
the whole lot of them troop out of the room. Finding the emergency
cigarette she kept in the cup of pens on her desk, she lit up, smoking rapidly out the window—inhale-exhale-inhale-exhale—inducing
a head rush. She killed the cigarette and took two painkillers
instead. Then she sat on her bed, holding her Zippo.

Flick-spin-scritch! The flame snapped into life like a genie, but
it didn't grant Jess any wishes, least of all relief. *Snap!* She needed
a bigger genie.

Each room she searched on T-floor was both deserted and a

mess, like some great catastrophe had happened during the day, the zombie apocalypse, rather than just a music festival. When she reached Allie's door, she pulled it open and headed straight for the dresser, upending a basket full of toiletries.

"Help you there?" a voice asked, and Jess leaped into the air with an "Oh shit!"

Leanne. She was lying on Allie's unmade bed, half-hidden by the quilt, dressed in a sports bra, shorts, and socks. A star had been drawn in black marker around her belly button, which meant she'd been on Team Star Belly Sneetch. She was holding a phone— Allie's presumably.

"Where is everybody?" Jess asked, running a palm over the things she'd tipped from the basket, looking, looking . . .

"Food run."

"Why aren't you with them?"

"Why aren't you at your aunt's?"

"I just got back." Jess sensed rather than saw Leanne look her bathrobe up and down, its pockets full of the things she'd just scavenged. "And changed."

"Your eyes are red."

"So are yours." Jess found what she was looking for and threw everything else back in the basket. "Right. I'll be on the roof."

"Right. Me, too." Leanne got out of bed and slipped the phone into Allie's tote.

"You can only come if you bring beer. I know you've got some. And matches."

Leanne rummaged through the pigeonhole above Allie's desk and threw Jess a box of matches. "You're not supposed to drink after you've had a concussion."

"Are you qualified to give medical advice? Because last I checked you were studying psych."

"Ooh!" Leanne said, making jazz hands. *"Raging Flash."*

"Sorry," Jess apologized. "I'm just a bit—"

"No, it's better. Otherwise you're just, like, *always* with the fucking smile . . . Meet you up there in ten."

Jess set up in their regular spot, on the tail end of the roof, where the crowns of several gum trees dropped litter onto the concrete and the siding served as a windbreak. It was needed, because the wind had strengthened, sending clouds scudding across a sky lit by a half moon. When she'd finished stacking paper, twigs, leaves, and branches in the old washing machine cylinder they used for fires, Jess sat on the ventilation housing, brushing dust and bits of wood off her bathrobe, thinking she should have changed instead of just pulling on panties and her cowboy boots. If college was all about having the right bathrobe, hers was a classic—thick, white, and expensive, hotel style—and it would probably get wrecked. Leanne had changed, though. When she arrived, carrying a six-pack of beer, she was in jeans and her Knight Rider jersey.

Typical, Jess thought dully.

"Catch," Leanne said.

Jess did, cracking the can open and sucking foam from the top. She looked sideways at Leanne as she took a seat next to her. "Hey, we're in a bad joke. A sociopath and a pyromaniac were having a drink together . . ."

Leanne clinked cans with her. "You think I'm sociopathic?"

"Ish."

Leanne seemed to take that as an insult. "You're not a real pyro, either, you know."

Jess nodded. "I can control the impulse. And it's not about the fire, anyway. It's more about the way it starts. The flare. That's where I get off."

"*Please*. Do demonstrate," Leanne said, every bit the interested scholar.

"Well, Leanne, tonight, I'll be doing a little variant that I like to call doggie style. First, disperse your accelerant, like so . . ." Jess poured three bottles of nail polish remover over the material in the cylinder, then sprayed it liberally with the insect repellent she'd found in Farren's room. "Prepare your match, like so . . ." She lit a match, shielding it with her hand.

"You should totally use your Zippo," Leanne suggested in a helpful voice.

"Hah. Nice try." Jess threw the match into the cylinder, taking a step back. *Woof!*

———

LATER, WHEN THE fire had died down, and they were onto their second beers, and Jess had achieved a warm sort of numbness, Leanne said, "This can't be just a sore head."

"Try another part of my anatomy."

Leanne flicked an empty bottle of nail polish remover, making it spin. "Heard of masturbation?"

"No, I was thinking more—" Jess thumped her chest.

"Oh, *gross*, Jess. Keep that shit to yourself." Leanne sounded truly disgusted, but also embarrassed for her, as if Jess had just said she'd peed her pants.

"Try a little compassion, Leanne," Jess hissed. "It might come in handy in your future profession. *Com*—meaning shared. And *passion*—meaning feeling."

"Latin?" Leanne asked, impressed.

"Aunt Heather studied it at school." Jess drank a lot of her beer, thought for a while, and then poured the dregs over the dying fire, causing it to steam and hiss.

"Was that necessary?" Leanne asked.

"Yes, because it was symbolic. I'm a phoenix, rising from the ashes—"

"*Squawk!*"

"—because you are totally right. I am being pathetic. What I need is to get laid."

"See? There I can help you. That's the easy part." Leanne got up and leaned over the handrail. She waited for a while, then put two fingers to her lips and gave an ear-splitting whistle. "Brent! Hey, Brent! Would you do Jess?"

"What?" came the shout.

"Jess Gordon! Would you sleep with her?"

"In a flash. Ha, ha!"

Jess looked skyward.

"What about you, Ticker?" Leanne yelled.

"Affirmative."

Leanne returned to her seat. "Problem solved. Brent and/or Ticker."

"I feel sorry for your future patients."

Leanne took a swig of her beer, unperturbed. "I'm not interested in people's problems. I'm going into the research side so I can experiment on them. Hook them up to electrodes and give them electric shocks and shit."

Jess stood to squash her empty can. "You know what my problem is? I can't cut the sex stuff off from the feelings."

"Actually, that's considered healthy; sex plus feelings—I'll have to try it sometime."

Jess sat down with a thump. "It's not doing me any good."

"I'm assuming all this drama is related to the Fahrenheit dude," Leanne asked. Jess looked away, and Leanne prodded her with a finger. "Why's it such a big secret?"

"Because it's a big nonevent." Jess, agitated, rubbed her hand rapidly up and down her calf, like she was trying to start a fire with her own skin. "What's it mean when a guy won't kiss you?"

"He doesn't smoke."

"What if it's not that?"

"He's a prostitute." Leanne raised her can to her lips, her words sounding tinny: "Doesn't want to confuse sex with intimacy."

Jess grimaced. "What if he's not having sex with you, either?"

Leanne started to cough, spurting beer everywhere. Jess whacked her on the back until she eventually managed to wheeze, "Virgin?"

"I'm probably the only girl in the world he hasn't slept with."

"So you're friends?"

"No, he'll touch me. But that's all we do. There's been no sex, and no kissing." Jess gave the squashed can a moody kick. "Touching, though? That's fine. Touching's safe."

"That is the most fucked up thing I've ever—*ow!*" Leanne glared down at Jess's fingers, hooked deep into the sleeve of her jersey—or rather, Julian's jersey.

"That's it," Jess told her, wide-eyed. "Touching is safe."

"What's that mean?"

"No idea." Jess pried her fingers out of Leanne's arm. Sighed. A gust of wind made it over the siding, causing a flurry of sparks.

"You want my professional opinion?" Leanne asked and then burped. Jess thought that might have been it, but then she added, "The only thing you can do is stop wanting things to be different. Because you can't change people. You can't help people. And you definitely can't save them. They have to do it themselves."

Jess frowned. "You're studying *psychology*."

"That's what makes it so good. Feel better?"

"Not one bit."

BUT WHEN SHE returned to her room that night, the first thing Jess did was make her bed, then she got back into it and slept like a baby, so perhaps she did feel better. She didn't regret talking to Leanne until four days later, when she returned home from work to find a gift-wrapped package on her desk.

Inside was a hot-pink vibrator with "8.5 inches of sensuous glitter."

Along with a card that read: *With compassion. For your phoenix.*

29.
Rendezvous

Late on a Thursday morning toward the end of second semester, a stranger tapped on Jess's shoulder during the break in her lecture. He was standing on the walkway behind her—the Abel Smith theater having been designed to be filled from the top down, the lecturer's podium at a subterranean level. Students were streaming in through the entranceway behind him. Unlike them, Jess hadn't gone outside. It was too chilly.

"Are you Jess Gordon?" he asked, sounding suspicious, as if she didn't meet the description he'd been given. When Jess nodded, he held out a folded piece of paper. "This guy outside asked me to give it to you? Said you'd be sitting in one of the back rows? Said he's afraid of heights? Well, not heights, exactly. More of a structural thing?"

Jess forgot to thank the guy. She'd reached the point where she hadn't expected to hear from Mitch again, so she was in shock. She opened the note grim-faced, expecting some kind of tidying up. Instead, what was there made her laugh. Which was worse.

Dear Miss Gordon,
GREAT ENTRANCES, UNFORGETTABLE EXITS
is available for collection. You can pick it up
after your lecture.

Yours cordially,
The Co-op Bookshop

After she read it, Jess sat very still. She felt hot, her breathing too shallow. And she remembered what Leanne had said during their conversation on the roof, all those weeks ago. Was it possible Mitch had changed? She smoothed the note out and placed it carefully between the pages of her notepad, like you might press a flower, because if he hadn't, that note had just become a souvenir.

———————

SHE FOUND MITCH lurking in Young Adult fiction. RÜFÜS was on the sound system, and the music made the moment seem cinematic, as did the fact that Mitch's eyes widened when he saw her, taking in her high-heeled boots, her black pencil skirt, her fluffy mohair sweater, her beating heart—no, that would be the push-up bra—her hair, clean and glossy, styled in an artfully messy side braid. She'd finished the ensemble with an extra spray of the perfume she favored, Dolce and Gabbana's Light Blue, and Mitch probably saw that, too, because he was looking damn hard enough. Maybe he didn't recognize her. Any other day, she may well have looked like shit.

Viewed that way, you could say it was fortunate Mitch had decided to resurface on the one day of the year when Jess had a date. Otherwise you'd have to concede it was fucked. She was due to meet Darwin, a PhD student who shared Erin's office, for coffee at twelve thirty. Unfortunately, as soon as Jess had read Mitch's note, she'd known she wouldn't make it.

"Hey, so you look . . . wow."

"Thanks," Jess said briskly. "You look good, too."

Mitch was in jeans, his Timberlands, and a Knights jersey identical to the one she'd stolen, and he actually looked so handsome it was ridiculous.

"How's the head?" he asked.

"What? Oh. That was ages ago." Jess lifted the book he was holding so she could see the cover. *The Book Thief*. "You know what would be funny? If you actually stole that."

"Yeah, that would be funny." Mitch shifted his weight from one foot to the other. "How was micro?"

"Two hours of a foreign language."

He nodded. She nodded. He shelved the book. "Look, I'm sorry I haven't been in touch."

Jess said nothing. She wasn't trying to make Mitch uncomfortable, although it seemed to have that effect, she just knew that whatever he said next would tell her all she needed to know.

He cleared his throat. "Things have been really hectic, hey. Didn't even realize it'd been so long, but then—"

"It's all good."

Mitch laughed, shaking his head. "Now I know I'm in trouble. When you say that."

Jess gave him a half smile. Relaxed. No, resolved. "You're really not."

Mitch frowned, looking for the catch. Frowned again when he realized there wasn't one. Jess's eyes were clear, her face open. Her smile stretched a little more in sympathy.

"Jess?" he said, uncertainty in his voice, and there was the same little pull between his eyebrows that she'd first noticed in the photograph of him and Julian.

"Oh, hang on. I've just got to . . ." Jess pulled her phone from her tote and started composing a text. "Sorry," she said apologetically, typing as she talked. She took a deep breath, trying to release a sudden constriction in her chest.

"Who's so urgent?" Mitch asked with a hint of disbelief.

"Darwin."

"That's a name?"

"Maybe he was conceived there. I've never asked." Jess glanced up at him with a smile. "I'm supposed to be meeting him for coffee in fifteen minutes," she explained, and Mitch's eyebrows signaled some kind of adjustment. He seemed even more surprised when she admitted, "It's a one-off. Besides being too old for me, he's also a bit too economics." She turned her attention back to her phone.

"I wondered why you were all dressed up." Mitch seemed to reconsider, adding, hurriedly, "I mean, not that you don't look good normally, but . . ."

"It's okay, I knew what you meant." Jess hit SEND, snapped her phone case shut, and gave him another smile. It was easy really. Leanne had been right. The only person you could change was yourself.

"So where are you off to instead?"

"Oh! I just assumed you had something in mind." Jess laughed. "That was a bit presumptuous, wasn't it?"

Mitch stared at her. When he spoke, he sounded subdued. "Not really." He patted his pocket and there was the crunch of keys. "Adrian's away for work—for real this time. He's in Melbourne, and I rang this morning to make sure he's still there. I thought you might want to come over to the apartment with me. But maybe I'm the one being presumptuous."

"No, not at all. That'd be good." Jess's voice was untroubled, as regular and even as her breathing. "Where have you parked? I'll meet you there. I've just got one thing to do first."

30.
High-speed

Jess took the path that led past the main lake, where spray from the fountain fanned gracefully in the wind and much of the water's surface was covered in water lilies. As she neared Sir William MacGregor Drive, she could see Mitch up ahead, sitting on the hood of Adrian's car, a sleek-looking shark of a vehicle set against a backdrop of gracious old trees and the river. He got to his feet when he saw her. Jess felt like she was in a movie.

"You took a while," Mitch said when she reached him, opening her door.

You took six weeks. "Had to buy something."

A round of nervous throat-clearing from Mitch. "Just thought you might have changed your mind."

Once they were on their way, he asked, "So what have you been up to?"

"Same old, same old. Basketball starts after the break. That's good."

"Basketball, huh? Are you any good?"

"Why do people always have to be good at something? Why can't they just do it because they like it?"

"I was only asking."

They were halfway to Adrian's before Mitch spoke again: "Are we going to talk or what?" And his voice was so hostile that Jess, staring out of her window, was startled. She looked across at him, but he was focused on the road, changing lanes, and she realized how fast he was going.

"Can you slow down, please?" she asked. When he did, she said, "I'm not playing games, Mitch. I just think we should cut back on the talking, that's all. Otherwise we're kind of coloring outside the lines, don't you think?"

Mitch was looking at her like she'd changed shape. Again. But if she had, it was partly his fault.

"Fine. Have it your way," he said, and he jabbed the radio on, and Elliot Moss filled the car, and he sped up again, and Jess didn't bother telling him to slow down this time, just rolled her window down and let the cold come rushing in.

———————

"CURTAINS OPEN OR closed?" Mitch asked.

"Sorry, do you mind if we close them?" Jess put her bag down. "Make it a bit darker."

"Don't mind at all. If you'll stop saying sorry." He pulled the curtains closed, a thick layer of clotted cream, his movements terse. The room became gloomy, not dark.

Jess unzipped her boots and pulled them off. She dropped her skirt and peeled off her sweater. For once, she was wearing Big Occasion underwear: champagne satin and lace, French panties that matched her push-up bra. When she reached these last two items of clothing, she just stood there, rubbing her arms. Mitch was on the other side of the bed, still fully dressed. His eyes flickered over her lingerie.

"So straight into it, then?" he asked, not sounding happy about it.

Jess nodded, and he peeled his jersey and T-shirt off as one item. He pulled off his Timberlands and socks. But when his hands went to his belt, she said, "I'll do it, if you want."

He came around to her side of the bed and stood in front of her, too close. It was meant to intimidate, nothing else.

Jess unbuckled his belt. Had trouble unbuttoning his jeans. "Sorry, can you . . ."

"*Enough* with the sorry shit." Mitch unbuttoned and unzipped, then dropped his hands back to his sides. Jess knelt, pulling down his jeans until they were bunched at his ankles. Then she carefully maneuvered his black boxers down to join them. He lifted one foot and then the other while she pulled them off.

She glanced up at Mitch, but he was staring across at the mirrored closet. Jess looked, too, and saw the scene they made, knew why he was growing hard. But when she took hold of him, moistening her lips, Mitch's hand gripped her hair, jerking her head back so he could frown at her.

"That's where we were up to," she told him, wincing.

He exhaled, letting her go, and said in a sour voice, "Fine then."

Jess began. She wasn't super experienced, but she'd done it a few times for Brendan. The hard way, she realized now, courtesy of Mitch's hand-job lesson. She licked her palm and used it, too, and it made things easier, and she eventually established a rhythm. After a while, Mitch groaned, sounding helpless, and he touched her hair again, but gently now. And even though her jaw was hurting, Jess might have enjoyed herself then—if everything else had been different.

Still it was hard not to feel choked at times. At one point she gagged and had to stop. She breathed for a moment, looking down at the thin rug separating her from the floorboards. Rough on the knees.

Mitch lifted her chin. "You all right? Stop if you want."

"No, I'm okay," she said, eyes downcast.

"You sure you want this?"

"I'm doing it, aren't I?"

"Yeah, and if you keep doing it, I'll come, but it doesn't necessarily mean I've enjoyed myself."

Jess met his gaze. "I want to do it," she said coldly.

"Why?"

"It's symbolic."

"What's that supposed to mean?"

"You wanted me on my knees when you first met me. And here I am."

"Oh, fuck you, Jess," Mitch spat angrily, pushing her away. He sat on the edge of the bed, one hand pressed to his groin. "Don't put this on me. You're doing it to yourself. You won't talk to me, but you're straight into giving me a blow job? Who are you?"

"I would have thought that makes me your perfect woman."

Mitch made a harsh coughing sound, his blue eyes boring into her. "You're unbelievable. That's bullshit and you know it. I've changed."

"No, you've just learned something, that's all!" Jess realized how angry she sounded—how angry she *was*—and she dropped her head, rocking back on her heels and staring down at her hands, now folded in her lap.

"Hey, what's going on?" Mitch's voice was gentle now. He leaned forward, taking hold of her shoulders, trying to pull her up. "God, you're freezing. Come here. Look, I know I shouldn't have left it this long, but things have been pretty full on with training and games and assignments, and we've been doing a bit of pre-season training for Knights, as well, so—"

"Stop it." Jess pulled away from him abruptly. "You don't have to explain yourself. This is not a relationship."

"Yeah, but that doesn't mean I haven't missed you. Like crazy, actually."

"*Mitch, please*," Jess begged, all the frustration she felt compressed into those two words.

Mitch studied her, the little crease present on his forehead.

She sighed. Stood up.

"You're not going," he told her as she crossed the floor to her bag.

"No," Jess said. Strangely, she felt calm. She rummaged through her tote until she found the packet of condoms she'd bought at the university pharmacy and then turned back to him, pulling off the plastic wrapping.

Mitch's voice changed abruptly, from coaxing to abrasive: "What the fuck's that?" Jess took out a single foil and threw the rest of the packet onto the bedside table. Then she slipped off her underpants and removed her bra, and as she was doing it, Mitch was moving away from her, scooting backward until he couldn't go any farther, pressed up against the headboard. She clambered onto the bed, kneeling in front of him.

"It's an ending," she told him, holding the foil in her fist. "I want you to fuck me. Now. Right now. If we're lucky, it'll be awful."

Mitch made a disbelieving noise at the back of his throat. "Are you kidding?"

Jess looked away and then back at him. "Kiss me then."

"Jesus, Jess, for the last time, I don't do that!" he snapped, his voice rising, but he looked uneasy.

Jess rubbed at her eyes, teary all of a sudden, but they were angry tears, hot tears, the result of months of feeling stuffed around. She was a long way from calm now. "Well, they're your only two choices. You can kiss me, or you can fuck me. But there's no more talking and no more touching, no more safe. So if you won't kiss me . . ." She tried to hand him the condom.

Mitch knocked her hand away. "When it's like that, it's about as personal as a one-off. You don't want that."

"That is *exactly* what I want—"

"Don't be stupid."

"—because you will use me like a tissue and throw me away and I won't have to feel anymore."

Mitch rubbed a hand over his face, his voice grim. "I'm not sleeping with you, Jess."

"Why? Aren't I good enough? Oh, that's right. I'm not. 'I doubt it'—that's what you said, wasn't it? That day in the laundry room. Because I'm not hot enough, or slutty enough, or whatever it is that you want."

"Can you hear yourself?"

"Yes, I can! And I hate the fact that you've reduced me to worrying about shit like that. But that's what you've done to me, Mitch. You have *reduced* me. I just got down on my knees and sucked you off to make a point, for fuck's sake!" Jess slapped him in the chest, once, twice, tears running down her face now, dripping from her jaw, and he grabbed her wrists. Her voice rose: "And I used to like myself before you came along, but now I can't even—" She howled, the noise coming from deep down in her chest, something primal and awful about it.

Mitch shushed her, trying to pull her into a hug.

"Don't shush me." Jess pulled away from him, feeling like she was about to be overcome by great wracking sobs, fighting the feeling as hard as she'd ever fought anything in her whole life.

And she won. Regained some kind of control. She took a deep, shuddering breath, wiped her face with her hands, and then spoke without looking at him. "I'd like to go back now. Please."

Mitch touched her shoulder. "Jess, I'm just trying to do the right thing."

"By who?"

He dropped his hand.

31.
Oblivion

"I don't get it. I thought you'd be happy," Jess said with a frown, chalking her cue.

"I am happy," Allie said, avoiding eye contact. "At least it's official now."

"Updated-your-status official?" Leanne asked. She turned her attention to Jess, who was lining up her shot, and hissed, "Softly."

"You go softly," Jess said with a meaningful look at Allie.

Allie, oblivious to this, started to play piano on the felt edging of the table, looking hurt and restless. "Sorry," she said, taking a step backward.

Jess lined up the purple four again. A night out at Lucky's was a good thing—being in the Valley, away from St. Lucia, was a welcome distraction. She took the shot, hitting the cue ball softly, as Leanne had wished. It kissed the four, which fell into the pocket with a satisfying plop, leaving her with a reasonable chance of getting the seven next.

Leanne stalked around behind her to take a look. "Don't even think about it, glory whore. Just block the hole. Speaking of which, had sex lately?"

Jess pocketed the seven. "Nope." And deliberately messed up her next shot.

The two guys they were playing had stopped paying attention when it became obvious they were about to get spanked. Although one of them, a tall, studious-looking guy in a *Doctor Who* shirt, kept glancing at Allie a lot. His turn was next. Jess handed him her cue, then sat on a barstool, swinging her legs. She wanted a cigarette, but she wouldn't give in. She'd told herself she was giving up for running. Really, it was another distraction, an alternative ache to focus on.

A chorus of raised voices came from the other side of the pool area—most of them belonging to Unity people. The place was unusually empty for Student Night, and things had an end-of-the-world feeling. People were probably at home, chained to their desks. Reading week started the next week, and after that, exams. Jess wondered again whether she should have joined Farren and the Z-floor guys for a movie at the Eldorado rather than drinking so she was fresh for studying the next day. But she wasn't going to get drunk, she reminded herself.

The Doctor was trying to talk to Allie as he lined up his shot. Jess felt sorry for him; he seemed like a nice guy. Normally, even if she wasn't interested, Allie was always kind. He mishit the cue ball, which rolled a couple of inches and stopped short of actually connecting with anything, and Jess hoped he could at least appreciate it as a metaphor for his night.

"Thanks for coming," Leanne told him, snatching the cue. She got down to business, pocketing balls in rapid succession. Amateur hour was over and the hustler had arrived.

And that was when Jess saw Dud. Or maybe she heard him first. He was at the head of a large group of people who'd just entered the pool area; mainly guys, but there were a couple of girls as well. They were loud and noisy, a few of the guys mock scuffling with one another, and a bouncer drifted across to eye their approach. Dud saw Jess then, and she kept her gaze nailed to him. He took it as some kind of challenge, giving her the bird in response. But it wasn't that. Jess was afraid that if she looked anywhere else she might see Mitch. Then the group converged on the bar and Dud was swallowed up.

Leanne lined up the eight ball, but she was looking at Jess as she took the shot, her eyes narrowed. The eight ball ricocheted around the table before finding the middle pocket. The cue ball had stopped on impact, still spinning on the spot. Watching Leanne play pool was like watching a cartoon.

"Knights," Jess said, by way of explanation.

"What are you worried about them for?" Leanne demanded. "I *want* them to come over here so that they get to pick glass out of their foreheads."

"I'm not worried," Jess said. "Back in a sec. Going to the bathroom." She wound her way through the club on legs that felt watery. Once inside, she stood beside the girls who were primping in the mirror and frowned at herself for a while. There was no need to panic. Mitch might not even be here.

She left and walked straight into him coming out of the men's bathroom.

Jess stopped dead, unable to keep the shock off her face. Mitch's reaction was more circumspect. He blinked and then raised his eyebrows, giving her a sleepy smile. Despite it being officially winter and a crisply cold night, he wasn't wearing a jacket, just a button-down shirt over jeans.

"*Heeey*, you," he said, as though they didn't know each other very well. Maybe he'd forgotten her name. "Been here long?"

"A while. I saw your friends come in."

"The boys? Yeah, we're celebrating."

Jess could see that. Mitch's eyes were bloodshot and his joints seemed loose. She could smell the booze on him. "What's the big occasion?"

"Knights' first game tonight. My first game as captain."

Jess nodded. "Congratulations."

He frowned. "I didn't say we won." Then he smiled, like he was being clever. "But we did."

"And you're drinking again?" she asked, like you might say, *And you're well?*

"The team that drinks together, stays together." Mitch glanced at the room behind her. "Or maybe it's 'plays together.' I don't know, some bonding shit." He finally met her eyes, and it was like an electric shock. Jess dropped her gaze.

"Well, you're back on track then," she said, sounding shaken.

"Like nothing ever happened. Good to see you, Just Jess."

When he'd gone, Jess looked around blindly, feeling like she'd forgotten something. It was some time before she noticed the person leaning against a mosaic-covered column watching her, her flaming-red hair backlit by the lights.

"I worked it out ages ago. You're too uptight to get involved with somebody else's boyfriend, so the only other reason it'd be a secret would be if it was a knight," Leanne said when she reached her.

"It's not what you think."

"Are you saying he's not Fahrenheit?"

"I'm saying it's over," Jess said. "So you can tell Farren if you want, but there'd be no point."

"Do the knights know?"

"I doubt it. He swore on his dead friend's ashes that he wouldn't tell them."

"That's a bit dramatic." Leanne watched Jess closely. Then she asked in a voice that Jess had never heard before, "Want to blow this hole and go to The Beat? Dance?"

Jess shook her head.

"Do you want to go home? I'll get a cab with you."

"Oh God, don't do that." Jess pressed her fingertips to the corners of her eyes. "You'll make me cry."

"I'm just talking transport."

"No, you're not. But I won't tell anyone." Jess took a deep breath, pulling her shoulders back. "Let's just get drunk."

"Thatta girl." Leanne sounded approving. "We were here first."

The two girls made their way out to the rooftop area, where a swimming pool glowed an unearthly blue in the chill of the night, and rejoined the Unity crowd, baking under a couple of heaters on the opposite side of the bar from the knights. Mitch was standing with two man mountains, the three of them forming a rough semicircle. There was a lot of back slapping going on. Loud voices. Besides the eight or so knights, there were at least four girls that Jess could see.

Leanne lit a cigarette and blew the smoke over Jess's head. "Did you ever find out why he wouldn't have sex with you?"

"No." Jess took Leanne's cigarette and appraised it for a moment, noticing how badly her hand was shaking before she took a deep drag.

"Probably because he cared about you."

Jess looked at her sharply. "Why would you say that?" A stream of smoke accompanied the words.

"You've given up," Leanne reminded her, taking back the cigarette. "He's a knight. They're not supposed to care about women. They've got standards."

"They're not all like that," Jess said, looking in vain for Tipene. Instead, the person she saw was Sylvie, taking mincing steps in shiny red heels toward Mitch and mock tackling him from behind. Mitch regained his balance with difficulty, looking back under his arm to see her like he was worried he was going to step on her, his face amiable. Sylvie looked tiny next to him, impossibly fine. She was as drunk as he was.

"Who's she?" asked Leanne.

"No one," Jess said, getting an echo of memory. In a flash of jealousy that felt like a burn, she wondered if Sylvie and Mitch would end up having sex later that night. Julian was dead, so what would it matter? And if Mitch was drinking again, meaningless sex couldn't be that far behind.

———————

TIME WASN'T A reliable thing when Jess was drunk. That night it slowed right down, and nothing made sense. She felt like she was trapped aboard a lurching ship, the good ship *Lucky's*, viewing everything with a peculiar kind of tunnel vision, so that people seemed to appear and disappear around her at random, and there were gaping holes in the night's continuity. As she reached for what she hoped was her drink on one of the tall tables, she saw that in a feat of magic the place had suddenly become full and a DJ was playing. When did that happen? Even more puzzling, Michael Azzopardi was beside her, enthroned on a bar stool, and they were evidently midway through a conversation.

". . . their rugby team?" He pushed dolefully at his glasses. "We're gonna get killed." Jess squinted at him. "Looking pretty drunk there, Flash."

"No, I'm okay," she said, tottering forward and then tottering back.

"Well, while you've got your teeth out, I want to ask you about Farren."

"Don't you mean Allie?" Jess asked, confused.

Michael shifted on his stool, seeming uncomfortable. "No, that's a different thing. I'm thinking about running for president next year. It's my last roll of the dice, you know? And I wondered if you knew what Farren's plans were. Is she staying on or moving—"

"'Cause I think we should talk about Allie," Jess said, smacking the table, suffering a slight time delay.

Michael bristled, looking around impatiently like a million other people were clamoring for his attention. "God, don't you start. I'm doing everything right and I say one little not-quite-perfect thing, and she gets the shits."

"So you *are* together?"

Michael shrugged. "You tell me. She hasn't talked to me all night."

"What did you say to her, exactly?"

"I told her that I wasn't interested in anybody else."

"But that's good! Well done, you."

"No, wait." Michael spoke in a rapid monotone. "Then I said, 'I know there might be better-looking girls, but I just want to be with you.'" Jess made a gargling sound. "I know, I know," he said, shaking his head. "Believe me, *I know*. I didn't mean it the way it sounded." Jess was laughing now but trying to stifle it, a helicopter in trouble. "It's not funny!" he roared.

"It so is!" She slung an arm around his shoulders. "You poor, clueless bastard. I would actually feel sorry for you if your standards weren't *way* too high."

"Look, I know Allie's hot. All I meant was that if someone even hotter than her came along, I wouldn't even look at them."

Jess made a weird snorting noise and sagged against him. "Oh God, oh God," she breathed. "Of all people, the one person you shouldn't have said that to was Allie. Do you know how many selfies you've just spawned? You've probably—" She broke off as someone pushed her roughly and looked over her shoulder to see Mitch. His gaze flickered over the two of them in a way that made Jess wonder if he'd misread the situation: her arm around Michael's neck, her body pressed against his.

"Oh, hey, man." Michael twisted around, holding out his hand.

"Michael Azzopardi. We played each other in first year. How's your season looking?"

Mitch ignored him, his eyes locked on Jess. "Sorry to interrupt. You dropped this." He handed over her Zippo, then stalked off.

"What's up his ass?" Michael asked in a wounded voice. "Does he think I'm not up to his level or something? I'll fuckin' show him."

"Just likes everything his own way," Jess said flatly.

———————————

THE WRONG END of the night. Everything spinning, getting faster and faster, as though they were all about to be sucked down a drain. Jess swam against the current to reach the bathrooms. Inside, the music was muted, but the ringing in her ears was loud. Toilet paper all over the floor. Then she was back outside, walking into a remix of Grimes—she loved that song! And she saw Mitch, evidently waiting for her, propped up by the wall. He looked bleary-eyed—from drinking, from lust, all his old bad habits. But when he touched her hand, he looked wistful, and Jess crumpled.

"Oh God, Mitch, look at you. Please don't do anything stupid tonight."

"I just wanted . . . to tell you," he said, with some difficulty, placing one word after the other as slowly and carefully as dominoes, "that it's . . . all . . . okay now."

Jess squinted, pulling her hair back so she could see him clearly. "What is?"

Mitch nodded, as if confirming the question. "That's, like . . . if you want." He rubbed at his face. "Let's just . . . have sex."

When Jess finally spoke, she took as much care with her words as he had. "Mitch, I have to go now, okay?"

32.
Little Secrets

Jess woke with a headache, grainy eyes, and a sense of disorientation. Something was wrong. As she checked her phone, she realized that she must have turned her alarm off and gone back to sleep, because it was a quarter to eight. Her microeconomics exam started in fifteen minutes.

For a moment there was only the horrible cold feeling she got when faced with a situation she wanted to believe wasn't happening, then she leaped out of bed, ripping her flannel pajama pants off and tugging her jeans on, pulling her college jersey on over her pajama top. She jammed her feet into her high-tops without socks, not bothering to tie the laces, and pulled her hair back in a ponytail. Then she hunted around frantically in the chaos of books and paper on the desk for pens, a calculator, and a ruler. She finally found her student card under a little reminder note she'd written for herself that said: *The state of your desk reflects the state of your mind. Do not go into exams with your mind a tangled mess!*

THE EXAM WAS in the Parnell Building, and Jess sprinted the whole way there. By the time she passed the physiology refectory, the crisp morning air was making her nose run, she was gripping her side because she had a horrible stitch, and her palms were a mess of gravel, blood, and chipped skin. She reached the crowd of students waiting to enter, hardly able to believe she'd made it in time, and doubled over. She thought she heard someone say her name but couldn't tell over the sound of her own loud and labored breathing. Then Jess recognized his Timberlands. And his legs, even though he was wearing jeans.

There must have been a law or commerce exam as well that morning in one of the other rooms, because, like her, Mitch was holding pens, pencils, and his student card. Unlike her, he'd obviously rested, showered, and eaten breakfast.

"You okay?" he asked, a look of concern on his face.

And in any other circumstances, Jess would have found talking to him hard—she hadn't seen him since that night at Lucky's. But in exam time—that endurance test of stress, cramming, too much coffee, and not enough sleep, when nothing was as it should have been—seeing Mitch again, talking to him, was suddenly the most natural thing in the world. He was a friendly face in the middle of a nightmare.

"I slept in! I still had to—I must have turned the alarm off, but I—" Jess broke off, making a gurgling, swallowing noise. "Oh God, I can't remember anything. I had to go over all this stuff on—"

"Jess, take a breath."

"—Edgeworth Boxes, and the Pareto thing again, because that'll be on there for sure. Seriously, I woke up fifteen minutes ago. I can't even—"

"*Shh.* Just breathe," he said, clamping one hand on her shoulder and squeezing it. Not hard enough to hurt, but hard enough to ground her. "Take a big breath. Come on, with me."

Jess inhaled in time with him, staring into his eyes. So blue, so sure, so steady.

"Again. Breathe," he told her. But Jess was distracted, because people around them were starting to shuffle forward. The exams had been called, and she hadn't even noticed. "Heaps of time," Mitch said firmly. He gently brushed the gravel out of her palms. "What'd you do, fall over?"

Jess nodded, her hands stinging. Eyes stinging now; heart, too.

"Okay, well, I want you to do something for me. I want you to stop thinking. Everything you need will be there when you need it." As he said this, Mitch tucked the collar of her pajama top beneath her college jersey. "And when you first sit down, just concentrate on filling out your details properly—your student number, your name, all that. Then, when they let you read the paper through, do that and only that. Make sure you read the questions properly, understand what it is you've got to do, but don't think about the answers yet." He was squatting now, tying the laces on her high-tops, and Jess felt like a child being dressed, but she took a stupid comfort from it anyway. "When they tell you to start, that's when you think about them. But not all at once. Just tackle one question at a time. Maybe do the easiest first." He looked up at her. "What do you think? Can you do all that for me?"

Jess nodded, then glanced at the last of the stragglers making their way inside. "We've got to go." She took another deep, gulping breath. "Thank you."

"No need for that." Mitch straightened so that he was looking down at her and suddenly very close. And for the first time, he seemed thrown. He frowned.

Jess was frowning, too. "Mitch? I'm really glad that we saw each other one more time. Like this. I mean, like friends." He nodded slowly. "Would have liked to have been a little more groomed, perhaps." She gave him a wan smile. "Haven't slept for two days, or even brushed my teeth. But, hey, I think I was looking this sharp when we first met, so it's probably perfect for the good-bye."

Mitch just stared at her. Jess grimaced, realizing he didn't need all that right before an exam, and he probably didn't care, either. The point about good-byes is that they usually don't require saying.

"Anyways," she said. She walked away.

Mitch said her name. She looked back.

"Just breathe," he said.

JESS WAS WOKEN for the second time that Wednesday when someone opened the door so abruptly, the change in air pressure hurt her ears. She groaned, burying her head under the pillow, feeling sick in a turned-inside-out kind of way that was due to a cumulative lack of sleep.

"It's me, my little flower!" a female voice trilled. Farren. Accompanied by Passion Pit. She jumped on the bed and started to bounce—higher and higher and higher and higher.

Jess removed the pillow, squinting at her. "God—I'm—tired. What—time—is—it?"

Farren stopped jumping, pressing her phone's screen to kill the music. "Just after three. In the afternoon. Do you want to go back to sleep?"

"I have to get up. I've got no choice. Seriously, I can't believe they jammed my two hardest subjects in one after the other. Fucking fuckers. Maybe I should have a shower. What are you doing here, anyway?"

"I miss you," Farren said, looking around Vanessa Ng's room as she spoke. Vanessa had family in Brisbane and stayed with them during reading week and exams. Like Jess, she knew that if you wanted to make high grades, the first thing to do was get away from your usual festering partners. Jess was using Vanessa's G-floor room as a base for the exam period. Farren, in turn, was using Jess's room. If that was working, it had to be on the basis of novelty alone, given Farren was only making a twenty-meter shift.

Farren was still in her pajamas, a scarf wrapped around her head. "What's the G-spot like, anyway?" she asked.

"No direct sunlight," Jess said. She waved at the CDs on the shelf above the desk. "And a lot of P!nk."

Farren laughed a lot harder than Jess thought was strictly necessary. "P!nk!" she gasped. She was probably cracking up: Last Jess had checked, she'd resorted to putting lists of cases in plastic sleeves and taping them to the walls of her favorite shower and toilet stalls. When she recovered, Farren opened the window, turned off the heater, and then returned to the bed—sitting down this time. Getting settled in.

"No offense, but I came over here for a reason," Jess told her.

"Ooh, I love it when you get all Type A. I just want to tell you a little story."

Jess put the pillow over her head again. "La, la, la, not listening . . ."

"Well," Farren said. "It started when I was studying in your room today, and Leanne came in—"

"*Farren.*" Jess ripped the pillow away. "I told you not to let her in there while I was gone. She gets into everything!"

"—and she was all like, 'Ever seen Flash's vibrator?'"

"Oh, you are kidding me."

"—And I'm like, 'Hello! I'm her best friend. I think I'd know if she had one.' And then she opened your third drawer and pulled out the clothes you'd put on top of it, and I was all, 'That's disgusting—'"

"She gave it to me."

"—who has a *pink* vibrator? With glitter? But then, about two hours later, you had a visitor." Jess sat up, suddenly tight in the chest. "And when I heard the knock, I yelled out, 'Come on in, you big stud!' The door opened, and this guy was standing there—" Jess made a small noise. "—and when he saw me, he was all like, 'You're not Jess.' And I was all like, 'And you, sir, are no Davey!' Then I gave him a look—like this, see?—that just cut through all the crap. And he said, 'Mitchell Crawford, nonpracticing knight.' And I said, 'Farren Ghosh, ferocious best friend.' "

After that, everything was still. Farren stared at Jess, and Jess stared at Farren. Farren drew first, raising her eyebrows.

"I'm so sorry. I know I should have told you. But how could I have told you that? A knight."

"He wasn't involved."

"Still, it's not very loyal."

"I think I can forgive you. And then hold it over you for the rest of your life."

Jess rubbed her chest. Maybe she was asthmatic. "What did he say?"

"Ooh, wouldn't you like to—"

"Farren, I swear to God."

"He said that you'd been together a couple of times, but you'd kept it quiet because you didn't want to hurt me, and also because you'd look like a doofus in front of the Unity girls. Actually, he didn't say that last bit; I did. Then he said that he'd been an idiot."

"Did he?" Jess felt lightheaded. She frowned, cleared her throat.

Farren got a bottle of water from the desk, handing it to her. "And I said, 'Well, what makes you so sure she'll want to see you, then?' And he told me about this morning, and he said he'd wanted to check you'd done okay in your exam. And I was like, 'Wow, I'm so moved.' Then he said—and I'll quote this bit, because it was embarrassingly over the top—'All right, I wanted to tell her that when she said it was good-bye this morning I thought I was going to fucking die.' "

"Oh," Jess said, with difficulty.

"I *know*." Farren bounced up and down a couple of times, her brown eyes very bright. Then she wrinkled her nose. "Of course, I had to explain that you've quarantined yourself, because despite all appearances you're actually a driven, high-achieving type of person, and that you have your econometrics exam tomorrow, and you're really stressed about it."

"Oh," Jess said again, sounding deflated.

"I told him I could take him to you, if that's what he wanted, but personally I wasn't in favor of it. He said I was probably right, he shouldn't disturb you. And then I said—and I'll quote this bit, too, because it was kind of cool—'But that doesn't mean you can't disturb her some other time. Arise, Sir Mitchell of Knights, you have my blessing to pass through the corridors of this college unharmed.' "

"You did not."

"Well. That was the gist."

When Farren said nothing more, Jess prompted, "And that was that?"

"Actually, no. He did say one more thing. He said he was sorry about the way I'd been treated. I thought that was quite good."

Jess nodded slowly. "That is good." She took a deep breath, trying to release her constricted chest. "God, how am I going to get my head together now? I almost wish you'd waited until after my exam to tell me that story."

"I tried, but then . . . you know . . . no impulse control."

Something occurred to Jess and she froze. "That's two

stories." She eyed her friend suspiciously, her voice sharpening: "Tell me that was two stories."

"What? Oh! No, I just forgot the best bit. Because what Leanne and I did was get your vibrator—with tissues, of course, to protect our hands—and we put it on the shelf above your desk, jutting up in all its glory, an eight-point-five-inch rocket ship, so that when you came back you'd see it straightaway, and you'd get embarrassed, or really paranoid about who'd been using it."

"Please tell me you're joking."

"I just forgot it was there! *He* was too polite to mention it. I mean the whole conversation was meet-the-parents serious. He *might* have thought it was mine."

Jess stared at Farren, openmouthed. Farren made a *what?* face. And then Jess lost it, laughing so hard she would have peed herself if she hadn't been dangerously dehydrated—*wukka-wukka-wukka*. Farren joined in.

"You all right?" Farren asked when they'd wheezed to a halt.

33.
Busy Earnin'

"What have you got in the way of hours next week?" Georgie asked Jess, sliding a full rack of dirty glasses onto the bench.

Jess started loading the glasses into the fresh tray she'd set up over the sink, wiping rims to remove lipstick stains, tipping out dregs. "All the performance nights and the double shift on Wednesday and Saturday. I told Vivian I wanted to pack the work in while I'm on break. How about you?"

"She's only given me my usual," Georgie pouted, tapping the stainless-steel bench with her long plum nails. "The *dragon*." Georgie was studying drama. Not that it showed, much.

Jess, used to her performances, smothered a grin. "Did you tell her you wanted more work than that?"

"She *knows*, Jess. I've told her *before*." Georgie's fingernails reached a crescendo and stopped abruptly. She applied another layer of dark plum lipstick using a knife as a mirror. Georgie always seemed to have a full makeup kit in the front pocket of her apron, in addition to the waiter's friend corkscrew and pens carried by everybody else. With her baroque eyelashes and frizzy auburn hair, her theatricality carried over to work; dressed in her black and whites, she was more *Rocky Horror* than *Rocky Horror*, the current show at QPAC.

"Hey, did you do the terrace?" Jess asked.

"She never *listens*, even though I've said it a *million* times," Georgie drawled. "I can always be relied on to *fill* extra shifts—"

"But, sadly, not always to work," a clipped female voice commented, and Georgie and Jess both jumped. Vivian, their boss, appeared at the marble counter, impeccably groomed as always, in a suit jacket and skirt, her silver hair shining. "Nearly done? Good. You can sign off when you come down. Don't forget to bring the trash." With that, she was gone.

The two girls collapsed in silent giggles. Then Jess said, in an unnecessarily loud voice for Vivian's benefit, in case she was still in range, "Would you mind doing the terrace, Georgie?"

"Make me, you big *suck*." Georgie held out her fists. "It's *freezing* out there."

"Fine." Jess held her fists out, too. "One . . . two . . . three!"

Georgie, ever slippery, subverted the rock-paper-scissors paradigm and fingered a *W*, telling Jess, "Whatever."

But Jess, on a lucky streak that night, trumped her with the double bird.

Georgie rolled her eyes, grabbed a tray, and flounced off. Jess threw a wet cloth after her, hitting her in the back. "Wipe down the tables, too."

"Pushy fucking Aries." In Georgie's catalog of astrological transgressions, being an Aries was second only to being a Taurus.

Jess finished the tray of glasses and slid them into the dishwasher, then sprayed the bar top and wiped it down, staring out at the city and the river, the freeway lights, haloed by the cold. She loved working at the Performing Arts Center for the view alone. And for the smells: the heady mix of the patrons' perfumes and after-shaves, ground coffee, the sweet-sour of spilled alcohol. Even the marble seemed to have a smell, or if it wasn't that, it was the air of the large, open architectural space.

By the time Georgie returned, her tray filled with the usual assortment of terrace crime scenes—cigarettes drowned in the dregs of coffee, cigarettes snuffed in cake—Jess had done every-thing else.

"Okay, we do this, and then we do the *thing*," Georgie said.

"What if Viv comes back?"

"She's already busted us. What would she come back for?"

"What if the usher comes out again?"

"Fuck the usher. He shushes me one more time? I scream."

Jess scraped food and trash into the trash can while making faces, wiped rims, and restacked everything. Georgie played on her phone. Teamwork.

"Done?" Georgie placed a tumbler on the marble counter and positioned her phone against it carefully. "Our time, okay?" she said to Jess, who nodded, an intense look in her eyes. With that, Georgie pressed the screen, and Jungle started playing.

She took her position beside Jess, and the two girls watched the screen closely, arms by their sides, bouncing on the balls of their feet to the music.

"It's good how there's the intro bit," Jess said. "So you can get prepared, you know?"

"Quite excited, actually," Georgie murmured. "I think we're get-ting better."

At thirty-four seconds, the dancers on-screen came to life, slid-ing to the side. Jess and Georgie slid with them. They kept up through the side-steps, the crossover behind, the forward heel taps—one side and then the other—the little jump across . . . but slowly they began to lag. If the film clip was the actual show, they were the live telecast. Knee tucks, attitudinal nod . . . it was all starting to run away from them.

"Push through, okay," Jess urged. "If we make it to the body wobble part, we can catch them."

"Focus on *yourself*," Georgie snapped. "Not giving in here." But in contrast to her words, she slowed. And then stopped.

Jess kept going. "Don't worry about it. Just make the jump. Hands on hips, Georgie. Come on!"

Georgie still didn't move, and Jess glanced up.

Mitch was standing near the head of the stairs. Jess stopped dancing and felt like she was falling instead—a rapid, wind-rushed, out-of-control feeling that wasn't entirely pleasant. He looked good: his hair freshly trimmed, his usual jeans and Timberlands teamed with a black denim jacket that seemed to accentuate the width of his shoulders. He also looked nervous, not seeming to know what to do with his arms: crossing them, letting them fall by his sides, rubbing at his elbow.

But then Georgie got it together and said, in a regal and well-projected voice, "Bar's *closed*, I'm afraid. Unless you were here for the *performance*?"

At that point, Mitch actually looked like he was about to be shot. Jess could only see his face, nothing else around them—the sheen of sweat on his forehead, that little crease—but it took her a moment to connect with his eyes. When she did, he opened his mouth and his jaw moved, but no sound came out.

"He looks like a Leo," Georgie said. "A malfunctioning one."

"Might be," Jess said, her eyes still locked with Mitch's.

"Challenge you for him?" Georgie asked, holding out her fists.

"Not this time," Jess told her.

Mitch made a sound like a car that wouldn't start and then managed, "I'm here to give Jess a ride home. If that's what she wants."

"Let me check for you," Georgie told him. "Jess?"

Jess nodded.

"*Careful*, kids," Georgie purred. "That's how something starts."

34.
My Car

"So you just bought it?" Jess said.

"Yeah." Mitch sounded puzzled. "I'd borrowed Mum's car to go to town and do some stuff, and I thought, *Fuck it, I need my own car*. Getting to games has been a pain in the ass. And then I remembered I had that money from working last year. So I went into the dealership and picked this."

"This" was a white Subaru Impreza. A couple years old, although it still smelled new.

"You like it?" he asked.

"I'm just glad it's not a Holden, because we're Ford people. If it was a Holden, I couldn't be seen with you in case Dad found out." Jess coughed. "Sorry, I'm just talking crap. I like it." Her palm was itching for her Zippo, but finding it in her bag would have involved a bit of rummaging, and she wasn't up to rummaging. Instead she exhaled—quietly, so Mitch wouldn't hear.

They pulled up at a set of lights, both of them staring straight ahead, and Jess started to feel like they were trapped in a jar. So far the trip had featured more hesitation than conversation. For the first time ever they seemed to be having difficulty finding things to say to each other. It was awful.

Mitch turned on the radio. Tear Council blared out, and he hastily turned it down. The lights changed and they moved off. Thank God.

Jess asked, "So how did you know what time I finished?"

"I called and put myself at the mercy of Vivian."

"That would have hurt. But how did you even know I was in Brisbane, not home?"

"Farren. She said you were going home for a week, but you'd be working for the rest of the break."

"Did she? That's interesting. She did not mention that." Jess felt a sharp burst of love for Farren, which was then wiped out by a wave of worry that it all might have been in vain. They couldn't *talk* to each other. What the fuck was that?

"Yeah, I paid you a visit after that exam. Didn't she tell you?" Jess didn't answer, overcome by another coughing fit. "How'd the exam go, anyway?"

"Um . . . better than it should have. I'll probably still fail, but at least I'll fail well. Thanks to you."

"I told you, no need for thanks."

They reached Birdwood Terrace, and Jess directed him to her aunt and uncle's house. Mitch pulled up outside. She thought he might leave the car running—always advisable in a getaway situation—but he switched it off. They pickled in silence again, and Jess started to feel like the jar was running out of air.

Mitch must have felt the same way, because he cleared his throat, but instead of speaking, he took her hand. They finally looked at each other then, both of them testing their weight on something that felt new and fragile.

"Is that okay?" he asked.

Jess nodded, dry-mouthed. "Are *you* okay?" she rasped.

Mitch shook his head. "Not without you." He took a breath. "Jess?"

"Yes?"

"Can I have your number?"

———————

"JESSIE! YOU'VE GOT a call, sweetheart. You left your phone in the kitchen. I only answered because I thought it might be your work calling." Jess surfaced slowly, fighting to open her eyes. Eventually, Heather gave up waiting, pressing Jess's phone into her hand and guiding it to her ear, then leaving.

"Hello," Jess said in a croaky voice, eyes still closed.

"It's me."

"Hello, you," Jess said with a soft sigh, snuggling farther beneath her quilt. "What time is it?"

"Just after eight."

Another sigh. "You're calling early."

"But that's good, though, right? I could have just texted, but I'm *calling*, you know?" Mitch waited. "Jess?" Jess started to breathe more deeply, her mouth going slack. "Are you there? *Jess!*"

Jess came to with a start, making snuffling noises. "Sorry, what?"

"Did you just go to sleep while you were talking to me?" Mitch demanded.

"What? No." Jess stifled a yawn.

"Seriously, do you plan this shit?" Mitch sounded incredulous.

Jess groaned. "I'm sorry. I'm just terrible at mornings. And I didn't get any sleep last night." Her voice changed, growing husky. "Kept thinking about this guy . . . drives a white Subaru . . ."

"Soft. Real men drive Fords."

Jess gave a sleepy laugh. "Hey, how come you're in Brisbane, anyway? I meant to ask you last night, but you were talking so much I couldn't get a word in."

Mitch snorted, seeming much more relaxed than he had the night before. "Rugby. I got a week off, but I can't miss more than that. I would have had to be back for training on Tuesday anyway, but I came early, because I wanted to give you a ride home."

Jess absorbed that. It was worth absorbing—it's not every day that the guy you like drives five hours to give you a ride.

"I'm staying at Adrian's until we go back." Mitch cleared his throat, suddenly all business. "Anyway, I was calling to ask you something. Can I take you to dinner tonight?"

Jess's eyebrows rose. "Dinner?"

"Something wrong with dinner? I just thought because it's Sunday you're probably not working—"

"No, I'm not working. Where would we go?"

"Aria."

"That fancy place on the river? I'd feel like I was pretending to be a grown-up."

"I thought that was what you're supposed to do. Nice restaurant, flowers."

"Hmm," Jess said.

"I want to see you," Mitch said.

Jess thought for a bit. "I've got an idea. You're not going to like it, though."

———

WHEN JESS ANSWERED the door that night, Mitch still seemed dubious, but he looked great: collared dress shirt, jeans, freshly polished RM Williams boots.

"Quick, come in out of the cold. Why aren't you wearing a sweater, you maniac?" Then, when he was inside: "You dressed for it. That's so many points right there."

"You didn't," Mitch said, giving her the onceover. She was in her lucky Black Milk Hell Yeah leggings, which clashed somewhat with her blue-checked flannel and black-and-white striped socks. The effort Jess had made was more subtle: freshly washed and blow-dried hair and an extra spray of Light Blue.

"I know, but if I'd dressed up, you would have known I'd dressed up, and I would have felt dumb," she said, pulling her hair over one shoulder.

"Thanks."

"You know what I mean. You have to make an effort because you're the guest. And, look, more points." He held a bottle of wine in his right hand, his arm wrapped around a generous bunch of tulips. "They're lovely."

"They're not for you. They're for your aunt."

Jess wrinkled her nose. "Really?"

"This is for you, though." Mitch brought his left hand out from behind his back, producing a bundle of twigs fashioned like a bouquet, wrapped in delicate paper and finished with ribbon.

"Oh! Thank you," Jess breathed, taking her bouquet and glancing at him—he seemed pleased with her reaction. "I like them so much I won't even burn them."

Mitch hugged her then—awkwardly, because he was still holding the tulips and wine. He put them down and tried again, and Jess wrapped her arms around his neck, still holding her bouquet, and it felt almost unbearably intense. It was the first time they'd touched, this time around, apart from holding hands the previous night.

They were taking it slow.

"I can feel your heart," he told her.

It's yours, she wanted to say. "I'm thin-skinned." She pulled back to look at him. "Mitch, can I ask you something? Who's feeding you this stuff? I mean, dinner, wine, flowers . . . call, don't text."

Mitch grimaced, clearly embarrassed. "Mum."

WHILE MITCH MADE small talk with Heather, Jess watched the way he looked around, casually taking in the polished wooden floors and white-paneled walls, the covered back deck with its rattan furniture and luxurious ferns, the landscaped swimming pool, the view of the city. Appreciative, but not seeing it as anything out of the ordinary.

"Was it you guys who renovated the place?" he asked Heather.

"Yes, it was." Heather used the tip of a knife to gently prod a piece of salmon. "Well, Tony handled the structural things. I was more involved on the decorating side."

"We've got a Queenslander, too. Mum spent a lot of time doing it up. Wanted it to be a restoration, not just a reno, in keeping with its history and stuff."

"Oh, I wonder if she'd approve of this then," Heather said lightly.

Mitch gave a small jolt. "No, that's not what I meant. She'd think it was great."

Mitch and Heather were different generations from the same world, that much was obvious. The thing that surprised Jess was how diffident Mitch was being, the crease ever-present on his forehead.

But then Jess's uncle Tony came bustling into the kitchen and shook Mitch's hand vigorously, looking excited in a way he'd never been with Brendan, saying, "Get you a beer, Mitch?" Tony was a tall, bald workaholic of a man, fighting a losing battle with a slow-creeping thickening brought on by his love of good eating and good drinking. He was as impatient as Heather was placid and held the strong belief that there was no social occasion that couldn't be improved by Powderfinger—that night's dinner no exception.

His arrival seemed to relax Mitch instantly.

"Come on, I'll show you around the place." As Tony led Mitch out of the kitchen, he said, "What do you think our chances are against the All Blacks? Get tickets for the game?"

"Yeah, I did, actually," said Mitch. "You?"

In their wake, Heather said to Jess, "Nice of you to find Tony a friend."

"What? Oh. I wondered why he was asking me all those questions about Mitch and rugby. Hang on, is that why he's wearing that green and gold thing?"

"It's called a Wallabies jersey, darling. Tony probably picked it out specially."

"God, how embarrassing," Jess groaned. Then she said, "I don't get the rugby thing."

"Evidently. Stir this for me, would you?"

Jess did as Heather asked, glancing at her questioningly.

Heather pretended to ignore her for a little longer, taking the warmed plates out of the oven. Then she said, casually, "Mitch seems like a nice boy. Lovely manners."

"Oh, Auntie, he's the catch of the season," Jess said in a breathy voice, but she quickly dropped the act. "You do like him, don't you?" she asked, worried.

"Of course I like him," Heather laughed, then hugged her so tightly that Jess knew she'd smell like Obsession for the rest of the night. In a perfume-off, the shoulder-padded, power-packed eighties scents always won.

Jess pulled away. "There's a 'but,' isn't there?" she asked, quietly devastated. "How can you not think he's right for me? He's perfect."

"You know that, and I know that." Heather suddenly seemed as impenetrable as the Sphinx. "He's the one who's not sure."

Jess felt a little twinge, which meant it was the truth. She gave her aunt a sidelong glare. "Well, it's not his call. If I think he is, that's all that matters."

Heather, unperturbed, poked her in the ribs. "It's probably positive. He'll try harder."

"Honestly, you have this special talent for making the simplest things sound dirty."

Heather also had a great laugh, rich and throaty. She blew Jess a kiss, as though she was going somewhere, her face oddly poignant. "I like your Mitch, very much. He's gloriously special, just like you. An unwritten book—even if he doesn't know it. But he's also completely unarmed, so be kind to him, Jessie."

"He's just nervous because he's meeting you guys."

"Hmm," Heather said, and Jess realized just where it was that she herself had picked up that particularly annoying verbal tic.

"No, truly. Mitch doesn't exactly lack confidence."

Heather's voice was calm. "That doesn't mean he might not need reassurance."

35.
Open

After dinner, Mitch and Jess helped with the dishes and then retreated downstairs to the family room. Tony did look at Jess like a puppy whose bone has been stolen, but Heather made sure he stayed put. She knew what "watch TV" meant.

"See? If we'd gone to your fancy restaurant, we wouldn't have been able to do this," Jess commented.

"What? Burn shit?" Mitch asked.

She smiled, not taking her eyes off the teepee of split wood she was constructing in the combustion stove. "Hang out."

"Why don't you use the firelighters?"

"They don't *whoosh*, no flashback—says so on the packet. So there's no point."

"Explain the pyro thing."

Jess flicked her Zippo on and held it to the balled-up newspaper at the base of her teepee. "Don't know really. I've liked fire since I was a kid. But I was always careful, like I never would have burned the house down or anything. It's more a fascination than a compulsion, if you know what I mean." Jess glanced across at him. He'd made himself comfortable on the chaise part of the large modular lounge, his hands resting behind his head. Her phone was docked in the stereo, providing mood. "At home it's just something we do, sit around in the backyard, talking around a fire. Maybe I just do it now because I get homesick."

She fanned the fire with a newspaper to give it some help. When it was burning well, she added two chunks of thicker wood, closed the door, and adjusted the flue. Then she skated over to Mitch, sliding across the wooden floor in her socks. She sat next to him on the chaise, her knees raised like his, her chin resting on her crossed arms, her body pressed against his. Touch. Why was it so comforting?

"So you survived," she said.

"They're great."

"Tony's in love with you."

"Rugby—Tony's in love with rugby."

"Mitch?" Jess said, not listening. "I'm so glad you're here—and I don't just mean at my aunt's and uncle's. I can't even believe it, really."

Mitch nodded, drawing his teeth across his bottom lip. When he spoke, his voice was rough. "Jess, stuff got in the way. I don't want to talk about it now, okay? It's nothing to do with you, though."

Jess wanted to know. Badly. Because she suspected it came back to Julian. To her, he was like a beautiful snake, hidden in the shadows, and she badly wanted to shine a light on him, see him clearly. But Mitch met her curious gaze, his face intense, his blue eyes unblinking, a wordless plea for clemency. Things between them were so fragile still. It wasn't the time. So she told him a truth instead, made herself as vulnerable as he was.

"Well, no matter what it is, I just want you to stay. Because if it's hard to believe you're here right now, it's also easy to believe you might disappear again."

She saw him swallow. "Is that for real?"

"Of course," Jess told him, and what surprised her was how much he looked like he needed to hear it. How did Heather get to be so smart, anyway? She watched his face relax and thought, *No time like the present.* "Can I ask you something? What did your mum say comes after dinner?"

Mitch's gaze slid away from hers; a form of evasion. "I think I'm supposed to ask if I can see you tomorrow. Actually, she didn't say that. That's just me," he admitted gruffly. "Can I see you tomorrow? "

Jess rubbed his knee, charmed. "I want to see you all the time, stupid. Make it your starting assumption."

"I might take you up on that," he said, sounding even more gruff, and Jess gave him a shy smile, suddenly, uncharacteristically, lost for words. "I've wasted too much time, Jess. I want to see you every day. And I don't just mean during the break; I mean when we go back, too. I know we're taking things slow, but I want to get this locked in. You know what I'm asking, don't you?"

"I think so," Jess said in a small voice.

"I want it to be us. Okay?"

"Okay," Jess said, and Mitch exhaled. "On one condition," she added.

Mitch abruptly switched to retreat. "Aw, come on. Cut me some slack."

"That's what comes after dinner," she said firmly. Mitch didn't look like he was buying, so she added, "I don't even smoke any-more, so that's good."

"Yeah? How come?" he asked, interested in spite of himself.

"Just thought it was time." Jess moved closer. "I'm waiting."

Mitch sighed with very bad grace. "You'll be sorry," he told her, taking hold of her shoulders.

"You won't be," Jess said, beneficent, calm, and very sure of herself.

Mitch lunged. His lips were slippery, and their teeth clacked together, and then his tongue was pushing its way into her mouth— or maybe it was all the way down her throat—her head forced back so roughly, so abruptly, it actually hurt her neck.

Jess pushed him away, gasping for breath. "Jesus!" She wiped a hand across her mouth. "That was the worst kiss I've ever had. You slobbered all over me! I think you broke a tooth."

"It's not like I didn't warn you," Mitch shot back, but he dropped his head.

"Oh, this is tragic." Jess stared at the ceiling. "Why? *Why*? Why is everything always the wrong way around with us?" Her head snapped back to look at Mitch, eyes narrowed like she was sighting him with a gun. "I won't accept this. This is the one time when it'll go like it's supposed to. I'll make it happen." She sniffed. "Right. Let's get started."

"Where are you going?" he asked as she got up.

"Not as far away as you'd like," Jess told him firmly, skating across to her phone. She flipped through the playlist until she found Rhye and set the song to repeat. "We need suitable music."

"That's it. I'm out of here," Mitch snapped, starting to rise.

Jess bolted back to him, sliding the last two meters and knocking him onto the chaise again. He muttered something that she chose to ignore. When she was happy with how they were positioned—facing each other like before, only now with her kneeling between his legs—she said, "Now close your eyes."

Instead, Mitch glared at her. "I refuse to do this."

"Just . . . *relax*," Jess said, with the faintest of smiles, echoing another time.

"I'm not used to relaxing," he said, following the script but forgetting to add humor.

Jess slid her hands onto his shoulders, her eyes beseeching. "Please? Because I really like you, Mitch." She blanched. "Oh God, sorry, that was so high school."

"That's all right," Mitch said, his face thoughtful. "High school was good." And just like that, he closed his eyes.

Jess blinked. Then she touched his face. "It's only going to be soft to start with, okay? So don't feel you need to do anything. Just let me do it to you. You can trust me." With that, she pressed her lips to his, like a promise.

They kissed their way through the song once. They kissed their way through it again, and by the end of the second time, something magic happened. They *kissed*, slow and deep, like they were falling into each other, a willing sort of drowning.

Finally, Jess eased off, bringing it back to soft. She gave him an ellipsis, three little kisses, as she started to pull away. But Mitch followed, leaning forward, and then farther forward, his eyes still closed. She smiled, pressing her forehead to his, watching his eyes open.

"I knew it would be good," she told him, dazed but also victorious.

SO FOR ALL that week, and the next, they saw each other every day and every night. Work shifts, rugby training and games, and sleep were the only major interruptions. Mitch drove Jess to work and picked her up. She tried to give him money for gas, but he told her not to be ridiculous—he only accepted sexual favors. She liked to sit with her feet up on the dashboard.

"Yeah, those things. I like those things," Mitch said, pulling the hem of her skirt a little higher.

"They're called stay-ups."

"You had them on the night we went swimming."

"I thought you weren't looking."

"*Of course* I was looking."

ON THE DAY that grades came out, Mitch arrived early, waking Jess up for her to discover she'd gotten a credit in microeconomics, and then reminding her, when she started to whine, that she'd thought she hadn't even passed. To celebrate, he took her to Aria for dinner, as threatened. She took him to McDonald's for lunch.

They played tennis, a match filled with epic rallies, dodgy line calls, swearing, and other displays of bad sportsmanship. They played half-court basketball, which was even worse. They went running together around Kangaroo Point.

"You know what I rate?" Mitch said. "The fact you're sporty. I never realized you could do this stuff with a girl."

Sadly, Jess, red-faced, heart rate going through the roof, keeping pace on the basis of pride alone, had no breath to spare, and had to content herself with rolling her eyes instead.

Afterward, they walked for a while to cool off, holding hands. A pair of older ladies passed them, and one of them sighed and said, "Young love is so sexy," and Jess got the giggles.

THEY TALKED A lot, about everything and nothing. Sometimes important things.

She said: "You're generous."

He said: "Is this another rich thing?"

"No, it's completely unrelated to your economic bracket. People are either generous or they're stingy. You're generous. Farren's generous. Brendan was stingy. You know, like, when a group of you are going rounds at the pub, and there's one person who always deliberately avoids their shout. I don't think Leanne's paid for a drink in her life."

"Yeah, I know what you mean. If there's just two of you, they never shout first, because they've worked out that that way they'll never come out behind. Dud's like that."

"I hate that guy."

"Why bother? He's harmless."

"Not by choice, though."

"You know what, Jersey? I'm actually not generous, at all. I'm only generous with you." A pause. "There it is. There's the smile." Another pause. "Your ears are generous."

"Oh, fuck off."

He said: "The night of the toga party—I knew you were something even then."

She said: "I knew you were lonely."

"Thought I needed your company?"

"Thought about jumping your bones."

He said: "Tell me how you broke your nose."

She said: "Never."

MAINLY, THOUGH, WHAT they did was kiss.

They shared kisses in the sun, kisses in the dark, kisses in the car, kisses on the lounge, kisses in the kitchen, kisses on the run. Salty, buttery popcorn kisses, sticky ice cream kisses, furtive kisses, brazen kisses, sexy kisses, silly face-licking kisses. They held unimaginably long and intense kissing sessions that caused them both sharp discomfort that they were too polite to mention— wind pains caused by not breathing properly. Sometimes Jess would look up to see Mitch watching her like a cat watches a bird, and he'd kiss her like his life depended on it and then ask if it was the best kiss she'd ever had, and she'd have to tell him not to be so competitive.

They kissed each other senseless. But Jess could not kiss Mitch better. Because there were kisses on the kitchen calendar, too—an old habit of Heather's—and as those crosses marched toward the return to campus, the crease of worry on Mitch's forehead returned. And sex came back on the agenda.

ON TUESDAY OF the second week, Mitch arrived for their run with a change of clothes in his car. With Heather and Tony both at work, they took a long shower together afterward, one that used up all the hot water. He went down on her; she went down on him. That night, he picked her up from work when he'd finished training, and they drove to the top of Mt. Coot-tha—erratically, because he was steering one-handed. They parked at the highest lookout, but if there was a particularly nice view of the city to be seen from up there, they certainly didn't notice it.

The next afternoon, Mitch was unusually silent as he drove Jess to work. Then he cleared his throat, and announced, in a faux casual manner: "Hey, I was just thinking, it's a shame you're not on the pill. You know, for when . . ."

"Oh my, that's subtle," Jess drawled, arching an eyebrow at him. "Why do guys always assume that women want to clean up after them?" Mitch focused on the road, red splotches blooming on his neck. After she'd enjoyed his discomfort for a while, Jess laughed and said, "I'm just messing with you. I don't like condoms, either." And she laughed again at the reproachful look he gave her.

A couple of minutes later, she said, "As a matter of fact, I'm on the pill already. But I'd like you to get tested. No offense, but you've been around, and I'm super careful. Got tested before and after Brendan."

"No, that's the thing. I'm clean. I got tested when I was at home for the year. And I haven't been with anyone since."

Jess felt something go through her so suddenly and strongly, it was like the air had been sucked from her lungs. "You haven't had sex with anyone in all that time?"

Mitch shook his head.

"Oh, come on. *You?*"

"It's the truth." Mitch frowned at the road ahead of him. "I'll swear on Julian's ashes, if that's what you want."

"Don't say that. That's horrible. I didn't like you doing it the first time."

"Well, why doubt me?" he asked, his voice sharp. "I wouldn't lie about that."

"I'm not, it's just . . ." Jess pressed her lips together, but couldn't stop herself. "That night at Lucky's—I was sure you were going to end up with Sylvie."

She saw his chest rise, fall. "She was Julian's girlfriend, Jess."

"So?"

"We were best friends. We played together." Mitch glanced across at her, his voice harsh. "Knights don't fuck their best friend's girlfriend. Knights don't fuck their teammate's girlfriend. Knights don't do that shit."

"I'm sorry, I . . ." Jess faltered, feeling helpless. "I don't know what's wrong with me. I think I'm just really jealous. But I never used to be. It's only with you."

Mitch looked at her, then back to the road, to her, to the road, as though torn. "Don't you get it? I would never, ever do something like that to you."

Jess saw the muscles working in his jaw. She touched his cheek. "Let's not talk about it anymore."

THAT NIGHT, WHEN Mitch picked her up from work, he announced, a little stiffly, "Adrian has invited you over for dinner on Friday night."

"The alien?" Jess said, looking like she'd smelled something bad. And then: "Sorry."

"No, you're not."

"Do I have to?"

"He's my brother. And last time wasn't his fault. He wasn't prepared."

"He doesn't like me."

"That's just Adrian. He doesn't like anybody."

"But that'll be our second-to-last night together, before we have to go back."

"And I've been spending all this time with you, and Adrian would like to meet you properly."

"I've got to work," Jess said sullenly. "I won't be finished until nine thirty."

"He always works late. That's perfect."

"Yeah, but what about for you? Don't you have a game Saturday?"

"Not this one. We've got a bye week." Mitch turned the corner into Birdwood Terrace. "I thought you might want to stay over, too. It'd save me having to drive you home."

Jess's mouth formed a perfect circle. "Oh," she said, nodding slowly.

36.
Ordinary

As Mitch retrieved her overnight bag from the trunk of the car, Jess stared up at the rectangle of light she was pretty sure was the kitchen window in Adrian's apartment and exhaled heavily, her breath making a cloud in the cold night air.

"Trust me, it'll be fine," Mitch said, slamming the boot closed. "He wants to get to know you. He wouldn't have invited you otherwise."

But the person who needed to be reminded of that was Adrian, Jess thought, when he answered the door seeming flustered and incredibly irritated. There'd obviously been no time to change: He was still wearing his tie, although he'd rolled up his shirtsleeves.

"Jess." Shaking her hand in his quick, chalky way. "Good to see you again. How are you?" Without waiting for a response, he snapped at Mitch, "Did you get the wine?"

At least he'd got her name right, Jess thought, feeling bleak.

"Jess brought some." Mitch dropped his keys onto the sideboard, and Jess lifted the bottle of red she was holding.

Adrian frowned. "What about the parmesan, the eggplant, tomato—"

"Oh, come on, does it really matter?"

"Well, *kind of*. Just a little bit. Given we're having veal fucking parmesan."

"All right, all right. Don't have a breakdown," Mitch muttered, picking up his keys again. Adrian disappeared without a response— unless you counted the violent banging that issued from the kitchen a moment later. Mitch rolled his eyes at Jess. "You coming?"

"No, it's okay, I'll see if I can help. Do you mind getting more wine, though?" Jess made a face. "Like a *lot* of wine."

"I'll see what I can do," Mitch said, giving her a warm look that made her feel heroic. Then he kissed her and left.

Jess entered the kitchen, putting the bottle of wine down on the bench. It started jumping immediately because Adrian had a meat mallet and was banging the crap out of several pieces of veal, his tie flung over his shoulder. He didn't show any signs of having noticed her, so she retreated to the lounge room and rummaged around in her bag.

"Here!" she shouted, nudging his shoulder when she returned. Adrian stopped, looking down at what she was offering him: her work apron. "So your shirt doesn't get stained."

"Thanks," he said stiffly, letting the mallet clatter onto the bench. He tied the apron strings with quick, jerky movements, reminding Jess of an enraged stick figure. "I thought you'd gone with Mitch."

"I figured you might need some help. And before I forget—this is for you. I know people usually bring flowers when they come to dinner, but I didn't think you'd be into that, so . . ." Jess held up the LP she'd purchased from Rocking Horse Records on her break earlier that day. 'The Preatures. I love their stuff. Isabella Manfredi is the only woman I'd turn for. Seriously. Anyway, I noticed you didn't have them." She gave a nervous laugh. "That makes it sound like I was going through your stuff, but really I only went through your collection. Um, I mean . . ." Adrian didn't seem to be listening so much as waiting for her to finish. "I'm talking too much, aren't I?"

"Thank you for that," Adrian said without even looking at the LP. "Perhaps you could put it on—seeing as you already know where everything is. I haven't had time to do anything about music yet. I'm a little behind, as you can see. Had to rush here straight from work."

Adrian said this with such hostility that Jess blinked, taken aback. "Maybe we should have done this another time."

He used his forearm to wipe his dark floppy fringe back from his face—his hands were covered in splatters of veal. "Well, this is the only night that suited you, apparently, so you'll just have to put up with me playing catch-up."

Jess stared at him in horror, finally realizing what was going on. "Oh God, I'm so sorry. Mitch told me . . . You know what? Don't worry about dinner. When he comes back, I'll just go. I feel awful."

Adrian shrugged. "Up to you. You're here now."

"Actually, no. *You* are making me feel awful," Jess said, jabbing a finger at Adrian, whose mouth snapped shut in the face of the sudden transition. "And for something that's not even my fault. Mitch said you'd invited me over. He insisted I come. But he must have told you that I'd invited myself." Jess shook her head. "I'm going to kill him. Do you really think I'd volunteer? When you were so welcoming the last time we met?"

Adrian hadn't moved, the freckles on his pale skin standing out in the kitchen's LED lighting. He gave a nervous whinny of a laugh, his nostrils flaring.

Jess held out her hand. "I want my apron back. I need it for work. You can keep the wine, though. Shove it up your ass, for all I care. I'll wait downstairs."

"You're not going. Don't be silly. Look, I wouldn't normally have been so rude, but it's been a shit of a week at work, and . . ." Adrian shook her outstretched hand. "Great to see you, Jess. Glad you could come."

She snatched her hand back. "I don't want to touch that! You've got dead calf all over it. You're supposed to cover the meat with plastic wrap before you pound it."

"See?" Adrian said, a smile tugging at the corner of his mouth, just for that moment reminding her of Mitch. "If you hadn't come, I wouldn't have learned that."

"It's not funny. I feel like crying—"

"Please don't. Mitch will kill me."

"—I was so nervous about coming here, and it's been even worse than I expected. Why would he do that to me?"

"I repeat—*please* don't cry. Look, I know my brother better than you do, and—"

"What? We're competing now?" Jess asked, incredulous. "God, you really are brothers."

"My point is," Adrian said, speaking clearly and calmly—like a lawyer, in fact, "Mitch has got everything he's wanted his whole life. So he does whatever he wants, when he wants, because he'll probably get away with it. He wants us to get on? Great, he'll just throw us together and hope for the best. He's incredibly immature, in a lot of ways."

"That's something, coming from you, Mr. Courtesy," Jess snapped. "I think he's lovely."

Adrian glanced down at the floor for a second while he stifled a smile. "Well. Let me kick things off by apologizing for last time we met."

"We weren't having sex, by the way. Just for the record. We were cuddling."

"Ah . . . fine. Good. Great!" Adrian cleared his throat. "The thing is, you're the first girl Mitch has ever brought here, so it was unexpected, that's all. I've never met any of the girls he's been with—and there have been a few. You're unique."

"If that oxymoron is meant to be a compliment, then it's back-handed," Jess said, distinctly unimpressed. Adrian was impressed, though: His eyebrows twitched. "All right then, I'll stay," she told him, grim-faced. She grabbed the bottle of wine and twisted the cap sharply, like an action hero breaking someone's neck. Adrian flinched. "But I'm going to require a very big glass of wine. I bought it, so I'm allowed to have some. I don't care what you say."

"What if I said I'd like a very big glass of wine, too?" Adrian asked.

Jess looked him up and down and then sniffed. "I'd say you need it."

LATER, WHEN THEY were midway through their second round of very-big-glasses of wine, and Adrian was crumbing the veal, and Jess was rinsing lettuce for the salad, and The Preatures were play-ing, Jess said, "Adrian, you should do something with this place. I mean, you're a single guy and you've got this great pad. You should make it more . . . cool."

"But I am not cool, Jess. That's Mitch's department. I'm ordinary."

"Oh yes," Jess said, taking a large sip of wine. "Mitch is Mr. Cool, isn't he?" And they both snickered. Then they snickered again because there was something funny about being in cahoots. Neither of them had eaten for hours, so the wine was doing its job quickly.

"You're not ordinary, at all," Jess told him, and he made a face at her. "Compliment! But I also can't believe you two are brothers."

"Thanks," Adrian said—not in response to what she'd said, but because she was holding up his wine glass. His hands were covered in egg wash, flour, and crumbs. "I take after our mother: no sport-ing ability, no strut, and I burn if left in the sun for five minutes."

"What's your mum do?"

"She used to be in marketing, but she hated it. Too much mar-keting. When she met Dad she was working for a pharmaceuticals company. Now, she's happy managing—all of us."

"So Mitch is like your dad?"

Adrian sipped, seeming to think it over. "Yes and no. He's gone a lot further with rugby than Dad ever did. And Mitch not getting into med school was probably a good thing—Dad would agree. Rocked little bro's world, though. First time he ever failed at anything."

"I thought your dad might have leaned on him," Jess said.

Adrian shook his head. "You don't know our father."

"What's he like?"

"Dad? Dad's just . . . decent. He's a good man. Much nicer than his sons. You'd like *him*."

Jess rewarded him with a smile. "So where did it all go wrong?"

"Our mother," Adrian said, nodding. "Spoils us rotten. Loved having Bub back with her for a year, I can tell you."

Jess's eyes widened. "She does not call him Bub."

Adrian winked. "You didn't hear it from me."

"If I told my parents I was taking a year off, they'd go ballistic."

Adrian frowned at her. "No, Mum and Dad made him take it. They wanted to keep an eye on him. We were worried he'd do some-thing stupid. Final. You know, after Julian."

"Oh my God." Jess pressed a fist to her chest. "Adrian."

Adrian looked as if he was sorry—not only for shocking her but for saying too much. "Anyway, that's all a while ago now." He turned away, washing his hands more thoroughly than necessary. "Mitch had a lot of time to think in that year, and he hasn't been the same since. I mean that in a good way. Look, it's a terrible thing to say, but Julian's death might have been the best thing that could have happened to Mitch. If he ever strikes you as being an arrogant little shit now, you should have seen him back then."

Jess, though, wasn't diverted. "Adrian? Can you tell me what happened?"

"You know most of it, don't you?" Adrian asked briskly, drying his hands with a paper towel. "What's Mitch told you?"

Seconds dripped away. "Why? How many versions are there?" Jess asked, and Adrian paused for a moment but wouldn't look at her. "I mean, was Mitch even at the party that night? I thought he must have been, but then, what would I know? The only reason I know anything at all is because I looked it up online. I'm scared to bring it up with him, because I know he'll get upset, and I always seem to say the wrong thing, so I always end up feeling like I should just—"

"Back off," Adrian finished for her, but he was warning her, too, even though there was sympathy in his brown eyes. "I can understand it must be frustrating, Jess, but it's up to Mitch to fill you in—if he wants to. Not me."

Jess scowled. "Do you even know?"

"When something like that happens, you're there for each other. I am his brother. Anyway, I was home for break, too. Didn't go to the party, though. Too old."

"So Mitch *was* at that party."

"Yes, he was there."

"And does he feel he should have stopped Julian from driving? Is that it?"

"He feels very responsible for what happened."

Jess stared at him. "Are you a lawyer or a politician? Can you please answer my question?"

Adrian just cut her off with, "Jess." Said kindly, but also firmly.

They fell silent. Jess poured the rest of the wine into their glasses. Adrian began to fry the veal in batches. Jess turned her attention to chopping cucumber and capsicum for the salad. She took a sip of wine, glanced sideways at Adrian. "What was Julian like then? Can you tell me that?"

"I didn't like him," Adrian said, with no malice but also no hesitation. "He didn't bring out the best in Mitch, either. But they'd known each other for a long time, and there was the whole rugby side of it, too. You know Mitch plays fly-half? Well, Julian played scrum-half." He noticed Jess's blank look. "You have zero idea, don't you?"

"Less than zero. Like, negative one hundred."

"They're the two most tactical positions on the team. Together, they control the game—when it works. And it worked with Mitch and Julian. They'd played with each other for a long time. So it was a pretty close relationship. Close, but also competitive and a bit fucked up."

Adrian drained his wine glass, picked up the empty bottle, and then put it down again. "But now," he said, grinning at her suddenly, "Mitch has you." Jess dropped her gaze, chopping the capsicum more violently than was necessary. "You do know he's never had a girlfriend before, right?" Adrian continued, a teasing note in his voice.

"No wonder, if this is how you were going to carry on."

"Where is he, anyway? We need more wine. Actually, hang on, I think Dad left some here. You look—it's in that bottom cupboard on your right."

Jess dug around and found two bottles. "Shiraz, or cab sav?"

"Fuck it, let's have both. Knowing him it'll be the good stuff," Adrian said, suddenly looking quite rakish.

"Maybe we *can* be friends," Jess told him with a smile. She opened the shiraz, inhaled the wine's scent—it was the good stuff—then refilled their glasses. "I think you're burning that veal, by the way."

"Let it burn," Adrian said grandly, holding up his glass. "Here's to you, Jess Gordon. I take back what I said before, about Mitch and his year off—I think *you* might be the best thing that's ever happened to him. And you are welcome here anytime."

"Thank you," Jess said, touched to the point of it being painful. "Now, stop it." They clinked, and she gulped her wine.

Adrian started to turn the veal, pushing his fringe back again with his arm. "You're a bad influence. He's been acting like a lovesick dickhead."

"Here, let me fix that for you," Jess said, wanting to distract him because she was starting to feel disloyal to Mitch. She loosened Adrian's tie and then repositioned it as a headband. "Better?"

"Brilliant. I should wear it like that to work," Adrian said, checking his reflection in the oven door. Then he gave a start, saying, "Shit!" And he turned the oven on. "Are we a brilliant team in the kitchen or what?"

Jess laughed, and they clinked glasses again, drank some more.

Adrian gave her a sharky grin, starting to look a tad inebriated, not least because his teeth stained easily. "But back to you—the bad influence. Do you know what I caught him doing the other day?" Jess shook her head warily, knowing something good was coming by the way his eyebrows twitched. "Well, I came home early for once. And you must have been working, because he was home. He was in the shower, right? So he didn't hear me come in—"

"This isn't going to be rude, is it?" Jess interrupted.

"No, no," Adrian said with a dismissive wave of his hand. "He had music on. You know Rhye? The guy that sounds like a girl?"

"I love Rhye!" Jess cried, and then blinked as she made the connection. "Oh wow, that's actually really romantic."

"Yeah, but, listen, listen—" Adrian stopped for a second, overcome by his whinny laugh. "Mitch was *singing along*."

Jess's eyes widened. *"No."*

"Oh yes," Adrian breathed, his eyes as wide as hers. "And Mitch can't sing for shit—sounds like a baby seal being clubbed to death—but believe me, he was putting everything into it. *Ooooh! Aaaah!*" Adrian lost it then, dragging Jess along with him for a while.

"But he's Mr. Cool!" she gasped. "Mr. Cool does not do such things."

"Oh fuck, oh fuck." Adrian breathed rapidly, his face scrunched up as if he was in pain. He looked like he was giving birth. "But it gets better. Because then he just stopped, went quiet, and I got a bit worried—"

"You said this wouldn't be rude!"

"No, no, stay with me. So I crept up to the bathroom door . . ." As Adrian said it, he leaned toward her, looking quite maniacal now, eyes too bright, teeth red.

"And?" Jess breathed, leaning toward him.

"And I saw . . ."

"What?"

"Mitch kissing his own hand."

"The corner place was closed, so I had to go to Ascot."

Adrian and Jess froze, staring at each other with horrified faces, then Adrian launched into another round of rapid breathing, and Jess viciously pinched her own skin.

"And they only had one person on the bloody registers because they must think people like standing around in supermarkets all night long."

Mitch arrived in the kitchen, thumping his bag of shopping down on the bench and placing a second bag down more gently. The bottles inside clinked.

"This veal parmesan better be—" he stopped short, taking in the mess the kitchen was in, the empty wine bottle on the bench, the two bottles next in line, Adrian and Jess huddled together near the oven, staring back at him with guilty looks on their faces, wide-eyed, obviously a bit tipsy, Adrian wearing his tie as a headband. . . .

And Adrian, unable to help himself, snickered.

Mitch frowned at his watch and then at Jess. "Seriously, you've only been here for fifty minutes."

37.
Island

Mitch entered the kitchen holding a stack of dirty dishes and cutlery. "That's all of it," he announced, sliding it onto the bench beside Adrian, who appeared to either be taking part in a washing-up speed trial or just splashing water on the floor. Mitch frowned at him for a second and then came to stand behind Jess, his hands closing on her hips. He rested his chin on her shoulder while he watched her wipe and polish a wine glass. Then he pressed his lips to her ear and murmured, "I'm going for a shower."

Jess, getting a wave of goose bumps, gave an involuntary shiver. "Okay."

He waited, and eventually she looked at him, and when she did she flushed.

"And . . . do you want to come with me?" he asked, with a smile and the flicker of a frown.

"Mitch." Jess, embarrassed, glanced pointedly at Adrian, who didn't show any signs of having heard them as he sloshed a long-stemmed and expensive-looking wine glass around in the sink. He was dancing on the spot in a special, jerky, stick-figure kind of way—Du Tonc was playing so loudly that people three blocks away could dance to it, too, if they were so inclined at one in the morning.

"No. He can't come," Mitch told her firmly.

Jess laughed, but her gaze slid away from his, focusing again on the glass she was wiping. "I should help clean up. We can't just leave it all to him."

"We can. He fully deserves it," Mitch said dryly.

"I won't be long," she assured him. "You go."

"Do you want me to take your bag to the room?"

"No, it's okay. I'll get it."

Mitch still didn't move, and eventually she glanced at him again. He looked as if he wanted to say something more, but then he just kissed her on the shoulder and left. A moment later the music's volume dropped dramatically. It brought Adrian out of his inebriated haze.

"Nobody likes a spoilsport, Mitchell," he called, his voice a mock whine. "We're the fun ones. You're the un-fun."

Jess grinned, just for a second feeling some residual fizz from their night. She was quiet until she heard the bathroom door close, placing the clean glass on the bench beside the collection of items she'd already wiped. Then she said, shaking her head, "I cannot *believe* you played Rhye."

Adrian gave a start, as though he hadn't realized she was still there. He looked at her, tilting his head back to see her, apparently having some trouble keeping his eyelids up, and retaliated with: "I cannot *believe* you sang along."

She rescued the wine glass from his hands. "Well, you shouldn't have kissed your hand," she scolded. "That was terrible."

"You shouldn't have laughed."

"Poor Mitch."

"Fuck, don't worry about it," Adrian slurred with an unconcerned wave of his hand, flinging suds everywhere. "He secretly loves it when people give it to him. Anyway, he wanted us to get along. He should be glad."

"I think he is glad," Jess said with a smile. But her smile faded quickly, replaced by the breathless anxiety that had started as soon as they'd begun to clear the table. Everything had been amazing all night, and then, for Jess, the weight of the occasion suddenly arrived and steamrolled her. She'd stopped drinking not long after Mitch had arrived back with supplies, but now she almost wished she hadn't.

Adrian's head might have been drooping—lower, lower, lower—but he certainly seemed impervious to doubt and worry. He frowned down at the sink, a toy with flat batteries. Then he plunged his hand into the water and pulled out the plug. "Leave this. We'll do it in the morning." He was still wearing her apron, and he wiped his hands on it. Then he grabbed the open bottle of wine on the bench by the neck. "I've got a date with the couch and Billy Bragg."

"Who's Billy Bragg?"

Adrian froze, then looked at her out of the corner of his eye. "You're hurting me, Jess. I thought we had something. Billy Bragg. Singer. Socialist. Music best enjoyed with a bottle of expensive red, courtesy of my father, the dick doctor."

"Is that irony?" Jess asked, briefly distracted.

"Probably. Come on, you. Enough man time. You've got a boy waiting." With that, Adrian lurched out of the kitchen.

Jess stared after him, all too aware that Mitch was waiting for her, paralyzed by the thought, actually. She turned back to the sink, ran more hot water, feeling like a coward and a failure. Only when she'd finished the pile of dishes, leaving them to drain in the rack, did she venture out of the kitchen. By then, the bathroom door was open, a pool of golden light spilling out of Mitch's room. Adrian had fallen asleep and was snoring soundly, the empty bottle of wine nestled against his chest like a baby. Jess turned off the music, set the heater to low, and left one lamp burning in case he woke later and decided to go to bed. She picked up her bag, feeling her legs turn to water. And then, losing her nerve, she put off the inevitable by deciding to take a shower, too.

When she emerged, a towel wrapped around her, she was greeted by a heavy stillness. Mitch's bedroom was in darkness, the doorway gaping like a cavity in the white wall of the hall. Jess took a slow breath, exhaled it on an unspoken prayer, but for what, she couldn't say—some kind of mercy?—then slipped inside, placing her bag on the floor and closing the door softly behind her.

It took a moment for her eyes to adjust. The curtains were open, the room washed with the otherworldly light of a full moon. Jess could see Mitch's shape under the covers, the gleam of his blond hair, but not the expression on his face. He was lying on his back, one arm tucked under his head. For an odd moment, they just looked at each other. At least, Jess assumed he was looking at her. Maybe his eyes were closed.

"Mitch?"

"You okay?"

"Yeah, I . . . I thought maybe you were asleep." She dropped her towel and climbed onto the bed, sliding under the covers, shivering with cold and nerves. Mitch lifted his arm so she could tuck into him, her head resting on his shoulder, and then hugged her tightly. His chest was bare, but he wasn't, as she'd initially thought, naked: He was wearing a pair of track pants. They were silent for a little while, Jess rubbing her cold feet against his warm ones. That was another thing that Mitch was generous with: his warmth.

"I was starting to feel like you were avoiding me," he said.

"I'm just . . ." Jess couldn't even finish the sentence. Her skin felt stretched; her heart beating too hard beneath it. Surely he could feel it? The words came out in a rush: "I'm so nervous about this, Mitch. Honestly. I'm dying I'm so nervous."

He shifted so he could look at her, and Jess responded very maturely—burying her face in his chest. "What are you nervous about?" he asked.

"You know," Jess said, her words muffled.

She felt his chest rise, fall. Then he kissed her head. "We don't have to do anything," he told her, his voice low, reassuring. Jess made a noise like a laugh. "We don't. It doesn't matter. We said we were taking things slow. We've never spent a whole night together before. So that's still pretty good."

"But we set it all up."

"Maybe we shouldn't have. Too much pressure." Mitch paused and then added, "I'm nervous, too, you know."

Jess, feeling a little better, a little braver, raised her head to look at him—in the moonlight, close up, their faces were visible to each other, but smudged, softened by shadow. So much easier that way. "What are you nervous about? You've had heaps of sex."

He shook his head, and she heard the rasp of his hair on the pillow. "Not lately."

"Don't say that. Say something nice."

"Okay. Not like this, then."

"What's that mean?"

There was thin, reverberating silence, the sort of delicately plucked note that isn't heard, but felt in the heart.

"With my girlfriend."

"Oh." Jess smiled at Mitch, her eyes burning, just a little. "That's really lovely. I like you calling me that."

"I mean it."

"I know you do." She kissed his lips softly and studied him some more. Then she took a noisy breath, released it, and when she spoke, her voice was much less subdued: "I'm sorry for wrecking everything. I have, haven't I? We can't do it now."

"Might be a bit hard to make it seem spontaneous," Mitch commented, and she giggled. "Look, let's just cuddle. Wake up together."

"Okay," Jess told him, snuggling into him again, feeling weak—not with relief, more from the release of tension. She started to rub her feet against his once more, marveling that even that simple thing could feel so good. There was something hypnotic about doing it, relaxing. Time drifted, and there was only that sound, the soft susurration of skin on skin. But then Jess grew aware that Mitch's breathing was deeper, slower, and she stopped rubbing abruptly.

He's fallen asleep, she thought. *Unbelievable. He's actually fallen asleep.*

Bastard.

She made a noise in the back of her throat, kicking her legs and rolling on top of him in a quick flick of movement, but she didn't get a chance to speak. Because Mitch reached for her, one hand pressed to the back of her head, rising up, bringing his mouth to hers. And he kissed her desperately, with more passion than she'd ever been kissed with in her life. She kissed him back with the same lack of restraint, losing herself, and she knew then he hadn't been going to sleep at all; he'd been waiting and wanting in the dark. But it wasn't a conscious thought, more a feeling, because that kiss left no room for thinking—it took everything. It went on and on and on, and Jess never wanted to break it, never wanted to stop, her whole body tingling, drunk with feeling, and if Mitch had asked her then, she could have told him honestly it was the best kiss she'd ever had.

And then Mitch was rolling her off him, his hand still cupping her head, keeping the kiss going even as he attempted to take off his track pants one-handed. There was the snap of elastic, and Jess reached for his waistband, suddenly impatient, and he broke away from her, sliding his pants off quickly and kicking them away. He pulled her back on top of him, except that as he did it, she was trying to pull him on top of her, so that for a moment they were nearly wrestling, and they laughed. He succeeded, though, and then, suddenly, they were still.

Jess looked down at his face, saw he felt it, too. Reverence. The naked length of her pressed against the naked length of him. She could feel his erection on her inner thigh, and that seemed beautiful, natural, and made her feel even more close to him.

"Stay there," he whispered, and she knew what he meant.

She widened her legs, straddling him now, reaching down to guide things, leaning forward at the same time so her lips met his again as he started to push inside her, not kissing now, just pressed there, both of them concentrating on the other pressure. He dipped his hips slightly and then pushed again, small movements, trying to get her to ease for him. Until finally, she moved, bearing down, and when she did, Mitch said her name in a shot of breath, and she gasped, shocked by it, too. The feeling of it was so intense, so much more than pleasure.

Then slowly, surely, they began to find a rhythm together.

———

AFTERWARD, FOR A long stretch of time, they didn't speak at all. Jess lay motionless on top of him, her head turned to the side, feeling the heat trapped in his skin, feeling his lungs working, slowing as he recovered, while he ran his hands over her back in lazy sweeps. Eventually, though, Mitch took a deep breath and exhaled it again, whispering, "Jessie, Jessie, Jessie," and she raised herself up so they could smile at each other.

Because after two weeks and five months, they had not just had sex for the first time: They had made love. And it had been perfect.

38.
My Delirium

Jess and Mitch finally emerged late the next morning, their bodies glowing pink and still steaming from a shower together, their eyes smudged by shadows but painfully bright—that special look shared by new mothers and new lovers, after tender, sleepless nights.

Adrian, by contrast, seemed a little wilted. He was slumped at the dining table, his chin propped on his hand, still in what he'd been wearing the night before, including Jess's apron, something orange fizzing in the glass on the table in front of him, a pair of sunglasses shielding his eyes. The window framed a ruthlessly beautiful winter's day. Hell for the hungover. Heaven if you were in love.

"Is he dead?" Jess asked.

"Could be," said Mitch.

But as they passed him, Adrian's lips moved. "Morning." And then, when they were in the kitchen and out of sight, continued in an undertone: "Rabbits."

Mitch, about to kiss Jess on the forehead, smiled.

Jess snickered.

———————

MITCH DROVE JESS to work that afternoon, heading there straight from Hamilton. The sun was setting, the sky bruised indigo and blushing crimson, and it was already dark enough for the lights of the city to be reflected in the river. Ladyhawke came on the radio, and Jess turned it up. They were against the traffic, the sunroof was open, even though it was winter; they were free.

"I should be there by ten thirty, hopefully," Mitch told her. "Eleven at the latest. Just depends on how long it takes to get out of the parking lot when the game's finished."

The Wallabies were playing the All Blacks that night at Suncorp Stadium. Jess was on top of all that, she just didn't know who the All Blacks were.

"No worries," she said. "Just text when you're close. I'll call Heather on my break, tell her I'm not coming home tonight."

"Actually, I said I'd meet up with Tony for a drink before kick-off." Mitch glanced across at Jess. "What are you smiling about?"

"I don't know. It just makes me happy that you know my uncle and aunt, and I know your brother. Is Adrian going to meet you there?"

"I'm picking him up after I drop you off."

Jess wrinkled her nose. "I can't believe he went into work on a Saturday."

"He was giving us a little privacy."

The way Mitch looked at her then, drawing his teeth across his bottom lip . . . Jess flushed. Mitch focused on the road again, well aware he'd made her spark just by looking at her. And she knew that he, like her, was thinking about the fact they'd be in the same bed again that night—the things they might do to each other. It was almost too heady to bear. She reached through the sunroof, letting cold air rush through her fingers.

"I don't want to go back tomorrow, Jess," Mitch said abruptly.

"Let's keep driving then. Run away to the Gold Coast and be beach bums."

"Be serious."

"I can't be serious! I'm too happy. Aren't you happy?"

After a moment, Mitch nodded, his face softening. He glanced across at her. "It's not going to change anything, is it? I can still see you all the time?"

Jess smiled at him, happy he'd voiced it, because she'd been a little worried about what going back meant for the two of them, too. "Of course." Her smile faded. "The only thing is . . . Well, I don't really feel comfortable about staying over at Knights. I don't know if I ever will."

Mitch frowned, focusing on the road again. "God, I wouldn't put you through that. I'll come to you." They were silent until they stopped at the Ballow Street lights, and then he said, "Don't go to the RE tomorrow, Jessie. I'm not going to make a habit of asking you to change your plans for me, but just this once, be with me instead. I don't want to share you with other people yet."

Jess beamed at him. "Of course," she said again.

JESS SCUFFED HER way through the reading room, her feet jammed into high-tops that she hadn't bothered to lace, twisting hair that she hadn't bothered to brush into a knot on top of her head and securing it with a pen, buttoning her flannel. The only good thing about being so late to lunch was that she wouldn't have to stand in line. She reached the courtyard, glancing through the dining room's plate glass windows, wondering why Allie and Leanne hadn't bothered to wait for her. They'd banged on her door not long after Mitch had left, running late for his first lecture.

Inside the service area, she grabbed a tray, greeted enthusiastically by the kitchen staff, chatting to them about how her break had been. Then she helped herself to a large slice of lasagna, suddenly ravenous—she'd missed breakfast thanks to Mitch, although the chance of making breakfast was a fifty-fifty proposition for Jess on the best of days. She made her way to the salad bar, piling food onto her plate, moving in a dreamy way, not so hungry now, thinking of him, a little smile playing around her lips. She glanced around the tables, still unable to see Allie or Leanne. Then she spotted a couple of freshman girls who'd signed up for the Unity basketball team and decided on them instead. At the same time, one of them saw her and nudged her companion, nodding in Jess's direction.

Jess froze, realizing that of the hundred or so people who remained in the dining room, there wasn't one who wasn't looking at her. She blinked, not seeing a single friendly face. They were eyeing her as though she was a giant slug come to join them for lunch.

A slow hand clapping started behind her, and she turned to see Leanne making her way inside from the outdoor section.

"Ladies and gentlemen, there can only be one. I present to you Unity's real Knight Rider."

At that, everybody started applauding, and Jess realized it had been a setup. She shot Leanne a look. When the applause continued, along with whistles and shouted obscenities, she put down her tray and bowed to the room.

"Just thought it was better out in the open," Leanne told her.

"You're probably right," Jess agreed, bowing once more.

———

THE FOLLOWING MONDAY night, the Unity girls' basketball team played their first game of the season. Midway through the second quarter, playing man-on-man defense, Jess snatched the ball cleanly from her opponent, dribbled past her, and sent a long pass to Farren, who missed it completely because she was gazing in the other direction.

"What the fuck are you doing?" bawled Jess, because they were already sixteen points down, and manners and civility had fled the court long ago.

Farren pointed at Mitch, recently arrived and trying to pass undetected, hovering behind the paltry group of Unity supporters, and her face crumpled with mirth.

"Farren!" Jess roared, because the other team wasn't waiting for her to get it together. They seized the moment and scored. Jess seized the moment and then received a caution for barging—it should have been a foul, but she'd done it to her own teammate.

And Farren, lying prone because Jess had knocked her over and she was laughing too hard to get up, raised her head long enough to wheeze: "Oh my God, he's being supportive. That's hilarious!"

39.
Love Is to Die

The wake-up call, when it finally arrived for Jess, was both literal and ugly. Five weeks into the semester she was jerked out of sleep by an urgent knocking, the sound unbearably insistent—a woodpecker hammering at her sleep-fogged brain. She blinked into focus, looking around groggily for clues as to what might be going on. She was in her bed at college, as normal, but the bed itself seemed unusually spacious. Mitch was gone. She checked her phone: Tuesday, 7:46 a.m. He had a lecture at nine. He usually took a shower around now, so maybe he'd locked himself out by accident.

As another round of knocking started, Jess squinted at the door, noting it was unlocked. Then she realized it was probably one of her floormates; they no longer just barged into her room now that Mitch was in the picture. "It's open," she called in a hoarse voice, turning over and burrowing into her pillow. "Take whatever you want," she added as the door opened, "but do it quietly."

"Morning, Miss Gordon," a male voice said. Jess's eyelids flicked open, and she stared at the bricks in front of her, but other than that she couldn't move. "I'm looking for a friend of mine. You know him? Goes by the name of Killer—at least, he used to. Doesn't like being called that anymore. You haven't seen him around, by any chance? He's been disappearing every night like a vampire, and we've been kind of curious about whose blood he's been sucking."

Jess sat up, clutching her quilt to her chest, feeling vulnerable for many reasons, not only because she was naked beneath it. Dud stood just inside the door, wearing a navy hoodie and jeans, a backpack slung over one shoulder, his face amiable beneath his curly hair. But his eyes hadn't changed, nor had the insect that lived behind them.

Dud stepped closer, squatting down to peer at a pile of clothes like a tracker studying spoor: jeans, T-shirt, an old rugby jersey . . . He pulled a pen from his back pocket and used it to lift Mitch's black trunks.

"Well, he might not be here now, but he's been here." As Dud said this, he grinned up at Jess like they were friends, inviting her to play along.

And the terrible thing was, Jess did. She forced a smile, although it was difficult, her face doughy and unresponsive, because at the back of her mind was the irrational thought that this guy was from Mitch's circle, so she couldn't embarrass herself. If she screamed at this creep, told him to get out of her room, he'd report back to the others: *Completely unhinged. Acted like I was going to rape her or something.* And she was just hopeful enough to think that if she did this thing, pretended his being in her room wasn't entirely unreasonable, she'd win Dud over. Like a kid trying to convert a bully. Maybe he was there in some kind of lame attempt to bridge things with her. There was always that little testing period at the start between you and your new boyfriend's friends, some careful circling, right?

Dud, encouraged by her smile, became grandiose. "What have you done with him?" he mock scolded.

"He's in the shower."

"What? Here?" Dud asked, temporarily jolted. "In a girls' bathroom?"

Jess gave him a laugh. Not a real one, but a close imitation. "Well, yeah, but . . . Bathrooms don't really have a gender at Unity."

"Fucking classic. Turn up at Unity, and he's off showering in the girls' bathroom." The way Dud said it, you would have thought Mitch was in there with a harem. Jess realized that he wasn't saying these things to her, but rather rehearsing, playing to an invisible audience: the guys he intended to tell this to later. And she felt sick.

Dud dropped Mitch's trunks. "So . . . how long's this thing been going on?"

Mitch hadn't told them about her.

When she didn't answer, Dud seemed to read it as some kind of shameful admission, his voice taking on a nasty edge of triumph. "All right, Killer."

He straightened, glancing around the rest of the room, talking once again to those invisible others. "I knew something was going on, knew he had some dirty little secret—acting all cagey. But fuck if he didn't walk right through the Unity gate. Knew the code. Straight up the stairs, easy as."

"Get out."

Dud acted as if he hadn't heard, stepping closer to the desk, peering at one of the framed photos on the shelf above it. The one of Jess sitting on Mitch's lap at Heather and Tony's place, his arms around her, their smiles wide, faces relaxed. Heather had taken the shot, and she'd printed it out for Jess on the last day of the break, just before driving her back to Unity. As Dud studied it, he rubbed a hand over his grin, which stayed fixed in place—a mask.

"I said, get out," Jess told him, panicked now, because for

some reason him looking at that photo made her feel even more vulnerable than him casting her in the role of conquest.

But Dud's gaze had dropped to her trash can. For a moment he just stood over it, staring down at the mound of balled-up tissues inside. Then he glanced at Jess, his eyes too hard, too bright. Knowing. "All right, Killer," he repeated.

He left then, as quietly and carefully as a thief—made it a joke even, tiptoeing out of the room. He didn't bother closing the door behind him. It was because of that, Jess heard them.

"Here he is now. How are you, big man?"

"Jesus, Dud. What are you doing here?" Mitch sounded shocked.

"Followed you last night." Dud sounded absurdly proud of himself. "Knew something must have been going on." His voice rose, becoming excitable. "How long have you been giving it to her? Since the fucking toga party, I bet."

"Dud, look—" Mitch dropped his voice, his tone conspiratorial, man to man: "I'm going to have to ask you for a favor. Keep it on the down low for now, all right?"

"Yeah, all right." Dud sounded surprised, but flattered, too. "Roger that, Killer. What's the big . . ." Jess didn't catch the rest, because their voices faded. As if Mitch was showing him out.

———

THAT NIGHT, UNUSUAL for a Tuesday, Jess had to work—filling in for Georgie, who had something to do. As she slid into the Subaru afterward, Mitch stared at her expectantly, waiting for the kiss that was her normal greeting when he picked her up. When it didn't come, his face hardened, a match for Jess's expression. "We went into overtime," he said, pulling away from the curb. He was still in his training gear, his hair spiked with dried sweat. "Did you get my text?"

"Yes."

"Were you waiting long?"

"No."

"How was work?"

"Good."

"I left as soon as I could." Mitch reached across, taking hold of Jess's hand and placing it on his thigh—something she also usually did.

She pulled her hand away. "I told you, I was happy getting the bus."

"I didn't want you getting the bus," he said, grabbing her hand again. She tried to wrestle it free, but he tightened his grip, swerving the car abruptly out of traffic and pulling up at a bus stop. He turned toward her, and they scowled at each other, continuing the tug of war, Jess resisting, Mitch's strength winning, so that he slowly pulled her palm toward his thigh.

A sharp blast from a horn made Jess jump. She glanced back. "There's a bus waiting. You've got to move."

"Not until you put your hand on my leg."

Jess glared at him a moment longer and then acquiesced, gripping his thigh as hard as she could, digging her fingernails in. "Happy?" she asked.

"Ecstatic," Mitch told her, flicking on his indicator. He pulled out into the flow of traffic.

"You know this is not about you being late," Jess said, turning toward him.

"What's it about then?" he asked, his eyes on the road.

"Oh, come on. It's about this morning."

"We've talked about that." Mitch turned up the radio and Warpaint flooded the car.

Jess turned it down again. "That was hardly a resolution. You telling me I was overreacting and then scurrying off to your lecture."

"Tutor."

"Whatever! How do you think it felt having that thing standing in my room? Counting the sex tissues in my trash can. Like he was going to report back on how many times we've—" Jess broke off as Mitch tapped the brakes hard, then just as abruptly accelerated so that the car lurched forward again.

"Seriously, Jess, it's just Dud. He's nobody. Nothing. He's just a . . . a *dud*. Like I said, I'll have a word with him. Tell him not to bother you again."

"It's not just that."

"What now?" Mitch asked, managing to convey disdain, irritation, and weariness with just two syllables.

"Why haven't you told them?" Jess hated the note of hurt in her voice. It meant she was vulnerable, and she didn't feel like she could afford to be vulnerable. That's where things were at between them: right back to the start, like nothing had changed at all.

"Because I don't answer to them," Mitch snapped, glancing across at her. Then he was forced to brake sharply, narrowly avoiding hitting the car in front of him as it stopped at a set of lights. The quiet that followed was red, prickling. "Let's talk about it when we're back to your room. I'm going to have an accident in a minute."

Jess rubbed her chest. Why hadn't he acknowledged their relationship to anybody? Was it even a relationship? Maybe she'd misread everything. The traffic started to move again, and she said, "Why don't I come to Knights tonight? You always come to Unity."

"You're not coming to Knights."

"Of course not. Because then I might exist."

"Don't be fucking ridiculous." He accelerated, zigzagging through the traffic, changing from lane to lane.

"Please don't speed," Jess said.

After a moment, Mitch slowed, but he was breathing hard, his nostrils flared.

"How is that ridiculous?" she asked, back to the subject at hand. "What's ridiculous is that I haven't even seen your room yet." She felt like she'd been uncorked, all these things she'd only half realized flowing out. "We haven't been seen in public together— anytime there's the opportunity, you make an excuse, unless it's a Unity thing. You come to all my basketball games, but I've never watched you play rugby once."

"You said it would bore you shitless!"

"Well, I bet if I'd wanted to, you would have put a stop to it somehow. Even my uncle's watched one of your games, but not me. God, why didn't I see this?"

"See what?"

"You tell me. There's something going on. I just don't get what it is. You're not being honest."

Mitch rolled his eyes. "There is nothing going on."

"Don't do that. You always make me feel like I'm being stupid when it's something you don't want to talk about. Explain it. *Please*. I can't understand why you'd be keeping me a secret. Unless you're ashamed of me or something."

Jess waited for him to respond, but Mitch was silent, his face hard, muscles working in his jaw. She pulled her hand back, and this time he didn't try to stop her.

"You know what? I think I should be alone tonight," she said.

"Don't play games."

"We haven't had a night apart since we got back. Maybe it'd be good for us."

Mitch glanced across at her, his top lip curled, showing his teeth, and in that moment he looked so much like the guy she'd met in a laundry room once that she felt sideswiped. When he pulled up outside Unity, he left the engine running. Jess stared at him, her mouth dropping open, unable to believe that he really was going to just leave things there.

"You said you wanted to be alone," he reminded her, looking straight ahead, his hands tightening on the steering wheel.

"Oh, fuck . . . you," Jess said, the words weak and breathless. She grabbed her bag and got out of the car, slamming the door harder than necessary, and then stood on the curb, staring at him through the window, feeling her eyes start to burn. There was a faint whirring noise, and the window rolled down.

"Look . . . I fucking *love you*, all right?" Mitch said it angrily, as if it was her fault.

The fact that he'd told her that for the first time, in those circumstances, in that way, was unbearable. "Then why would you feed me to him?" she asked, her voice wavering, eyes welling over. "Because that's what you did this morning. It was like that night on the bus, all over again. Why choose him over me?"

"It's not that."

"What is it then?"

But Mitch just shook his head, his eyes slitted, his face leached of color. And somehow Jess knew she'd lost him. Even before he drove off. She just didn't understand why.

MITCH CAME, THOUGH. At just after two in the morning, wide awake and restless, Jess checked her phone for the umpteenth time, wishing he'd text or call, too proud to text or call him. She dropped the phone back on her desk and then curled into the fetal position, buried deep beneath her quilt. Her closed window was covered in a layer of condensation.

Her door opened abruptly. She hadn't locked it.

She sat up wordlessly, recognizing his silhouette, even though it was too dark to see his face. She watched him kick off his shoes and pull off his jacket, and she lay back down again, hearing the rattle and snake of his belt coming off, the rasp of denim over skin as he shucked off his jeans, the snap of elastic as he pulled down his boxers. Then he was lifting the quilt, pushing her across to make room. She wrapped her arms around him, and his skin felt cold and unyielding, like he was made from stone. He tasted of beer, his kiss hard and demanding. He pulled off her T-shirt, and she raised her hips to help him tug down her underpants, and he was rolling on top of her, and she could hear him breathing, his leg nudging hers apart. He started to push inside her, taking care with it, more than he needed to, because she was growing wet.

"Stop," she said, but Mitch ignored her, moving his hips, pushing harder. He tried to kiss her, and Jess turned her face away. "No, stop," she said, louder now, and he was still.

He rolled off her. She leaned across him and turned on her reading lamp, angling it away from the bed. Mitch shaded his eyes, looking irritated by the light, but Jess felt it was the scrutiny he didn't want.

"Mitch."

He shifted, dislodging her from his chest, moving backward, sitting up. And Jess moved too, kneeling, putting her hands on his shoulders, trying to keep him there.

"You heard what I said? I love you." Mitch gripped her wrists as he said it, like it was a plea of some kind.

"I love you, too," Jess said, sounding scared. She was scared, her heart pounding. She could feel the ground shifting beneath her feet. "I just don't understand why you'd act like that."

Mitch let go of her wrists—violently, as if he was casting her away. "Because the last person I had sex with was Sylvie. And now you know, all right?"

Jess made a sound like she'd been punched. "Since you've been with me?"

He shook his head. "No. Before."

And Jess remembered then that he had a before, and that

she'd only known him in the after. But if she was stunned, it was because she'd known. She'd always suspected it. And she could understand how something like that might happen, if they were around each other a lot, if they were friends.

Mitch looked stricken, his lips thin, his eyes glassy. She recognized it for what it was: grief.

"Did Julian find out?" she asked softly.

He leaned back against the headboard, wrapping his arms around himself, drawing his knees up. "He couldn't believe I'd do that. It killed him."

Jess swallowed. "I'm so sorry, Mitch."

He didn't give any sign of having heard her. Just frowned at the ceiling, as if trying to read something written there.

"You're always sorry," he said suddenly, his voice flat. "You are always sorry, but you never shut the fuck up."

Jess looked away, her eyes skidding off things in the room without seeing them at all. Finally, she found the photo of the two of them on the shelf above the desk, and she blinked at it, having trouble bringing it into focus. "Do you still have feelings for her? Is that what this is about?"

"God, why are you so fixated on her? It's not even about her. We were just drunk. Off our faces. She didn't mean a fucking thing. That's the problem."

"You said you didn't want her knowing about us. That night in the parking lot."

"She's a loose cannon. I didn't want her overreacting. Telling the boys."

In the silence that followed, Jess could hear her own breathing. It sounded too loud, not really human, like it was coming from an animal.

"The boys."

"They wouldn't understand. Sleeping with your best friend's girl is a low thing to do. Sleeping with a teammate's girl is possibly even lower."

"You wouldn't be captain material."

"That's not it." Mitch looked sick, his skin grey, the light sheen of sweat on his forehead. "I did a really bad thing. I didn't want them to know about it because it would change everything. Instead, I tried to be different."

Jess pressed her fingertips to her temples, staring at him. "So you stopped drinking, and you stopped having sex, and you thought that was being different?" She lowered her hands, studied the way they were shaking. "What about being honest, Mitch? That would be different. Because you having sex with Sylvie? That's just a mistake. It means you're human. But you're not, are you? Because if you were, you'd treat people with some decency."

Mitch opened his mouth to speak, but she cut him off, her voice rising: "You just said that Sylvie didn't mean a thing. You just said that it wasn't even about her. So you must think that. Of course it's about her! Julian was her boyfriend, and that means she lost him, too. But for some reason, in your eyes, all that means is that she's his property. Some fucking sex toy that the rest of you aren't allowed to touch. *God, Mitch.*" Jess exhaled. "You make me sick."

Mitch was silent.

After a long time, Jess looked at him again. And when she did, her face was empty, expressionless. Mitch stared back at her through lowered lids, his head tilted against the headboard. And they were both naked, their bodies touching, skin against skin. But there was no warmth or compassion, no intimacy.

Only the sense that they'd exhausted each other.

40.
Wish I Was

Nine days later, Jess split the cab fare home with three other Unity residents who'd gone on the Economics Society pub crawl with her. Then she dragged herself up the seven flights of steps to T-floor, wishing she was drunker, or drugged, or anything else that might render her oblivious. She heard someone playing Ayla softly on S-floor as she passed, but apart from that the college was quiet, most rooms in darkness, a halo of mist around the security lights. And as Jess climbed, her steps became slower and slower, because thinking you might be coming home to a cold, empty bed and actually arriving there were two different things. So her heart lurched when she saw the silhouette of a tall, well-built guy sitting with his back against a door halfway down the hallway.

But the guy was Michael, not Mitch, and the door was Allie's, not hers, and hope drained away.

"Flash," Michael said in a gloomy voice. His arms were resting on his knees, and he didn't look at her, but stared at his fingers. "Don't even ask. Talk about high maintenance."

"Who? You or Allie? What'd you say this time?"

"Fuck if I know. Something." Michael gave a sniff. "But you girls—you've got to start looking at actions, not words. I mean, whatever it is that I said, I'm sitting out here, aren't I? Waiting for Her Majesty to relent and open the door. 'Cause if I don't—if I just go back to my room and get some sleep, which would be the rational course of action—there'll be hell to pay for that, too." He glanced up at her and his eyes narrowed. "Are you pissed?"

"I don't know," Jess said in a thick voice. "But I think I'm going to cry."

"Aw, Christ, not you, too." Michael patted the carpet beside him and Jess sat down. "Problems with Crawford?" he asked, a note of curiosity in his voice.

"You know?"

"Well, I got used to seeing him around." Michael's voice deepened, almost imperceptibly. "Used to run into him in the bathroom sometimes. We'd talk rugby and stuff."

Jess pressed her fingertips to the corners of her eyes. "People must be laughing their heads off," she told him, not actually caring, just trying to divert his attention from the fact that she was losing it.

"Why would they be laughing?"

"Have we met? I'm the girl who was making speeches at the toga party pregame."

"Not really," Michael said with zero guile. "They're still trying to work out if it's all off."

"Yeah, me too."

"Call him."

"How many times? I've left so many messages. I'm sure his fingers aren't broken."

The first two messages Jess had left Mitch had been harsh and full of demands. The next eight or nine had taken a different tone. She'd told him she missed him. She'd told him she loved him. She'd said things like *Can you just come and see me? Talk to me?* And as time passed, disbelief had turned into a quiet, permanent state of panic. She knew she'd ripped into him the night he'd come to her room, and the memory of his face, just before he'd shut down, shut her out, haunted her. But surely he wouldn't just leave things there, cut himself off from her without further explanation?

Then again, maybe he would. He had form for it. That's how he'd treated every other girl he'd been with, so why not her?

The last time Jess had called him had been two days ago. By then she couldn't think of anything new, and the message she'd left had been a short period of nothing, eloquent in itself.

"Go see him. Now, if you want—I'll walk you over there." Michael shrugged. "Got nothing better to do. Just sitting here, getting carpet burn on my ass." Jess smiled at that. Then her smile faded, and Michael pushed at his glasses, asking nervously, "What did I say wrong now?"

"I don't even know his room number."

Michael's eyes widened. "Man, that's ruthless."

"Arm's length, right?" Jess asked, feeling winded. Michael nodded. Jess took a shuddery breath. "Guess that makes it official then. Not only have we broken up, but we were probably never really together. Wish I was smarter."

"Sorry, Flash," Michael said with genuine sympathy. After a while, he added, "If it makes you feel any better, we've broken up, too."

"But you guys probably break up a lot, right?" Jess pointed out, and Michael nodded, conceding the point. "I think we're only going to break up once." She went quiet, her eyes burning, then she made a small noise, something like a whimper, and whispered, "Oh fuck, it hurts, Michael," and he gripped her shoulder and squeezed it hard.

They sat like that without talking for a long time, Jess crying noiselessly, Michael politely pretending not to notice.

"You know what's funny?" he said suddenly, seeming strangely shy. "I used to wish that I'd gone there. To Knights. Because it meant you were the best or something."

Jess sniffed. "Well, I'm glad you didn't. Because you're a good guy."

He pushed at his glasses. "I'm not really."

She patted his leg. "You're good enough."

41.
Fire, Meet Gasoline

"Will we be wanting to Instagram this?" Leanne asked Jess. Jess shrugged, not really holding a view either way. They were on the roof in their normal spot, sitting on the ventilation housing, and what Leanne intended to capture was the scene in front of them: the Unity girls at the pregame, all of them dressed for the Business Ball, but in a Unity kind of way, which meant sequins and satin had been paired with Docs and tiaras and wands and fairy wings and amazing stockings and the occasional sash. And the hair: tipped pink, tipped blue, rainbowed, messy side braids, pixie cuts, feathers, chain headbands. There was a roaring fire in the cylinder, but it wasn't necessary for anything other than mood on a balmy spring night in September. Jugs of Ginger Mule were doing the rounds, choked with limes and mixed strong enough to kick, and the student council's speakers were blasting out Sia.

The T-floor girls had organized a thrift shop crawl especially for the occasion. Jess had gone for boho glam, matching a cream lace corset with a skirt made from layers of tulle, finishing the ensemble with a deep-red satin cummerbund and her cowboy boots. But best of all were the strings of crystals and fake diamonds she'd wrapped around her neck and wrists, glittering every time she moved.

Leanne showed Jess the caption: *That one time when we ate Cinderella.* Jess frowned. "Exactly how long have you had my phone, by the way?"

"Only had a couple of calls to make. Nothing expensive."

"Jesus. I can't believe you've lasted the whole year without one," Jess drawled lazily, tilting her head back to view the night sky. She stayed that way, transfixed by stars that seemed to pulse and spin.

"You feeling it by any chance?" Leanne asked.

Jess's laugh was low and throaty. "Girl, I am feeling it."

"What the actual fuck is the theme of this ball, anyway?" Leanne asked.

Jess turned to look at her, her cheek pressed to her shoulder, and said, in a dreamy voice, "The bold and the beautiful."

Leanne frowned. She was wearing a bow tie and a black velvet smoking jacket over a kilt and fishnet stockings, her red hair slicked down. "So what are we then?"

"Bold *and* beautiful."

Leanne grinned suddenly. "Your pupils are ridiculous."

Farren joined them, taking a seat beside Jess, resplendent in blue taffeta and lace. "What are you two deviants talking about?"

Jess prodded her in the cheek. "About how you can't leave us next year."

"Don't be needy," Farren said. To Leanne: "Her pupils are fucking ridiculous."

"That's what I said." Leanne gave a jolt. "Whoa. We've got a call. I set it to vibrate. Get it?" She flicked the phone's cover open, frowned at the screen, and then closed it again. "So who are these girls you're moving in with?" she asked, leaning forward to see Farren.

"They're doing my course," Farren said.

"Hang on," Jess said, blinking. "Who was trying to call?"

"We'll have to meet them sometime," Leanne said, continuing her conversation with Farren but with a grim look on her face.

And Jess knew then.

———————————

THE BALL WAS held at the Brisbane Conference and Exhibition Center, a cavernous space festooned with thousands of balloons, swathes of satin, and hundreds of tiny lights twinkling from a ceiling that was vast and high and crisscrossed with catwalks. There were close to two thousand people there, the ball committee having caved to pressure to open the event up to students other than just those enrolled in business, economics, and law. Predictably, the Unity crowd arrived late, missing the sit-down dinner and speeches, and by the time they got there, the T-floor girls were at full steam, needing to dance or die. They danced and danced and danced for what seemed like years before people started to peel off. Allie was the first when Michael came up to claim her, whispering something in her ear that Jess hoped was the right thing to say. Farren was the second to go, when she found out one of the freshman girls was already so drunk she'd vomited and had been spotted by security doing so, which meant having to find someone to escort her home. And not long after that, Jess came to, realizing she was thirsty. It was as she was heading to the bar that someone tapped her on the shoulder.

"Hey, Jess." Mitch was holding a beer and had obviously been drinking, but his speech was clear, his eyes were almost too bright, and he looked painfully good in a tux. He'd broken away from his group to talk to her: Four guys stood in a rough circle behind him.

Tipene was one of them; the others Jess hadn't seen before. They glanced at her and Mitch and then continued their conversation.

"How are you?" Jess asked, getting jostled by the people behind her. Mitch put out a hand to steady her and then stopped himself when she flinched.

"I'm glad you're here," he said.

Jess shrugged. "Well pretty much everybody at college decided it was an event, so . . ." She looked around as if somebody was waiting for her and then back at him.

Mitch nodded, his lips pressed together, obviously wanting to drive things in a certain direction, just not sure how. "You look beautiful," he said, his eyes making too much of the compliment, and Jess realized with a sudden lurch in her stomach just where he might be trying to go.

"Thanks, but I'm hot and I'm sweaty, I'm wearing cowboy boots, and my hair's all messed up," she said flatly. "You've been drinking."

"Not that much. Listen, I tried to call you tonight. I wanted to—"

"Sorry, but I'd better—"

"Come and meet the guys," Mitch said abruptly, slipping his arm around her waist. Before she could stop him or protest, he'd pushed her into the group, interrupting their conversation to make the introductions, starting with Tipene.

"I think we've met before," Tipene said in his deep voice, shaking her hand.

Jess nodded, giving him a tight smile. "Thank you for what you did that night."

Mitch moved on to the next guy, who turned out to also be from Knights. He kept his arm around Jess, making her feel like she was a ventriloquist's dummy, having to nod and smile and pretend to be interested. The other two were guys Mitch had met playing Rugby Sevens at the university games. The four of them in turn seemed almost too polite, carefully respectful, and Jess started to suspect that they might have been prepped for the occasion.

"These guys all play front row," Mitch explained.

"Great," Jess said, glancing toward the bar area.

"You don't know what that means, do you?" Mitch asked, his voice falsely cheerful.

"No idea," Jess said, and they all laughed. She didn't; she needed to get away so badly she felt sick. It wasn't the guys. She could tell they were all right, nothing snide or covert in their faces. They were just guys. Guys trying to pretend a situation was something it wasn't, for the sake of their mate. The person Jess needed to get away from was Mitch. Seeing him again was like being kicked in the chest.

Tipene said, "So how's economics working out for you?"

Jess stared at him blankly.

"Mitch talks about you a lot," he explained, trying to keep things rolling. "I mean, that's how I knew."

When it was apparent Jess had nothing to say to that, one of the Rugby Sevens guys asked, "How do you and Mitch know each other, anyway?"

"We used to sleep together," Jess told him abruptly. And then, to Mitch: "I can't do this."

She broke free of his hold, starting to push her way through the crowd, not sure where she was headed, just desperate to get away. Mitch followed, grabbing the chain of her gold mesh bag, so that it bit into her skin, and she turned to tell him to leave her alone. But if she felt desperate, Mitch looked the same way, grabbing her by the shoulders.

"Jess, nothing's changed."

"What?"

"I love you. I just had shit I couldn't deal with, that's all. I was scared. But I can't do it anymore. I don't care what happens now. I've just got to let it all fall down."

"You must be mad," Jess said. "Everything's changed. You can't just leave someone up in the air for weeks and think they'll be okay with it."

Mitch shook her slightly, and then pulled her close, his face right in front of hers. "No, I know! I know that wasn't okay. You've got to hear me out. Let me explain. And you'll understand then, even if you don't want me. But not in here, okay? Come outside with me. *Please*."

Jess clamped a hand to her mouth, thinking she might actually vomit she was so upset, and she was dimly aware that the people around them had turned to stare. But when she slapped Mitch as hard as she could across the face, they turned away. She'd shocked them. She'd shocked herself. The only person who didn't seem shocked was Mitch. He didn't even seem to have felt it.

"Just talk to me," he told her, the red imprint of her hand clearly visible on his cheek. But then someone bumped into the two of them, nearly knocking Jess off her feet. It was Dud, no jacket, his shirt untucked and missing a few buttons, so drunk he was slurring already.

"What's going on?" he asked, looking from Jess to Mitch, his arms slung around their shoulders, so that Jess sagged under his weight. "Secret lovers' reunion?"

"Fuck off, Dud," Mitch said, his eyes on Jess. "I mean it."

"You don't have to worry," Dud told Jess. "I kept it on the down low. Just like young Mitchell here asked me to." He laughed, spraying her with spit. Jess pulled away. And as she turned to go, one of them slapped her on the ass.

Jess wheeled around, thinking for a second it might have been

Mitch. But when she saw Mitch punch Dud in the stomach, she knew it hadn't been.

"She hates that," Mitch hissed, an ugly look on his face, and Dud doubled over with a hoarse coughing sound, his arms crossed over his stomach. Mitch punched him a second time, driving his fist into Dud's gut so viciously that his body jerked upward. Then he pounded his elbow on Dud's back.

"Jesus, Mitch. Don't!" Jess grabbed at his arm, feeling sickened, and frightened, too, because Mitch looked like he'd lost it, all the frustration he'd shown with her spilling over onto Dud. She thought he mightn't stop, but he did.

Instead of hitting Dud again, Mitch grabbed a handful of his hair and pulled his head back to look at Jess. "Apologize. And don't ever fucking touch her, or talk to her, again."

All Dud was capable of was a whimper. Mitch let him go, and he barged blindly through the crowd, still doubled over. Mitch stared after him, his blue eyes burning, his posture stiff with anger. But as he focused on Jess again, saw how shaken she was, his eyes softened, his hands reaching for her.

"Are you all right?"

She batted his hands away. *"Who are you?"*

"Jess, it's me. You know that."

But she was looking past him at the two security guards who'd suddenly appeared, one on each side of him.

"Sorry, sir, but that behavior is not appropriate," one of them said, politely enough—while they sharply twisted his arms up behind his back. "You're going to have to leave."

Mitch started to kick and struggle, swearing at them, which did not help his case. Half lifting him, half dragging, the two guards bulldozed a path through the crowd, heading toward the entrance, Jess slipstreaming.

"Excuse me." She touched one of the guards on the shoulder.

"Hey, can you just listen? It wasn't his fault. That other guy— Would you just stop?" The guy ignored her, so she gripped his sleeve instead and leaned back with her full weight: "Let him go. You're hurting him!" She sounded shrill and drunk and rabid. She'd turned into *that* girl.

The guard glanced back at her, the whites of his eyes showing, his face red with the effort of trying to control Mitch, and spat polite words at her in a tone that was full of aggression. "Hands off, please, miss. I said, don't touch. Unless you want to join him?"

Jess stopped in her tracks. She didn't know what she wanted. She didn't even know what had just happened. And then the three of them were gone. She looked around her, seeing a wall of curious faces, not feeling embarrassed exactly, more like blinded, completely unable to distinguish any individual features.

42.
What Kind of Man

Away from the noise and press of bodies, Jess had the space to sway, and she had to touch the tiled wall to steady herself before she made it to the sinks. She turned on a tap, cupping her hand beneath it and drinking deeply, terribly thirsty. She drank for ages, dimly aware of the other girls around her. Then she straightened, looking at herself in the mirror. She was a mess—flushed, disheveled, all her makeup long gone—and her head was even worse.

She made her way into one of the stalls, slamming the door shut and kicking the toilet seat closed. Then she sat down, the tulle of her skirt puffing up around her like a life raft inflating. No sooner had she done so than her phone began to ring. She took it from her bag and flipped the cover open, her hands shaking. Mitch. She didn't answer, letting it ring out. A short pause followed, and then it started to ring again and Jess turned it off. The feelings were the same: her heart pushing him through her blood, like it had done for every beat in the last thirty-two days. But if he'd hurt her by staying away, he'd hurt her even more by just popping up and saying that everything was okay now. What kind of idiot did he think she was?

After a while, Jess slipped her phone into her bag and stood, pushing down her skirt. She hit her hip on the door as she opened it, trying to squeeze through before there was enough space to do so. She knocked into another girl as she passed, telling her breathlessly, "Sorry, sorry." Mitch was outside—there was no way the bouncers would let him back in—and she had the feeling he'd wait for a while. What she needed to do was find Farren or Leanne or Allie, or even Michael or Callum or Davey—just anyone she trusted—so she could ask them whether she should go out there and hear what he had to say.

But Jess was too late. Because before she made it out of the bathroom, Sylvie walked through the door, one hand pressed to her cheek. When Jess saw her, she stopped dead, her skin going cold all over, like she'd just passed through a ghost.

"We've got to stop meeting like this," Sylvie told her. But her green eyes showed no surprise at all. "Stay for a second. I want to talk to you."

She crossed to one of the sinks, taking up position in front of the mirror, ignoring the three girls who were already there, glancing only at Jess to check she wasn't leaving. She was wearing vivid red lipstick and a little black dress, and, in contrast, her skin seemed as white and smooth as porcelain. Funereal. But when she took her hand away, Jess saw the angry mark on her cheekbone, and she had a disorientating moment of déjà vu.

Sylvie grimaced, sucking air through her sharp little teeth. "Son of a *bitch*. Can you believe a guy just hit me in the face?"

"Not Mitch," Jess said, feeling sick, because even though she didn't think Mitch would do something like that, she was smart enough to know she knew nothing. She'd realized it as soon as she'd seen Sylvie walk through the door.

Sylvie ignored the question, splashing water on her cheek. "Love the look. Not so sure about the boots this time, though. I saw the show outside." She glanced questioningly at Jess in the mirror. "Did he get a chance to tell you?"

Jess said nothing, too tense to speak. But Sylvie waited. "If you mean about him and you, I already knew," Jess said eventually.

"Not everything." Sylvie studied her carefully. "No, I don't think so. But he was going to tell you. That's important. Especially for Mitch." And all the while the other girls were chatting and laughing as they fixed their makeup, seemingly oblivious to the fact that Sylvie was about to tear Jess's world apart. Because Jess already knew it was going to happen. She just didn't know how. She thought Sylvie was going to tell her that she and Mitch had been together again. That she was the reason for thirty-two days of silence.

She was wrong.

"He called me today," Sylvie told her. "You know how they say better late than never?" She paused, as if expecting a response, so Jess nodded. "Well, it's actually not true. He was too late. He's let so much time go past that I am more angry at him now than I was at the start. I actually hate him now. But he did mention when he called that he would be talking to you, too. What I'm trying to say is that he told me." Sylvie sniffed delicately, a flicker of hurt on her face for just a moment. "About you two."

God, she's still got feelings for him, Jess thought. She took hold of the basin, needing to feel something steady.

"You know what's funny?" Sylvie said, just for a second dropping her guard, the only time Jess had ever seen her vulnerable. "I kind of knew. That night on the bus, he kept looking at you." She cleared her throat, hardening before Jess's eyes like she'd been varnished. "Anyway, because he didn't get a chance to clear things up for you, I'd better do it. All hell is going to break loose soon, so you might as well know what is going on."

"What are you talking about?"

"I'm talking about what happened to Julian. What we did." There was something poignant in the way Sylvie said it. "The truth."

The three girls finished up, and Sylvie waited for them to leave. Each of them glanced furtively at her as they left. Jess, by comparison, couldn't look at her any longer, her gaze sliding to her own reflection. Her face was so anguished she barely recognized herself. Fear, she realized. And then it was only the two of them, alone with Sylvie's truth.

"Did Mitch cause it?" she asked, in a voice that made her sound much younger than she was. "I mean, the accident. Did he tell him that night? At the party?"

Sylvie shook her head, and now her green eyes seemed too bright, backlit, fixed on Jess with an intensity that was eerie. Jess had seen that look on Mitch. It was grief. "Not intentionally."

And in that moment her beauty was impossible, bone-sharp, so precise, while Jess felt smudged and blurred and ground down. But Sylvie was also laid bare. Because Jess knew then. "You were there that night."

Sylvie nodded. Carefully. Her guilt wasn't hot and raw like Mitch's; it was a cold, brittle thing, something that could shatter. "Oh God, Sylvie." Jess crossed the floor in two quick strides and hugged her. Fiercely at first, and then more gently, because it was like holding a bird. Sylvie didn't resist. She went limp, as though Jess had taken something from her.

"I was up there visiting Julian," Sylvie said, her face buried in Jess's neck. "The three of us went to the party together." She made a small sound as if something was hurting her. Jess still held her, however loosely, like they were friends, or sisters, or lovers. "Mitch and I had already slept together by then. But only once. Afterward, he was over it. You know what— Well. Seems you don't know what he's like. But, for the record, I didn't even feel guilty. Julian had done the same to me. I think I'd sort of planned it, really. And I liked Mitch. We used to talk a lot, you know. I knew he'd . . ."

"Never had that before," Jess finished for her. Sylvie nodded, pulling back to look at her, and Jess dropped her arms. "Mitch told me there was a girl he used to talk to. I knew she must have been special." Jess meant it as an acknowledgment, every word a burn, but Sylvie took it as a kindness, and she didn't like that at all— backing away from Jess until she found the edge of the sinks.

"Oh, I was special," she said. "Right up until we slept together. Sometimes I wish we'd just stuck to talking. We talked about how much we liked each other for a long time before we ever did any-thing, and it was so sweet. Mitch said nothing could ever happen, and I pretended I felt the same way. But in reality, I kept turning up." Sylvie's eyes were glittering now, but she stayed unblinking so the tears didn't fall. "That's how it all started. If I went to Knights and Julian wasn't around, I'd go see Mitch instead. After a while, I started to go when I was sure Julian wouldn't be there. But every-thing changed after that first time. Mitch wouldn't talk anymore." Sylvie exhaled. "On that night, though . . . New Year's Eve. We were smashed, of course. And Mitch fucking relaxed for once. He was— well, happy, I think, because the three of us were there together. Kept telling us we were his two favorite people. And it was true. Because he might have cared about Julian, but he definitely cared about me." Sylvie said this angrily, as if Jess was arguing with her.

"I know," Jess said.

Sylvie pressed her fingertips to her forehead, as though she had a headache or another pressure in her head that wouldn't go away. "I was so stupid. I thought he might have changed his mind. You know how when you're drunk, you'll convince yourself of anything?" She stared into space for a second. "The party was on a farm, and he'd gone up to the house for some reason—everybody else was down in the shed. I followed him up there. And I tried to talk to him. But he got angry, and then we started arguing, and we didn't realize that Julian was standing there, listening. I can't even remember what Julian said. Isn't that crazy? I can't remember his last words at all. I just remember turning around, seeing him, and thinking, Oh shit." Sylvie shook her head, her face tight with pain. "He had the keys in his pocket."

"You can't carry that," Jess said, and then stopped as a pair of girls entered the bathroom. They glanced from Jess to Sylvie as they crossed the floor to the cubicles, their eyes curious.

Sylvie stared them down defiantly, but Jess had the feeling she was buying time, trying to harden again.

"Oh, come on," she said to Jess eventually. "You must judge me."

"For what?"

Sylvie met her eyes, and her face looked so raw. "Why not?"

"If Julian had treated you better, maybe things wouldn't have come to that. You didn't make Julian drive, and you didn't make him speed, and none of us should drink like we do. It's just a tragic fucking waste, that's all. Judging you is the easy way out."

"What about Mitch then?" Sylvie's voice was spiked with more than curiosity.

Jess dropped her gaze. Mitch believed he'd killed his best friend. That crushed her. If she'd just shut up on that last night, maybe he would have told her then. He did tell her, in a way. *It killed him.*

When she didn't answer, Sylvie said, in a sour voice, "Do you know he never talked to me about it afterward? Not once. What kind of guy treats people like that? He treated me worse than dirt, like it was all my fault. Just completely avoided me." She started to blink rapidly, as if her eyes were burning, and the tears finally broke. "And now, because he wants you back, he thinks I'll be cool with everything? That I'll shut up for him?"

Jess touched her arm. "What did he say to you today? Can you please tell me?"

Sylvie gave a flat laugh. "Oh, of course. You think he's changed. Well, I don't. He's only got himself to blame for what happens now, though. Remember that."

"What are you talking about?"

Sylvie stretched her lips. It wasn't a smile. It was a grimace. "Maybe he even hoped I'd tell them for him."

Jess felt that coldness again, crawling over her skin. "Who hit you, Sylvie?"

"Dud."

Jess's voice was hoarse. "What have you done?"

"Told the truth."

———————————

OUTSIDE, EVERYTHING SEEMED impossibly crowded, chaotic, the scene washed through with red lighting that was too dim and pulsed in time to Florence + the Machine, adding to Jess's sense of disorientation. She pushed through the crowd, so panicked that for a moment she lost her sense of direction, whirling in a circle, up on her tiptoes, trying to see the exit.

Someone grabbed her arm, and she turned on them, shaking them off. She'd thought it was Sylvie, but it was Tipene.

"Where's Mitch?" he bellowed at her, looking wild-eyed, fierce.

Jess, frightened, just shook her head.

He jammed his face into hers. "No, listen! They're after him. Some of the guys. Where is he?"

And Jess realized he wasn't wanting to hurt Mitch but wanting to help him. "The bouncers threw him out! But I can't even find the way—" She broke off. Tipene wasn't waiting for her to finish but barging his way through the crowd, and, before she lost him, Jess grabbed hold of the bottom of his tuxedo jacket, getting pulled along. As the crowd thinned, Jess let go, keeping pace with him, the coldness she'd felt when she'd first seen Sylvie inside her now, spreading through her chest. She bolted past security and pounded her way down the length of red carpet that led to the building's main entrance. Outside, things seemed compressed, the air too quiet, too still. Jess's ears were ringing so loudly that she couldn't hear anything at first, and she turned back for a moment when she realized Tipene wasn't with her. She saw him coming through the doors, bringing two of the bouncers with him, maybe the same two from before.

Then Jess's ears cleared enough to hear the sound of a scuffle, swearing. She whirled, spotting them. Someone was shouting: "What kind of man does that?" It was Dud, egging the others on. A soft *thud, thud,* like someone plumping a pillow.

Then Jess screamed, a loud, piercing noise, wanting to cut through the pack of them.

Make them stop.

43.
Tough Love

L ate the next morning, someone knocked on Jess's door.

"It's open," Jess called in a dull voice, not moving. She was lying on her bed, still in the corset and tulle skirt she'd worn to the ball, wishing she could sleep, wanting to crash out of reality for a while, but the world was too noisy: Allie's empty room blasting out Jessie Ware, a group of gamers engaged in an energetic discussion on the floor below, the sounds of distant traffic as the campus's commuter students came and went. How amazing that life just carried on as usual.

It was Farren. Unlike Jess, she'd showered and changed and looked none the worse for wear after the night before. For some reason, that annoyed Jess greatly. She rolled over, facing the wall. But then Farren lay down beside her, boots and all, and hugged her ferociously hard from behind.

Jess swallowed. Every time she closed her eyes, she could see it: Mitch pinned, arms pulled back behind him, while a guy punched him in the stomach, in the face—the others crowded around, looking on. And every time, she felt the same overwhelming sense of panic, helplessness, and she had to remind herself it was over.

"You all right?" Farren asked after a while, raising herself up to rest her chin on Jess's shoulder.

Jess glanced 'round, giving her a wan smile.

———————

TWO DAYS LATER, Jess met Adrian for coffee. She'd been typing up lecture notes while she waited, just trying to keep her mind occupied, but when she noticed him coming, she froze, her fingers poised over the keyboard. It was odd to see him in casual clothes—jeans and a jacket. He'd tucked his T-shirt in, and it made him seem thinner than ever.

He ordered and then collapsed into the chair across from her, placing a stand tagged with the number twenty-seven on the table. "Well, I've packed up his room. Got everything. He won't have to go back there."

"What about the headmaster? Did you talk to him?" Jess asked.

"Yeah. That was a bit tricky." Adrian gestured to her empty cup. "Should I have gotten you another one?" Jess shook her head impatiently. "I know him from my time there, so that helped. I told him that Mitch, unfortunately, felt he needed to leave. That he hadn't lived up to the standards set by some of his fellow knights."

"Being human?" Jess asked, disgust in her voice. She snapped her laptop shut. "You shouldn't have made it sound like it was his fault."

Adrian didn't react, just rubbed his eyes, looking tired. "I think he could read between the lines. He asked me if there was anyone or anything he needed to be made aware of."

"Did you name names?"

"No. I promised Mitch I wouldn't."

"Why's he protecting them?"

"I think he wants to move on, Jess. And for some of those guys, it was just the situation. Alcohol plus shock. They'd all been good friends with Julian." Adrian frowned, cleared his throat. "Actually, I did give him one name: Owen McCaffrey."

"Who? Oh. Dud." Jess's face clouded. "I hate him."

"Only met him once and couldn't stand the guy. Felt like fucking him up for fun."

"He hit Sylvie."

"Class. I'm not surprised. I don't think the headmaster was surprised to hear his name, either. Young Dud might find himself under a bit of scrutiny from now on."

"Won't change anything," Jess said dourly. She systematically ripped her empty sugar packet into small pieces and let them blow away in the breeze.

Adrian watched her do it. "Don't you want to know how he is?"

Jess and Tipene had taken Mitch to Adrian's in a taxi, and Adrian had dropped them back to campus the same night, after he'd gotten Mitch settled with ice packs. The next morning he'd sent Jess a photo of what Mitch looked like: one that clearly showed his black eye and swollen, split lip, the bruising to his cheekbone. So Jess already knew the physical damage, knew that wasn't what Adrian was referring to.

"Of course I do," she told him. "It's just that he hasn't called and—"

"His phone's broken. They smashed it."

"Pretty sure there's a landline in that apartment of yours."

"Exactly. And we're listed. So you could have called him."

Jess shook her head. "I'm scared."

"And he's not?"

"Of what? Me?"

"Absolutely. At a guess, I'd say he's pretty terrified about what you think of him right now. Because, as we all know, you're a woman of strong opinions." Adrian smiled as he said it, more teasing than trying to provoke her. "You *are* still into him, right?"

Jess gave him a look.

"Good," Adrian said.

"Yeah, but that's why it's scary! Because when he just disappeared, I kept thinking that I should have known better, I was an idiot. What if it happens again?"

Adrian's chai tea arrived, and he stuck a finger into the foam, then licked it. "Why would it?" He sipped. "Having everyone see you for who you used to be might be a hard thing to face up to, but he's done it now. The only person left to face up to is you."

Jess shook her head, suddenly firm. "No. That is not true. And that's the other reason I haven't called. The person he's got to face up to is Sylvie. Because I've talked to her, Adrian. She's a human being. She deserved to be treated so much better. And she's been damaged by this." Jess took a deep breath, exhaled. "But I can't say that to Mitch, because I don't want him doing it just because I said so. If he *has* changed, he'll do it himself. I know he's talked to her already, but I'm worried it was because of me . . . or maybe just to keep her quiet. I want him to face her now, after this, after what she did, by his own choosing. That's my bottom line. Because I don't think what happened to Julian was Mitch's fault, even if he does. Julian chose to drive—God, Mitch drives like a fucking idiot sometimes and that's when he's sober. But what I really hate is the way he's treated Sylvie."

Adrian studied her for a moment, his face hard to read. Then he leaned back in his chair, his hands behind his head, reminding her of Mitch. "Yeah, I forgot to mention that," he said casually, glancing around at the other tables. "He caught up with her yesterday. Asked her to meet him for coffee. Bub drank his through a straw, apparently."

Jess was quiet for a long time. "That's good," she said finally.

"I know," Adrian agreed, his voice placid. "For both of them, I'd say." He met Jess's eyes then, and they shared the kind of look that only two people who love the same person can share. "Does that change things at all?"

"I missed him so much, Adrian. It still fucking hurts."

He nodded. "Well, be angry, but don't be stupid. Anyway, I told you Mitch is immature."

"You know who sounds immature? You, right now."

He arched an eyebrow, looking knowing. "But you missed me, too, right?" Jess laughed, surprising herself. "That's better," he told her, warmth in his voice.

Jess took a sip of his chai and made a face. "So what happens now?"

Adrian clapped his hands together, suddenly all business. "Well, for the rest of the year, he'll live with me, focus on his classes, and try to get his head together. At least the rugby season's over, that's one good thing. He's not keen to return to campus for a while, though, so I'll find out what he needs in the way of lecture notes and readings next week, but it won't be hard with so much online." Adrian paused, then cleared his throat, suddenly seeming shifty. "But if you meant as far as you and he are concerned . . ." He leaned forward in his seat, taking something out of his back pocket and placing it down on the table like he was laying down the winning card. A couple of sheets of paper, neatly folded.

"A letter?" Jess asked, eyeing it warily.

"For you." Adrian's eyebrows twitched. "Jessie."

Jess blinked. She stared at him, her face incredulous. "*Adrian!* I can't believe you! You're as bad as he is! What is it with you guys and other people's letters? It must be hereditary."

"Possibly," Adrian said, sounding thoughtful. "When I told Mum about it on the phone, she made me read it to her, too. I wasn't going to, but she insisted. She said it was okay, because in a way she's kind of dated you." Adrian grinned at Jess's shock. "Don't worry, it's not dirty or anything. Just soppy. When Mitch least expects it, I'm going to quote key sections back at him."

"That's *disgusting*, Adrian. A complete betrayal of trust."

"I know," Adrian said, sounding quite pleased with himself. He glanced at her, his eyes amused. "Welcome to the family."

44.
Summer

"And here we are. Same bat time. Same bat place," Leanne intoned. "Same bat sheets." She was stretched out along the ventilation housing on the roof, her head on Allie's lap, a beer resting on her belly. She was wearing a swimsuit and shorts and had fashioned her sheet as a turban.

"Why don't you let me do your toga for you?" Allie asked. Her toga, of course, was immaculately wrapped. "You're a third year now. Time to grow up."

"Hell, no. Then I'd be like them." Leanne cocked a finger at the large gathering of girls on the section that looked across at the river, the hum of their voices competing with shrilling cicadas and a sound system booming out Calvin Harris. Leanne sat up. "Have you talked to the freshmen this year? They're not even the same species as us. Seriously conservative. Those two girls on our floor? Fucking *scary*."

"Imagine what they make of you then," Jess said from her position on the siding. Unlike the other two, she was sheetless, wearing a floaty little cotton dress, her hair piled on top of her head in an effort to stay cool. She swatted at a fly. "I miss Farren."

"We miss you," Leanne said dryly.

"Give me a break," Jess said, picking at the label of her beer. "Things will settle down."

"Come tonight then."

Jess shook her head firmly. "Not the toga party."

"Farren's not that far away," Allie said, lagging a little in the heat. What she said was true, geographically speaking—Farren and two girls from her program had rented a house in Indooroopilly, only a couple of kilometers away. But they all knew it signaled the end of an era.

"You know how the Z-floor boys are in the next street?" Jess asked, and Leanne and Allie nodded. "I went over there with Farren the other day. Instead of washing up their plates, they just put them in the fridge and reuse them."

All three of them shuddered.

"Actually, maybe it's better if you don't come tonight," Leanne said to Jess a short while later. "You might blow our cover."

Jess frowned. "What are you talking about?"

"Knight Rider challenge, phase two." Leanne took a large swig of her beer.

"You can't! You know Michael's clamping down on that stuff," Jess said sternly. "He's pushing an avoidance policy. He's getting Farren and me to talk to the freshmen later this week. Boys, too, not just the girls—thank Christ. About choosing wisely, looking after your friends, that sort of stuff. Treating people the way you'd like to be treated yourself. And we're going to talk about sex— someone has to. Get it out in the open. Because pretending people are sex toys isn't doing anybody any good. Farren's so impressed. His heart is definitely in the right place."

Allie sat a little straighter, smiling proudly. So today was a good day then. At other times, from what Jess could gather, there was some niggling tension over the demands of Michael's new role.

Leanne burped. "That'd be right. What this college really needs is a good war. Bloody Mikey."

"*Michael*," said Jess and Allie.

———————

Z-FLOOR SEEMED DESERTED, the place eerily silent. It was probably because most people were at the pregame, but right then it seemed appropriate to Jess: the place a graveyard without the Z-floor boys. She started down the long, gloomily lit corridor, enjoying the coolness after the heat of the roof. Every door was closed except for one midway down. The door belonging to Z6—Callum's old room.

Jess knocked on the slatted wardrobe door blocking the doorway, calling, "It's just me." Then she slid the door across. Late-afternoon sun flooded the room, filtered by the blinds, making everything golden. Mitch was lying on his bed, holding a battered-looking book with a rose on the cover: *Shakespeare's Sonnets*.

Jess stopped dead. "Are you for real?"

"Nah," Mitch said, throwing the book on the floor. He picked up the book he'd really been reading: *Ponting: At the Close of Play*. A sports biography. "Found it in the closet when I was unpacking."

"Very funny." Jess slid the slatted door closed again. "Wow, there's just no breeze, is there?" A small fan was swinging lazily from side to side on the desk, but it didn't seem to be doing much more than causing dust mote flurries.

Mitch shifted closer to the wall, making space for her, and patted his shoulder in the way that meant, *Your head here*. Jess kicked off her scuffs and lay down.

"Your hair's hot," he told her.

"Trapped sunshine. I've been up on the roof. You've got to come up there sometime."

"Yeah, four stories up. Not going to happen."

"You get up to my room all right. And it's three stories up."

Mitch looked at her, giving himself a double chin. "There's an incentive."

And in that moment Jess was struck by the changes in him. He seemed older. Thinner, too—although rugby preseason training had already started, so he'd soon regain the condition he'd lost during the off-season. His hair was longer, and she liked it that way. And there were other, more subtle changes. The guy she'd met in the laundry room a year ago had gone. Mitch never seemed intimidating to her anymore. His face was calmer, warmer, and there was something in his eyes that hadn't been there before: humility.

Grief, it seemed, was something carried, not spent.

Mitch noticed the way Jess was studying him and kissed her on the lips—but quickly, just a peck. Eager, she realized, to return to his book. He did just that, murmuring, "Your hair's hot, *and* you taste like beer."

"I had one with the girls. Pregame. I shouldn't have, though. It's made me sleepy." Jess reconsidered. "Well, really, it's your fault I'm sleepy."

"Are you sure you don't want to go tonight?" Mitch asked, not listening.

"Couldn't think of anything worse. Listen to that traffic. I'd hate to live on the first floor. So much road noise." Jess yawned. "God, I'm tired."

"Why don't you sleep then?" Mitch said, an edge to his voice that made Jess figure his motivations weren't completely selfless.

She smiled. "Too hot."

"Well, how about you just lie there and be quiet instead?" Mitch said. "I've only got a couple of pages to go."

"You know, I never really believed you were a reader," Jess

mused. "I thought you were just trying to impress me." Mitch grunted, turning a page. She grinned. "Is it any good?"

He ignored her. But after a minute or so more, he interrupted himself anyway. "I had some visitors today."

"Who?"

"First, Michael Azzopardi—"

"I meant to tell you that," Jess said with a jolt. "He's totally in love with you, you know. He was asking me about you yesterday. Wants you to play rugby for Unity. I think that's why he went with Farren to put a word in for you at the office."

It was Farren, though, who'd largely been responsible for getting Mitch into Unity. As the outgoing president of the student council, she had a bit of pull, but Jess suspected it might not have been that much of a hard sell. Everybody at Unity, even those in the office, probably liked the symbolism of a Knights golden boy moving to Unity.

"Yeah," Mitch said. "Michael mentioned that. I think I will." Jess stiffened, about to argue, but he cut her off. "You don't have to worry if I do. Tipene dropped by, as well. Said to say hello."

Jess sat up. "Really? I would have liked to have seen him."

"We'll catch up. He was here on an official capacity."

Jess tensed. "You mean as a knight?"

"Well, as a messenger, anyway. The others wanted me to know that there are no hard feelings. That sort of stuff. They thought things went too far. So, it's done. Move on."

"You mean the ones who did it?" Jess asked, her voice hard.

He shrugged. "Some of them."

"Is Dud back there this year?"

"No, that was funny. Tipene said he didn't get his residency approved. It couldn't have just been what Adrian said to the headmaster. I don't think Jarrod Keith ever liked him, either."

"Huh," Jess said. After a while, she asked, "Do you think you'll miss it? Knights?"

Mitch shook his head. "I don't miss places. Just people." They stared at each other for a moment. Jess touched his face.

"So what do you want to do tonight?" she asked, lying down again.

"I'll be reading, if you can just be quiet for five minutes."

"So rude," Jess murmured. She buried her face in his cotton T-shirt, breathing in the smell of him. "You know what? You are my favorite season."

"And you are noisy," Mitch said, turning a page.

Jess dropped her arm over the side of the bed, patting around until she found Shakespeare. She opened it and intoned, "My boyfriend hath got summer skin." Mitch grunted. "He did not want to let me in." Jess thought for a moment. "But he was cracked. And I was . . ."

"Whacked," Mitch suggested, unkindly.

Jess let Shakespeare fall and turned toward him. "So I put on my boots, and kicked his fucking heart open."

At that, Mitch finally relented, tossing his book to the floor and turning to face her in one smooth motion. Then he kissed her. Tenderly.

Acknowledgments

Thank you to my agent, Catherine Drayton. You are, and always will be, a total Boss Goddess. Thanks to Anna McFarlane, Jen Dougherty, and the team at Allen & Unwin. Thanks to Anna Roberto and the team at Feiwel & Friends—it is exciting to be working with you. And I am hugely grateful to Debra Billson for creating the. Best. Cover. Ever.

Thanks to the Creaghe, Eagar, Nott, Cash, and Lewis families— so many surnames, but really just my extended family. Thanks to all of my writer friends, with special thanks to Cath Crowley, Trish Doller, Belinda Jeffrey, Rebecca James, Gab Williams, Rebecca Lim, and Vikki Wakefield for acts of personal generosity that went above and beyond.

Thanks to the friends I went through college with—your energy was irrepressible, and I can sense it still.

To all of my surfing mates—I don't know what I'd do without you guys. You have given me a community, and it makes all the difference. Likewise, thank you to my other community of readers, booksellers, students, librarians, teachers, YASS, Stella Schools, and the #LoveOzYA crew. And a very special thank-you to the readers in the States who have championed my work since Raw Blue was first published. I will forever be grateful.

Most of all, thanks and love to Jason and Charlee Bean and Harper Jay.

Thank you for reading this Feiwel and Friends book.

The friends who made **SUMMER SKIN** possible are:

Jean Feiwel, Publisher

Liz Szabla, Associate Publisher

Rich Deas, Senior Creative Director

Holly West, Editor

Anna Roberto, Editor

Christine Barcellona, Editor

Kat Brzozowski, Editor

Alexei Esikoff, Senior Managing Editor

Kim Waymer, Senior Production Manager

Anna Poon, Assistant Editor

Emily Settle, Assistant Editor

Hayley Jozwiak, Managing Editor